"I have brought robes to keep you warm during told the white soldier, placing the items at his feet. He looked at her with admiration, and that pleased her.

John's eyes raked over her, drinking in her beauty. The white doeskin dress clung closely to her tall form, setting off her blue-black hair and large blue eyes to perfection.

"You seem to be feeling better, Yellow Hair. I am glad for that," she said, settling beside him and touching his forehead for signs of fever and relieved to find none. "You call me by name. By what name are you called?"

"My name is Major John Hanlen. I'm a warrior, just like some of the men in your tribe." He could sense her sudden tension. "My mission is to protect my people. Please understand."

"We want no war!" she exclaimed, her fear evident. "We are peaceful and want only to be able to roam freely and hunt the buffalo."

John wanted to put her at ease, to make her understand he was grateful for her help and would not hurt her. Gently, he touched her arm and pulled her close, his lips brushing hers lightly. When she leaned closer, he captured her in his strong embrace, deepening the kiss and savoring her awakening.

Skyraven had heard of the white eyes' courting gestures, but had never experienced a man's kiss before. Nothing prepared her for the jolt of sweet fire that swept through her veins as their passion deepened, and, closing her eyes, she gave in to the pleasure of his touch . . .

SWEET SAVAGE SURRENDER

KATHRYN HOCKETT

ZEBRA BOOKS
KENSINGTON PUBLISHING CORP.

ZEBRA BOOKS

are published by

Kensington Publishing Corp.
475 Park Avenue South
New York, NY 10016

First printing: February, 1990

Printed in the United States of America

This book is dedicated with loving appreciation to Kathryn Falk who has given me so much encouragement and been so very helpful not only to me but to so many writers. A heartfelt thanks.

"O, swear not by the moon, the inconstant moon,
That monthly changes in her circled orb,
Lest that thy love prove likewise variable."
—William Shakespeare, *Romeo and Juliet*.

Foreword

The Plains Indians of North America were hunters. Living in a land of high mountain ranges, dense forests, fertile river valleys, and wide grassy plains, they developed skills and traditions which best suited their natural environment. Wildlife was plentiful, wild plants and berries also abundant. They lived as one with the plants and animals as nomads and hunters.

The mainstay of the Indians was the buffalo, which provided them with food, clothing, bones for dishes, and ceremonial rattles. The skins were used for shelter. The buffalo was held sacred as a source of life. Without the buffalo they knew they would perish. Sadly enough they were right.

Several families usually lived together in conical tents made of buffalo hides sewn together and draped around poles. These were assembled and disassembled, constructed for easy transportation, for the tribes were constantly moving about, following the large, powerfully built animal that was the core of their existence. Once a year, at the beginning of the summer hunting season, several groups of the same tribe would come together for communal festivities and religious ceremonies, an eight-day celebration culminating with the sun dance. In the autumn the tribes separated again and took to river valleys or the foothills of the Rocky Mountains to seek shelter from cold winter winds and snow sweeping down from the north.

With the coming of the white man into the plains, the Indian way of life changed drastically. The buffalo began to vanish, the grasslands were covered with buildings such as forts and settlements. Times grew hard for the Indians, for the buffalo was their life's blood, and as the herds lessened, the Indians suffered as a consequence. When the Union Pacific railroad was to be built upon hunting lands owned by treaty, the idea of sending the Indians to reservations took hold. Like a swarm of bothersome gnats, the Indians were swept aside.

Thus it is that two lovers face the ultimate test. She, an Indian girl, granddaughter of the medicine man, and he, a soldier, must test the strength of their love for each other.

Part One:
A Heart Held Captive

Colorado Territory

1863

"The heart has its reasons which reason does not know."

— Blaise Pascal, *Pensées*

Chapter One

The early-morning sun was just visible upon the horizon as the large band of Indians traveled along the plains toward their summer grounds near the South Platte River. At the head of the tribe, astride horses as black as night, rode the tribe's two foremost leaders — their chief, Left Hand, and the *wicasa waken,* or medicine man, called Buffalo's Brother. Acknowledging their leadership, the others of the tribe followed closely behind. The warriors rode in a double line side by side, the colorful feathers adorning their lances dancing in the breeze. Following them came the women and children, dogs, spare horses, and horses pulling travois piled high with household goods. For generations they had repeated this same journey, long before the white man had poured into the territory seeking the "yellow metal" in the mountains nearby.

At first the Arapaho had not been bothered by the white man's presence. They were a peaceful tribe. But with the coming of more white settlers, followed by soldiers and their families, even the trees and grasslands were disappearing; the trees were cut to build forts, houses, and fences, the grasslands trampled, burned, or fenced off. Only a few moons ago the buffalo herds had been so plentiful that they resembled a tremendous black storm cloud in the distance. Now the buffalo, an animal held sacred to the Indians, were vanishing, the plains littered with their white sun-bleached skulls.

From the back of the caravan but heading the procession of women, Skyraven, the medicine man's granddaughter, viewed the passing landscape with dismay. It was as if a swarm of locust had passed through, stripping the area of its vegetation. Perhaps her tribe's enemy, the Utes, were right after all in what they said—that the white man should be run off so the Indian nations could stay. But no. Her grandfather, the wisest man in the tribe, had steadfastly held on to his vision of peace. The Arapaho were skilled with weapons, but as hunters, not as instigators of war, he had said.

Peace was the answer, her grandfather had insisted, and the chief had listened. How then could Skyraven argue? Her grandfather was a wise man, a holy man, called by Man Above for a lifetime of service. He did not carry any weapons, only the peace pipe. He brought not only physical healing but mental and spiritual fulfillment as well. Squaring her shoulders, lifting her chin, she felt pride in their kinship and in her duties of aiding him in his ceremonies. Within the tribe she held a position of prominence and was much respected for her own merit. More than one brave had already asked for her as wife, but so far Skyraven had not found the warrior she wanted to share her life with.

A warm breeze stirred the air, blowing Skyraven's long black hair into her eyes. Like all the Arapaho women, she wore her hair hanging free, unbound. It hung nearly to her knees, covering her shoulders and back like a thick blanket. As was the custom among Indian women, Skyraven had never shorn a single lock of her tresses but washed and combed her maidenly glory frequently to show its beauty. Now she sighed as she let the wind whip the long strands about her face. It had been a long, tedious journey and she was tired, anxious to reach that large, triangular site formed by the South Platte River and Beaver Creek. Soon the sun would be high in the sky, and she longed for shelter before the torturing rays were at full strength. Hopefully the white man would have left some foliage in her treasured oasis.

A beautiful girl of eighteen summers, Skyraven was tall and sleek, her lively blue eyes reflecting the color of the sky. It was to her mortification that white blood ran in her veins, merging with her Indian heritage. It proclaimed her different from the others. Her skin was lighter, her cheekbones not quite as boldly pronounced. Even so, her grandfather often told her she was pleasant to the eyes, that she greatly resembled her mother.

Skyraven tried to imagine the parents she had never known. Had her mother's love for the white trader really been so fierce that she would have died of heartbreak when he broke his promise to return for her? Anger battled with awe in her mind at such a thought. To perish from passionate longing was foolish. Certainly *she* would never languish for so silly a reason. She had learned to be strong, to go out on her own if necessary. Let the braves stare boldly at her. She would take her own time in choosing a mate. Until then, she was quite content with the pattern of her routine of gathering the necessary roots, leaves, grasses, and barks for her grandfather.

Watching the first puffs of a cloud rising to touch the clear azure sky, Skyraven was reminded of her grandfather's sacred ceremonies. In his possession was the peace pipe, the most sacred of all things and the heart of the Indian rites. The smoke represented the voice of the people, rising from earth to Man Above. How then could she look upon her grandfather's noble form without feeling a large measure of pride? But it was far more than that. He was her sun and moon. Except for her two cousins he was really the only one of the tribe she could call family. From the time she was two years

13

old he had given her the protection of his lodge, had guarded her and given her his love. Even now, when he looked her direction, he granted her a smile. Have patience, his eyes seemed to say. We will reach the campgrounds soon. Touching her heels to the flanks of her mare, Skyraven did all she could to speed up the women so that they would not lag too far behind.

When the sun touched the mountains, Skyraven was granted her wish. Pausing on the ridge of a hill, she welcomed the sight that met her eyes. It was still the same. The white man had left this area alone. There were trees rising up like tall warriors to protect them. The fluttering of birds in the highest limbs and a soaring eagle caused her to whisper gratitude to the Great Spirit who lived in the sky. The foliage, rocks, and clear waters had not changed since she had been here last summer. It was just as if she had never left.

As the caravan approached the Platte River near the massive cottonwood trees, Skyraven prepared herself for what was to come. She watched as her grandfather dismounted ever so slowly, then walked to the sacred ground. Dipping an eagle feather in a mixture of sweet grass and water she had prepared earlier, he sprinkled it on the ground in a purification ceremony. Only when this was done could the others in the party dismount from their horses.

Skyraven swept toward her grandfather, her ankle-length skirt of softest deerskin brushing against her legs as she walked. Skyraven had decorated the dress herself with porcupine quills, beads, and embroidery. Her moccasins were attached to long leggings, making it more comfortable when riding horseback for long periods of time. Without the leggings, the tender skin of her thighs became chafed and sore.

"Ah, little one. Skyraven," her grandfather greeted her. His voice was caressing and soft, as soothing to the ears as it was when he was immersed in his chanting. "It is good to my eyes to look upon your smiling face. The

14

long ride has shaken up my bones until I feel as if I might fall apart, but the sight of you is good to a man who has passed many summers."

Looking at him with concern, Skyraven noticed a grimace of pain etched around his mouth as he stretched his arms and legs. He was growing old, his face pale and lined. Even so, he was a magnificent sight. He was simply dressed in a buckskin shirt and leggings and beaded moccasins. Around his braided gray hair was an elaborately beaded headband with a thunderbird design, a group of short feathers protruding from the front. Skyraven had worked the beading and felt pride whenever he wore it. Two round silver earpieces were attached to each side, from which flowed strips of dark and light tanned animal skins reaching to below shoulder length. Around his neck, a close-fitting necklace of silver squares completed his attire.

"You will pass many more summers, of that I am certain," she told him, her eyes gentle as they met his. She could not imagine life without this wise and brave man.

"Enough summers to see you married to a brave who will protect you as I have all these years." He tugged at a stray tendril of her hair in a gesture of affection, his expression brightening as he recalled the years she'd spent in his lodge. He had witnessed her birth, had heard her first wails. From that very first moment he had loved her. He saw her as a creation of incomparable beauty. Her hair was shining like the black wings of a raven, but her eyes had been as blue as the sky, not the onyx of his people. Skyraven, he had named her, wrapping her in deerskin and putting her in her mother's arms.

The fate of his granddaughter was a constant worry to him because of her white blood. When the whites had first come into the area he had foreseen marriages between white and Indians, especially since the whites had not brought their women with them. Buffalo's

Brother had hoped that this mixing of blood would bring peace, would bind Indians and their white brothers closer together. He had been wrong. "Take, not give" was the white man's creed. They looked upon the red men as little better than the ants that crawled upon the ground. His daughter had given her heart to a white trader, had married him only to be deserted soon after their child was born. The medicine man had taken the two females into his household, had trained Skyraven in herbal potions, instilling his wisdom in her head. She had not disappointed him.

"You have become a lovely young woman," he whispered, his gaze scrutinizing her delicate features. Her complexion proved her mixed heritage. It was a light creamy olive, a shade between the skin hues of her parents. "But then I suspected you would rival the sunrise for beauty. And you have. . . ." He smiled as she blushed. "We must find a very special husband for you."

"Husband?" She shrugged her shoulders. "I am in no hurry. I'm happy to stay with you." Being a squaw could be a life of drudgery. Skyraven wanted to let a few more summers pass before she had little ones clinging to her legs.

"We'll see." He could not help but notice how many male eyes were turned her way. Lone Wolf, Eyes-of-Night, Lame Rabbit. Each would make a good husband for her. All were handsome, as the people of the southern Arapaho were comely. Tall, stately, and slender of build, not short and squat as were their enemies the Utes. "We'll talk of this tonight."

They ended their conversation, for it was time to set up the ceremonial lodge. Only after it was completed could the personal lodges be assembled. Braves, children, and women were smiling, for it was a joyous occasion. The summer hunting would begin after the eighth day of the sun dance celebration.

The trunks of the massive trees swept upward toward the sky, their thick foliage filled with chirping birds.

The din of voices from the camp blended with the woodland sounds as soft strains of music sounded and the pungent smell of burning wood wafted through the air. From across the camp, Lone Wolf proudly stuck out his chest and strode about with manly pride. Skyraven did have to admit that he was handsome—tall, proud, and impressive. In his long black braided hair was one lone eagle feather. His tan deerskin shirt and leggings rippled with the strength of his muscles. Lone Wolf was the chief's son, the eldest son of Left Hand's loins. Skyraven had to smile at his pride. She had grown up with him, romped, climbed trees, and raced him on her pony. They had joined in games such as spinning bone or wooden tops, whooping and hollering, chasing and teasing each other. Then they had reached the age of twelve and assumed adult responsibilities. Lone Wolf had become a warrior and a hunter at thirteen summers and could participate in the hunt. Since then, they seldom spent time in each other's company.

Lately he had taken to preening himself before her, however, much like an overproud quail, just as he was doing now. And yet he had a reason today. It was an honor to be chosen as one of the four young men to find and bring back the white oak central pole for the Offering lodge. The pole was sacred and could not be touched by human hands after it was felled. Instead, it had to be transported quite cleverly by carrying it with sticks.

"I see the way you are looking at him!" A voice hissed behind her and Skyraven whirled to find herself looking into Whispering Wind's scowling face. The dark-eyed Indian girl had proclaimed herself Skyraven's rival on more than one occasion. Now it appeared she had set her sights on Lone Wolf. "But he is mine!"

"You may have him, I care not." Skyraven shrugged her shoulders. She wasn't about to spar like a she-wolf and bare her claws for any brave.

"Then keep your distance! You with the tainted blood. White man's spawn!" The squinting eyes were flashing with jealousy and malice. Whispering Wind had always been hateful to her, though Skyraven did not really understand why.

"Silence your tongue or I will do it for you," Skyraven warned the girl now. It was a time for religious ceremonies so she did not want to quarrel, but neither would she take any insult from this spitting wildcat.

"Lone Wolf would never choose you," Whispering Wind persisted. It is good that you have resolved yourself to losing him. You are too pale, too fragile. He will want a strong woman to warm his bed and give him sons. Just remember that when you seek him with your eyes." As a final warning, she pulled Skyraven's hair before she ran away. Skyraven would have chased her at any other time, but now, as her grandfather motioned her to him, she fought her anger. She would not foul the air with her angry words.

Skyraven watched as the pole was brought back and the sacred lodge built. Even after the pole was secured in the ground, no one was allowed to touch it. The sick and troubled were allowed to sit inside the lodge and were offered healing by prayers, gourd rattling, and the roots offered them by her grandfather. Skyraven put away her hostilities toward Whispering Wind as she took a place by the medicine man's side. It was during the sun dance ceremony that the tribe put themselves in touch with the spirit world, with her grandfather acting as the link. Closing her eyes, she leaned against a rock. The soft splashing along the banks of the Platte River was a comforting sound, as if Man Above was walking in its depths. Skyraven gave herself up to the mood of contentment, but was startled suddenly by a strange feeling that swept over her. A strange foreboding, an uneasiness, as if something unforetold was going to happen.

Opening her eyes, she looked around. It was quiet.

Peaceful. Why then was she uneasy? Putting her fingers to her eyes, she pressed on the lids, as if forcing the thoughts away, concentrating instead on the soft chanting around her. It was no use. Over and over again she was overcome by the awesome feeling that somehow the soothing routine of her life was about to change.

Chapter Two

The distant mountains were a purple backdrop against the sky in the early-morning twilight. They could make good time today, Major John Hanlen thought as he led his men single file up the canyon which formed a natural gateway to the otherwise impassable barrier of bluffs and deep ravines bordering the Platte River. Their first day's ride had brought them to a tributary of the Republican River where the cavalrymen camped for the night. Now they were ascending from the valley to the plateau overlooking the same valley they had left.

Hanlen knew that smaller groups of men moved more quickly than larger ones. That was why he had hand-picked ten cavalrymen and one guide, making an even dozen when he included himself. Bending close to the churning muscles of his horse, he sought a firm grip on the reins, thinking again how little he liked this errand he had been sent upon, to spy upon the Indians. He had been advised to lead his tiny group of men into this desolate area, to work himself into the Indians' confidence and report all that he had heard, promptly. It was his mission to discover the main camp, a job that made him nervous and wary. Still, he was determined to accomplish his purpose and would, if hard riding and keen watchfulness would bring about success. They were riding through unknown country. The Indians here were generally reported to be friendly, although lately other scouting parties had reported seeing a few hostile ones here and there.

Taking off his French-style major's cap with the tall yellow pompom, he ran his fingers through his long blond waves, attuning his eyes to any danger. He had no doubt that coming across a group of galloping wildmen would be an unsettling experience. Facing a group of yahooing rebels was bad enough, but at least the Confederates were somewhat civilized. The same most certainly could not be said for the red men.

Major Hanlen had been a Union Cavalry officer stationed in Missouri, his home state. When it was learned that the Confederates were trying to persuade the Indians toward their cause, however, he had been quickly given a change in assignment and sent into Indian territory before he could blink an eye. His job, and the job of his comrades, was to keep the savages out of the Confederates' sphere of influence. Even if that meant killing them like the vermin they were, the colonel had said. The thought was unnerving. He had no wish to take part in a slaughter, but a soldier had a duty to perform and he meant to do his best.

Until now he had rather enjoyed being in the Colorado First Cavalry unit. It had been a welcome relief from the constant fighting broiling at home. Then, when the Pacific Railway Act was passed, it became necessary for the soldiers to oversee an important section of land, earmarked for the railroads, two hundred feet wide and running through the buffalo grazing land. It was a necessary evil if the West was going to be connected with the rest of the lands, he supposed. Still, the knowledge that the government would use the Fort Wise Treaty to extinguish the Indians' rights to land that was theirs bothered him. The land was legally owned by the Arapaho and Cheyenne. It had been granted to them as hunting ground by the same government that now wanted to undo what they had done.

21

"Unfortunate!" the territorial governor John Evans had said when Major Hanlen had asked about it, "but you must remember no other land offers such opportunities for the vast accumulation of wealth. There are settled towns here, gold-mining camps and open plains that promise expansion to a steadily growing country."

Later he had found that the government held hopes that the tribes would cede the land. Hanlen's job was to see that they did. Only a small group manned Fort Lyon now. Many troops had been called back to active duty in the War Between the States and were now serving east of the Mississippi. The few remaining cavalry personnel were expected to do whatever they were called to do. The situation was tense. Already some Indians were openly displaying their disfavor of a peaceful settlement. There had been cattle raids, looting, burning of fields, and other atrocities. Tempers were beginning to heat up. So far the chiefs had been successful in counseling restraint, hoping that some acceptable settlement of the land question could be made, but how long would the peace last? He could only wonder.

Riding as silently as they could so as not to stir up trouble, John Hanlen and his men watched as the first rays of sun came over the hilltops. It gave him a feeling of relief knowing it would soon be light. It was much safer if they could see where they were going. Hanlen's company had been instructed to bivouac at each day's end, with two men standing watch. They were to travel in the dawning hours of the morning, through early afternoon.

Unable to talk much while proceeding in single file and lulled by the monotonous movement of his horse, Hanlen let his thoughts wander. It seemed only yesterday that he was a law student at Harvard, the middle son of a career general. He'd had a hell of a time convincing his father he didn't want to go to West Point. He nearly had been disowned. Then his mother, God bless her, had taken his side. He'd been granted his wish only to find himself in uniform after all when the war had started. What a rueful irony! Now he was finishing his term of enlistment in this godforsaken territory. Ah, well. He'd signed up for three years and had only served one. If he survived, perhaps he could go back East and continue his education. One thing was certain, with all this expansion, the West was going to need lawyers. He'd sure as hell rather be slinging a law book than a gun any day.

A chorus of twittering birds and the contented hoot of an owl far away soothed him. The early morning hours seemed quiet, peaceful. Suddenly Major Hanlen was disturbed by a less tranquil noise. Reaching down, he patted his trusty Spencer rifle which was always at his side. As he listened, he heard the sound of horses' hooves coming closer and closer until they echoed in his ears. Indians! It had to be. No crickets or birds or owls. Owls were nightbirds! Why hadn't he realized? That peaceful sound had been the Indians' way of signaling his advancing party.

"Ho. . . ! Ride! Get the hell out of here, men!" He'd been instructed not to issue the first shot. If they could only outride the Indians they might have a chance. Thank God it was daylight!

John Hanlen rode with his men at a furious pace. Their death sentence—that was what it could mean if they were caught. Drenched in perspiration from the exertion of the chase, he looked over his shoulder and saw the band of war-painted Indians coming upon him from the rear. No peaceful hunters these! Feeling the pulsating rhythm of his horse's flanks beneath the high leather of his boots, he plunged onward, but the Indians, about fifty of them, had taken advantage of a ravine and had managed to approach quite close before being discovered and thus held the advantage. There was no way his soldiers could outride them now. One of his men had already been run down and the entire war

23

party had galloped ruthlessly over his body. The speed of the Indian ponies and the expert horsemanship of the Indian warriors was too much to compete with, but they couldn't just give up and be slaughtered. At least they would go down fighting, he thought. Hanlen ordered his men to dismount and form a circle, using the horses as a barrier between themselves and the redskins. The war whoops were falling clearer and louder upon the soldiers' ears, mingling with the sound of gunfire.

Soon the soldiers were surrounded by the superior force of the savages as the Indians, obviously on the war path, circled around and around. The loss of two of their warriors, both slain by one trigger-happy soldier, compounded their hostility. After several warriors had dismounted and dragged the bodies of their fallen companions from the field of battle, they soon were back in the saddle again, dangerously eyeing their captives. Hanlen knew it was an Indian custom in battle that warriors would risk their own lives to prevent a fellow warrior's body from falling into enemy hands. They believed that if a slain warrior were not retrieved, he could not go to the Happy Hunting Ground but would be suspended between earth and sky in a sort of limbo.

John Hanlen searched the area with his eyes for his men and was thankful to see that most of them had made it safely to the circle. They had miraculously survived this long.

"I'll be goddamned, Major," a soldier next to him was saying. "I've never seen the like. Just look at them redskinned bastards."

The Indians were arrayed in full war costume. Their faces, arms, legs, bodies, and even their horses were painted various bright colors and on their heads were brightly colored war bonnets. They had a hideous, frightening appearance now that he could see them from a closer distance. Some were carrying lances and all had round bulletproof buffalo-hide shields fastened to their left arms. The bullets seemed to just glance off the shields. They were well armed, which made for a more precarious position for his soldiers, Hanlen thought. They carried not only bows and arrows but carbines and revolvers as well.

Despite the Indians' weapons, however, he held off the order to fire. Suddenly, with a wild ringing war cry the Indians bore down upon the little party of defenders, shattering any hope whatsoever that there could be any peace. They rode boldly forward as if preparing to dash over the mere handful of cavalrymen.

Hanlen heard their shouts and the plop of their horses' hooves and prepared himself for the inevitable. "Steady men . . ." he commanded.

Not a soldier faltered as the painted warriors came thundering upon them. They dropped upon one knee, took aim, and fired. Several warriors were brought down by gunfire, but moving at such rapid speed and coming like a swarm of ants, it was difficult to bring them down. Their expert riding and well-trained war ponies were certainly superior to anything the soldiers had seen before. Throwing themselves to the side of their war ponies, the warriors were able to fire from above or beneath the horses' necks and were themselves well protected. The few who had lost the horses beneath them in the firing were now fighting on foot.

Edging toward the cluster of remaining men, an Indian with bear claws around his throat raised his tomahawk and grabbed a young, wounded sergeant by the hair, preparing to scalp him. Major Hanlen sprang into action. "Leave him be, you savage bastard!" he screamed. Cocking his gun, he took aim but was struck from behind before he could even fire a shot. Three jabbering, painted Indians were babbling in his ear as he slumped to the ground. His last coherent thought was that he was about to die.

But they didn't kill him. Instead, he awoke to find

himself at the center of a desolate clearing, his hands roped together and tied to a post behind his back. The Indians surrounded him, knives drawn. John Hanlen had the feeling it might have been better if they *had* killed him.

"My men. . . !" he said aloud. As if somehow understanding his question, one of the braves pointed to an area lit by firelight. There, lying in a heap, were his blue-coated soldiers. Dear God, he'd never meant for it to end this way. Stevens, LaMoine, Bently. So young to have died so violently. Good men, all. Dear God, why? And why then had he been kept alive? He could only wonder.

Once again the Indians gave vent to their chattering. How he wished he knew what they were saying. They were pointing at him, growling like animals. Stomping their feet, jeering at him, they seemed to be offering insults. They showed extreme interest in his hat, as if somehow they knew he was the leader of the group. Therein lay the reason he'd not been murdered, he realized.

A sudden twist of the wood thrust through the knots holding his wrists made him cry out. Over and over again they twisted the knot, cutting off his circulation. Soon his wrists were numb and blue with bruises. Whooping and dancing around him, they brandished their knives and made obvious their intentions.

"Dear God, give me strength!" he called out. The horror of it all swept through him as he realized what his fate was to be. They were going to torture him to death.

Chapter Three

The early-morning sun hovered in the sky like a ball of fire. As she lifted the flap of the tepee to gaze outside, Skyraven squinted at the glare. At last the living lodges had been constructed, comfortable tepees of buffalo skin sewn together and draped around sturdy pine poles. The flaps of the dwellings always faced the east so the sunrise was the first thing one saw when leaving the lodge in the morning.

Although it was still early the entire camp was ablaze with activity. Several men were galloping through the village astride their horses, in a hurry to be on their way to scout for buffalo herds and to return before nightfall. Everyone except the small children and babies had some kind of work to complete before the evening came and the ceremonies could begin.

Skyraven walked toward the river with ceremonial robes to be washed and dried before the day turned to night. As she made her way through the camp, a group of young children playing throw-the-hoop called out a greeting to her. Her attention was momentarily diverted and she did not have the chance to acknowledge Lone Wolf's hand raised in greeting. He was tying a quiver of arrows around his war pony's neck in preparation for the mock battle to be fought later in the day, but he stopped for a moment to look longingly in her direction. The look did not go unnoticed by Whisper-

27

ing Wind. That scowling Indian girl had been preparing pemmican from strips of buffalo meat mixed with fat marrow and chokecherry paste, but she quickly put aside the gut casings she was filling with the mixture and hurried to Lone Wolf's side. Her eyes blazed possessively as she brushed his arm. She was disappointed that Skyraven continued on to the river's edge to commence her washing without taking notice of her rival's supposed victory.

The water was cold, but Skyraven ignored the discomfort as she submerged her hands in the river, concentrating her attention on her grandfather's shirt. Soaking it and pounding it with a bone mallet, she soon had it clean, then paused in her labor. It was a magical morning made for daydreaming. She could take her time laying the garments out in the hot sun, which would dry them quickly. Indeed, the sun danced and sparkled upon the surface of the water, and she splashed some of the refreshing moisture on her face only to be startled as she peered into the river's depth. She could see the same image she had seen in her dreams the last two nights but shook her head trying to chase the vision away.

"No . . . no." She stared into the blue depths for a long time, completely mesmerized by the vision that met her eyes. "I do not want to see," she mumbled softly, speaking to the images in the water. To her horror the images seemed to talk back, issuing her a warning. Like one gone mad, she talked back to the voices, trying to push them away. "Leave me!" Instead of obeying, the images hovered before her eyes and she was immersed in a living dream.

Her soft doeskin dress was wet with perspiration, her dark hair tangled around her face like a thick rope when at last she jumped up with a start. Her blue eyes were wide with fright at that which she could not fully understand. She looked around, raising a shaking hand to her mouth in an effort to calm her fear. There was no

28

one nearby. She was all alone. She must have imagined the voices, and yet it had all seemed so real.

She had seen a golden-haired white man surrounded by Indians. It was as if the Great Spirit had called upon her to aid him in freeing the man, just as he had in her dreams. It had been so real that she had fully expected to find someone lurking within the deep blue waters. Just to make certain there was not, she frantically slapped at the water, sending it into frenzied waves, then rose to her feet. She had to find her grandfather.

On trembling legs she walked to the entrance of the lodge. "Grandfather!" Lifting up the flap, she scanned the room. On the southern side, with its head west, was her grandfather's bed. Above it were painted pictures of things he'd seen and done during his lifetime. Near the bed were several buffalo robes to sit upon during the day or for warmth at night, but her grandfather was not in the lodge.

Skyraven's eyes were drawn to the glowing embers of the fire. A fire always burned in the center of the tepee just as one continuously burned in the middle of the camp. She sniffed the air and could smell the scent of the meat and wild vegetables which had simmered over the hot flagstones in iron pots all night long—white man's cookery that the squaws used sometimes. It reminded her that she had not yet eaten, but strangely, now she was not hungry. Fear and apprehension had wiped her appetite away.

Foolish woman, she thought. Like a child she had run to her grandfather's arms, but all around her seemed peaceful. Still, she felt uneasy, as if she could still feel the presence of danger—danger not to herself but to the white man who had appeared in the water. She had to question her grandfather about the matter. Was it possible that she had inherited his ability to see the future? Was this how he felt when he gave himself up to his visions, his chants?

Wandering about the camp as if in a trance, she tried

to put some meaning into her vision. A man with hair as pale gold as the spring corn had been surrounded by a ring of warriors not of her tribe. She shuddered as she contemplated the man's fate. But what had he to do with her? Why had she seen herself there also? It was a thing she could not help but wonder.

This was the fourth of the eight days of ceremonial activity. Already the young warriors had begun the mock battle. As usual, Lone Wolf was the boldest of the braves. Like a fluttering sparrow, Whispering Wind was as close to the edge of the doings as she was allowed. Twittering, swaying her hips whenever she walked about, she tried to draw his notice, but Skyraven didn't care. In some ways they deserved each other, for both were exceedingly vain.

"Skyraven . . ." Her grandfather had called to her. A look of mild irritation clouded his wrinkled face. As she came near him he held out his hand. "The leather pouch of herbs was torn during our journey. I did not discover it until just now. I have no wild sage for the ceremony tonight."

"I know a place not far from here where it grows thickly. I have gathered it there before. I'll go, but it will take me some time to get there and back." Looking up at the sky she calculated that she would have plenty of time. The ceremony would not begin until sundown. The crier would ride through the village, stopping at each of the one hundred and fifty lodges to call the people to assemble for the dance ceremony and give thanks to Man Above for a safe journey, but not until it was dark. This day had just begun. "I will ride like the wind and be back before the sun is high overhead," Skyraven promised.

Her reply brought a smile to her grandfather's lips. "And so you shall be. I can always depend on you, Granddaughter." He patted her on the shoulder, turned, and left before she had a chance to mention her vision. She had wanted to ask him about what it could

30

have meant, but now he had his own worries so she did not follow after him. Perhaps time alone with her thoughts was what she needed. A horseback ride always cleared her head.

Putting her two fingers into her mouth, Skyraven made the shrill sound that always brought her painted mare to her. The large animal was beautiful and gentle, yet as fast as the wind. That was the reason Skyraven had named her Running Antelope. As the mare approached, Skyraven patted her head, then sprang upon the horse's back with expert nimbleness.

Tossing her head fretfully, the mare nickered in greeting, showing her eagerness to run. Skyraven let the animal have her way and breathed in excitement as horse and rider became one with the racing wind. The tepees of the camp soon looked like huge pine cones in the distance.

Onward they galloped, past the creekbed, beyond the steep incline. She thrilled at the feeling of freedom she always experienced when the whole countryside was open to her. Her disturbing dream and all her fears and worries were swept away as the horse responded to her owner's soft whisper and light touch on her mane. When they finally came to the edge of the clearing, Skyraven slid from the horse and busied herself with gathering the plentiful herbs, including wild sage, red root and milkweed. Soon the pouches were filled, but off and on as she worked Skyraven was assailed by unsettling feelings of impending danger. She tried to ignore the voice that called her but a power seemed to be urging her onward.

Once again she mounted Running Antelope, intending to return to the village, but the mare seemed to be leading her farther into unfamiliar country. Was it magic that pulled at her or her own inner thinking? Her grandfather had asked her over and over again if she ever saw visions, as if he expected that she should. Now she could tell him that she had. The gift seemed to be working for her also.

Running Antelope stopped abruptly and raised her head, her nostrils flaring. Smoke. Skyraven could smell the faint pungent odor of buffalo chips in the distance and strained her ears and eyes. Were her senses deceiving her or could she hear the distant sound of chanting being carried in the wind? Carefully she slid from Running Antelope's back and tethered her to a tree near the tall grass where they would both be well hidden from view. Skyraven crept forward on her hands and knees for quite a distance, then lay down on her stomach and carefully parted the tall grass. As she gazed through the thick cover, the sight before her caught her stomach to churn and her legs to tremble. The image again had returned to haunt her. She made an effort to hide her fear but all thought evaporated into thin air.

Skyraven's throat became constricted. She was almost afraid to breathe. Then she realized that the sight before her was *real*. It was not imagined or just a vision. Even from this distance she could see him, the man in her vision. He was tall and strong in appearance, as powerfully built as any warrior. A group of eight brightly painted warriors stood in a menacing semicircle around the light-haired white man. Utes! Like the Pawnees, they were enemies of her tribe. Oh, how she hated them, she thought.

Cautiously she moved forward for a better look. The Indians were stripping the clothing from the white man's body while making gestures and talking in grunts she could not understand. The white man was nearly naked, wearing only the strange undergarments his people were said to wear. They looked much to her eyes like red leggings. Skyraven could not help but stare. His shoulders were wide, his legs long, and his body glistened with perspiration, emphasizing its beauty. In truth, the white man was a fine specimen of manhood. She doubted he had succumbed easily to his captors. No wonder there were so many of them, she thought with scorn. It would have taken more than one squatty Ute warrior to subdue *him*. Oh, he was handsome for a white man, but it was his hair that drew her eye. Catching all the rays of the sun it looked golden, like corn silk or flax. How she would hate to see those beautiful yellow waves adorning a Ute's belt!

It is none of your concern, woman, she chided herself, and yet something about the white man drew her. His head drooped to one side, his eyes were closed, and for just a moment she could nearly feel his pain. Was there anything she could do? She attuned her ears to the sounds floating around her. She could hear more voices and chants far away. There must be more of them than she thought. She didn't dare to look. Not now. All of her teachings came to her aid as she willed herself to remain stiff and still as a stone, watching.

They had roughly tied him to a tree, leaving him stripped of all clothing except his underwear. One large warrior raised his lance and shouted something she decided must be "Come, let us bring back the others to help us decide what we should do with our prisoner." She could not really understand what the large warrior had said, but it really didn't matter. All that mattered was that seven of the warriors had climbed on their horses and galloped out, leaving only one warrior to guard the prisoner.

Utes! They disgusted her. Even their looks were repulsive. They were short, squat, and ugly, not tall and graceful like her people. She had to be wary, for they were always on the prowl for women of her tribe. Being carried away by a Ute would be a humiliating trial.

Skyraven remained immobile until the sound of horses' hooves, which had been so loud before, became muffled and sounded distant. She breathed a sigh of relief. *I should leave,* she thought. Why should the Great Spirit want her to help this yellow-haired man? The whites had come to the area searching for their yellow metal, pushing the Indians farther and farther from

33

their hunting grounds. They had killed the buffalo and caused much destruction. *Leave him! Let the Utes have him.* So thinking, she turned to go, only to retrace her steps. A war raged in her soul. She was torn between leaving him and saving him. Something about the white man was compelling, tugging at her heart. Perhaps because she was half white herself, she surmised.

Now that the main party of warriors had gone, she would creep just a little closer to get a better look. Frantically fighting the apprehension that coiled in her belly, she made her way through the foliage until she was nearer the stranger.

He was dirty, bloody, and unconscious. If the Utes had their way he would be shattered by the tortures he would be made to bear. No! She couldn't let that happen. Not to this golden man. She couldn't let him be mutilated by the sharp knives and cruelty of her enemies. That her own tribesmen might be blamed was another thought that crossed her mind. The spirits had instructed her to save this man and somehow she now knew why. He was to be a part of her destiny.

She felt so small. Could she rescue him? *If only I had a dagger,* she lamented. She was barehanded. It would be sheer folly to try to rescue him without a weapon. Perhaps she could free him if she could somehow get the knife away from the one warrior who was left to guard him. That thought was tempting.

Skyraven planned her strategy as she surveyed the Ute. The short, squat warrior was bent over, peering at the white man from a crouched position. The laughter rippled from his throat as he tried on the white man's plumed officer's hat. Skyraven thought how silly he looked as he folded his arms across his chest. He seemed quite pleased with himself, however. *As if he could ever measure up to the white man's strength,* Skyraven scoffed silently. He began fumbling through the man's discarded clothing until he found the white man's black boots. Pulling off his moccasins, he put his feet into the boots, which came well above his knees. Foolish, foolish Ute! He had put the left foot into the right boot and the right foot into the left boot, which made walking clumsy and difficult. How like a Ute to do such a simple thing wrong, Skyraven thought sourly. Hopefully he would prove to be just as incompetent in fighting. That she would soon find out, for he was headed in her direction.

The Ute approached her hiding place behind a clump of bushes. Spotting a large rock at her feet, she hefted it, preparing to defend herself in case he discovered her. Walking in the boots made him less than sure-footed and his eyes were on his feet as he continued his approach. As he was near enough, Skyraven brought the rock down full force on top of his head and watched as he fell to the ground with a great thud. As she groped for his weapon, she felt the Great Spirit smile, her fingers caressing the knife. She waited for a moment, watching to make certain there were no other braves lurking, then she hastened toward the man.

"White eyes. . . ?" she murmured questioningly.

The white man's chest muscles rippled as he breathed, but he did not acknowledge her. Carefully she cut the leather thongs that tied his hands. He slumped to the ground, moaning. Overcome with sympathy, she knelt and touched him, speaking to him in whispered tones. Shaking his shoulders gently, she tried to rouse him to consciousness. She could get him away from here much faster if she didn't have to drag him.

"Please!" she urged, but it was no use. Hurrying to a small stream that bubbled through the area, she dipped the edge of her doeskin dress into the water and returned to wring its moisture in his face. She was rewarded for her effort when he opened his eyes.

"No! Go away!" he moaned. Major John Hanlen looked beseechingly at her, pleading with her to leave him alone. He had suffered so much. Dear God, he was not afraid to die, he was a soldier and had been trained

35

in the art of warfare, but to be picked at and poked at until he lost his mind, to be cut apart piece of piece while he was still alive frightened the living hell out of him. It was too gruesome an end. He had heard stories about these heathens and their devilry, but he had not realized until this very moment that the fearsome tales were really true. Was this another of the heathen band come to watch him suffer? Perhaps. The warriors of this tribe were sadistic, why not their women as well?

"Listen to me!" she persisted. "You must stand! You must . . ."

"No! Leave me be."

"I've come to help you escape!"

John Hanlen felt light-headed, weak and dizzy, but he shook his head to clear it of its spinning. Had he heard her right. She did not mumble and grunt in words he could not understand. She spoke English. Did he dare to hope? Looking full into her face, he was startled by the blue eyes looking back at him.

"If that's true, then thank you," he choked. Thank God she spoke English. She was no savage, then, but an educated woman. The thought made him smile. As he did, it was Skyraven's turn to be startled. He had a lovely mouth and fine, strong teeth, but she was foolish to notice such things.

"Stand up!" She barked as if to order, then quickly added, "If we do not hurry, we will both be victims of the Utes." As she spoke, she grabbed his clothes from off the ground and put them under her arm. She did not want to take the time to remove the hat or boots from the body of the fallen warrior lest he awaken. She was not sure whether she had killed him or simply knocked him out.

Struggling, John Hanlen called upon his inner strength, somehow managing to get to his hands and knees. With the Indian girl's help he crawled through the thick undergrowth toward the mare she had carefully camouflaged. She placed his clothing into a leather saddlebag, then helped him onto Running Antelope's back.

John Hanlen felt the softness of her hands as she pushed and pulled him onto her horse, then he sensed nothing more. Black swirls danced before his eyes. He fell victim to the darkness once again.

Chapter Four

Skyraven guided her horse along at a furious pace, holding to the reins with one hand and keeping the other wrapped securely around the white soldier to keep him safely in the saddle. She knew that she must put as much distance between herself and the Ute warriors as possible. When they returned and found their captive had escaped, the Utes were sure to send out a search party. She and the white man could be in dire danger if she did not act carefully.

Even the added weight of the soldier's body did not slow down Running Antelope's fast pace. She was a well-trained horse, always obeying every command. Skyraven had cautiously judged just how far the mare could travel and how much weight the animal could carry. Several times she doubled back, and whenever possible would travel in the shallow creek in order to confuse anyone tracking them. The Utes would soon find that their quarry had vanished with no telltale signs left behind. That thought made her smile and wish for just a moment that she could see their faces when they realized they had been so easily duped. Foolish Utes, they were no match for an Arapaho, she thought. Her people were much too wise.

As she neared the low-lying hills just to the west of her tribe's campgrounds she knew just where she was going to take her precious burden. Though she would have preferred taking him to the sweat lodge or the medicine lodge to be tended by her grandfather, her instincts warned her against such a brazen move. Some of the braves did not like the white eyes and might stir up trouble, Lone Wolf for one. They might resent her for bringing him to the village. This was a time of change, when more white men were coming, threatening to alter the Arapaho's traditional nomadic way of life. She could not be assured that this white man would be totally safe among her people. She remembered a small cave she had discovered while searching for herbs. She must take him there, to the special place she thought of as *her* cave, where she often went to be alone. It wasn't a deep cave nor a wide one, but it would do as a hiding place. As far as she knew, no one else was aware of its existence. The cave was not too far away from camp, yet it was not so close that searching eyes would discover it.

Somehow the thought of the white man being enclosed within Mother Earth in this shallow cave and watched over by the Earth Spirit gave Skyraven the hope of a speedy recovery for the yellow-haired stranger. It was as close to a sweat lodge as she could manage, considering the circumstances. Clasping her medicine pouch closely to her chest she guided her horse to a stop close to the mouth of the cave. Positioning the white man safely on Running Antelope's back, she carefully slid from the animal.

From the medicine pouch she took a small handful of the sage she had collected for her grandfather and walked to the mouth of the cave, sprinkling the pungent-smelling herb along the way. At the mouth of the cave's entrance, she turned in the directions — east, then west, then north and south — chanting softly. When the cave was purified she collected some fallen branches and fashioned a bed, taking her own buffalo robe from her saddlebag and using it as a cover, then hurriedly collected some wood and started a fire to bring warmth to the chill of the cave. She managed to rouse the soldier to consciousness long enough to get him inside. Once inside the cave, she tried to make him as comfortable as possible. He had drifted in and out of consciousness throughout the ride, and now he moaned as he tossed his head from side to side. Leaving him only for a moment, Skyraven gathered some of the horse mint which grew abundantly just outside the cave, chewed the leaves, and placed the moistened vegetation on his most severe wounds to reduce any swelling and stop possible infection. She secured the leaves by tying them to his limbs with wide rawhide strips. He winced and cried out from time to time as she tended his injuries but drifted into a deep sleep, relishing the softness of the buffalo hide as soon as she had completed the treatment. Somehow he seemed to sense his danger was over.

Skyraven let her eyes roam over what she could see of the white man's body. His skin was several shades lighter than her people's, yet dark where it had been exposed to the sun. His arms and chest were well muscled. Fine golden hair covered his broad chest and trailed in a thin straight line down to his navel. The strange red leggings kept her from seeing further, yet she couldn't help but wonder if he was as well endowed below as the braves she had seen bathing in the river. She supposed all men were much the same. That unmaidenly thought caused her face to flame, for it was more like Whispering Wind's boldness than her own resolve. She hurriedly pushed such questions from her mind as being unseemly for a young woman who held such high honor in her tribe.

While he slept, Skyraven went outside and climbed to the edge of the ridge near the cave and peered over. Down below she could see the trail of smoke which rose from her village swirling into the air. There were more than a hundred tepees shining white and clean in the sun. Skyraven could see lightly blanketed women gathering firewood, while others worked at their looms or meat drying racks. Children ran about. Although most of the men seemed to be away from camp, there were some sitting near their lodges, restringing bows and repairing their weapons. On the flat land near the river, the horses were grazing peacefully. From her vantage point, the people and horses of Skyraven's camp looked like miniatures, small enough to put in her pouch and carry away. That thought made her smile. When she was a child her grandfather had fashioned just such a tiny village for her play. Whispering Wind had maliciously trampled Skyraven's most precious possession, but that she-wolf would not now have the chance to practice her malice on the yellow-haired white man. He would be Skyraven's secret. Just the thought gave her an inner glow.

From this position on the ridge, she could observe all the activities in the camp. She felt safe here and knew that the golden-haired soldier was safe, too. *But I must be careful lest my absence be noted,* she thought. She could not stay with the white soldier too long. She would be missed and searched for if she failed to get the sage to her grandfather in time for the evening's dancing and thanksgiving ceremony. Nor could she ever shirk her duties to her grandfather for any reason, even one as important as this white man who the Great Spirit had sent into her care. By the position of the sun, however, she knew she still had a long time before nightfall. Rising from her crouching position on the ridge, she returned to the white soldier's side to keep watch until it was time to go.

Sitting on a rock by the fire, Skyraven let her eyes touch on the white man, caressing him with her gaze. It was really the first time she had studied him in detail and she found him most definitely pleasing. She had seen white men before at the trading posts, but none with such pale hair. He was handsome in an unusual kind of way, different from Lone Wolf's sullen dark

41

comeliness but just as muscular. Whereas Lone Wolf's hair was dark and long, the white man's wavy golden hair was cut just below his ears. His eyes were closed now, but Skyraven remembered that when they were open they were the color of the sky, like hers. Lone Wolf's brows went from eye to eye without end; the white man's were not as bushy. Both men had high cheekbones, but Lone Wolf's nose jutted out like a rough stone while the soldier's nose was carefully chiseled. It was what grew beneath the white man's nose that fascinated her, however: Yellow-colored hair as thick as that on his head grew on his upper lip. None of the braves had such facial hair.

"How strange!" she said aloud.

Skyraven could not help reaching out to stroke the golden hair to see if it was soft or scratchy. It was smooth and pleasing to her fingers. Cautiously she ran her fingertips over the entire length of the mustache, then just as quickly pulled her hand away as if she had been scorched by the contact. What was this feeling in the pit of her stomach? Just touching this man caused her to tremble. With sudden fear she drew away and walked to the mouth of the cave. This white man must have potent magic to so affect her, she mused, folding her arms across her chest as she frowned. The feelings his magic stirred within her breast made her wary. She should flee, return to her people. He didn't need her anymore. She had done all she could do for him. All he really needed now was rest, she decided, rising to take her leave.

Hurrying to Running Antelope, she untethered the mare and started to mount, yet something caused her to pause. He might be dangerous, she thought, but she was not afraid of the white man's potent magic. She was the medicine man's granddaughter. She could counter any spell he might be able to weave. If she ran away right now she would be admitting that his magic was greater. That she would not do. Squaring her shoulders, holding her chin high in the air, she retethered the mare and returned to the cave and her vigil, maintaining a cautious distance.

"No! Dear God, no!" The sound of the white man's murmuring as he thrashed his head from side to side brought Skyraven closer to his side. Overcome by sympathy, she knelt beside him and reached out to soothe his brow, thankful that there appeared to be no fever.

"Rest, white eyes. None will harm you here," she said gently.

The soldier's eyes flew open as if responding to her voice. "Dead. All dead . . ." He started to sit up, but Skyraven pushed him back down.

"No . . . leave me be! Heathens. Goddamned savages!" He twisted and squirmed, trying to escape from the firm hand that pressed against his chest, but Skyraven maintained her hold on him. At last he ceased his struggles as fatigue seemingly drained him of energy. Even so, his eyes remained open, focusing at last on her. "Who are you?"

Skyraven was wary. "Why do you ask?"

"I . . . I just want to know by w-what name to call you. That is all." John Hanlen's eyes raked over her, remembering vaguely that in some way she had come to his rescue. Certainly she was a welcoming sight, a striking, beautiful woman.

"My name is Skyraven, white man." There could be no harm in telling him, she thought. "I brought you here. You are safe from those Ute devils who tortured you."

"Utes?" Not quite believing her, he lifted his head and looked around as if expecting a war party to fall upon him again. He was in some sort of cave. With a shudder, he recalled what had happened to him. Would he ever feel safe again? "Where am I?"

"In my secret cave." As if reading his mind, she added, "Far away from the Ute camp. Near my people's village."

43

"Your people?"

"Arapaho." She said the name proudly. "The Utes are our enemies. They are warring. We are peaceful."

"Peaceful?" he croaked. Were any Indians really peaceful? After his experience, he couldn't help but wonder.

"Our name means traders. We have kept our word to the white man." A frown creased her brow. "They have not always done the same." The old hostilities assailed her, and for a moment she could not bear to even look at him but his wracking cough renewed her sympathy. His throat must be dry. He needed water. She had with her some pemmican and a water pouch made of the lining of a buffalo paunch. The vessel had a small wooden hoop at the mouth to keep it open, and a stick across the hoop acted as a handle. She fetched it now, giving him the comfort of its soothing moisture. "Here . . ."

John Hanlen was amazed at how gently her hand touched his as she aided him in taking the water. To drink from the pouch he had to raise his head and put his mouth to the opening while she pressed the pouch between her palms to bring the water to the top. Once or twice his fingers encountered hers and he found the contact to be pleasant. Savage? That word most certainly did not belong to this young woman.

"The taste. . . ?" he asked. It was not unpleasant. He drank tentatively at first, then gulped it down, letting the water quench his parched lips and soothe his dry throat.

"There is a sprig of mint to give the water a mild flavor and cooling taste. Do you like it?"

"Yes." He liked this woman as well. His eyes took in all of her—the full, firm breasts, long legs, small waist, well-rounded hips. Even the shapeless leather gown she wore could not hide her curves. For a moment he could imagine her dressed in a bright blue ballgown, twirling in a waltz on his arm. She would dazzle them in Mis-

44

souri. Dark hair framed a slightly rounded face that couldn't have been more perfect if it had been painted by an artist on canvas. Her nose was straight, perfectly sculpted, her chin was firm, her eyes large and blue surrounded by thick dark lashes, her lips full and sensuous. "You are lovely . . ." he blurted, feeling like a fool the moment the words were out.

"What?" She drew back at his words in startled surprise.

He thought he had offended her. "I . . . I'm sorry." He closed his eyes, feeling as if every drop of blood had been drained from his body. "Ungentlemanly of me to . . . to be so bold."

She had not been offended. Indeed, she was secretly pleased by the compliment, though she didn't tell him that. Instead, she continued tending him, moistening her fingers with water and soothing his brow. "Are you in great pain?" she asked.

"My . . . my hands feel as if they were cut off at the wrist and there are places on my body that sting." He looked at the leather strips tied to his wrists and arms. "You did this?"

"Healing herbs." As if to give credibility to her ministrations, she said quickly, "My grandfather is medicine man for our tribe. I am his helper."

"Then I am in good hands . . ." With a deep sigh, he closed his eyes, wishing suddenly to do nothing but sleep.

Skyraven's voice was stern. "I cannot stay with you all the time, white man. I must leave now. But I will be back. You must wait for me here and not leave the cave. Do you understand?"

Hanlen nodded weakly.

"Tonight there is a ceremony I must attend, but when it is possible, I will slip away and return to you. Wait here until then."

"I will wait." In truth there wasn't much else he could do. Damned if he wasn't as weak as a newly born calf. It

45

was aggravating and humiliating to be so dependent on a woman, and yet he was, at least for the moment. If he had to rely upon any woman, however, he could not think of one who was as pleasing as Skyraven. He watched her as she moved about, bending and stooping as she did all within her power to make the cave pleasant for him. Then the weight of his eyelids forced his eyes to close and he could see her no more.

Skyraven knew the white man was asleep when she heard the gentle rumble of his breath. Though she knew she should leave she nevertheless watched him protectively as he slumbered, glad now that she had not let the Utes have their way. She liked this man and not just because he had called her lovely. Her grandfather had often told her that she seemed to have insight into men's hearts. If that were true, then she sensed that the golden-haired stranger was a good man, even if he was a blue-coated soldier. Her eyes were gentle as they touched on him again and again.

When at last Skyraven peered outside the cave she was startled as she saw by the sun's position that more time had elapsed than she might have supposed. She had to hurry lest her grandfather became anxious. Taking just one last look over her shoulder at the white man, she hurried to her horse. Mounting the mare, she rode at a gallop back to the camp and found her grandfather alone in his tepee, a long-stemmed clay pipe sticking from his mouth. Silver circles of smoke drifted overhead.

"Skyraven?" he asked, wondering why she had been so long. In that moment she wanted to confide in him, tell him about the white soldier and her brave rescue of him from the Utes, but something silenced her. Now was not the time.

"I have filled a new pouch with sage, one with red root, and one with horse mint," she said, putting her arms around his neck as if that was the explanation for the length of time she had been gone.

46

"Ah, the spirits will be pleased," Buffalo's Brother answered with a comforting smile. Taking her hand, he pulled her down beside him, giving her a puff on his peace pipe just as he had since she was a child. It was a delicious secret that bound her to him spiritually and made her feel as if she were part of his visions. His love gave her a deep sense of peace. She was happy here. For the moment, at least, she pushed all thought of the yellow-haired white man from her mind. Soon she must go to her own tepee to prepare herself for the evening's ceremonies.

Chapter Five

Already the drums were beginning to sound as Sky-raven left her grandfather to prepare for the ceremony. Before she entered her own smaller tepee, right next to her grandfather's, she watched while a few dancers dressed in their ceremonial attire hastened toward the center of the village where the ceremony would take place. After they were out of sight, she glanced up toward the sky. It was just now turning dusk and a few stars were beginning to appear and the full moon looked silvery white against the graying sky. For just a moment her eyes traveled toward the faraway ridge where the cave was located. She wondered how the white man was feeling by now, if he was resting or if he was thinking of her just as she was thinking of him.

Disturbing thoughts! Thoughts that made her feel all tingly inside, just as she had felt when she'd touched the white soldier. Determined to put him from her mind, she stepped inside her own tepee, thinking how she could love no other dwelling in the world as much as she loved this home of hers. She had constructed not only her tepee with her own hands, but her grandfather's as well. She had tanned the buffalo hides, sewn them together with sinue, and even cut the poles to the proper length.

Looking around inside her tepee she realized how very fortunate she was that Buffalo's Brother was her grandfather. It was not just any woman who was allowed such a splendid display of buffalo hide and hair ornamentation. Such "medicine" was meant to call the buffalo herds to this vicinity and to her tribe. She was a special woman. Her grandfather was *wicasa waken* and she was his helper in training. She was expected to show outstanding character and to be an example to the other women and girls. Being artistic in decorating her lodge and the "medicine lodge," as her grandfather's lodge was called, was part of her duty. She had done the artwork in both. Only the outside of his medicine lodge had been drawn and painted by her grandfather. His tepee and the tepee of the big chief and the lesser chiefs were the only tepees allowed to display bear, buffalo, wolves, and such other sacred paintings on the outside. This was in order to distinguish them as outstanding tribal leaders from the other members of the tribe.

Along the walls of her tepee were beaded pouches of all kinds and beautifully decorated rawhide boxes called parfleches. The boxes contained many personal items such as clothes, feathers, porcupine-quill combs, moccasins, and other things necessary for personal grooming. They were also meant to make the tepee colorful and attractive.

Skyraven knew all the white men looked at the Indians' dwellings with scorn, foolishly preferring to be cooped up inside all day long to enjoying the sky, air, earth, and vegetation Man Above had given them. She supposed the white soldier would think much the same. But why the white people would want to live in those square or oblong structures made of wood or stone with only a fireplace for warmth, Skyraven could not understand. A tepee was a much better home. They could withstand terrible winds without falling over, and driving rains without becoming flooded and wet inside. Not only that, but they could be moved from place to place. The white man's permanent structures were big and bulky and not anywhere nearly as warm as a tepee.

How smart the Indians were to be able to take their homes with them while following the buffalo herds. This was true freedom, a wonderful way to live in harmony with nature. *Why couldn't the white men just go back where they came from and leave them alone?* she wondered.

Even the golden-haired white soldier? an inner voice asked. *Yes, even him!* Skyraven thought with irritation. It bothered her that every now and then his face would somehow sneak inside her head. She shook her head as if to clear it, glancing around her at everything she treasured. That seemed to bring her peace and a glow of pride. Everything here had been cut from rawhide and embroidered with porcupine-quill embroidery or painted by her own hand. She stepped around the firepit lined with stones where a fire smoldered and walked to the pair of beautifully decorated and fringed parfleches against the back wall. Here was where she kept her clothing while they were in camp. When they traveled from place to place her garments were folded over and carried by the packhorse, a parfleche on each side.

Carefully she unfolded the large rawhide bag and took out her most beautifully beaded ceremonial costume of soft white doeskin and laid it aside while she searched through the other rawhide cases and bags. She needed three yellow feathers for her hair, her jewelry, and her new moccasins. Seeing a pair of her grandfather's high-topped moccasins that she had just recently finished beading, she placed them by the front flap of the tepee with the thought in mind of taking them to the small cave. Even now it seemed the white soldier invaded her thoughts. He needed shoes, thus her grandfather's "surprise" would just have to wait a while longer.

Her grandfather had not seen the moccasins yet, so he would not miss them. "Forgive me, Grandfather," Skyraven said aloud. Right now the white eyes needed foot coverings more than her grandfather did. She had left his boots behind on the fallen Ute's body, thus felt it her duty to replace them. Along with the moccasins she laid out two buffalo robes, planning to take them as well when she returned to the cave later on.

Pouring some water from a buffalo-skin bag hanging upon the wall into a small wooden bowl, Skyraven lathered a yucca plant, undressed, and sponged her naked body. She tried to tell herself that it was not because of the soldier that she was taking special care in her grooming, but she knew it was. He'd said that she was lovely and she wanted him to continue thinking so. Also she had heard that the white men sometimes referred to the Indians as "stinking savages" and she wanted him to be able to notice that her people were not dirty.

"We were so close together," she whispered, remembering the touch of his hands as she gave him a drink of water. She found herself hoping that she would have reason to be that close again. "To help him return to his full strength," she quickly amended, refusing to admit how strongly she was attracted to him.

Throwing a buffalo robe over herself, she sat down on her willow-branch bed and leaned back against the tall buckskin backrest. *Does the soldier have a woman?* she asked herself, frowning the moment that thought touched her mind. It didn't matter. Why should it? Once he was healed he would return to his soldiers and she would never see him again. That was the way it must be. Why then did that thought cause such a feeling of loss?

Because I am tired and I am vulnerable to the white man's strange magic, she thought. Placing two buckskin pillows decorated with porcupine quills and tassels behind her back, she closed her eyes. She must get back her strength, both physical and mental, so that she could combat these potent feelings. She would lie here quietly for just a moment to think and rest for a while. It had been a strenuous day and the evening's activities were just getting underway.

Skyraven willed herself to think about the night's ceremony, but her thoughts were unruly, touching upon that moment she had first seen the golden-haired soldier instead. Even then she had been drawn to him, had known somehow that he was special. But in what way? Why did the Great Spirit lead her to save him? How was his life going to intertwine with hers? Her grandfather had often told her that nothing that happened in life was an accident but well planned out by Man Above. Did that include her meeting with the white soldier?

All her life Skyraven had held a resentment for her white blood, remembering that her father had deserted her mother and his child. She had thought of the men with light skin as greedy and cruel, and yet there had only been kindness in the golden-haired man's blue eyes. "And a gentleness in the touch of his fingers," she murmured, conjuring up that moment again. If only . . .

She was so comfortable that she let her thoughts wander with imaginings. Dreamily she thought of how it might have been were the soldier part Indian as she was. For a brief instant she pictured him in buckskin, wearing feathers in his golden hair, riding a strong horse and looking at her as boldly as Lone Wolf often did. She would not give *him* up to Whispering Wind!

"Never! I would fight that she-wolf for him." She listened to the constant drumbeat and the soft, faraway chanting. Suddenly she shuddered, for the chants made her recall the fearful events of the day and the Utes' haunting singing. Her eyes flew open. If she had been captured she no doubt would have been forced to marry one of the disgusting Utes. And the white man . . . It was too fearful to even think about.

Skyraven turned her eyes upward. She would not wait until the thanksgiving ceremony to give thanks to Man Above but would thank him now. He had given not only her but also the white man protection from the Utes. How awful it would have been for the yellow-haired man had she not happened to be out collecting medicine and been led by Man Above to that very place. Or had Man Above planned every detail of what had happened? Had the medicine pouch been torn by accident on the journey or had it been part of Man Above's plan?

The drumbeats, the chanting and the rattling of gourds, became more and more intense, coming closer. There was no more time left for pondering such matters. The ceremony would soon begin. Skyraven struggled to her feet, quickly donned her ceremonial dress, smoothed her long black tresses with a porcupine comb, placed the three feathers into the beaded head-band on her head, and darted out from beneath the tepee flap, closing it securely. Quickly she went in search of her grandfather.

She found Buffalo's Brother standing in front of the huge buffalo robe that was stretched between two poles. He was now wearing his ceremonial robe and buffalo-horn headdress and seemed to blend in with that awesome sacred symbol as he immersed himself in chanting. Skyraven looked upon the huge medicine wheel painted in the center of the buffalo robe with pride, noting the four symbols of the elements painted on each corner. Fire, a bright orange triangle; Earth, red line; Air, a white arrow; Water, blue rippling lines. The powers of the earth and Man Above's blessings. A bleached buffalo skull hung in the middle of the painted robe. The buffalo, the provider of all the necessities of life.

Buffalo's Brother was shaking rattles, scattering sage, and chanting thanks to Man Above for the buffalo when she came up beside him. Skyraven walked quietly, hardly daring to breathe for fear of distracting him. Watching him, she felt the power of his wisdom and once again was tempted to tell him about the white

53

soldier, but a voice inside her head told her that now was not the time and thus she made the decision to wait.

When her grandfather had finished, he turned to face her and moved to stand with her in the circle. His wrinkled, leathery face relaxed into a smile, his happy eyes telling her she was his pride and joy. Skyraven felt a warmth of affection as she returned his smile. Of all the people on the earth, her beloved grandfather was the most important to her.

Chief Left Hand captured the tribe's attention as he moved forward to say words that would inspire the warriors of the tribe. As he spoke, his eyes touched on each face, resting for longer than usual on Skyraven's visage. For just a moment she feared that somehow he knew about the white man, but just as suddenly his eyes drew away. After the chief finished addressing the crowd, her grandfather returned again to the center of the circle. "We thank Man Above for our brother the buffalo," he said, "He supplies us with meat to eat, with skins for robes, with horns and bones for our equipment, weapons and eating utensils, and with everything we need for our very existence."

The buffalo they shot in the summer would carry the tribe through the winter months. The summer months were a time for fellowship and pursuit of crafts. The men spent their days hunting, repairing weapons, or making new ones. Women tanned hides, gathered berries, fashioned containers, cooked, tended babies, and gossiped. Young children and older boys and girls performed chores such as gathering wood, carrying water, or caring for the horses. After that, they were free to play. At night they all gathered to tell stories and dance. It was also a time when young people courted one another. Skyraven sensed that Lone Wolf might seek her out, but that thought did not make her smile. Was it because of Whispering Wind's possessiveness or was she foolishly remembering her dream of the white man? Whatever it was, she felt an aversion toward the cocky, self-assured brave.

As if confirming her intuition, however, when Buffalo's Brother finished speaking, Lone Wolf did catch her eye and smiled at her. It was as if he had been waiting to show off for her. Now that he knew she would see his performance, he strutted about like a rooster.

"Ayee!" he crowed. He and two other braves crouched low and, with a leap, sprang into the middle of the circle to perform a buffalo-hunt dance. Lone Wolf had made sure that Skyraven had seen his face before he placed the make-believe rawhide buffalo-head mask over his own head. It was an honor to be chosen for the dance and for the scouting which followed, and he made it obvious he wanted her to be aware of his honor. Skyraven took great delight in ignoring him. Let that cool his pride!

Whispering Wind watched from her place on the opposite side of the circle of dancers, giving Skyraven her usual frown. As the dancers moved slowly around in the circle, she had seen an expression of desire for Skyraven reflected in Lone Wolf's eyes. He had not even glanced in Whispering Wind's direction, and this angered her. The chief's son was making it all too evident that he wanted Skyraven for his wife. Whispering Wind succumbed to her anger and resentment. It would not be! She wanted him. That half-white, blue-eyed girl would not take her brave.

"I must do something to show Skyraven at a disadvantage," she said to herself. Somehow she would find a way, she vowed, scuffing the toe of her moccasin in the dirt. She would watch and wait, for surely Skyraven was much too sure of herself and the power she held because of her grandfather's prominence in the tribe. Hopefully it would lead her into some foolishness that could be reported. With that thought in mind, Whispering Wind determined to watch Skyraven's every move.

Unaware of her rival's intent, Skyraven looked upon Lone Wolf and the other two dancers as they came to the end of their ceremonial movements. The dance ended, the three braves removed their masks and jumped astride brightly painted and decorated horses, galloping away from the village. They would be away hunting for the buffalo herds for three days or more as part of the ceremony. As he galloped past her, Lone Wolf bent low and touched Skyraven's forehead with the tip of his feathers. It was the beginning of what she had sensed was inevitable. But how was she going to graciously deny him without causing ill will? Though at times the handsome brave annoyed her with his arrogance, his father was a man she deeply respected and didn't want to anger.

Oh, if only I were already spoken for, she thought. The white man intruded once again into her mind, dressed in the same ceremonial dress Lone Wolf had worn. A foolish dream. He was a soldier, she scolded herself. As far away from being an Indian as the earth was from the moon. His kind scorned Indians. Hadn't such words passed from his lips? He would never even look twice at an Indian girl. She must not allow her thoughts to indulge in silly visions. Truth was truth. He was white and she, though sharing white blood, was, in spirit and manner of living, an Indian. And as such she would take an Indian husband. But not Lone Wolf!

Skyraven watched as Lone Wolf's departing form became smaller and smaller, feeling a sense of relief that he would be gone for a time. It had been her concern that somehow he might learn about the white man and cause trouble. But for the moment he would be elsewhere occupied.

The braves were well on their way, and the male children and maids who wished to attract the departing warriors' attention followed after the retreating horsemen. With all the excitement going on, now was the time for Skyraven to slip away. She left the circle of dancers and returned to her own lodge just long enough to reach inside the front flap for the moccasins and robes she had placed there earlier. She was so anxious to return to the stranger that she did not notice the dark, brooding eyes watching her as she filled a leather pouch with meat and vegetables before leaving the camp.

"So," murmured Whispering Wind, noting Skyraven's actions, "she has something very important going on during the night. Something that requires new moccasins and two robes." The figure in the shadows smiled a cruel, calculating smile. Those moccasins were too large for Skyraven's small feet, nor did a woman take such care with her grooming unless a man was in her thoughts, Whispering Wind observed. Was it possible that Skyraven planned a meeting with one of the braves left behind? How she hoped that was Skyraven's plan! Lone Wolf would be deeply angered to find himself second in Skyraven's thoughts.

Whispering Wind wanted no more dancing now that Lone Wolf had galloped away. She had more important things on her mind as she left the Indian women. She could hardly believe how quickly Skyraven had dared to act, and yet, even now, Skyraven walked rapidly toward the outskirts of the camp. Perhaps before returning to her own lodge, Whispering Wind would find out just where Skyraven was going, and why.

Chapter Six

The evening air was turning chilly, awakening John Hanlen from his deep slumber. He opened his eyes slowly, fully expecting to be within his camp tent, but instead was surrounded by dirt and rock. Dear God! He was entombed within the earth. At first he did not know where he was. His heart quickened as he lifted himself up on his elbow and glanced around at his surroundings. A cave! His eyes darted back and forth across the small opening as he remembered how he'd gotten there. A chill ran up his back as he realized how close he'd been to death.

The Indian girl, where was she? Clenching his jaw, he tried to remember. She had spoken of a ceremony, had told him to wait for her here. She was coming back, or so she had said. *Trust me,* he remembered her telling him. Trust an Indian after what he'd gone through? Bitterness threatened his reason until he remembered the gentleness in her large blue eyes. He recalled what had happened earlier in the day. Those leering savages, his dead comrades, and the tortures he would have endured — if not for the lovely Indian maiden! She had rescued him at the risk of her own well-being. He owed her his sanity, his very life.

"Skyraven. Beautiful raven-haired, blue-eyed Skyraven." He repeated her name over to himself. His countrymen would call her a savage, a squaw. Still, he had never met anyone more gentle or sincere than she.

Unconsciously he rubbed his hand over the stubble of his beard. What he wouldn't give for a razor right now. He laughed softly to himself. What a ridiculous thought. The stubble of beard was the last thing he should be worried about. He was lucky to be alive. Never had his life meant so much to him as it did now.

Images flashed before his eyes as he vividly recalled the bodies of the soldiers who had not been as lucky as he, but he quickly banished them from his mind. It was over now. Torturing himself with such visions would cause him helpless anguish. All he could do was pray for the dead and make a vow that they had not died in vain.

But a corner of his mind screamed for vengeance. Ride back to Fort Lyon, gather a troup of soldiers, and retaliate for what those heathen bastards had done. There were some people who said that all Indians were alike and that the only good Indian was a dead Indian. But no! That kind of thinking would only make the rivers run red with blood.

The lovely Indian girl who had saved him had told him the Utes who attacked his soldiers were her enemies, too, that they were vicious warriors. It was logical. How could all Indians be alike any more than all white men were identical? Hadn't he known some men who were real bastards? Indeed he had. Suppose he was judged as being of the same tawdry mettle? Skyraven had said that her tribe was not like the chanting naked heathens who had murdered his fellow soldiers and taken him captive in order to torture him. He believed her. They couldn't have anyone as gentle and kind as Skyraven among them if they were nothing but heathen savages.

She had put her own life in jeopardy to rescue him. She didn't have to do that. She didn't even know him. She told him that the spirits had led her to him, that her grandfather was a *wicasa waken,* a healer and holy man, and that her tribe, the Arapaho, were buffalo hunters, not warriors. She had blue eyes and spoke English fluently. She was hardly savage.

His whole concept of Indians was changing since he had met her. He would have a message for those who thought Indians were all alike. When he got back to Fort Lyon, he could tell them that he had learned firsthand that it simply was not true. From now on it would be hard for him to listen to the stories he had heard. He would want to judge things for himself.

"Oh, Skyraven, there is so much more I must learn about you and your people," he murmured. He could still feel the gentle touch of her hand upon his brow. The wounds and bruises on his arms felt much better now thanks to her knowledge of medicine.

She had left her buffalo robe, a bowl, a knife, some food and drinking water for him. Taking a bit of pemmican from the pouch she had left by his bedside, John scooped it into his mouth and began chewing. He couldn't say that he liked the taste. It was quite tart and unlike anything he had ever eaten before. In time he could probably get used to it if he had to. Right now he had no choice. Food was food. His nearly empty stomach was crying out for anything to fill it. It had been damned nice of her to leave anything at all. Reaching for the water pouch, he took a big drink to wash the pemmican down then pulled the robe tightly around his shoulders as if by doing so he could hasten her arrival.

The cave was much cooler now. He slipped his light-blue trousers on over his underwear. His dark-blue coat had been torn and one of the epaulets was hanging by a thread but the garment was still wearable. Only his hat and boots were missing, but hell, Hanlen reflected, he'd been lucky to escape with his skin. Certainly he wouldn't have if the Utes had had their way.

The light of the full moon shone down, illuminating the mouth of the cave. Peaceful. He could hear a bubbling brook nearby. Everything was calm and serene, like the lovely blue-eyed Indian girl. Her touch had been gentle yet strong, and her voice as melodious as the night wind through the trees. John Hanlen found himself anxious to see her again. There were so many questions he wanted to ask her, so many things he wanted to know about her people, about *her.*

A sudden rustle in the undergrowth outside the cave disturbed his reverie, his training as a soldier instantly putting him on guard. "Damn!" he muttered. He'd be easy prey for a mountain lion, bear, or two-legged kind of predator, he thought, as weak as he was. Picking up the knife the Indian girl had left, he prepared to at least make an effort to defend himself. He heard footsteps and waited. It was the Indian girl. He could hear her voice calling to him.

In a few moments Skyraven appeared at the mouth of the cave, a big smile of greeting on her lips. The sight of the blond-haired white man made her feel lightheaded and lighthearted as none of the young men of her tribe did. Somehow the feelings she had for this man were different from anything she had ever experienced. Perhaps because he was so unusual.

"It's you!" John Hanlen let the knife slip through his fingers. It made a soft thud as it fell to the ground. "Skyraven . . ."

"I have brought you something for your feet, and robes to keep you warm during the night. It can often grow cold."

She stepped closer, placing the moccasins and the two buffalo robes at his feet. He was looking at her with the same expression he had when he'd first opened his eyes and gazed upon her face. Only this time he seemed to hold even more admiration for her, and this pleased her.

John Hanlen's eyes raked over her. Oh, how lovely she looked tonight. The white doeskin dress with beautiful beading and long fringe clung closely to her tall

61

form. Around her head was a red beaded headband with three yellow feathers. Her blue-black hair framed her pleasingly round face and tumbled down around her shoulders, ending far below her waist. Her smile was a joy to behold, her teeth were gleaming white, her lips full and sensual. Her large blue eyes were surrounded by thick, long black lashes and black arched eyebrows. While she was away he had almost forgotten how truly beautiful she was, but now he feasted his eyes.

At first he was speechless, tongue-tied. Her beauty took his breath away. Finally, he managed to say, "I missed you while you were gone."

"You seem to be feeling better, Yellow-hair, I am glad for that." She stepped closer, feeling his head for any signs of fever. There were none. Lowering herself gracefully to the ground, she took a seat beside him. "You call me by my name. By what name are you called?"

"My name is John."

"John?" Picking up one of the buffalo robes, she held it out to him. "John." She seemed to like the feel of his name on her lips.

"John Hanlen," he said. His fingers touched her wrist as he reached for the robe, then moved down to wrap around her hand in a gesture of affection and gratitude. Her long, slim fingers offered no resistance as he entwined them with his. "I'm a major."

"A bluecoat, a soldier. Yes." A frown touched her brow.

"I'm a warrior, just like some of the men of your tribe must be." He could feel the tension in her hand that spread all through her body. "My mission is to protect my people. Please understand."

Skyraven saw by the look in his eyes that he was deeply troubled. So, she was right to be cautious, she thought. "We want no war!" She drew away slightly. "We are peaceful. All we want is to be able to hunt the buffalo and to roam freely as we please."

Things were so complicated, more so than he could explain. He wanted to promise her that her people could live as they wanted to but knew if he said such a thing it would be a lie, and so he remained silent. Gently touching her arm again, he pulled her toward him, hoping he could make her understand that he was grateful, that he would never do anything to hurt her. His lips brushed hers lightly. When she did not pull away but responded by leaning closer, he captured her lips in a long, passionate kiss.

Skyraven had heard about the white man's courting gestures but had never experienced any man's kiss before. Nothing had prepared her for the jolt of sweet fire that swept through her veins as his mouth explored hers, but she liked what he was doing. It was a pleasant sensation. Closing her eyes, she enjoyed the spark that was kindled between them.

John Hanlen reluctantly drew away. Was he dizzy because he was weak, or was the Indian girl's loveliness to blame? Certainly the innocent yielding of her mouth was deeply stirring. He wanted to deepen the embrace, but instead, with a regretful sigh, he let his head fall back upon his makeshift bed.

"Thank you for saving my life, sweet Skyraven," he whispered.

He did not want to be too hasty in his lovemaking and frighten her away. Perhaps it was better that he had very little strength. Besides, she deserved better than just a rough tumble in the hay. An Indian she might be, but no one deserved more care and attention than this beautiful, gentle, understanding person before him. Undoubtedly there was at least one brave, or two or three, who had this young woman in mind for a wife, if she wasn't already spoken for. Closing his eyes, he tried to put the thought out of his mind, for it was strangely troubling. It was as if he wanted her to belong to him, but that was foolish. Allowing himself to have tender

63

feelings for her was dangerous.

Skyraven carefully folded one of the buffalo robes and placed it under the white soldier's head. "You must sleep now," she said, watching as he closed his eyes. For a long moment she sat beside him, touching her lips, watching the rise and fall of his chest as he eased into sleep. She decided that she liked this joining of the mouths. The white men were right to enjoy such a thing. Though she knew she should not even think about it, she wondered if the white man might kiss her again.

If he does, I must push him away, Skyraven thought, angry at herself for such musings. She was Indian and this John Hanlen was not a proper man to share a tepee with. Her grandfather would not approve of such a match. He would counsel her to keep her distance from the white soldier. In the past, mixed marriages had only led to trouble. Didn't she know that by having watched her mother's pain?

Rising to her feet, Skyraven tended the fire, then looked outside the cave to be sure everything was quiet. The sky was clear, with not even a sign of a cloud. Only white puffs of smoke, the village fires, disturbed the perfection of the darkness. She should go back, she thought, but somehow the day's excitement had finally caught up with her. She was much too weary to make the journey just now. She would rest just a short while and then she would return. Yes, just a short while. Her eyelids were heavy and her body was weary. Lying down beside John Hanlen, she closed her eyes, and was soon fast asleep.

Chapter Seven

The wind moaned like a woman in pain, sweeping through the cave, joining with John Hanlen's groans as he thrashed in the midst of a nightmare. The eerie harmony awakened Skyraven from her sleep and she opened her eyes. The white man! A poignant compassion possessed her as she turned her head toward the man who lay beside her. He had endured great suffering, more to the soul than to his body. Seeing one's companions struck down so cruelly must have been a painful experience, she thought, one that might lie hidden while one was awake but came back to haunt a man in the depth of sleep. Her grandfather had witnessed such things and told her about them, for it was at those times he had need of his most potent rituals.

"No! Leave him be." The soldier seemed to be struggling with his attackers again. "He's little more than a lad. Don't! Oh, God! Not that . . ."

"Hush." As he moaned in his sleep, she reached out to him, her hand soothing his tortured murmurings. "You are safe here. It is just the wind." Her voice, whispering in the darkness, seemed to soothe him, for he quieted. The soft rumble of his breathing told her he was asleep.

For a long time it was peaceful, only the sound of the wind disturbing the night. It was as if for just a little while they were the only two beings in the world. She relaxed and listened to the sound of the breath of life coming in and out of his lungs and felt at peace.

Skyraven peered out of the cave and tried to judge the night cycle by the position of the stars. The stars were important to the Indians. It was by their movements that they judged the changing of the seasons, how soon the morning would send its glow to the horizon. From the stars they took their directions when they were forced by circumstances to travel at night. One particular cluster fascinated Skyraven, and it was to these stars she cast her eyes now. There were many stories of how those stars came to be. Lone Wolf pridefully proclaimed that the stars were seven warriors who danced so fast they swirled up into the sky and remained there dancing forever, but Skyraven preferred the story her grandfather told her that they were seven beautiful sisters, the daughters of the sun and moon. By those stars she could see that it was late.

I should return, Skyraven thought. In truth, she had dozed off for much longer than she had intended. She couldn't take the chance of being missed, and yet she couldn't bring herself to leave — not yet! She soothed her trepidation by telling herself that the village would be asleep. *Her* village! Somehow it seemed suddenly remote and alien to her, as if it were here and not there that she belonged.

I am inviting danger, she thought. *These feelings stirring in my breast for the golden-haired man must be stilled.* She was risking her grandfather's anger by being away from her tent. If her absence was noticed by the women of the village who kept an eye on the unmarried maidens, how would she explain that she had been absent all night? Would she tell them that she had been communicating with the voice of the wind? Walking about the camp? Could she tell such a falsehood to her grandfather? No. Lies were the white man's invention. Until the white eyes had come to the land there had been no word for liar in the Indian tongue.

She didn't even want to think about it, for she could not have done differently. The white soldier had needed her and she had answered that need. Now a fierce feeling of protectiveness surged in her heart. With a sigh she sank back down on the buffalo robe and nestled into the crook of his arm. She could feel the warmth of his breath on her neck, ruffling her hair, his strength beside her, and she experienced a tingling sensation down the whole length of her spine. She could hear her heart beating so loud that she was certain it would wake him. Soon, the warmth of him, the whisper of the wind, relaxed her as she closed her heavy-lidded eyes, and she slept once more.

Dreams assailed her, and she tossed and turned fitfully during the night. When she awoke, snuggled close against the white man, she remembered her dream. John Hanlen was the great "golden man" in the legends of her people, and she the skymaiden—the sun and the sky, who had fallen so much in love that they could not be separated. They had wanted to remain together and thus the Great Spirit had lifted the golden man up to be with his beloved. It had been decreed by the spirits that it would always be so. Would such a thing happen to her? Would the spirits intervene and bring forth a happy ending?

Sleepily she rubbed her eyes, stretched her slim arms above her head, yawned, then sat up to take a look at the man the spirits had delivered into her care, just as they had the sun into the sky's embrace. It was then she knew without a doubt the potency of her feelings. Somewhere between the darkness and the dawn she had fallen irrevocably under the spell of this white soldier called John Hanlen.

She studied his face carefully, looking down at his sleeping face and tousled golden hair, glad that she had been able to spend the night with the handsome white man. Surely she would not have had a wink of sleep had she not, for she would have been besieged with thoughts of him and would have worried. But now, upon awakening, there were only happy thoughts. She sighed as she remembered his strong arms around her and the feel of his warm lips upon her own. The very thought of being here so close to him caused her a great deal of joy.

It was her favorite time of day, the time that she spoke of to her grandfather as the "golden hour," that time between dark and light. The moon had fled across the sky with a swiftness that surprised her. When she was with her soldier the precious moments moved much too quickly, but now she knew beyond a doubt that she could not linger here in the cave with him much longer or she would take the chance that her secret would be discovered. Even so, she couldn't quite leave. Not yet.

"If only . . ." she whispered, wanting to tell him of her feelings but not able to bring herself to say the words. He might not feel the same way about her. What if she was wrong about her thoughts? A frown creased her brow as she thought of how the white men looked at Indian girls — fit to warm their beds but not quite suitable for wives. She would not be any man's "squaw woman." For just a moment her happiness was spoiled. What if John Hanlen did not share in her dreams for the future? What if his heart had not been likewise touched by the Great Spirit?

How do you feel about me, John Hanlen, she wondered? Swiftly their moments together ran through her mind as she tried to answer the question. Oh, he had kissed her and she had responded, but he hadn't told her that he wanted her for his own. *Oh, if only he would,* she sighed. *What would she do?* She could only wonder.

Rising to her feet, Skyraven started a small fire inside the cave. She looked into the flames, deep in concentration as she debated her emotions toward John Hanlen. Her feelings welled up inside her. She wanted him to be with her, wanted him to be part of her life. To

68

share her dreams, know her joys. Was it possible? She felt that hope surge with her. When she turned around to look at him again, she found that he was awake. His clear blue eyes drew her to him in an almost hypnotic way. Skyraven's eyes met his steadily.

"So you are not a dream," he told her softly. "You are real. I thought I was just imagining."

"No, I am not part of your dreams, John Hanlen. I am real." Shyly she smiled, then, bending down, she reached out her hand as if to give proof. He clasped the offering tightly. Once again she was encompassed by a comforting warmth. It seemed as if nothing existed beyond this magical circle of their closeness.

"Very real and very beautiful." He was thoroughly captivated, just as he had been last night. Her large, almond-shaped blue eyes focused on his face without guile. She was as fresh and soothing as the morning air. "Utterly lovely," he said.

His compliments and his intense scrutiny suddenly made her nervous. "Are you hungry, John Hanlen?" she asked quickly, shyly avoiding his gaze lest he guess her thoughts. "I can gather some fruit and berries and be back in no time at all."

John didn't want her to go. She was such a beauty and such pleasant company, and somehow she soothed his loneliness, like a balm to his soul. Her big blue eyes fascinated him. They were so expressive and seemed to be telling him that she, too, held tender feelings. What he really wanted was to gather her into his arms again and make love to her, but he didn't say so. He said only, "Well, yes, I guess I could use a little something to eat."

Pulling her hand away, she left the cave and soon returned with a bag full of wild raspberries and some buffalo jerky she had taken from her saddlebag. "There now, that didn't take too long, did it?" She smiled sweetly as she held the food out to him. "I picked the berries; the jerky was left over from that I brought last night."

"Anything would taste good." Perhaps his hunger was a sign that he was healing. Longing for the touch of her hand again, he reclaimed it, pulling her down to sit beside him. As they ate he asked her several questions, wanting to know all about her. He was as hungry for information about this lovely woman as he was for food. "You told me your father was a white man," he began.

"Yes."

John was not surprised to learn that her father was of his kind. He had suspected that she was part white because of her pale olive skin and blue eyes. Even so, her face had just enough roundness to it to speak of her Indian heritage. The blending of Indian and white had produced an exotic beauty.

"He promised to return for my mother, but he never did," she went on. Even now, that thought was strangely painful.

"Then he was a fool! Seeing you now I pity him for all that he has missed."

"You do?" His soft voice mesmerized her. The blue eyes staring into hers were sincere.

"The greatest blessing a man has is to watch as his child grows up. From sprout to blossom, my mother used to say." He traced the line of her profile from forehead to chin with a smile. "I'll bet you were pretty right from the moment you were born. You sure are now."

"I never felt that I was." She remembered Whispering Wind. "There were some who taunted me for having white man's blood."

"They did?" He was taken by surprise. He'd heard of being condemned as a "half-breed" by the whites, but never for being half *white*. It gave him a different perspective on the matter. "Was your childhood a happy one, Skyraven?" he asked.

"Oh, yes! My grandfather is the best of men. He made me all sorts of wonderful playthings and let me go

70

with him when he collected his herbs and magical weeds, teaching me just the right ones to choose." She thrust back her shoulders in pride. "Now it is my duty to gather his roots and leaves and berries. And soon I learned that having white blood was not quite as bad as I had first supposed. In time I relished being just a little different from the others. It gave me my own identity."

They talked for a time, Skyraven opening up a bit of her heart as she talked about the heartache of her early childhood and the pain of growing up without a mother or a father. As the sun began to peek into the mouth of the cave, however, Skyraven knew that she must return to the village below. She could never let it be known that not only had she saved the life of a white man, but she had spent the night with him. Even if they were quite innocent of any lovemaking, her tribesmen would never understand. It would be a slight on her honor.

The Arapaho were gentle people for the most part, and deeply religious. A few of the young bucks, such as Lone Wolf, thought war was more exciting than making peace. They were young and sometimes hard to handle, but so far her grandfather and Chief Left Hand had kept them under control. She could not take the chance that Lone Wolf might be infuriated by John Hanlen's presence. That the brave considered her "his" would only add more heat to the flame. A misunderstanding could easily undo everything Buffalo's Brother and Chief Left Hand had been able to accomplish.

I must go back, she thought. *I have been selfish and foolish to take such a risk.* Skyraven made up her mind that she would return to the village and go about her chores as if nothing unusual had happened. But could she do that? Right now her heart was ready to explode with excitement. Could her heart carry such a secret and not give it away? She had to try.

John had been asking her about her grandfather's duties as medicine man when he noticed a faraway look in her blue eyes. "Your thoughts seem to be somewhere else."

"Yes. I was thinking that I must go!"

"Just like that?" He wanted to learn more about her, had been enjoying their conversation.

"If I am missed, there might be trouble." Rising from her seat on the buffalo-skin robe, she took his hand one last time and squeezed it hard. "I must go down to the village now, but I will return at sundown. I cannot let anyone know that you are here in the cave."

"No, I don't believe you should." He was still a bit wary of all Indians, even peaceful ones. Besides, he looked forward to having her all to himself. He didn't want anyone else intruding. So far it was just the two of them, and that was exactly how he wanted to keep it.

"You will not leave?"

"I can't go very far. I never have been much good without a compass." He laughed. "So you see, you have me at your mercy, sweet Skyraven."

"Rest while I am gone."

"Rest. Ah, yes, I will. God knows I'm too weak to do anything else." He raised his eyebrows, wondering what she would do if he told her how much he wanted to make love to her.

"The rest will help you to regain your strength. There is dried buffalo left if you hunger." She could see by his expression that the idea was not very appealing. "Tonight I will bring you a great feast," she promised. "In the meantime, keep the pouch of pemmican, the rest of the uneaten berries, and the jerky to calm your hunger pangs." Now that it was time to leave, she did so reluctantly. It was as if an invisible thread tied her to this white man, a fragile thread.

"I'll miss you the moment you are gone." He smiled, watching her as she walked to the mouth of the cave. "Good-bye Skyraven. It seems we are always saying good-bye." He had known her for only a short time and yet when she left, it seemed as if a part of him had gone with her. An emptiness consumed him. It would be a long day without her company. For once, he mused, the darkness could not come too soon.

Skyraven rode down the steep slope to the cottonwood forest below, not daring to look back for fear of wanting to turn back and return to John Hanlen. Instead, she kept her eyes riveted on the pathway. This area of the campsite was a kind of oasis, hidden in the shelter of giant cottonwoods. It was one of Skyraven's favorite places. There was plenty of shade, plenty of water, and plenty of grass for the ponies.

It was still early enough in the morning that the villagers were just beginning to stir. Only one or two women and a few small children were to be seen, and that fact relieved her anxiety. From the look of things, most of the men and young boys had apparently already left for the antelope hunt, for many of the horses were missing. Skyraven had overheard some talk a few days before of an antelope herd which had been spotted just north of the village.

Sliding from her horse's back, she walked to Buffalo's Brother's lodge, lifted the flap, and peeked in. She was relieved that he was not there, for the thought of making explanations had troubled her. "He has gone on the antelope hunt," she said to herself. Although her grandfather was a holy man and carried only the peace pipe, no weapons, he was expected to accompany the hunters to bring the spirit of a good hunt. Now she would not have to worry about answering any questions. If he had accompanied the hunters, and she was certain that he had, he would have had things on his mind other than watching after her. If he had come to her tent he would probably have assumed that she was out walking and put her absence far from his mind.

"So you have decided to return." A voice she knew too well disturbed her sense of well-being. Turning, she saw Whispering Wind sitting in the shadows, a small wooden loom on her lap. Her arms moved gracefully as she pulled the horsehair thread to complete the headband she was making.

"Yes, I have just returned from an early-morning ride. Running Antelope and I both enjoy the early-morning air." It was true. She had been on the horse's back, it was not a lie. Still, Skyraven avoided the other woman's glaring eyes. She felt no need to explain her whereabouts. Her activities were really none of Whispering Wind's business. They were both unmarried women with no obligation to report to each other on their comings and goings. Still, Whispering Wind's remark did cause her some concern. She hoped with all her heart that she did not know more than she was letting on. The Indian girl had already proven herself to be a treacherous enemy and might take great delight in reporting any wrongdoing to the squaws.

"As you say. And a late-night ride as well."

Skyraven's body was as taut as a bowstring. Was the woman making accusations? Or was she just too sensitive because in her heart she knew she did have a secret? Whatever it was, Skyraven walked away from Whispering Wind without a backward glance, going about her morning tasks, making herself highly visible to the other women as she performed her fair share of the day's duties. Not only was she responsible for keeping her own lodge in order but her grandfather's as well. She beat the buffalo robes with a wooden adze till they were soft and pleasant to the touch, then replaced them on the tepee floor. She walked to the river to fill the water pouches, taking a little time out to bathe and comb her long black tresses. When she returned, she scraped hides, gathered wood, then straightened her grandfather's medicine lodge.

Although she tried to keep herself busy, the hours seemed to drag by. Her thoughts were on John Hanlen alone in the cave, and she longed to be there with him. It was a temptation to sneak away, but after Whispering Wind's remark, she knew she wouldn't dare. Instead, she worked herself into exhaustion trying not to think about the golden-haired man, but delighting in her secret. Sitting down outside her grandfather's medicine lodge, she admired the colorful pictures painted on his tepee as she at last took time to rest. Her grandfather was a very good artist, she thought. How she wished she could show his fine work to John Hanlen. It would make him fully understand how special Buffalo's Brother was.

"Grandfather is an artist as well as a fine medicine man," she said aloud. The big red spot at the top of the tepee represented the bear's den. Claws and tracks were painted in red and black along the bottom. The green, yellow, and blue zigzags around the middle represented lightning and storms. The bear was the patron of wisdom, magic, and medicine. The Indians knew that the bear stayed strong and well by eating certain herbs and roots. They followed him, watched him, and learned. The buffalo head on the other side of the tepee, at the top, was painted in black. The buffalo was the patron of courage and the provider of many necessary things such as tepees, pouches, and moccasins.

Moccasins! Suddenly she remembered that she had taken her grandfather's to the white man. She had wanted to have them finished for him but now would have to start from the beginning. Perhaps now, before it began to turn dark, would be a good time for her to cut out the soft skin. Then she could begin to bead them. That would help her to pass a few more hours.

Drifting smoke carried the aroma of meat and vegetables simmering in cooking pots heated by stones from the firepit. Later she would take a little out of each pot and carry it back to the cave for John Hanlen. He was in need of some solid food if he was going to heal quickly. The fact that he was not too fond of pemmican had not escaped her notice, though she hadn't said a word. This time she would bring him something delicious.

Ah, yes, she was anxious to return, she could not

argue that. It was all she could think of as she worked, though Whispering Wind's words gave her reason for caution. It was possible her rival suspected and might watch her comings and goings. Even so, she was determined to take the chance, treasuring for the moment her precious secret.

Chapter Eight

It was silent, so quiet that John Hanlen could hear the sound of his breathing as he lay with his hands tucked behind his head, staring up at the ceiling of the cave. He was bored. Now that he had had time to rest he was quickly recovering his strength and that made him fidgety. It just wasn't in him to hibernate like some mangy old bear while the hours passed by. And yet, what else was there for him to do?

Leave? He frowned as he looked around him. The truth was he didn't have any idea just where he was. It would be easy to get lost wandering about in unfamiliar territory. Besides, he didn't have a horse and he wasn't strong enough to walk any great distances, that much was for certain. He was getting stronger, but he wasn't that steady on his feet. Most important, there was a whooping, hollering bunch of Indians out there who might just take him into their custody again. If they did, he might not escape with his skin this time.

"The Utes!" he whispered angrily. Their images hovered before his eyes when he was awake and haunted his dreams. He wondered if he would ever recuperate from the hellish ordeal they had inflicted on him and his soldiers.

John suspected that the cavalry from Fort Lyon had followed hard and fast upon the trail of the soldiers in an effort to find his little band. He had not been in contact with the fort for nearly a week, and surely that would set them to wondering. When they contacted Fort Wallace, the next fort up the stream from Fort Lyon, and found out that he and his men hadn't come to renew their needed supplies, surely there would be concern. The forts were few and far between, strung out with nothing but prairie land, gama, and buffalo grass, bluffs and low-lying rolling hills between them.

"They'll ride out to find us, and then those red devils will pay for the murder of my men!"

How he hoped the cavalry would catch and bring every one of those murdering savages to justice, just as they had in Missouri a short while ago when they had hanged thirty such offenders. One part of his heart wanted such vengeance, but, in reality, he knew the Utes would be nearly impossible to track.

The scouts and guides had led his men on a trail unknown and untraveled by anyone else from Fort Lyon. Even more important, it was entirely possible that if the Utes discovered that they were being pursued, they would break up into smaller groups and would never be found. Damn those savages all to hell, they knew this country like the back of their hands, and although John hated to admit it, they were by far better horsemen and fighters than the young, untrained cavalrymen in this Indian territory. Most of the more experienced cavalry soldiers, with a few exceptions such as himself, had chosen or had been retained to fight the War Between the States, as there was no glory to be had in fighting these Indians. All the medals and honors were going to the heroes of the war across the Mississippi.

Hell, the people back in the States have their hands full with their own problems. They probably don't even know that the cavalry is fighting anywhere else, John thought. Even the settlers and farmers in these parts didn't really seem to appreciate what the soldiers here had to endure. It was a thankless, depressing, and seemingly hopeless situation. The young enlisted men at Fort Lyon, and the other forts as well, had volunteered for duty here thinking they would find adventure. Most of them had already become disillusioned when they had found what they were up against, including John himself.

Just like all the others, not wishing to fight his own kinsmen, he was relieved when he had been transferred out west. He'd hoped to get this job of Indian fighting over with and then be on his way home to Missouri, had hoped the War Between the States would be over by then. He'd heard glorious tales about the West and the chances for a man to succeed. So far, however, he had found uncomfortable living conditions, lack of understanding or appreciation from his countrymen for the sacrifice he was making, and the threat of ambush from every scouting expedition.

But neither I nor the others could ever have guessed that they would meet their deaths, he thought, tormented by that moment once again. God, how he had hated to see those young men massacred. It wrenched his soul, tore at his stomach with a haunting sense of loss. It would be one of his agonizing duties when he got back to see to it that their next of kin were told. "Goddamn heathen bastards . . ." For just a moment, hatred and anger took complete possession of his emotions, at least until he stared down at his feet, at the soft leather moccasins, and thought of her.

"My angel of mercy," he said softly, remembering how dutifully she had taken care of him. That memory tempered his anger and helped him to see things clearly. As he'd told himself so many times during the last few days, not all Indians were violent. She was all that was gentle and good in the world. Deep emotion stirred in his heart at the thought.

He had increased in strength and was by now close to being fully recovered, thanks to Skyraven's tender care. The lovely dark-haired beauty was not like the chanting, naked, painted savages who had fallen upon him.

She had come to his rescue like some legendary Indian princess, exhibiting her daring and bravery, just like Pocahontas or Sacagawea in the stories he'd read. John Hanlen knew if he lived to be a hundred he would never forget her.

He wanted her with him right now. Every evening she had returned to the cave to bring nourishing food and see to his needs. He could never have survived without her. He knew that he should be getting back to the fort. In fact, he was probably strong enough to make the journey now. She was the reason why he lingered on, he realized. Somehow the thought of leaving her tore at his heart. By the saints, he finally had to admit to himself that he was in love with her.

Certainly she was unique. There was only one Skyraven in this world, he thought. She was beautiful, intelligent, and as brave as anyone he had ever met, woman or man. It took a lot of courage to take a chance on angering her own people by helping him as she was doing. John knew her tribesmen would be far from pleased were they to find them here together. Even so, she had risked their anger every night to come to him.

Just being with her was an experience that had taught him much about the Indian culture. Until now he'd had the idea that Indian squaws were treated as beasts of burden, always walking behind the men, working themselves to an early grave. Skyraven had made him understand the importance of a woman's place in the Indian society, every bit as important as any other woman was to a household. He had been surprised to learn that the woman ruled the tepee. Skyraven had told him that a woman of her tribe had the power to evict an errant husband if he was guilty of a misdeed. The small conical tent was the woman's and not the man's home, and she had the right to say who would dwell within. *Just as this cave is Skyraven's,* he thought with a smile, wondering what it would be like to share a dwelling with her, be it cave or tent or house.

He found the idea pleasant. The very idea, however, would no doubt shock his family, his friends, and, most of all, his commanders.

"Have you taken leave of your senses?" he could almost hear his father say, a man very set in his ways with unalterable ideas on things. Unfortunately he would judge Skyraven without even knowing her, would think of her as a heathen, just as all the other officers would. Heathen? She was as far from being a heathen as anyone he'd ever known. She was graceful and intelligent. Skyraven spoke better English than some of the white immigrant horse soldiers the Army had requisitioned. Hell, some of the American troopers in his outfit were barely intelligible. Skyraven had told him that not only she but her grandfather, the chief, and some others of her tribe spoke English also.

As he looked out from the mouth of the cave toward the Arapaho village, he could almost see her face before him, registering her pride as she had said, "After all, we have traded with the whites for a long time now. My people learn very quickly." She had smiled as she had added, "But very few of your people have been able to learn our language, John Hanlen." Indeed, she had tried to teach him a few words, but he had stuttered and stammered so pitifully that he had given up on the idea.

John Hanlen immersed himself in his thoughts, finding it exceedingly pleasant to think about the Indian girl. He was anxious to see her again and was growing very impatient. Shadows were darkening, and he knew it was getting late. Where was she? Rising to his feet, he peered out at the horizon, issuing a sigh of relief as Skyraven's slender form came into view. She had tied Running Antelope to a tree below the cave and was scurrying up the bank through the undergrowth.

"Skyraven! Skyraven!" He wasn't even aware of saying her name until she looked up to where he was standing and waved. It was the most natural gesture in the world. His heart leapt in response and he yearned to take her in his arms and make love to her right there on the vine-entwined hillside. With the breeze whipping her hair around her shoulders, she was mesmerizingly lovely. As she walked tall and proud toward him, John fought to gain control of his emotions. The one thing he must not do was to pounce upon her like some animal.

"I am glad to see you up and about," she said as she handed him a cord-wrapped bundle. John opened it, besieged with curiosity. Inside he found a leather shirt, the workmanship flawless. "I have just finished it. It is yours to keep."

"For me? To keep?" He was touched by her charming gesture.

"So that you will not forget me."

Forget her? He knew he never would. He longed to take her with him, but there was such a wide gulf between their cultures. Reality was something far different from dreams. If not for the hostility such a match might bring, he would not have hesitated to make her his wife, he'd decided.

"Come, let's go back inside the cave so that I can put on your wonderful gift," he said, pushing the thoughts from his mind. In a gesture of gratitude, he took her hand, holding it tightly as they entered the cave.

Inside, the flames from the fire created a magical atmosphere, reflecting deep blue tones in Skyraven's long black hair as she sat next to him upon the painted buffalo hide she had brought the day before. It seemed she was always bringing presents to him. Generosity was another of her virtues, he thought. In truth, she seemed the perfect woman.

John was amazed at her knowledge and understanding. He sat spellbound now as she related to him the details of one of her grandfather's ceremonies, though his thoughts were more on her than what she was saying. Every time he was near her, his usually logical mind turned to pudding and all he could wonder about was how her skin would feel beneath his hands, how it would be to feel her supple form beneath him. As he watched her sensual lips form the words she was saying, he wanted to kiss her. Her lips had been so sweet against his own. So very, very sweet.

Oh, God, you tempt me so, Skyraven, he thought, and yet it would be impossible for them to stay together. Deep in his own thoughts, John took off his jacket and began to dress in the shirt his blue-eyed protector had brought, marveling at the workmanship. It was soft to his skin and beautifully designed, a souvenir he would keep in memory of the time they had shared.

Slowly John's attention turned back to Skyraven's conversation. She was explaining that the office of chief was not hereditary but that the males of each tribe chose their chief for the qualities of bravery, leadership, unselfishness, and willingness to do everything possible for members of the tribe. A chief could not be deposed unless the people lost faith in him.

"If your chief is chosen on those merits, then you qualify for chief," he said, drawing her head close to his own and laying his cheek upon hers for a moment.

"Oh, but that could never be!" she said with a laugh as she looked deep into his clear blue eyes. "Women do women's work and men do men's work. It was meant to be that way from the beginning of time. But I am pleased that you have found such qualities in me."

Skyraven went on to tell John that right now a sun dance was being performed and that the people would dance all night long in order to put themselves in touch with the Great Spirit. "I have hope that I will not be missed tonight. Lone Wolf might search for me with his eyes."

"Lone Wolf?" He seemed to recall hearing that name before, surprised as a surge of jealousy swept through him. He knew he had no claim to her, but the thought of another man looking at his Skyraven with the same longing he felt bothered him.

"The chief's son. I should have stayed but . . . but I wanted to be here with you. I must return before sunrise, however." With a sparkle in her eyes, she told him about the purpose of the ceremony. "These days of games and eating and young people catching the eye of their future husbands or wives will end at sunrise. Many of the braves will choose their wives before the buffalo hunt begins."

"Will choose their wives?" Again jealousy pricked him. Even though he knew that once he left they would go their separate ways, he just couldn't bear to think of her with anyone else. "Are you spoken for?" he asked softly.

"No, not yet, although I think Lone Wolf, the chief's son, has that in mind." His voice sounded so strange that she detected he was bothered about something. Did he care more about her than she dared hope? She cocked her head to one side and smiled broadly. "But if Whispering Wind has her way, that will never happen."

"Do you care for Lone Wolf?" It was a prying question, yet his turbulent emotions wrenched the words form him. He had no claim, he told himself again. She was merely a very beautiful woman who had saved his life. She had her own life to live, a life that did not include him. He had to get that through his head.

Skyraven could tell by the look on his face that he did not want her to be interested in anyone else and that greatly pleased her. She knew that sometimes women played on such feelings for their own gain, but she could not do such a thing. "No, he is my friend," she answered truthfully. "I grew up with him and know him well, but I do not love him. I am part white as I already told you. My father was a white fur trader, and although I never knew him, there are some in the tribe who feel that my loyalty is sometimes divided. Whispering Wind says that because of this Lone Wolf will choose her for wife. Who knows? Now I am free and I like remaining so, but someday I will choose." She measured her words carefully, gauging his reactions. "Whispering Wind says it is whispered that when I decide, I might choose a white husband."

"A white husband?" So, she did not oppose the idea. "Would you?"

"If he was not too unpleasing to the eyes." As she spoke, she raised her jaw in such a winsome, teasing way that John could not help himself. He gathered her into his arms in a loving, tender embrace, looking deep into her eyes. The depth of her emotions showed plainly and was as potent as any aphrodisiac.

"Oh, Skyraven, do you have any idea what you do to me?" He buried his face in the lustrous, soft strands of her hair.

"I make your heart beat rapidly," she answered, taking her hand and placing it on his chest. "Just as you do to mine." Taking his hand, she placed it lightly on her breast. "Two hearts that beat in a like way. But my heart is at war with my head."

"At war?"

"Remembering the way my white father deserted my mother makes me afraid."

"I would never desert you. Never!" he said fervently. "The spirits *have* brought us together. This was meant to be. I love you, Skyraven, and I want you to be my wife. Mine. Not Lone Wolf's or anyone else's. Just mine."

Skyraven opened her eyes wide in amazement. This was what she had desired to hear from the moment she had first seen him. "Yes, yes. Oh, yes!" She answered further by throwing her arms around his neck and hugging him closer. He was right in what he said. The spirits had brought them together, had led her to him. Now she understood why. This was meant to be. For just a moment she pulled away. "But first you must bring great gifts to my grandfather. That is the Arapaho way." Buffalo's Brother would be apprehensive at first, but somehow she would make him understand.

"Gifts?" John did not want to offend her by asking if the Indians bought their women in this way, so he remained silent on that point. "I will. Many gifts, for you are worth the world to me."

He loved having her so close to him. There was something magnetic about this woman. She was so childlike in many ways, and yet so knowledgeable in others. He could not help himself. He was drawn to her as he had never been drawn to any woman before. He loved her as he had never loved before.

Skyraven began chattering on happily. "Tomorrow I will take you to my village and let you meet my grandfather. Oh, he will like you, I know he will. And then—"

"Skyraven." He silenced her by putting his finger to her lips. He hated to put a damper on her enthusiasm, but even her beauty could not make him forget his responsibilities. "Before we can make any plans, I must return to the fort or I will be considered absent without leave."

"You must return?" She had known in her heart that he would say those words, had feared hearing them, but she understood. "But you will come back?"

"I will come back. It is a promise." Closing his eyes, he contented himself by holding her tightly for a long, long time. "While I am gone, I want you to remember that even though we must be separated for a short time I will return for you and will bring as many presents for your grandfather as I can carry back with me. You and I will become husband and wife."

It was an impulsive statement spoken from his heart and most certainly not his head. Though he was surely drawn to her, John Hanlen suddenly wondered what had possessed him to ask her to marry him. He had blurted out the proposal without really thinking. Jealousy of the brave named Lone Wolf? Most probably. Or the enchantment of the cave? For just a moment as reality invaded upon his dreams he wished he could take the words back, at least until he could think rationally about the subject. Above all, he did not want to hurt her. She had been deserted once by a white man and he didn't want to bring her such hurt again.

John Hanlen looked down into her face, and in that moment was lost. She suddenly reminded him of a soft kitten, purring with happiness as she succumbed to the dreams his proposal had unleashed. "I will come back," he said again. As he spoke, he made the wish that it would be a vow he could keep.

Chapter Nine

The night breeze was cool, the small cave cozy and pleasantly tranquil. John Hanlen sat across from Sky-raven, watching as she threw some logs onto the fire. *Just as she nourishes the small blaze, so does she kindle emotions in my heart,* he thought, catching a glimpse of her out of the corner of his eyes. He had never realized he could feel such strong emotion.

"Are you hungry, John Hanlen?"

"Hungry?" He watched her appreciatively, standing so regal and proud like an Indian princess. What would it be like to share his life with such a woman? "Yes, I am." Though for something other than just food, he thought. It was her company he welcomed more than the rabbit she was preparing for him. Just being with her was enjoyable and gave him a deep sense of peace.

"The meat should be cooked to tenderness now," she said softly, handing him the meat still on the spit. He took it thoughtfully, cutting it with a knife she had likewise given him.

"Rabbit is one of my favorites." Looking up, he caught her eye and smiled his thanks. She returned his smile, then looked away. It was as if both of them were still entranced by the embrace they had shared a short time before and afraid to break the spell by conversation. A fragile silence held them bound.

I hardly know her and yet suddenly she has become the most important person in my life, he thought. *We're from two different worlds, our customs and people are at variance, and yet I feel at ease in her presence, as if it is with her that I was always meant to be.* He pondered the matter over as he ate the moist, succulent meat. He'd never perceived that he would fall in love with a woman not of his own kind, and yet he had. There was no turning back now, though he knew what loving this girl would mean. Ridicule. Scorn. There would be difficult times ahead, for her and for him. Even so, he didn't want to change his mind. He had said he wanted to marry her and he had meant every word.

Skyraven's gentle laughter echoed in the cave. "You eat as if I have starved you." Without a second thought, she gave him her own portion. When he refused, she insisted. "I have eaten several times today, but you only this once. Please, take this, for I will enjoy seeing your hunger satisfied far more than I would enjoy satisfying my own."

"Well . . ." he hesitated. The dried meat and berries he had eaten earlier were filling but had not completely satisfied his appetite. As a soldier he was skilled in foraging for his own rations, but there had been little to be found on the ridge. *Soldier,* he thought silently, reality suddenly sobering his sense of happiness. He had an obligation to his commander and his fellow officers. He could not let selfishness justify his betraying his duty, though he desperately wanted to stay and never leave.

John stared into the fire, feeling depressed by the knowledge that the time had come all too soon. He had to leave. He had been at the cave for three days and nights, enough time to regain his strength. He couldn't, in good conscience, stay here any longer, even though it would take all of his fortitude to force himself to leave. Her face would forever be etched in his memory. She was a woman who could walk proudly beside him. He'd found the woman he'd always dreamed of, but now that he had found her he must leave her behind. It seemed a grave injustice. Tomorrow at the sunrise he would ask Skyraven to show him the trail to the fort.

Oh, Skyraven, he thought. Now he had to sacrifice the pleasure of her company to return to his own people. At least, however, the promise he had made would bind them until he could return. That was the only thing that soothed him. He would come back, and when he did, he would be prepared to take her with him.

Skyraven sensed at once that John Hanlen was troubled. All sorts of thoughts besieged her mind. Would he come back? He had said that he would. He wanted to, she could see it in his eyes. But would he? Perhaps when he left, it would be a final good-bye. For the first time in her life she came close to understanding her mother's turbulent emotions. She was experiencing similar feelings now. All the pent-up resentment she had once felt for her white father began to diminish a bit. Perhaps he had meant to return but could not. Perhaps, after all, he had loved her mother once. Was that why Man Above had chosen a white man to be her mate? So that she would think upon her father and mother's love more kindly?

Skyraven thought again about the white soldier's proposal, his promise to bring back gifts for her grandfather to initiate the marriage. *John Hanlen says he wants to marry me,* she told herself. *But will he once he leaves to join with his own kind?* She wanted it to be true, wanted to belong to him, but reality crowded in on her dreams. There was a chance that this would be good-bye. If that was true, then she wanted something to remember, one night of love to carry her through the rest of her days and nights without him.

She wanted to tell him what it was she wanted, but an unusual sense of shyness swept over her. As she knelt before the fire, her heart quickened and her legs suddenly grew weak with a trembling awareness of this man. She was acutely aware that she and John Hanlen

90

were all alone. The very thought gave her a warm glow, but she could not bring herself to voice her desires.

"Tell me about yourself, John Hanlen," she said, suddenly wanting to leave those thoughts behind. She knew so little about him, she realized, only that he was a soldier. "Are there brothers and sisters that once shared your tepee?"

"Two brothers and one sister, all much younger than myself. It's been a long time since I have seen them, or my mother and father." John didn't know what spurred him on to talk about himself; it just started. Once he began, the words poured out. He told her about his mother and her gentleness, his father's stern, unrelenting way. He spoke about all the times he had wrestled with his siblings, how he had always protected his little sister. He vented his feelings on how the war had devastated all of their lives.

"My grandfather says that war is very bad, that it causes much heartache," Skyraven responded. She told him that her grandfather, the *wicasa waken* had been called by Man Above to serve for his entire lifetime not just as healer but as a holy man. "He is peaceful, not a warrior. One of his duties is to conduct the peace-pipe ceremony."

John gave a thoughtful nod. He was very interested in the peace-pipe ceremony. Perhaps Skyraven's grandfather could help bring about peace between the whites and the Indians at some kind of conference. Surely, his own commanding general was a reasonable man. If a solution to this land war could be solved peacefully it would be much the better for both sides involved. Until it was solved he couldn't even begin to live his own life or think of a future with Skyraven.

"I hope when I ask for you that your grandfather will not deny me."

"Because you are a soldier?"

"Yes. I hope he understands that although I am a soldier by occupation, I, too, long for peace." He

91

reached for her hand and squeezed it tightly, as if he never wanted to let her go. "Just as all Indians are not like the Utes, not all soldiers are alike, either."

"I know. You are a special man, John Hanlen."

"Love makes me so."

"Love," she repeated softly. The word had a special meaning to her now. To join with a man meant the right to comfort him, the joy of making love, shielding and protecting him. Skyraven snuggled against him, curled into the crook of his arm. She was warm and content. For just a moment it seemed there was nothing beyond the charmed circle of their closeness.

"If only our love could—" he broke off, lifting the dark, glossy mane of hair that lay on the back of her neck and moving it to the side. It felt clean and soft between his fingers. On sudden impulse he put a handful of the dark hair to his lips and cherished it, just as he wanted to do to every part of her. "But until this feeling between the whites and the Indians is settled, we cannot go on with our lives."

"I must go back to the village and you to your soldiers." A poignant loneliness possessed her at the very thought and she turned to look at him. "And if our two peoples can not live together peacefully, then we may never see each other aqain."

Her voice sounded so wistful that it tore at his soul. "Perhaps I can talk to your grandfather about a peaceful settlement of the land situation." There had to be another way besides giving in to brutality. *Peace, such a precious word,* he thought. And now, since meeting her, it was even more so.

John could resist no longer. He took both of her soft hands into his own. The slender fingers offered no resistance as he entwined them with his own as if they were making love. He kissed the palm of each hand slowly, lingeringly. "Peace, Skyraven. We must do what we can to bring about peace so we can be together." Reaching up, he put his arms around her neck and drew her down beside him.

She smiled, showing her gleaming, straight white teeth. "My grandfather will help us."

"I hope to God that he can." He was suddenly curious about this *wicasa waken*. "Explain more about the ceremony and your beliefs so that I can understand."

"The peace pipe is our most sacred possession. It is really the heart of all our sacred ceremonies. Its rising smoke represents the voice of the people rising from Mother Earth to Man Above. The bowl represents man's mouth, the tobacco all living things on earth. The three-foot-long pipe stem is the connection between the sky and the earth. The stem is held in the right hand and is passed around in a circle in the direction of the sun circling the earth."

"And will this peace-pipe ceremony help to bring harmony between your people and my soldiers?"

"I believe it will be so. The spirits want there to be peace or they would never have led me to you." Her soul knew the gentle power of love. His caress upon her was an affirmation of life and contentment.

"I love you," he said softly. There was no doubt in his mind as he looked into the innocent, sincere questioning eyes gazing up at him. He loved this beautiful brave young woman with all his heart.

"And I love you," she managed to say before his lips were again upon her own, tasting the honey, the sweetness, and the softness. Their lips caught and clung in kisses of newly discovered love. His mouth moved across her mouth with a feathery lightness.

"Skyraven." He spoke her name softly, caressingly, then settled himself against the wall of the cave. Their kisses were tender at first, but the burning spark of their desire burst their love into flames. Desire flooded his mind, obliterating all reason. He was seized with an excitement that left him trembling, yet he was determined to maintain control. To do otherwise was to take advantage of the situation and of her trust.

They talked long into the night and he pretended to be content with just lying beside her. He was far from appeased, however, for her nearness was deeply stirring. He was mesmerized by her gentle, husky voice, entranced by the warm pressure of her body against his. How envious his soldier companions would be of this beauty, John thought to himself. No woman could match her beauty, and when they came to know her, they would find that none could match her gentleness, her knowledge, her understanding or her generosity. The thought of leaving once again filled his heart with sorrow, but he dared not think about that now. Tonight they were here and they were together. He must be content with what "the spirits" granted them. Resting his chin on the top of her head, he gathered her close against his heart as he stared into the darkness and pretended to fall asleep.

Skyraven, however, was not content. Rising up on her elbow, she listened to the steady breathing of the man beside her and felt a deep longing. The heat of his body had warmed hers as they curled up on the floor of the cave and she thought how perfectly their two bodies had fit together, as if they were formed to be so joined.

"You are the one I want to be my mate, John Hanlen," she whispered. Right from the first she had wanted only him. "I love you," she went on, her breath soft against his face. Just saying it gave her a sudden soaring sensation inside, a giddy happiness. Reaching out, she lightly touched his chin, then his lips, feeling the strange prickly hair that covered his upper lip. She traced his mouth lovingly and was taken by surprise when those lips moved against her fingers, nibbling gently in a kiss.

"I've been playing possum," he said.

"Playing possum?" She didn't understand.

"It's a saying that means I've been pretending to sleep."

She drew back her hand, but he reached up and put

94

her fingers back on his face. "No, don't stop. I like having you touch me." Skyraven felt a dryness in her throat and licked her lips, but before she could say a word, his mouth claimed hers in a gentle kiss. "My shy yet bold Indian maiden," he murmured against her lips. His hands moved along her back sending a tingling sensation up her spine.

Skyraven closed her eyes to the rapture. In that moment, his gentleness seemed to merge with his strength. Her grandfather had always said that such a combination made for a great man. Were he an Indian he would make a fine leader, she mused. But John Hanlen was a soldier. Soldiers and warriors were sometimes killed. What if he didn't return to her because he couldn't. If that happened she would regret never having fully given herself to him.

At that moment Skyraven came to a decision. Shifting her weight, she rolled closer into his embrace. How could she deny what was in her heart? She wanted to take him into her body so that she could experience the wonder that such joining brought about, the sensations she had heard the other women talk about.

His arm was a pleasant weight across her body. She felt the warmth of his breath on her neck. "Mate with me, John Hanlen," she said softly.

"What?" He felt her eyes upon him and welcomed her caressing gaze.

"I want you to mate with me," she repeated.

A moan issued from his mouth as he realized what she had just said. His arms closed around her. For a time that seemed endless, he held her to him, physically hurting from his desperate hunger to feel every inch of her against him, to take her as she asked.

"You are sure?" He didn't know what the Indian customs were, didn't want to harm or offend her in any way.

"I'm sure." She reached up to touch his face and his hand grasped her own. His firm touch caused a fluttery feeling to erupt in her stomach, like a butterfly, she thought.

He held her face in his hands, kissing her eyelids, the curve of her cheekbones, her mouth. "Skyraven, Skyraven," he murmured, repeating her name over and over again as if to taste of it on his lips. He shivered with pleasure, feeling as if for years he had been on a long journey but now he was home.

With reverence he touched her breasts, gently, slowly, until they swelled in his hands. It took all his self-control to keep his passion in check. He wanted to make it beautiful for her, wanted to be the perfect lover, husband, mate. With trembling fingers he tugged at the front of her soft leather dress to bare her beauty to his eyes.

By the light of the moon shining through the opening of the cave he admired her body. Her breasts were high and firm, and he worshipped their beauty as his hands explored the soft, velvety mounds. Bending his head, John gently kissed their peaks, pleasuring her with light, teasing strokes. Skyraven was caught up in the sensations of his caressing hand, making no effort to hide her breasts from his piercing gaze. Gone was her modesty. This was her fate, her destiny—to belong to this man. She felt that in every bone, every muscle, every sinew of her body as he touched her and gloried in the thought that her body pleased him. It was as it should be.

"I am glad that I please you, for you please me too, so very much." Her fingertips roamed over his shoulders and neck and plunged into his thick yellow hair. Once again he kissed her, a fierce joining of mouths that spoke of his passion. Then after a long pleasurable moment he drew away. She smiled as she watched him unbutton his jacket. So, he was as anxious to join with her as she was with him. That pleased her.

When he drew away for just a moment to pull off his clothing, her eyes swept over him, remembering the

96

first time she had let her eyes caress him. Had she hoped even then that they would at last be together like this? She knew that she had.

The flames caught and flared, illuminating the smooth skin on his chest. He was a muscular man, with a trim waist and narrow hips, and a broad chest. His thick, light-colored chest hair was soft as down beneath her fingers. As she caressed his chest, his hands wandered beneath her dress to her firm, flat belly and buttocks.

"Wait, John Hanlen," she said. Rising to her feet, she lifted her doeskin dress over her head and dropped it on the ground next to his discarded coat and shirt, then she removed her leggings and moccasins. John Hanlen watched her sensual movements, then quickly removed his breeches and long johns.

When both were completely naked, he rolled over on his side and drew her down beside him. "I like the feel of your skin against me," he breathed.

Skyraven was shattered by the all-consuming pleasure of lying naked beside him. A heat arose within her as she arched against him in sensual pleasure. Her breathing became heavier, and a hunger for him, a sweet, aching sensation, traveled from her breasts to her loins, a pulsing, tingling feeling that intensified as his hand moved across the smoothness of her belly to feel the softness nestled between her thighs.

Skyraven gave way to wild abandon, moaning joyously as her fingers likewise moved over his body. She felt a strange sensation flood over her and could not deny that before he left, she wanted their spirits to be joined together. She wanted him to fill her with excitement and pleasure. His strong arms were around her, his mouth covering her own. She shivered at the feelings that swept over her.

John felt her tremble. "You're not afraid of me?"

"No, I don't believe I ever have been, John Hanlen. Not really." She laid her head on his shoulder, moving

97

her palms over his muscles as if to know every inch of him.

The light of the moon illuminated their bodies, hers a smooth, deep olive, his muscular form a lighter hue. He knelt beside her and kissed her breasts, running his tongue over their tips until she shuddered with delight. Whispering words of love, he slid his hands between her thighs to explore her soft inner flesh. At his touch she felt a slow quivering deep inside that became a fierce fire as he moved his fingers against her.

Supporting himself on his forearms, he positioned himself on top of her and moved between her legs. Slowly he brushed his lower body against her thighs, letting her grow accustomed to the hardness of his maleness. Taking her mouth in a hard, deep kiss, he entered her softness with a slow but strong thrust, burying his length within the sheath of her softness.

As they came together, she was consumed by his warmth, his hardness, and she tightened her thighs around his waist as she arched up to him, moving in time to his rhythm. It was as if he had touched the very core of her being. There was an explosion of rapture as their bodies blended into one. She returned his caresses, exploring his body and feeling joy at his groans of desire.

From this moment on they belonged to each other. She wanted him and him only, and he vowed never to share her with anyone else. Each knew that they had found their other half. To Skyraven this was their wedding ceremony. After all, they did come from two different cultures, each having a different set of rules for becoming man and wife. He hadn't brought gifts to Grandfather yet to ask for her hand, but that would be taken care of in due time. The spirits wanted them together, had led them to each other. Surely they were smiling now at this union. The thought made her smile also. She was happy. Gloriously happy.

Throughout the night they held each other, made

love again, and finally fell asleep entwined in each other's arms, her head resting upon his soft golden chest hair. Neither wanted to remember that they must part before sunrise. Not even the chanting still going on down below at the Arapaho village kept them awake. They were content for the moment, and so much in love.

Chapter Ten

When the two lovers parted before daybreak the next morning they knew that their lives would never be the same. Now, truly, Skyraven could understand her mother's anguish when her father had left. But this time it would be different. John Hanlen would return for her as he had promised. After their wondrous night of lovemaking, how could she doubt it?

John held Skyraven close and kissed her tenderly, fighting to hold his emotions in check. Now that the moment had actually come, it pained him far more to leave her than he had foreseen. If only life could be simple and uncomplicated, he lamented. Instead, he was torn between his duty to his land and the woman he loved. He prayed that he would never have to make a choice. Would there be peace between the white men and Indians or would tempers flare over land ownership and war break out? Now he had a personal stake in the matter. It would be peace! Somehow he had to force any doubts from his mind and trust that his countrymen would see reason.

"I'm going to miss you," he whispered, nuzzling the soft dark hair that brushed against the nape of her neck. "While I'm gone, make a list of the items your grandfather requests for your hand in marriage so that I may quickly fulfill his wish."

"I will." She closed her eyes tightly to force back the

tears. She was Indian, she told herself, and Indians did not give forth weak emotions.

For a long while they stood silently, locked in an embrace beneath the pale moon, neither wanting to let go of the other but not really knowing what could be said. Good-bye seemed too sorrowful a word. Skyraven could only stare at him mutely, her blue eyes huge pools of misery.

John finally broke the silence. "I love you, Skyraven." He let his eyes touch on every curve of her face as if to memorize her beauty. Then with a muttered oath of frustration, he lowered his head and claimed her mouth with a soul-rending kiss. A jolt of sweet fire swept through his veins prompting him to give in to his passion one more time, but he pushed away. If he made love to her again, it would only prolong the agony. Still, he said, "You'll never know how it's tearing me apart to have to leave you. I don't know how long we must be apart, but I will come back for you. I swear that I will."

"The spirits brought you to me once before. I feel that they will again." Reaching up, she touched his face, running her fingers over his eyes, nose, and mouth like a blind person. "Walk in sunshine, John Hanlen."

Skyraven had prepared him well for the journey ahead. She had gone over and over with him the things that he should be aware of along the shorter and safer route that she had selected for him to take, describing the landmarks, streams, and other points that would keep him on the right trail. Not only had she provided food, water, and new high-topped moccasins but had given him her prized possession, Running Antelope, as well.

"You . . . you may take my mare," she had said, fighting tears. The animal was very dear to her, yet not as precious as he.

John knew how much the animal meant to her, and yet she freely gave it up in order to help him return to his soldiers. The thought that she would make that sacrifice deeply touched him. No one besides his mother had ever given him anything without strings attached, not even his own father. "When I return, I will bring Running Antelope back to you, along with many more horses for your grandfather," he promised.

"Yes, for my grandfather." She snuggled closer in his arms for just a moment, then quickly turned, wiping the moisture from her cheeks before he could see. Her heart seemed to be bursting within her chest, yet she fought to maintain her pride. She knew that it had to be this way but dreaded the parting, yet even as she said good-bye she kept her chin up, her shoulders back.

He was a soldier, he had to return to Fort Lyon, she told herself. She would not beg him to stay, and even if she did, he could not comply with such a wish. It was a truth she had to face. On the other hand, he had not asked her to go away with him, and while this pricked her heart, she knew that it was not that he did not want her—it was just the way things were. She accepted what had to be stoically, relieved that he had not asked her to leave her people. She could not have left him so quickly without making preparations. She was the medicine man's granddaughter, and as such had her own duties to the tribe. Her grandfather depended on her and he was getting older. Right now such a move would be unthinkable, for it would surely break his heart.

As much as I love you, John Hanlen, I would have had to refuse had you asked me to go with you this morning, she thought, closing her eyes. If only he were an Indian or she completely white, it would have been so much simpler, but they were what they were.

Skyraven trusted in the spirits to guard over her love and make things right, yet even so she had the impulse to run to her dear white soldier, to throw her arms around him and beg him to stay. Now that she knew what love was, it would be so lonely without him. *Oh, Mother, how terrible it must have been for you also,* she thought. Now at last she fully understood, for as he

102

moved with her toward her horse she nearly felt her heart break.

"It is a beautiful animal you give me, Skyraven. One more precious gift."

She moved away as John mounted the mare, watching as he pulled himself up and flung his leg over the horse's back. It was a different method of mounting than the Indian braves used. Running Antelope seemed ill at ease despite Skyraven's whispered words of calm. Unused to this man on her back, the mare raised her front legs high in the air and came down pawing the earth. The bucking action nearly threw John Hanlen to the ground.

Hurriedly Skyraven shouted out a command as she strode forward. Whispering in the mare's ear, patting her head affectionately, Skyraven calmed the horse down, enough to enable her soldier to attempt to control her again.

"Whoa! Easy, girl." John waited just long enough to be assured that the mare was indeed calm before starting on his way. Leaning over for just one more quick kiss, he galloped away, turning to look over his shoulder as he offered one last good-bye.

"Remember what I told you," Skyraven called back. "The Utes have moved on and are far to the west by now. Everything should go as we planned, but do be careful."

"I will," he shouted back, then he waved.

Skyraven watched as his figure became smaller and smaller, dwindling to the size of an ant. Only after he was well out of sight did she allow herself to vent her emotions. Sitting down on a rock, she buried her face in her hands and sobbed her heart out. Tears were foolish, she told herself, yet nevertheless great drops of sorrow fell from her eyes. Then when her emotions were spent and she had no more tears left, she stood up and began the long walk back to the village.

* * *

John raced at breakneck speed over the immense spread of land before him. Skyraven had selected a flatter, shorter route, one with little foliage and a few rolling hills covered by crisscrossing streams and buffalo wallows. He was headed toward the south and the valley of the Arkansas River, riding with the speed of the wind.

He was amazed at the strength and speed displayed by Running Antelope. Not one of the soldier's horses could even touch her for maneuverability, speed, and beauty. She had been well trained and it showed, he thought, marveling at how his beautiful Indian love had taught the animal so well. This Indian pony was a wonder, the finest horse he had ever ridden. Her mane and tail streamed in the wind like a flying banner, her muscles rippling under her glistening hide.

As he rode on, his thoughts returned again and again to Skyraven. He could almost see her beautiful face before him, and thought again what a unique person she was. She was strong yet gentle, full of wisdom, yet childlike in some ways, too. She was beautiful yet completely unaware of her beauty, and when it came to being a giving person, surely no woman had ever made the sacrifices that Skyraven had made for him. No other woman would ever take her place in his heart. He was sure of that.

Running Antelope's hooves thundered on the ground taking John farther and farther from the woman he loved so dearly. Even though he was thinking of Skyraven, his senses were alert to any danger. He vowed that he would never again be taken as unawares as he had been on that fearful day not so long past. Had he seen the eyes staring at him from a distance, however, he might not have been so certain.

Chapter Eleven

Tiny beams of sunlight danced across the sky, sending a soft, dim glow to the earth below as Skyraven approached the village. Usually she would have marveled at the beauty of the sky, but now it made her wary. Always before she had been cautious in her visits to John Hanlen, leaving when her camp was in darkness and returning long before dawn. Her nightly visits had gone undetected and she had grown overly secure in the knowledge that she had not been discovered. Would she now suffer for such foolish overconfidence? Had she allowed John Hanlen's tender words and lovemaking to overpower her own better judgment?

"As grandfather would say, I have made my own trouble," she scolded aloud as she walked along. Even so, she had to admit that had she to do it all over again, she still would have stayed with her soldier. Last night had been a wonder beyond belief, something precious to remember for the days ahead.

Dry leaves and twigs snapped under her feet and she cautioned herself to walk more stealthily, fearful of being intercepted and possibly questioned. She did not want such rebuke to spoil what had passed last night. But though she frightened off a foraging raccoon, none of her tribesmen seemed to linger about. Skyraven breathed a sigh of relief. The spirits were looking out for her, for no one was in sight. Her approach appeared to have been without detection.

In the distance she could hear chanting and knew that the dancing, greeting the approach of the first morning's light, had begun. That was the answer. Her people had already left the village to travel to the bluff to greet the dawn. They had been too engrossed in their ceremony to have noticed her absence. The camp was empty, at least for the moment.

The sun dance was the most elaborate festival among the Arapaho and Cheyenne. Already it had taken several days of preparation, every member of the tribe having had some part in it. Skyraven felt a twinge of guilt remembering that she had used this concentration and distraction for her own ends, to visit John Hanlen. Now the last day of the eight-day ceremony was to come to an end with one last celebration. Soon, when the first pink rays of the sun appeared over the horizon, her people would make an impressive parade back to the camp from the bluff and through the village. Skyraven planned to join in that procession, pouring forth her whole heart to atone for those moments her thoughts had been elsewhere during the rituals.

Quietly she lifted the flap of her tepee and went inside, hoping with all her heart that none of the women would be waiting to pry from her an explanation of her doings. She would have a difficult time explaining where she had been last night if it had been noticed that she was gone. Anxiously her eyes darted about, but again it appeared that the spirits were on her side. The tepee was empty, with no sign of anyone having disturbed her possessions. It was just as she had left it, a favorable sign which made her feel at peace. The women who kept their keen, watching eyes on the unmarried girls would have no scolding words or tattling tales to tell her grandfather. Facing her grandfather's anger when his goodwill toward John Hanlen was so important would have boded ill.

Nevertheless Skyraven waited for several moments,

watching the entrance to her tepee just in case she might have a visitor. She was greatly relieved when no one entered. So far, so good, she thought as she reached into her buffalo-skin clothes chest for her white doeskin dress. She would change into her ceremonial attire and join the others. If she timed her entrance right, no one need ever know that she had not been present the entire time. With so many others about, the women would very likely not even have noticed that she was missing. Skyraven laughed softly. They were too busy chattering among themselves, preening about in their beaded finery like strutting prairie chickens to concern themselves with her. For once she approved of such vanity.

The light in the tepee was dim as Skyraven slipped out of her soft beaded buckskin dress and leggings. The early-morning air was cool, and she felt her body come alive at its whispered touch, just as it had beneath John Hanlen's hands. Closing her eyes, she allowed herself the luxury of remembering the lovemaking they had shared for just a moment, then quickly returned to her task. Even so, as she brushed her hair and fumbled with her garments, she conjured up his face.

"Oh, John Hanlen, return to me soon," she whispered.

As soon as she had dressed she thanked Man Above for sending her the spiritual gift of dreams and vision, and for giving her the white man's love. She turned four times and asked the spirits to pardon her absence from the sun dance. No sooner were the words out of her mouth, however, when a cool breeze seemed to blow through the tepee whispering to her. She knew then that all was well. A voice from within her own head seemed to say, "You have saved a life and are in good favor."

Skyraven attuned her ears as she stepped forth from her dwelling. There were voices in the distance and the tinkling of bells. The women were coming closer now. The procession to the village had begun. The bells around their ankles kept time to the drumbeats, coming closer and closer. Slipping into the shadows as they passed by her tepee, Skyraven stealthily joined the throng of happy, smiling faces. She eased her way along until she was at her place in front of the other women.

"Skyraven!" Her grandfather's voice startled her out of her sense of well-being. Her heart beat as furiously as the tom-toms, but as she looked at him she realized he hadn't spoken. She had imagined his voice so vividly that it had seemed real, however. The spirits again?

I will make it up to you, Grandfather, she thought. She knew that she must confide in him all that had happened. He would understand. When he realized the spirits had led her to the white man, that it was a hope for peace, he would find it in his heart to be happy for her. She would soothe his mind and make him see that John Hanlen was her happiness.

Her eyes touched on her grandfather with loving eyes. He looked so splendid in the ceremonial dress that she had made for him just last year. It had taken her a long time to complete the quill embroidery on the yoke and down the front of the buckskin shirt. The fringe along the sleeves and around the yoke was longer than most fringe by at least a hand's length, but the simple buckskin leggings he wore had been easy to make. The beautifully beaded moccasins that reached to his knees were the ones she had just completed; he was wearing them for the first time. She had to admit with a sense of pride that they did add a touch of elegance. On his head was the buffalo-horn ceremonial bonnet with ermine and eagle feather streamers hanging down his back.

Her heart swelled with love. To her eyes he was the most magnificent sight of all the males, though Chief Left Hand looked splendid in his attire. He was dressed in a simple buckskin shirt, leggings, and moccasins, his war bonnet of eagle feathers reaching to the ground. Here were the two men to whom she had given her

108

complete adoration and respect, the only men she had loved until she had met her white soldier.

"Grandfather." For just a moment she reached out her hand as if she might touch him, sorrow weighing heavily on her mind. Could she leave him to make a life with John Hanlen? It was a question that marred the happiness she had allowed to consume her. Her grandfather would never make his way in the white man's world. He had said that again and again. Nor could she be so foolish as to believe John Hanlen would live among her tribe. A time for choices was at hand, and yet perhaps last night she had already chosen, she thought, as she joined in the singing.

After circling the entire camp, her grandfather, the chief, and the elders of the tribe stopped in front of the lodge of secret rituals. It was here her grandfather would conduct the peace-pipe ceremony and demonstrate his skill with offerings and prayers. The spring hunting season could not begin without this ritual asking for a good hunting season and escape from danger. Though it was a very solemn occasion, her grandfather made it known that he was aware of her presence by nodding in her direction before the leaders entered the secret ritual lodge.

Now as the drummers beat the drums and sang their chanting songs, the women danced in accompaniment. Skyraven was in the first of four horizontal rows of dancers. Each woman held an eagle feather in her hand. The dance was simple, just moving the body in place while lifting the eagle feather toward the sky and then lowering it to the ground. Even so, Skyraven was aware of her every movement. Her grandfather had always commended her on the graceful way she danced. As she gave herself up to the movements, she felt the spirit touch her again and she smiled. It was yet another sign that what had happened was right. The dance would continue until the peace-pipe ceremony had ended and the elders again joined the tribe outside

109

the ritual lodge. The people then would return to their own tepees to rest. Unlike her, sleeping in her lover's arms, they had been immersed in the ceremony all night long.

Skyraven was aware that the sun-dance festivities were almost over when the elders began to emerge from the ritual lodge. Only tonight's feasting around the communal fire remained. Tomorrow the buffalo hunt would begin. All of the able-bodied men would ride out on horseback leaving behind only the old and infirm men, along with the women and children in the village. Her grandfather would leave in the morning with the hunters, so she would have only a short time alone with him.

Skyraven approached her grandfather now but did not stop to talk with him. Several young braves had crowded around to seek his advice and she did not want to interrupt. Though she was anxious to reveal all that had happened she moved on, vowing to speak with him later. Till then she would gather her thoughts together so that she could speak her mind easily, truthfully, and in such a manner that she would receive her grandfather's favor.

"Skyraven!" She was headed to her tepee when Lone Wolf came up behind her. Taking her arm, he turned her around to face him. Leaning over, he whispered in her ear, "I have been looking for the most beautiful woman in the village and now I have found her."

"Have you?" Skyraven turned and smiled at the handsome brave, wondering just what Whispering Wind would think of his remark. Slowly her eyes appraised him, thinking again that he was a handsome warrior. Around his strong arms were metal bands of a golden color. He was wearing no shirt, just leggings, beaded ankle-high moccasins, and a headband with three eagle feathers. He was strong and powerful and she could understand Whispering Wind's attraction to him. Even so, she could not push from her mind another man's visage, a man with golden hair and eyes the color of the summer sky.

"Yes, I have found her," he repeated. His grip on her arm was tight, his eyes as intense as burning coals as he looked down at her. "I have always found you pleasing, Skyraven, as you must know."

"Such words flow from your lips as easily as honey from the honey pouch. But how do I know that you do not say such things to all the women?"

"Because I tell you now that I do not."

Skyraven met his gaze without wavering, knowing that this was no time for playful banter. She had noticed his eyes upon her, but until now, until she saw the same passion in his eyes that John Hanlen had exhibited, she had not fully realized the seriousness of his feelings. She had spoken lightly of his arrogance, yet now she didn't want to wound his pride, nor to hurt him. But it was too late. She had given her heart, her soul, her body to another man.

Lone Wolf's eyes narrowed and he walked around her, his eyes mirroring his appreciation of her beauty. "You will know tonight at the feast if you do not know by now. I want you for my wife. I will ask your grandfather and your cousins for their permission then."

"No!" The gasp escaped her lips, but Lone Wolf did not hear. He had turned and left without waiting for an answer. Women of the Arapaho tribe did have something to say about who they would marry and were never forced to marry against their will. Still, Lone Wolf's wanting her might very well complicate the matter of John Hanlen. Her refusal would sting Lone Wolf. When he found out that she had shunned him for a white man, there could be trouble. Better by far that he found her ugly, she thought as she watched him until he was out of sight.

"So, you think that you have won?" Whispering Wind seemed to come from out of nowhere, her face set in a treacherous smile. Somehow she had a way of knowing just what Lone Wolf was doing at every hour of the day.

"I do not think that I have won anything." Skyraven's jaw tensed with her dislike of this woman. "I have told you before and I will tell you again that I have no wish to be your rival, Whispering Wind."

"And I tell you again that I do not believe you. But no matter. Lone Wolf will change his mind about you, as will the others, when I tell about the yellow-haired soldier." Her voice was venomous as she pushed past Skyraven nearly knocking her to the ground.

Chapter Twelve

It was quiet in the camp. The chanting had stopped, the drums were silenced, the shuffling feet of the dancers were at rest. The next to the last phase of the sun dance was over and the people of the village were resting, sleeping like owls during the day so that they could celebrate again during the final night of the festival. But Skyraven could not sleep. How could she? Whispering Wind's hissed threats, Lone Wolf's bold appraisal of her and talk of making her his wife, and, more important, the memory of caressing hands and a body entwined with hers in the act of love churned through her mind. Conflicting emotions filled her breast as she restlessly tossed and turned upon her bed.

"I love you, Skyraven," the image of John Hanlen whispered. "I want to marry you, marry you . . . marry you."

"I have always found you pleasing, Skyraven, as you must know." Lone Wolf's image warred with John Hanlen's in her mind's eye. "I want you for my wife . . . for my wife. . . !"

"So you think that you have won?" Whispering Wind's menacing voice added to the tumult inside Skyraven's head.

"I will return for you and will bring many presents for your grandfather. I will return . . . will return . . . will return," John Hanlen's voice said.

"You will know tonight at the final feast if you do not know by now. I will ask your grandfather and cousins for their permission then." Lone Wolf's bold smile haunted her.

"I will tell them about the yellow-haired soldier . . ."

"No!" Skyraven's own mumbled voice jarred the silence. Deeply disturbed by the voices, she put her hands over her ears to block out the sound. Wide-eyed she tried to sort out her turbulent thoughts. Why was it so difficult? The answer was very clear, as much as the water that sparkled in the streams. She would refuse Lone Wolf, tell her grandfather about John Hanlen before Whispering Wind's vindictive voice could be heard, and speak before all of her intent to marry the white man she had saved. She would not let apprehension silence her. It must be done.

The solution decided upon, she curled up into a ball as deep fatigue at last claimed her. Closing her eyes, she at last fell into the sleep that anxiety had denied her. It seemed as if she had just fallen asleep, however, when at last night descended and the crier rode through the village announcing that the final feast was soon to begin.

Skyraven's eyes flew open, immediately conscious. She had the overpowering urge to mount Running Antelope, ride across the river, and scramble up the bank to the cave to see John Hanlen. That had become her pattern for the last several days. Sadly she shook her head as reality jolted her mind. He was gone. She had given up her mare to the white soldier she loved. Now, neither Running Antelope nor John Hanlen's open arms would be waiting for her.

"Gone" she said aloud, the word a soulful wail. However, she knew she must put sad thoughts behind her, at least for tonight. Tonight she must center her thoughts upon her grandfather. She would do her part to aid him in his ceremony, then she would talk with him. But just how should she reveal her secret love to him?

Skyraven was filled with mixed emotions. At first she feared that he would not understand, but she quickly chased that fear from her mind. She should not be feeling apprehensive. Her grandfather had always understood. What was she thinking of? His own daughter, her mother, had married a white man. Buffalo's Brother was a kind, gentle, wise man. She had never seen him display anger, certainly never at her.

Suddenly her heart swelled with love and pride as she thought of her grandfather. His eloquence and wisdom were valued as highly as bravery. He would counsel her, he might even be stern, but in the end he would wish for her happiness, knowing she would be content and find fulfillment at the white man's side. When he realized that, he would cease his gentle scolding and be glad for her. She left the tepee knowing that this was the way it would be.

As she walked toward the feasting place at the central fire, she looked up at the stars. Somewhere John Hanlen was looking at those very same stars as he traveled, and that thought brought her closer to him. Her eyes looked in the direction of the river, feeling certain that just as the waters at last flowed into one body, so she and her white soldier would one day be joined. Breathing deeply, she touched the eagle feather in her hair and willed it to be so. She had long ago learned the law and the mysteries of the sky, the earth, the water, and the air. Now she was learning the law of love as well, a law that decreed that soon the forces of life would bring two lovers together.

Eyes-of-Night, Lame Rabbit, Thunder-on-the-Hill, and several other young braves appraised her with their eyes as she passed them to join the other women who were finishing the cooking chores near the central fire. Their silent compliments soothed her heart and made her feel confident. Or perhaps it was knowing she was loved that put a slight bounce to her step, a smile on her face. The world had always seemed to her to be a beautiful place, but now it was even more so.

"Skyraven!" the women greeted as she approached. She was much admired by the other women. They reacted to her warmly now, which eased her mind of the apprehension that Whispering Wind's tattling tongue might already have been at work.

"You look so lovely," Morning Dew said.

"I wish I had your beauty so heads would turn when I walked by," added Doe's Eyes.

Skyraven raised her hand in salutation to the women, then, seeing her grandfather and Chief Left Hand, acknowledged them as well. The chief and the medicine man were sitting at a place of honor at the far end of the circle of tribesmen. She searched for Lone Wolf and Whispering Wind but they were nowhere to be seen. It was not a good sign, though she tried to tell herself it was not unusual that they would be together. Whispering Wind followed the brave like a shadow. Taking her place with the other women, Skyraven watched and waited, determined not to let the bad-tempered woman cause her any fear.

"Lone Wolf should have been here by now," Morning Dew said, voicing Skyraven's thoughts aloud. "Where could he be?"

"Both Running Hare and Red Dog have taken their places," Doe's Eyes added. The two braves who had accompanied Lone Wolf on the scouting mission had returned with a big buffalo bull for tonight's feast. No fresh meat had passed the lips of the tribe the last few days, as part of the ritual. It would make the offering doubly appreciated.

"We will want to thank the young braves for the feast they have made possible." With a barely repressed giggle, Morning Dew looked boldly at the tallest of the braves as if she meant to take on that pleasant duty single-handedly.

"No doubt Lone Wolf will outdo those fine braves. It

is just like him to bring in a buffalo twice as big as their offering. Mmm, I can hardly wait. But where can he be?" Doe's Eyes seemed agitated. "It is unseemly for him to make his father wait."

"Perhaps he had better things to do with his time," Morning Dew murmured suggestively. "Certainly the braves aren't the only ones stalking a prey." The Indian girl rolled her eyes.

"That bold one, Whispering Wind, she does not draw his interest." Doe's Eyes nudged Skyraven. "It is you who have drawn his gaze. He makes great show of attracting your attention, but you are wise to ignore him. The highest berry on the branch is the one that beckons to be plucked."

"But I don't want —" Skyraven started to tell the Indian girl that she was not seeking the chief's son's favor but broke off. Now was not the time. As for Lone Wolf, perhaps he would arrive late in order to make a grand entrance. It was just like him to do something like that. "He had better arrive soon or he will get nothing to eat," she said instead. As soon as the meal was over, it was part of his duty to help bury the buffalo hump which was thought to contain the animal's spirit. The pit had already been dug. Skyraven thought it would serve him right to go hungry.

Upon the fire the roast loin of buffalo, boiled buffalo tongue, and the buffalo leg marrow were ready for serving. Skyraven hit each leg with a hatchet in just such a way as to open its entire length on one side, exposing the rolls of well-done white marrow. Two youngsters grinned impishly as they gobbled a pilfered bit of food, but she reprimanded them with a frown. No one was allowed to eat even one bit before Buffalo's Brother placed a piece of meat on the rocks of the firepit and made an offering of thanks. It seemed, however, that no one else saw the children so Skyraven remained silent. Also something else had now gained her attention. Lone Wolf and Whispering Wind had joined the group, but they were not sitting together. Lone Wolf sat down in cross-legged fashion next to Lame Hare and Red Dog in the inner circle of honor. Whispering Wind joined her father, Watchful Fox, and his family at the far end of the outer circle.

Skyraven looked at Lone Wolf trying to assess what was on his mind. Perhaps, she thought, it would be better if Whispering Wind did tell him about having seen her talking to a white man. Then he might abandon his vow to make her his bride. It would make her life much simpler, she thought.

"Lone Wolf! So, he has come," Morning Dew observed.

"He is handsome, is he not, Skyraven?" Doe's Eyes asked.

Skyraven shrugged. He was muscular, strong, and handsome, but no more so than John Hanlen. She had to admit that she did admire him and that she was fond of him, but she did not want him for a husband, especially not now after enjoying her white soldier's lovemaking. Looking at him did not start her heart to thump the way that merely looking at John Hanlen had. With just a glance, John Hanlen could set her aflame, but the sight of Lone Wolf left her unaffected. She loved John Hanlen. She had given her heart and soul to the handsome blue-coated soldier and could never accept another.

"Does the wolf have your tongue, Skyraven?" Morning Dew teased, thinking her lack of response to be shyness.

"She doesn't have to speak. Lone Wolf's eyes speak of what is going on," Doe's Eyes whispered, nudging Skyraven so hard she was certain she would be wearing a bruise come morning.

"There is nothing between that bold strutting prairie rooster and me," Skyraven answered spiritedly, unable to hide her true feelings any longer. "As you will see when . . ." She quieted as the ceremony began. Her grandfather made the food offering to the Buffalo Spirit for providing the food, then went to Skyraven to sit by her side as he usually did at feasttime.

"You have been as elusive as a spirit," he said quietly. "We have been like the sun and the moon, seldom in a position to be together. When we do see each other your mind is troubled, I can sense that. Tell me. We have time now to talk."

"And I am thankful for that. I have many things to talk to you about, Grandfather." She answered in a whisper that only he could hear. "I had a vision."

"A vision?" He seemed pleased. "And voices also? Did the spirits speak to you?"

"Yes."

His smile was as bright as summer sunshine. "I knew it. I sensed that you had the gift. Now you fully understand what I am about."

"The Great Spirit communicated with me. It has caused a great change in my life." Noticing that Morning Dew and Doe's Eyes were eavesdropping, she said, "Come, let us sit over by those trees while we eat, away from the others so that I may tell you about it in privacy." They moved toward a group of cottonwood trees.

In between bites of food, Skyraven told her grandfather, briefly and as quickly as she could, all that had happened—the voices and vision that haunted her, the man whose life she had saved, her feelings of love for the man with golden hair. "So you see, when Lone Wolf asks for me to become his wife, I cannot do so, Grandfather."

His tone was stern as he answered. "As spiritual leader I will give you the same advice I would give to any other member of our tribe. We must all learn from experience. You are starting on a new turn of the medicine wheel's way, now that you have ventured into the spirit world. You must follow this inner voice, but remember that as far as Lone Wolf is concerned, nothing fires a man's blood more than competition."

119

"It is not a matter of winning a prize," she sighed. "Besides, my heart is already taken. I do not want Chief Left Hand's son as my husband. I want to choose my mate, and that will be the yellow-haired man whose life I saved."

"Skyraven, he is not—"

"One of our kind. Yes, I am all too aware of that. But I ask you. Why would the Great Spirit have brought us together if it was not meant to be?"

"There are times when we do not understand all, Granddaughter. We must let wisdom rule."

"Wisdom. Agreed."

A look of pain, as if he were wounded, flitted over Buffalo Brother's face. Skyraven reached out to take his hand. "Please, Grandfather, do not feel an ache in your heart when I feel so much love for John Hanlen in mine. I do not wish to hurt you." She reached out and entwined her long, tapered fingers with his firm, strong ones. "Your daughter, my mother, also fell in love with a white man, so I thought you would understand."

"I do, but . . ." Suddenly he seemed to be transformed before her very eyes, as if he had aged. He looked worried. "It pains my heart that the very thing I dreaded has happened. I thought you would have learned, would use caution."

"I did, but there are just some things that can not be controlled, Grandfather. I couldn't keep from loving him. I'm sorry if that has hurt you."

He was silent for a long moment, then said, "I must think about what you have told me and decide what is to be done." Skyraven was wide-eyed as she listened to every word, waiting as her grandfather looked lovingly at her, then dropped his hand from her own and lifted it to the sky. "I implore the spirits to be with you while I am away."

"You are leaving again, Grandfather?"

"Yes. Tomorrow Chief Left Hand and some of the lesser chiefs, Galloping Shadow, Caught-the-Enemy,

120

and Spotted Pony, along with some of the other elders, must go with me to have council with our friend, Lean Bear, and his Cheyenne. We will meet at the Cheyenne village just south of here to discuss the white men."

"And will the villagers be expected to go, too?" The fear that John Hanlen might come back and not be able to find her seized her violently.

"It is possible. Since returning from the scouting party, Lone Wolf and his companions have reported that the buffalo are moving father south toward the sandy creek area."

Skyraven's heart caught in her throat. "The sandy creek?" She did not want to leave here. Not now. How could John Hanlen ask for her hand in marriage if he did not know where to find her?

"We must go where the buffalo make their home. You know that." Cupping her chin with his hand, he looked deep into her eyes. "If that is to the sandy creek, then that is where we, too, will go. We must keep the buffalo in sight."

He explained that he would join with Lean Bear and the Cheyenne to scout the buffalo. If they were found in sufficient number at the creek, then there would be nothing to do but break camp and move there also.

"Then it is possible we might leave here when you return and move to the Smoky Mountains near the sandy creek?" Skyraven asked.

"Yes, Skyraven. That is what I am telling you." Though his voice was stern, his eyes were gentle. "I will be away for three days. While I am away, you must fast, search your own heart, and ask the spirits for the answer to your inner conflict. All the while you must remember what I am about to tell you now." Folding his arms across his chest, he looked forbidding.

"You know I always listen to you and do what you ask of me, Grandfather." Skyraven dropped her head, feeling sorrow that she had disappointed him. He most certainly did not approve of her relationship with a

121

white man.

"Your white soldier may ask that you throw off your savage customs and follow the ways of the white man. They have tried to get us to settled down and cultivate the soil. We Arapaho can never do that. We are hunters, not farmers. We are free and will always remain so. A caged bird can never be free. Think on that."

"Caged?" It was an unpleasant thought. "I do not think that John would ask me to do that, Grandfather. He seemed interested in our Arapaho customs."

"Perhaps he would not mean to subdue you. But you are foolish if you think for even one minute he could become like an Indian!"

She flushed as she realized she had been hoping just that.

"Your own father was a high-minded, kind-hearted Englishman. Even so, he spoke words he did not mean. Your mother did not believe it when she found that the easy acquisition of a squaw from our tribe had given your father the right to trap and hunt on our tribe's range."

"John Hanlen is different. He does not want—"

"Your father bought your mother with a horse, some fine English cloth, a few beads, and a white man's rifle. As if she were one of our fine buffalo robes, he bought her. *Bought* her, Skyraven."

"John Hanlen wouldn't . . ."

"He would trade our tanned skins, moccasins, thongs of buffalo leather, braided buffalo hair, and fresh or dried buffalo meat for other things that he wanted. No tribe is as adept at dressing robes as our Arapaho tribe. They bring a fine price in the white man's market. When the fur trade diminished, your father sold his trading post on the Platte River and left for Saint Louis. Your mother died a little each day that he was gone, and when he never returned, she gave up her life. She wasted away for love of him. Think, Skyraven. You are part white, but you are more Indian. You have been raised here with your mother's people, not among your father's. Might your young soldier not feel the same toward his Indian wife were you to marry?"

"No!" She might have further explained her feelings had not Lone Wolf appeared at that moment. The haughty brave approached them, his eyes flashing fire as he looked upon Skyraven. Obviously, Whispering Wind had told him something but Skyraven could only guess what had been said. Lone Wolf said nothing to her but addressed her grandfather as if she were invisible.

"Wise One, come, you are wanted. It is time to bury the buffalo hump to ensure good hunting." Though Skyraven expected him to speak further, Lone Wolf walked away instead, though he did look at her over his shoulder, an assessing stare that made her face flush.

Buffalo's Brother pushed himself up from his reclining position beside the cottonwood tree and followed Lone Wolf's steps. "Think on what I have said," he said over his shoulder as he walked away.

For a long while Skyraven sat silently with downcast eyes. Though her grandfather had not been scolding, neither had he easily been swayed. He had set her thoughts upon a road that needed to be traveled. She did have much to think about. How was she going to exist with the white man at her side? Would she leave her people and follow him into the white man's world or plead, scold, and try to talk him into living as an Indian. Neither way seemed right. But neither could they shut out the world. Give him up? No! Never that. What then? Her thoughts were disturbed as she at last walked toward the circle of tribesmen.

Chapter Thirteen

John Hanlen rode at breakneck speed over the immense tract of land, looking behind him from time to time for any sign of Indians, satisfied that he was not being pursued. His senses were alert, knowing well the dangers which lurked behind each tree, each ridge, each rock. He had vowed that never again would he be taken unawares, as he had been by the Utes. If death were to come, it would come to him on the run, for he would not stop for anything, at least until he had to.

The mare seemed impatient, eager to run. He was amazed at the strength and speed displayed by Running Antelope. Not one of the soldier horses, as cavalry mounts were called, could match the paint for strength and quickness of pace. She was the finest horse he had ever ridden. Her mane and tail streamed in the wind like a flowing banner, her muscles rippled under her sleek brown-and-white hide. It was little wonder that she had been Skyraven's pride. And she had given the animal up to him. What greater show of love could there be?

"Oh, Skyraven," he whispered to himself, "you will miss her dreadfully. But not possibly as much as I miss you." His thoughts were at war as he rode on, anxious to join with the cavalry yet yearning to see Skyraven once again, to hold her, make love to her. She would forever be branded on his heart, his soul.

As Running Antelope's hooves thundered over the ground taking him farther and farther away from the woman he loved, John's thoughts kept returning to Skyraven. He could almost see her beautiful face before him, feel her softness. Skyraven was a rare treasure. Though he had known well that he would miss her, he hadn't reckoned on the gut-wrenching pain that shot through him whenever he whispered her name. No other woman would ever take her place in his heart. Of that he was very certain.

And yet there are going to be problems, he thought. He would have been a fool not to realize that. But then was love ever really simple? "Hell, no," he said aloud. He supposed that in some ways they were a bit like Romeo and Juliet, then thought with alarm that he hoped their story had a happier ending.

He'd never meant to make love to her, not really. She had been a fantasy, a dream. He'd wanted to hold her, for what man seeing her would not want to kiss her, touch her. He would have held back, but she had given herself so openly, so completely, that he had been caught up in her spell without letting reality intrude. Now it did. She was an Indian, or at least half Indian, brought up in Indian ways. He loved her, God knew he did, but he had to go into a union with her with completely open eyes. Loving her would change his life. Indeed it already had.

Listening to the clipclop of horses' hooves against the hard ground, John reflected that he'd hardly planned for Skyraven to enter his life so completely. Of course he'd dreamed of meeting a woman someday — what man had not? Nearly every man wanted a woman to walk beside him, have his children, share his bed, and bring him the warmth of love and affection. It was just that he had envisioned meeting her in the future, when his livelihood was secure and he had something to offer a wife. A soldier's life was uncertain at best, and yet he had made a commitment, one he truly did not want to break.

"Somehow we will make it work. Someway." His cousin Reeve up north had married a southern belle. Surely there could not be any more strain on a marriage than that difference!

John was headed south to the valley of the Arkansas River, leaving the rolling foothills, canyons, and bluffs of the Platte River behind him. He had a good three days' travel ahead of him, which would give him more than enough time to think about what he was going to do. Bring Skyraven with him to the fort? It seemed to be the only answer, and yet somehow it seemed rather sad to take her away from her people.

He tried to put the whole situation out of his mind as he concentrated on the terrain, yet repeatedly his thoughts darted out of control. Skyraven was with him. Indeed he could almost hear her telling him which direction to take. Skyraven had directed him to follow the buffalo trails. With no compass to guide him, that made it much easier. The buffalo trails ran almost directly north and south; some of the trails pounded down into the soil nearly a foot deep. He glanced up toward the sky which was beginning now to shed its morning light, and prayed that it would not rain. A rainstorm could turn this trail into a quagmire.

For a moment he thought he heard the muffled thud of hooves. With reflex action he reached for his gun only to remember he no longer had one. What he wouldn't give for a breech-loading rifle and a chest of needle cartridges! Skyraven had given him the only two weapons she could find, a large knife and bow and arrows. The bow was made of buffalo bone wrapped with leather thongs, a strong bow which had been given to her grandfather. She had explained to John that her grandfather had never used it, for he was a peaceful man. It had merely been cast aside and he would never miss it. He couldn't hold back a smile when he recalled how she had gone about preparing him for this trip.

Skyraven was an adorable thief—or more accurately, a borrower, pilfering the necessary items for his journey little by little. Someday he would see that each item was returned to its rightful owner.

Once again he heard the rumble. Slowing for just a moment, stiffening in the saddle, he listened. Even with a bow as strong as the one he had, he knew that he would be no match for any Indian he might encounter, but at least he had some protection. He surveyed his surroundings as he prepared himself for ambush.

Suddenly a streak of light lit up the sky. Lightning and thunder! Relief swept over him—it would be far better to outride a storm than to face a galloping swarm of redskins.

John nudged Running Antelope to run until her sides heaved, then he slowed the mare down. Wind howled around him, and clouds shrouded the sky, but he had outdistanced the rain. He smiled with satisfaction as he looked back from where he had come and watched the lightning streak through the ominously dark clouds.

The part of the country he was now entering, northwest of Denver City, was unlike that settled part of the territory he had once visited. It was wild, without any sign of human habitation, Indian or white. The sparse grama grass had been trampled down by buffalo hooves. As he galloped over the rolling terrain, he sighted a large herd of wild mustangs kicking up the dust. The bellowing of a herd of buffalo could be heard, carried on the wind in the distance. He was cutting through the heart of buffalo country, just as Skyraven said he would.

Looking over a ridge to the south of Prairie Creek, he saw them. Their dark massive shapes blackened the horizon, creating an appearance of a huge black rain cloud in the distance. There were hundreds of them. He had seen wild grouse, sage hens, hare, and even wolves along the way, but this was the most splendid sight of all. For just a moment John was awestruck, suddenly understanding just why the Indians held these animals in reverence. They symbolized strength, life. He remembered Skyraven telling him that the Indians used every part of this magnificent animal for their needs and thus held the buffalo sacred.

"And we hunt them just for sport," he muttered, almost disgustedly. The white man always assumed he was in the right, and John had thought so, too, until Skyraven had opened his eyes. There were good and bad in both peoples, he supposed — renegade Indians, but peaceful ones also, and outlaw whites, but those who were honorable.

The day seemed to fly by as he galloped onward, pushing at a furious pace. When he could stand no more, when his body was exhausted beyond endurance, he pulled at the reins to urge the horse to a halt. Somewhere near Bajou Basin he came to a small area sheltered by a few overhanging rocks, reined in his horse, and hobbled her with a leather thong. Though his bow and arrow skills were lacking, he managed to bag a fat sage hen for his supper, then set about digging a pit where he could cook his supper.

Skyraven had given him some dried buffalo meat, some tallow, and some berries. The look on her face, when she had apologized for not being able to contribute more, had been such a sad one. As if she hadn't given him enough, he thought, she who had saved his life. She had said over and over again that she knew it would not be enough to satisfy his appetite. She had done the best she could and how he loved her for her efforts to help him. Now it was up to him to see to his survival. In this harsh country, what he needed most was endurance. He was on his own and far away from any help. Just one mistake could mean disaster. He would take no unnecessary chances.

Cautiously he set about making camp for the night. He had learned much from Skyraven and her Indian ways. She had told him that a pit would not give off as much smoke as an open fire, especially if it were lined with rocks. The hot rocks would cook the food but would not smoke. She had also instructed him to kick dirt over any fire when he was finished with it. The ashes should be covered over so that his trail could not be easily followed. As he moved about he did everything that Skyraven had told him to do, feeling a strange sense of her presence beside him. As he ate, he remembered her laughter, her smiles, the way her eyes widened as she told him about her people. Could he take her away from her grandfather? Would she even want to leave once she thought about it?

"If only life could be simpler," he muttered. Once again, the problems they would face assailed him. Even so, the idea of giving her up was unthinkable. But how would she fare in the white man's world wearing calico and ribbons instead of buckskin? Wearing her hair in carefully coiled curls instead of hanging freely down her back? Somehow he couldn't imagine Skyraven wearing corsets. No doubt she would wrinkle her precious nose in distaste if she viewed the white woman's instrument of torture, he thought with a smile.

John was bone-tired, in need of rest. Perhaps dreaming about his love would bring him solace. With that thought in mind, he returned to Running Antelope's side to get the buffalo robe Skyraven had given him. He scanned the horizon one last time before making camp for the night.

"What the hell?" he said aloud. What was causing that dust cloud up on the wide ridge just behind him? Dear God, he was not prepared for another Indian confrontation again, so soon. The memory of his recent ordeal with those painted savages and the mutilated bodies of his fallen comrades was still too fresh in his mind. Was he going to run, fight, or hide? Pulling himself up on Running Antelope's back, he made the decision to flee. He was far enough away to outride them.

John Hanlen took one more look. As the dots on the horizon came closer, he made a startling discovery — not Indians riding on the ridge, but soldiers!

"Praise the Lord!" he shouted, feeling instant comaraderie for those of his own. The dust cloud was caused by a cavalry column winding along the bluff in standard four-abreast formation. He could see the two officers in front and the standard bearer carrying the American flag, which flapped wildly in the breeze. He had never been so glad to see so many blue coats in his entire life.

Sliding from the horse's back, he ran out in the open and climbed a large rock where he could be seen more easily. John took off his blue coat and waved it in the air while he shouted, "I'm Major Hanlen. I'm Major Hanlen. Here! Here!"

One of the flank guards and an officer rode at a fast trot to meet him. As they approached, John quickly put on his jacket again. It would be needed for identification, for it was the only article of clothing he had left to substantiate his claim that he was indeed a major in the United States Cavalry. Standing there in moccasined feet John awaited his comrades, anxious to tell them all that had happened to him.

Chapter Fourteen

Young First Lieutenant Samuel Dunham, and the Second Colorado Company's trumpeter, Franklin Grier, eyed the man standing before them for a minute or two before speaking. Although he claimed to be a major in the First Colorado Cavalry Unit from Fort Lyon, he certainly didn't look like any major they had ever seen.

"Major John Hanlen!" he said again, his voice booming with an authority that seemed to say he was an officer of some sort.

"*Major* John Hanlen?" Just to be doubly certain they did not get into any trouble if he was a major, both men saluted.

"I ran into some trouble."

"I can see that," Samuel Dunham exclaimed.

John Hanlen was quite a sight to behold. He looked as if he had been in some kind of trouble all right. His blond hair was long, his mustache could have used a trim, his clothes were torn and dirty, and upon his feet were a pair of beaded, knee-high moccasins. Not boots but leather leggings like the Indians always wore. Moccasins! He was wearing no hat so they could not identify him as being in a cavalry unit, though he adamantly claimed he was. The black patch embroidered with gold crossed swords, worn by all cavalry members to indicate their branch of the service, was noticeably absent. The dark-blue double-breasted jacket with several buttons missing *was* an officer's jacket. One epaulet was hanging by a few threads, but the other indicated his rank insignia was that of major.

"First Lieutenant Samuel Dunham. Colorado Second Cavalry Unit, sir," the young, stocky, dark-haired officer said. He saluted again as he spoke. "You say that you are Major John Hanlen of the Colorado First Cavalry?"

"Yes." John Hanlen didn't know whether to be amused or angered by the two young men's reaction to him. He supposed he did look a sight. "I *am* Major John Hanlen."

Both men's heads snapped around as they searched the ridges, rocks, and crevices with their eyes. "Where are the others of your company?" the man holding the trumpet asked.

John swallowed the lump that was rising in his throat as he thought of his dead, mutilated comrades. "They are all dead, Lieutenant," he said solemnly. "I am the only survivor of a Ute ambush near the Republican River."

With that statement, the first lieutenant and the trumpeter removed their hats and signaled the others to do likewise in reverence for the dead. The silence stretched out to a long, agonizing moment. Memories crowded into John Hanlen's head, thoughts he had successfully buried but which now came back to haunt him.

"Poor souls," Lieutenant Sam Dunham said at last. He looked at John Hanlen quizzically. "How did you come to be so far from the Republican? Bijou Basin is at least forty miles west of that river." The look on his face seemed to ask just how come the major was still alive.

John answered quickly. "I was rescued from torture and death by an Arapaho Indian woman."

"Rescued from a band of marauding Utes by a woman?" Lieutenant Dunham and Trumpeter Grier glanced at each other in disbelief.

Their exchange did not go unnoticed by John. "It's a

long story that requires some explanation. If you two officers will but grant me permission to mount my horse and accompany you, I can fill you in on all the details as we ride. I assure you that what I said is true!"

The trumpeter was contrite. "Of course," Dunham answered. "Imagine you'd like some company, under the circumstances."

"Indeed I would." John made quite a show of mounting Running Antelope in proper army fashion, despite the lack of an army saddle. Once he was mounted, he frowned at the lieutenant. "She wasn't just *any* woman, Lieutenant."

The lieutenant looked sheepishly at the major and saluted again. "Forgive me for doubting your story, Major. It's just that dressed as you are, you don't look like a major in the United States Cavalry."

John glanced down at his attire. "You're absolutely right, Lieutenant." Had the circumstances been different, he might have found humor in the situation. He must have looked quite strange. "Absolutely right. But I'm lucky to be alive."

"Yes, sir!"

"Quite, sir."

Once again they exchanged a quick glance. It was obvious that they were very, very curious.

"I have quite a story to tell if you care to listen. It's a lesson to us all that such a thing can happen if we are taken unawares."

"Unawares?" The young trumpeter's face registered a slight twinge of fear as he looked hastily over his shoulder. It was obvious that the thought of what had happened made him more than just a bit edgy.

"Mount up, Major." The lieutenant saluted again. "Listen we will." A smile flickered across his face. "Truth is, we don't really have much choice. After all, you outrank any of the rest of us in this company."

John looked around him. "That's right, I do." He returned the lieutenant's smile, finally feeling completely

133

at ease among his comrades. "Then I guess you're going to hear the story. Who knows, you just might find it interesting."

"I wouldn't doubt that a bit!" The lieutenant motioned for the major to take the lead in the formation. "We may bend the rules occasionally, but we never break the rule of a senior officer's right to command." With a gesture, he indicated that the trumpeter should drop back into the next row. He and the major would take the lead.

John patted Running Antelope's nose to reassure the animal, then gave the command of "Forward ho!"

The sun was a faint glow in a deep purple haze. John was tired, but he somehow managed to sit tall and straight in his saddle. He would lead these men to a place of safety a little farther off, and there they would make camp. The spot that he had chosen was too small to accommodate so many soldiers. Besides, now that he had reinforcements, his plan had changed. Alone he had felt like a sparrow, but with these soldiers he was an eagle.

"We'll ride until we find a stream or pond for fresh water, then we'll make camp," he told the lieutenant. "Have you seen any Indians?"

"Indians! Yes, sir." As they rode, he and the young lieutenant exchanged stories about their recent encounters with the Indians, the lieutenant speaking first. It seemed that while John and Skyraven were together in the cave there had been a confrontation between some Cheyenne braves and a troop of white soldiers. "The troops were ordered out to scour the area when a report was sent to them by messenger that some cattle had been stolen. They were to pursue the Indians, disarm them, and recover the stock before resuming their search."

"Cheyenne?"

"Yeah," Lieutenant Sam Dunham explained. The group of forty men had divided into two groups of twenty men each. One of the group's lieutenants,

134

Dunham himself, had picked up a trail and followed the ten Cheyenne braves seen driving horses. They finally caught up to them near the American Ranch on the South Platte River about forty miles northeast of Denver City. Lieutenant Dunham sent a man ahead of the rest with a signal that they wished to parley. After some talk among themselves, one brave rode out to meet him. Both men dismounted and walked forward to shake hands, but when the young cavalry sergeant saw the Indian up close in full battle regalia, he panicked and tried to disarm the brave.

"Good God, man. No!" Hanlen exclaimed. To even try to separate an Indian from his weapon was considered an act of war.

"Unfortunately, yes. None of the soldiers had had very much experience in the field. Not only did they not know which tribe the Indians came from, but they did not know that when the young sergeant reached out to wrestle the rifle from the brave, that move was an automatic breach of friendship and a signal to fight."

"What happened then?" John Hanlen was extremely interested, after having experienced his own tragedy.

"Both sides began firing. The battle lasted for almost an hour. The Indians then retreated to the bluffs. Whew!" He shook his head. "Those Indian ponies very easily outdistanced our tired cavalry horses."

"I can well imagine." John Hanlen reached down to stroke Running Antelope's head. "I have seen both riders and horses in action. I know my men, and I sure as hell wasn't any match for them. That's how we got ourselves into a mess." He related the gruesome story of his men's fight with the Indians, their deaths, his own capture. "When I awoke, they had me tied up, and it was then I realized why they had kept me alive."

"Dear God!"

John Hanlen could see he understood. "They had some very brutal entertainment planned. To tell you the truth I don't know if I would have gone insane first or

135

died. Neither choice seemed agreeable to me at that moment."

"No, I don't imagine so. But how did you get free? You spoke about a woman?"

"A very beautiful one. Damned if she didn't risk her own life to come to my aid." He told his story, smiling as he remembered. "I've never met a woman like her and I don't think I ever will again. But taking me to that cave wasn't the end of it. She nursed me back to health. Fed me. Cared for me." He pointed at his moccasins. "Even brought me these shoes to replace the boots that fool Indian stole." His eyes had a faraway look as he remembered more intimate details of his relationship with Skyraven — things he could not, nor would not, reveal. "She gave me her horse and enough food for the journey, told me which direction to go, and sent me on my way."

The young lieutenant smiled. "If she was as beautiful as you say, at least you had some compensation for your pain. With my luck, she would have been as old as a hag."

"Skyraven wasn't old. She was very young and very beautiful."

"So tell me, are you a career man, your being an officer and all?"

"No. I got involved in the Army like most others, because of the war." John cocked his brows in question. "How about you?"

"I have always wanted to fight Indians since I was a child. Several days ago I had my first encounter with the real thing." The twenty-one-year-old lieutenant looked toward John with admiration. "Of course, my experience wasn't anything like yours. I can't imagine being captured, tortured, and left to die."

"I can tell you one thing, Lieutenant Dunham. I would go through it all again just to meet Skyraven." He smiled wryly. "Well, maybe not everything. I could do without those screaming Ute savages." He shuddered at the thought. For just a moment he could feel those ropes cutting into his flesh again.

"I'm sure you could, Major. A few days ago I also heard them give that bloodcurdling yell of theirs. It's enough to set your teeth on edge. Tell me, what makes an Arapaho so different from a Ute? An Indian is an Indian. I've heard tell that they are all alike regardless of what you call them."

"No, they're not. I used to think that way, too, until I learned differently from Skyraven. Many tribes are enemies. According to her, the Utes are one of the most vicious. The Arapaho are not a warring tribe but traders. Her grandfather is the medicine man, a peaceful man."

"A medicine man? That's the same thing as a witch doctor, isn't it?" He grimaced, making a frightening face.

"Far from it, Lieutenant." John held his anger in check. The young man just didn't understand, but how could he? People only understood their own ways. Perhaps that was one reason why there were wars. "We whites don't comprehend the Indian customs the way we should. A medicine man is *not* just a man who uses rattles and herbs. He is called *wicasa waken* — holy man."

"Like a preacher?" The lieutenant seemed amazed.

"I suppose you could say that." John Hanlen remembered Skyraven's pride as she talked about her grandfather. "The medicine man conducts the peace-pipe ceremony. He doesn't even carry weapons." He gestured to the bow he carried. "Skyraven gave me this, and these arrows that I am carrying. They belonged to her grandfather, but he had no use for them, she said, so she gave them to me."

"Hmm. So your Indian maiden was generous as well as pretty, and her grandfather is the preacher of the tribe. You say her tribe is peaceful and her grandfather a seemingly nice old Indian. They might not fight, but how about the rest of them?"

"I don't know, but I can tell you one thing. I feel a lot

137

different about the Indians now, even after what happened to me."

"Are you sure you were not easily convinced because of a pretty face?" the lieutenant said with a grin.

Scowling, John Hanlen answered, "She had nothing to gain by lying to me. Her pretty face matches her gentleness and her truthfulness. Her grandfather has as much influence within the tribe as the chief himself. I asked her to explain the peace-pipe ceremony to me. It was not her idea but mine." He shook his head, knowing at once that he sounded like a preacher now himself. "I just think we should work harder at making our peace with the Indians."

"Peace?" The lieutenant slapped his thigh. "Better tell that to the Indians. They're the ones always making trouble. Me, I'm a peace-loving man who wishes he'd never come here. All I want is to get my tail back home to Indiana where I belong."

It was dark when they paused to scout out a camp at the place where the South Platte River and the Arkansas River meet. By that time, John and the lieutenant had become friends, despite their differing view on the matter. John had tried to convince the young lieutenant that a peace parley with the Arapaho and Cheyenne could be worked out with the help of Skyraven's grandfather. Hanlen could tell the younger man was skeptical, but another few hundred miles and he would have him firmly convinced, he thought.

When they came to a clearing near the crook where the two rivers joined, Hanlen gave the command to halt and prepare camp. Soon all of the soldiers were busy setting up the large conical Sibley tent in which the fifteen noncomissioned officers and the privates would sleep.

After the horses had been fed and watered and the big evening meal eaten, one man was assigned to guard duty and to watch the horses. The major, the lieutenant, and the trumpeter set up their own two-man pup tents

138

and bedded down for the night. John and Sam would share one of the pup tents, Frank would sleep alone in the other.

"I'm afraid I won't be as good company as your Skyraven," Lieutenant Dunham whispered as he blew out the light in the lantern. "But I promise not to snore."

"As a companion you'll do just fine then," John responded, wincing as he stretched his arms and legs. The long horseback ride had made him a pincushion of pain. Lying down, he did what he could to make himself comfortable, trying not to think about Skyraven for fear of dreaming about her and talking in his sleep. A man had to have some secrets.

"Major?"

"Yeah?" He curled himself into a ball, exhaustedly hoping the lieutenant wasn't feeling talkative.

"I'm not being nosy about what happened between you and that Indian girl, but I do want to give you a word of caution, if I might."

"Speak your mind," he said.

"Well, I know you went through a hell of an experience and that you are grateful to that girl for saving your life and all. And after talking to you I can see that you are right in that the Indians are entitled to their point of view. But . . . but there are those to whom you can't talk as freely as you have to me." For a moment there was silence. "Be careful, that's all."

"I'll heed your warning."

"And . . . and, Major?"

"Yes," John Hanlen closed his eyes and sighed.

"If it means anything, I'm on your side."

"Thanks." As he turned over on his side, he felt the warmth of friendship. Somehow knowing that at least one man felt amiable toward the situation made him feel more relaxed. It was a start, John Hanlen thought.

Chapter Fifteen

Skyraven awakened to the new day filled with gratitude to her grandfather. Though he had been troubled over her news about John Hanlen, he had listened, given her stern advice, but had not scolded. In the end he had left it up to her to make her own decision. Little did he know she already had. The moment John Hanlen's hands had touched her she had known that he was her destiny. Her future was with him.

Lying in her bed, Skyraven tried to judge the time. The tepee was not as brightly lit with sunshine as usual, but this she knew could be because the sky was covered with clouds. Rising to her feet, she peered out of the opening, knowing that most of the others would sleep well past noon before they rose to begin their chores. It would take a few days to get back into the routine of rising early in the morning and sleeping at night. The sun-dance festival always disturbed the body's natural rhythms, though her grandfather said such a thing was necessary. For Skyraven it had been a blessing, giving her time to be with her yellow-haired soldier. Another stroke of good fortune had been the journey some of the leaders of the tribe were taking to the Cheyenne camp. It would give her time to be by herself without anyone's prodding. She didn't want Lone Wolf or any of the others to try to pressure her into giving the white man up. It was, as her grandfather said, her choice to make.

By now he and the Arapaho chiefs would be well on their way to the meeting with the Cheyenne chiefs.

As she dressed, she pondered the situation, then, stepping out into the cool midday air, she looked up at the sky. Just as she had supposed, a thick mist of clouds covered the sun. It was just as well, for it would give her traveling tribesmen shelter from the sun's hot rays, she thought. It was a perfect day for a walk, she decided as she dressed, knowing the exercise would help her think more clearly.

Skyraven entered the woods near the camp, taking in the sights of the untamed forest with its freshly budding beauty. The trees swayed in the breeze, their bright green leaves quivering. Hundreds of birds serenaded her with their wild, beautiful music as they flew from bough to bough. Was the world really a more beautiful place today or did this feeling of love in her heart for John Hanlen only make it seem that way? As if seeking the answer, her eyes were drawn toward the ridge where the cave was nestled among the trees. It would always be the source of a poignant memory, the place where she had experienced her greatest delight.

Skyraven ran toward the ridge, pausing as she felt total happiness consume her. She abandoned her dignified manner, and let herself go, jumping and twirling about joyfully, freely expressing her feelings. She wanted to dance, to sing, to give vent to her wonderful discovery of love.

"So, you are happy now," hissed a voice.

"Whispering Wind!" The other Indian girl's presence was the greatest invasion of privacy imaginable. "Did you follow me?"

"I did."

"Then you will be disappointed. My white soldier has gone." Filled with anger and frustration Skyraven reached down, picked up a stone, and hurled it at Whispering Wind. "And so will you be, for I will chase you off. Go on! Flee!"

141

Dark, flashing eyes poured forth fury as Whispering Wind ducked just in time. "You will pay for this! Your grandfather will not be here to shield you. Lone Wolf will—"

"Lone Wolf is gone." Just as she had when they were children, Skyraven made a face at her rival. "He went with the others."

"That is where you are wrong. After I talked with him, he changed his mind. Left Hand went instead."

"What? But last night . . . I thought . . ." The sky was not the only place where there were clouds. Skyraven's mood changed from happy to wary. Lone Wolf would be in charge of the village until they returned. Just the thought dampened her earlier enthusiasm. Such was Lone Wolf's rank in the social order. It was customary for the chief to leave his son to guard the village in his absence.

"He wants to speak with you. That is why I followed you just now. To tell you so." With a chuckle of laughter, Whispering Wind turned and left.

Somehow, just the thought of having to face Lone Wolf without her grandfather there to offer protection caused Skyraven's hands to tremble. The fierce Indian brave had a terrible temper, for which he had been reprimanded on more than one occasion. His reaction to the story about saving John Hanlen's life would be quite different from that of her grandfather. He would be angry. She just knew it. Though she wanted to run in the opposite direction, Skyraven hurried back to camp. If there was to be a confrontation, she had best get it over with and then be about her business.

Arapaho children were expected to become tough. They lived close to nature, traveled under the harsh sun in summer, and worked and played out of doors even in freezing weather. While they were very young, boys and girls played together, but as they grew older, most childhood play began to mimic adult life. Skyraven and the other girls had played with deerskin dolls and cradle boards. Lone Wolf and his boyhood friends pretended to go on raids, taking make-believe captives and counting coups like grown men. She had never noticed his temper until after puberty. By then his outbursts had become more and more frequent when he did not have his own way, or if he was thwarted.

When Lone Wolf reached the age of fourteen summers, he went on his first real hunt and killed a buffalo calf. His family praised him highly. His father, Chief Left Hand, had announced the news throughout the village, calling everyone to a feast in Lone Wolf's honor. Lone Wolf thought that he had become a man even though he still had much to learn. But strength was not the only proof of reaching manhood, Skyraven thought. There was such a thing as fairness and wisdom. Even the bravest warrior could not win all the time. Lone Wolf had not learned that lesson.

From the time of his manhood feast on, whenever he entered into games with comrades his own age, contests meant to develop endurance and toughness, Lone Wolf would often become angry when he did not win. Sometimes he would fly into a rage and cause the others to flee. Then later, when his temper cooled, they would all talk and laugh about it. Because he was the chief's beloved older son no one wanted to remain at odds with him for very long. Was it any wonder he thought he owned the world?

His temper had been one of the reasons Skyraven had not wanted to marry him. She feared his fits of rages, but she couldn't tell him that without causing much difficulty for herself. Marriage among the Arapaho was more of an alliance between families than a love match. She knew that her grandfather's prominence in the tribe would make her a likely candidate for Lone Wolf's mate. As son of the chief, and grandson-in-law to the medicine man, his power would be twice as great, and any children they might have would be twice blessed.

"Marry Lone Wolf?" She said aloud. Now that she had met John Hanlen and given her heart to him, she could never marry the fiery-tempered brave. She simply did not love him. That might not have mattered once, but after having experienced such vibrant emotions she realized she could never settle for a union devoid of love.

Pausing at the edge of the camp, she sat upon a rock and looked around her. There were many places to hide had that been her intent, but she was no coward. *I might as well get on with it,* she thought. *I can't stay hidden away in the forest forever. Perhaps if I go down by the river for a little while, I can think of what to say to Lone Wolf when I see him.* Holding on to branches and scrub trees to keep from falling, she crept as close to the water as she could.

Taking a seat on an old log, she watched as the leaves she threw into the water drifted down the stream like miniature canoes. When she was a child, whenever she was troubled, sitting by the river always filled her with a sense of peace. The soft roar of the water was soothing. Forgotten for the moment was the fear of Lone Wolf's temper. Somehow she would placate him. She would make him see that she was not the woman to take a permanent place by his side.

"Have you nothing better to do than sit idly watching floating leaves?" Lone Wolf's voice boomed through the silence.

Getting up from her crouched position by the riverbank, she turned to meet his gaze. Dressed only in leggings, a breechcloth, and moccasins, his arms folded across his bare chest, he looked to be an ominous foe. His eyes narrowed as he looked her over from head to foot. Neither of them spoke for a few minutes; they just continued to look at each other.

"It is my right to sit by the river if I so choose," Skyraven said at last. "It always brings to me a sense of peace."

He muttered beneath his breath, "You always were a

strange one, even when we were children." He leaned forward. "Or are you here for another reason?"

"I am here to watch the water, nothing more." So, she thought, he knew about her soldier. She could see it in his eyes.

"And not to meet a lover?" With the swiftness of a pouncing mountain lion, he fell upon her, his grip on her arm so tight she couldn't pull away. She could feel each finger squeezing painfully. So the moment had come.

She lowered her eyes in sudden embarrassment. "I wanted to be alone with my thoughts. My grandfather . . ."

With a derisive snort he interrupted her. "Didn't Buffalo's Brother tell you that we would be leaving here soon? There is no time to be alone."

"Leaving?" The very idea of going away was unsettling. If they broke camp, John Hanlen would not know where to find her when he returned. "No! It cannot be. We have just completed the ceremony. It would make no sense."

"There are not enough buffalo nearby to provide for our needs." He smiled at her in a gleaming show of pearl-white teeth.

Skyraven wondered if this was not just another one of his games. If they were going to break camp, why hadn't her grandfather told her so last night? "It is your decision to leave camp, no doubt?" Was he trying to exhibit his power to her?

"I gave council. As you know, without sufficient buffalo we cannot even think to stay here." He released her arm, but stood close to her. "But I do not need to discuss such things with a mere woman. You should be packing his rattles, skull altar, headdresses, ornaments, and other items he will not be using again right away. I'm sure you have much work to do. You should be packing his things and your own in parfleches and saddlebags instead of watching leaves drift downstream."

145

Skyraven tossed her head, sending her slender, dark hand whipping around her shoulders. "You are probably right, Lone Wolf. I do have much to do." She started to push past him, but he grabbed her wrists and turned her around to face him again.

"Not so fast, Skyraven. I have heard some disturbing news. Whispering Wind told me that early yesterday morning near dawn, she saw you kissing a white man who was seated upon the back of a brown-and-white painted horse." His dark brows jutted upward, forming a V. "She could not see him clearly, but he appeared to be a bluecoat."

Anger loosened her tongue and made her forget any fear of the well-muscled man. "Why was Whispering Wind up before dawn roaming around in the hills all by herself? And why did she come running to you with such a tale?"

His scowl relaxed. "Then it is not true." He seemed relieved.

"Whispering Wind is a spitting, sour-tempered she-cat!"

"Let us leave Whispering Wind out of this." He let go of her wrists but stood towering over her, his hands on his hips. "I am not concerned with her actions. I am concerned only with yours. I have never considered marrying Whispering Wind, only you." He reached out and grabbed her hand, but this time when he squeezed it tightly, he did so with affection and not with anger. "I do not have to tell you how I feel."

"No, you do not." For a moment she nearly felt sorry for him. Even though he was arrogant and overly proud, she didn't want to hurt him. "You are a strong warrior and I am very proud to be so honored." Skyraven's voice became almost a whisper. "But I have given my heart to another."

Despite the gentleness of her tone, he reacted just as she had anticipated. With anger. "To a *white* soldier."

"A white warrior, yes. Please understand, Lone

Wolf."

His voice rose to a shout. "How could you do such a thing? Everyone expects us to marry." Grabbing her shoulders, he shook her as if that would change her mind. "They always have since we were children."

Skyraven pulled away from his grasp. "Not everybody. Whispering Wind has long been my adversary in such matters. She wants you for herself."

Usually he would have preened at such a reminder, but now he was strangely subdued. "Then what she has told me is not true. You were just teasing me to scorn me for doubting you." He had misunderstood her statement, thinking that it was he who had captured her heart after all.

"No. My heart does belong to someone else."

"Then I will fight for you." Lone Wolf seemed to want to believe that it was another of the tribe who had caught her eye, for he knew that any one of those young men would have given her up were he to insist. "If that is what you want, to be quarreled over, then I will comply." Tangling his fingers in her long dark hair, he held her head immobile and gazed down at her. "Hurry and saddle Running Antelope while I saddle War Pony. We have been at this game long enough."

"Lone Wolf . . ."

"We can ride the short distance down to the grasslands. I will show you the horses that the Cheyenne helped me capture for your grandfather. These horses will make you change your mind and will seal our marriage."

"Horses?"

His smile was cocky. "Several Cheyenne braves along with Running Hare, Red Dog, and I took them from a white rancher. Some white soldiers followed us. We had a battle and several of the soldiers were killed, but they could not catch us. You would have been so proud . . ."

"Proud that you stole from the white man?"

His anger resurfaced. "It is not for you to judge,

woman, only to be thankful that I consider you worthy of so much trouble." Taking her by the hand, he pulled her along. "Now stop your foolish chatter. The day is already half gone."

He was so strong that she could not help but be pulled along after him. "Stop, Lone Wolf. Please stop."

He did and, in confusion, searched for her painted pony.

"I no longer have Running Antelope," Skyraven answered his unasked question.

Lone Wolf looked puzzled. "You no longer have Running Antelope? What happened to her?" Suddenly the realization struck Lone Wolf. "Whispering Wind said that the white soldier was seated on a brown-and-white horse when he leaned down to kiss you good-bye. You gave Running Antelope to a white man, didn't you?" Her silence only angered him further. "Answer me. Didn't you?"

"Yes!" Horses were the measure of wealth in the Indian society. A family was as rich as the number of horses in their possession. Skyraven might as well have given John a bucket full of gold nuggets as to have given him a horse, for she knew that warriors often valued their horses more than their wives. Even so, Skyraven thought with conviction, the animal had been hers to give if she so wanted.

"You gave such a fine animal to the men who kill and plunder our people. You are worse than a fool, woman!"

She tried to explain. "He was in trouble. I showed him kindness. I gave him food and . . . and my horse when he needed to get back to his soldiers."

"And what else did you give him? More than a kiss?" A Plains Indian man was the head and boss of his household. The Arapaho was a male-dominated society, but like the Cheyenne, the fidelity of their women was notable. In Lone Wolf's mind, he and Skyraven were already betrothed, and thus he considered it his

148

right to be furious. "Answer me!" His eyes closed to narrow slits of rage.

"I gave him my heart." Her voice quieted to a breathy whisper. "And my love." Now he knew the truth. She could no longer evade his questions. "I cannot accept your marriage proposal nor can my grandfather accept the horses. You are an honorable warrior and I admire you greatly. We have known each other since childhood, our families are close friends, but I have already given my promise to marry a white cavalry soldier."

Lone Wolf said nothing. Clenching his hands into fists, he seemed to be calling upon every measure of his self-control not to strike her. He simply looked right through her as if she were not there, then spit at her feet. Turning on his heel, he left her standing there alone.

Chapter Sixteen

It had taken the company of Major Hanlen and Lieutenant Dunham two more days of travel, due east along the Arkansas River, to reach Fort Lyon, a desolate, sun-baked outpost, far away from any civilization. Its location on the banks of the Arkansas near Smoky Mountain and Sand Creek made it a central contact between Indians, traders, and the military. Usually, military personnel stationed at the few military outposts found such places dreary and monotonous but not so the small company that was now approaching Fort Lyon.

"It's a welcome sight, isn't it, Sam?" John said to his traveling companion. During the days of travel, the men had gone from the formality of calling each other by their military ranks to "John" and "Sam," though usually Sam Dunham addressed John as "Major" when the other soldiers were around.

"Sure is, Major. After what we've been through, we will probably even welcome the five A.M. bugle call."

John shook his head. "I don't think I would go that far." Turning in the saddle, he raised his hand and brought the band of war-weary cavalrymen to a halt just in front of the arched passageway over the two gates of the main entrance, which today were open wide, not closed or barred.

"They must be expecting us," Lieutenant Dunham joked as they entered through the quadrangular fifteen feet of wooden wall and passed by the stone buildings. They galloped past the storehouses, corrals, stables, the sutler's store, and the enlisted men's barracks toward the parade grounds. As they came closer, they could see a five-piece marching band, outfitted in dress uniform, playing a lively tune of welcome.

Bringing Running Antelope to a slow trot as they came nearer, John turned to the lieutenant. "We seem to be getting a hero's welcome, Sam," he said.

Sam smiled and replied, "After what we've been through, every one of us, we've earned it." He whispered behind his hand. "Don't let the other men know, Major, but I arranged that little greeting. Let's just say one of those soldiers owes me a little favor."

"I see!" John hid his smile as he dismissed the other cavalrymen. He and Sam took their horses to the stables, dismounted, and gave the animals into the hands of the low-ranked soldiers whose duty it was to feed, water, and unsaddle the mounts. The soldiers would be in for a big surprise, he thought, when Running Antelope had her turn. It would undoubtedly liven up the conversation in the barracks when word got around that an Indian pony was on the premises.

"As hard as the beds are around here, it will sure beat sleeping on the ground," Sam Dunham said, trying to match John's long-legged stride. His legs were much shorter, his frame heavier, causing him to affect a sort of waddle. As the two men walked to the officers' quarters, a sergeant approached them. "Colonel Chivington wants to see you right away, Major," he said.

"Colonel Chivington," he repeated, looking at Sam Dunham as if to ask what the man was like. By the reaction the first lieutenant gave him, it appeared

151

that the colonel was far from being a likable sort of fellow. "An ogre?" John asked.

Sam shrugged. "More of a religious fanatic. Thinks he was called by God to clear the West of all the Indians. Think he has it in mind to be a hero."

"I see."

"I suppose we have to give him a chance. He's new here. He was a Methodist preacher a while back. Treats us a bit like his congregation. You know the type . . ."

Sam Dunham's look held warning. Still, John was determined to tell the whole story. He wouldn't allow anyone to force him to tell a lie just because of their prejudices. If a man could stand up against the slavery issue, then certainly he could speak his mind on the Indian situation. Wasn't it, after all, supposed to be a free country?

"You coming, too?" he asked Sam.

"Yeah, why not! It can't take too long," Sam answered. "I'll walk over to the administration office with you and wait outside. When you are through, we can go have that drink at the sutler's store I promised you."

John Hanlen mounted the steps and crossed the boardwalk. A guard with a rifle stretched over his chest stood in front of the door. "State your name and business," his voice boomed out.

"Major John Hanlen, First Colorado Cavalry Unit here to see Colonel Chivington. By request."

"Hanlen? Major Hanlen?" The guard eyed him up and down as if there had already been some kind of talk about what had happened to him. He made it a point not to look at the major's moccasins. "Enter." The guard flung the heavy door open. "The colonel is expecting you."

John approached the big black desk behind which a huge man with a barrel chest looked up to meet his eyes. His red hair, beard, and mustache glistened in

152

the sunlight which streamed through the open widow behind him.

John saluted. "Major John Hanlen reporting, sir."

"Yes, Major." He eyed him with distaste as if the major's tattered uniform appalled him. "I understand that you have quite an interesting story to tell."

"Yes, sir."

"Sit down and begin, if you please." His voice was so cold that it caused chills to bounce up and down John Hanlen's back. A premonition of trouble?

"I took a small band of men on a scouting mission. We were supposed to work ourselves into the Indian's confidence and report all that we heard. Seems the Confederates are trying to make use of the Indians to aid them in their cause. That's why I came here from Missouri. Well, sir, to make a long story short, we were taken by surprise." John related the story in entirety.

"You'll never win any medals with that kind of performance, Major." The colonel looked at him with eyes that were nearly black, a sharp contrast to his pale complexion and red hair. A former preacher, John thought. Surely the man looked more like the devil.

"We were ambushed, sir. Outnumbered. We didn't stand a chance."

"You should have been more careful!" Chivington barked.

"Well, sir, I have found that there are no manuals to be studied that can teach our soldiers how to fight Indians. Practical experience is the only teacher, and so many of the men are . . ."

"Are you telling me that our manuals are worthless?"

"No, sir. It's just that, well, for this kind of fighting, the Indians are strong, cunning, agile, have great power of endurance, and know the terrain very well. But I have found that some of the Indians want peace, and so if we were to work on that . . ."

"*You* were in command." It was obvious the colonel didn't want to listen to any words on making peace. "Losing so many men could call for a court-martial."

"If that's to be my punishment for surviving, then so be it," John Hanlen shot back, then tempered his tone as he remembered he was talking to his superior. "I wouldn't be standing here before you now, Colonel, if it hadn't been for a brave Arapaho woman by the name of Skyraven. I was tied up by the Utes, but she risked her own well-being to rescue me."

"Rescue you?" Picking up a pencil, he tapped it like a drumstick against his desk. "An Arapaho squaw showed such bravery for a white man. That is hard to believe."

"I don't know why. Our American women are showing their bravery every day by aiding in this war — some of them even marching off as soldiers, *sir.*"

Colonel Chivington shifted in his chair. "That doesn't have a damn thing to do with this situation." Again the pencil tapped furiously. "Arapaho, huh? Stepped right in and saved you from one of their own kind."

"The Ute and Arapaho are enemies, sir. The Ute are warring, the Arapaho want peace." He told the story of how Skyraven had smuggled him out of the Ute camp and taken him to the cave. He talked of how she brought him food and nursed him back to health. Chivington looked dubious. "It is true, sir. She is the medicine man's granddaughter. Some of her methods of healing are superior to our own."

"Superior!" Colonel Chivington stood up, showing his full height of six feet four, towering by at least four inches over John. By now he had fully realized that John Hanlen was a determined advocate of peace with the Indians. "You sound as if you're soft on the savages, Major. Superior, indeed. The Indians

154

are stinking heathens. Murdering, marauding swine! Do I make myself clear?"

"Not all of them, sir. Believe me, if you were to—"

"Silence." A vein in the colonel's neck pulsated, and for a moment John Hanlen feared it might burst. "That you would stand here before me defending savages is hard for me to swallow. Woman or not, an Indian is an Indian."

"Please, Colonel Chivington. She saved my life."

"Saved your life, be damned!" The colonel became red in the face. He shouted, "Damn any man who is in sympathy with any Indian, male or female."

"But—"

"That will be all, Major." Chivington looked down at the floor, and in that instant noticed what John Hanlen wore on his feet. "And take those damned moccasins off! Makes you look like an Indian yourself."

Standing outside, young Lieutenant Sam Dunham couldn't believe what the colonel was saying to his friend the major. As John Hanlen looked toward the window, he saw Sam peeking inside, his finger to his lips—a warning he heeded. But it was too late.

Calling for the guard, Chivington's words were chilling. "Lock him in the guardhouse."

"Sir!" Although he had expected a turbulent interview, he hadn't been expecting anything like this.

Turning toward John Hanlen, the colonel's voice was stern. "I'll check your story out, and if it isn't correct, you're in big trouble. To me, it sounds like an excuse from the lips of a deserter who wants to become a squaw man." The colonel sat back down, watching as the guards led the prisoner away.

Chapter Seventeen

Everything was in chaos after the chief, the elders, and Buffalo's Brother returned to the village. They had been away two days longer than they had originally intended. Much to Skyraven's dismay Lone Wolf's words about the camp being broken up so that they could move on proved to be true. Though Skyraven tried to sway her grandfather, he, too, said that moving on was best for the tribe. A thick herd of buffalo had been spotted to the southeast, and it was there that they would be traveling. Now they must hurry to break camp, he had said, and travel south over many miles of treeless grasslands to the Smoky Hills hunting ground, the area the chiefs had decided upon. There they would camp near the Cheyenne tribes.

Skyraven was reluctant to go. She loved this place more than any other. She had spent endless hours of joy along the cool, tree-lined banks of the South Platte River. She had enjoyed swimming in the cool water, running along the damp earth, gathering fruit and berries, but, most of all, she had enjoyed the time spent in the cave with John Hanlen and feared if she left the village, he would never be able to find her. For just a brief moment she paused in her work to look longingly up toward the cave. She couldn't help wondering just what John Hanlen was doing now. Did he miss her half as much as she missed him? Unconsciously, she ran her fingers over her mouth remembering the feel of his lips upon her own.

Skyraven was brought back to the present moment as Whispering Wind came dashing around the corner of the tepee nearly knocking into her in her haste. Why was she in such a hurry? Skyraven could only wonder as she continued to dismantle her grandfather's tepee and her own. The young woman's tattling tongue had caused enough damage. Skyraven couldn't help but wonder if the tribe would be moving onward had it not been for the ugly whisperings about her white soldier. She wondered even more if it was the buffalo that had caused the migration or fear of the white soldiers being nearby?

Perhaps the move to the Sandy River area would not be too bad after all, she thought, trying to soothe her troubled heart. It would bring her closer to Fort Lyon, where John Hanlen was stationed. The only problem was that he might not know where to find her now. The Indian women had little or no contact with the white soldiers. It was not as it had been a few years ago with the white traders. Now, with the raids occurring on both sides, the soldiers were as scorned as hornets, their forts avoided at all cost, like bees' hives.

Although she would be close to Fort Lyon, she would probably never be allowed to go there. There was a time when the whites and Indians had mingled together freely, with many white men having taken Indian women as wives. Now such men were known as squaw men, shunned by their own and some of the Indian tribes as well. The feeling between the Indians and whites was far from friendly.

And yet if the Great Spirit found a way to bring me together with my white soldier, he will aid me now, Skyraven thought hopefully.

She made up her mind that she would speak not another word about her reluctance to leave. She would be as docile as the white woolly creatures the white men sometimes let graze on their land. Later she could figure out a way to let John know that she was nearby. Now she had better get on with her work, for there was still much packing to be done. If she did not do her share she would come under severe rebuke, and Lone Wolf's anger was enough for her, she didn't want to anger Chief Left Hand and her grandfather, as well. With a sigh, Skyraven picked up her grandfather's possessions, carefully folding them, packing them away. To his pipe bag, she gave added reverence, since it had been his ever since she could remember, his most treasured possession with the exception of his peace pipes. Lifting, tucking, and folding, she bent to the task at hand.

All of a sudden there was a terrible commotion just a short distance away. Skyraven quickly stepped outside the tepee. Several people had gathered around to watch . . . something. Skyraven dropped the saddlebag she was filling and hurried to see what it was all about. She stopped in startled amazement as she saw Whispering Wind clinging to Lone Wolf and crying hysterically. Skyraven thought it to be a humiliating display.

She moved forward. She could not hear what Whispering Wind was murmuring, but as she came closer, Lone Wolf's voice could be heard very clearly. "No, I will not go to the Smoky Hills with you. I will ride with the Cheyenne warriors and drive the white man from our hunting grounds. Get away from me, woman." He pushed Whispering Wind so hard she lost her balance and stumbled backward. She did not fall, but with the grace of a wildcat, she stayed firmly on her feet.

"What is going on?" Skyraven asked Morning Dew.

"Chief Left Hand found out that Lone Wolf stole some horses from the white eyes, and he reacted in anger. They quarreled. Lone Wolf defended his right to have done the deed. In anger, he told his father he was leaving to join the Cheyenne dog soldiers."

"Oh." Even though she was troubled remembering her own confrontation with the arrogant brave, she still felt a twinge of sympathy. It was a terrible thing to leave one's tribe and wander alone. Lone Wolf could at times be annoyingly sure of himself, but he didn't deserve such a fate. "He'll come back once his temper has cooled." She looked toward her rival. "And Whispering Wind?"

"That bold one has been far from coy. When she found out about the horses, that Lone Wolf intended them as another bridal price, she offered herself to him. He refused. It is a battle of wills. Foolish woman, she would not take no for an answer but begged him to stay, to share her tepee once we arrived at the Smoky Hills."

"She said that?" Skyraven's interest was doubly aroused. In some ways Whispering Wind's unhappiness should have made her smile, but instead she felt a small measure of pity. Perhaps the young woman felt more strongly for Lone Wolf than she suspected.

Skyraven watched as Lone Wolf mounted his war pony to move away, but Whispering Wind would not give up. "Please don't go. You will only get yourself killed." The sun's rays revealed a sparkle of tears. "I love you, Lone Wolf. We could be happy together." She stood in the path of his pony. "Skyraven has deceived you, but I would not. I would forever be loyal. I can give you strong sons!"

Lone Wolf guided his horse forward, ignoring the Indian girl. "I have made it evident I do not want you, woman. Get out of my way." For just a moment Skyraven was afraid that Whispering Wind would be trampled by the animal's hooves, but she suddenly stepped aside.

"You are a fool, Lone Wolf!" she shouted, edging toward him again. In a final gesture of possessive defiance, she grabbed at his moccasin.

"Get away. Let me go." As the Indian shouted his indignation, he caught a glimpse of Skyraven standing there. She could see unhappiness in his eyes, and for just a moment truly believed that he held an affection for her, even after the unpleasant confrontation. She watched as Lone Wolf jerked his leg free from Whispering Wind's grasp, kicked his horse in the side, and rode off to join his three companions. Soon the four Arapaho braves were out of sight, leaving a red-faced and shamed Whispering Wind behind.

Skyraven knew that Lone Wolf's decision to ride with the dog soldiers was partly because of her refusal to marry him. How could she forget that it was for her he had stolen the horses and therefore quarreled with his father the chief? For just a moment she was tempted to ride after him, to add her plea to Whispering Wind's, but an inner voice told her not to interfere.

"There goes the handsomest man in camp," Morning Dew said, sighing regretfully. "But then I don't suppose it is possible those horses that he took could have been for me." She looked askance at Skyraven. "In all likelihood, they were for you, yes?"

"I wouldn't know . . ."

"They were! I saw the way he was looking at you. You should be ashamed." Though Morning Dew's words were meant to be teasing, they bothered Sky-

160

raven.

"I did not take the horses, or did I ask him to do such a thing. My heart is already taken." It was all she would reveal. In order to avoid being questioned, she quickly returned to her grandfather's tepee. Again the look in Lone Wolf's eyes came to her mind. He had acted in his all-too-familiar childish manner and they had quarreled. She was sorry, but she couldn't help it. She had promised to marry the man she truly loved. Was she to throw her own happiness away just to avoid hurting Lone Wolf's feelings?

Oh, John Hanlen, hurry back for me . . . she implored her thoughts, feeling a portent of tragedy tugging at a corner of her brain. She willfully swept it away, thinking instead that somehow they would find each other and when they did, she would be ready to become his wife.

That she-wolf got her due reward, Skyraven thought, remembering the girl's whispered threats. It served her right to be so shamed before the others in the tribe. Still, Skyraven couldn't help feeling pity for Whispering Wind. How could any woman humiliate herself that way? As much as she loved her yellow-haired soldier, she would never cling to him and beg as Whispering Wind had just done. But then, she thought again, in some ways it served Whispering Wind right. Perhaps Lone Wolf's anger was partly over having been told about the white soldier. No man liked to be reminded that the woman he loved had eyes for another. Perhaps he was taking his anger at her out on Whispering Wind, knowing well that he could, that her feelings were such that she would grovel just to keep him by her side. Maybe she had learned her lesson and would no longer be a troublemaker.

With downcast eyes, Skyraven worked on tearing down the tepees. First she undid her grandfather's tepee, and when that lay disassembled upon the ground, turned to her own. She carefully folded the buffalo-hide coverings, placed them on the travois along with the twelve-foot-long poles, then fastened them to her new horse's back. Skyraven had selected a black mare to ride on this trip and several other horses to act as pack animals. Her grandfather was rich. They had plenty of horses from which to choose, but oh, how she missed Running Antelope. She had never traveled without her beloved horse before.

On this move, as always, a few men and boys would herd the loose horses, feed and water them. The women would care for the pack and travois horses, the children and dogs. The braves would ride ahead to fight if they should meet any danger. The chief and her grandfather would lead them all. Nothing would be any different from before, and yet suddenly Skyraven had a strange feeling. For one brief moment it was as if she were viewing the journey as an outsider. Her people seemed suddenly remote, alien to her, as if she didn't belong. But that was foolish. She forced the thought out of her mind. She was Indian and would always remain so at heart, no matter where her love for John Hanlen took her.

It was a long way to the Smoky Hills. Skyraven had been given the duty of organizing the march. Leaving the campsite and the cave behind, she led the caravan on.

For one full day they journeyed, bedding down beneath the stars at night. Up early the next day, they continued their traveling, repeating the pattern the next day. Then at last, the weary travelers arrived at their destination.

Skyraven selected a choice spot near a giant cottonwood to set up her grandfather's lodge and her own tepee. Here, there was good drainage in case of a storm, and the sun would not shine directly upon the tepees during the hottest part of the day. The small stream nearby also gave them easy access to water, which pleased her, for she did not like to carry the heavy leather waterbags any farther than necessary.

Feeling quite pleased with herself, she stepped back to look at her handiwork. Living here would be almost as comfortable as the site they had just left. It was in Skyraven's nature to find happiness in her heart. Elsewise she would spend her life frowning, she thought, and look old before her time. She was still admiring the site when her grandfather came to her and placed his hand upon her shoulder, patting it affectionately. "The domestic atmosphere you have created for us is appreciated, Skyraven. How do you like our new home?"

She sought to please him with her answer. "I think I will like it here."

"It is good to stop our travels for a while. I tell you, Granddaughter, I am growing old. My bones are as brittle as dried buffalo bones."

"You old? Never!" She pointed to a spot where several of the women were setting up their tepees. "Look at how content the women seem to be. They are quite relaxed and eager to show goodwill. That pleases, me, Grandfather."

"And are you likewise content?" Though he didn't directly refer to her yellow-haired soldier, she knew he was in his thoughts. Still, she didn't want to speak of him. Not yet. So she ignored his question and gestured to the few naked children darting past them in pursuit of a butterfly. "The little ones are content to be here, too, it seems."

He looked at her for a long tender moment. "Ah, Skyraven, it was not too many moons ago that you were little and chasing after butterflies."

"Longer than I care to remember."

163

Buffalo's Brother sat down upon the ground near the huge tree trunk, leaned his head back, and motioned for her to do likewise. It was the kind of quiet time she truly appreciated, a time when they could just be together. "Let us rest for a while from our chores, Skyraven. After the long ride, my bones are weary." His eyes mirrored his concern for her. "You have worked very hard and must be tired, too."

Indeed she was, but even so, didn't want to nap. As her grandfather closed his eyes to catch a few winks, she looked around the campsite. Now that the camp had been set up, others were beginning to rest also. A few men were fishing along the stream, some others sat around telling jokes and laughing. The women visited and gossiped. A few mothers nursed their babies or placed the little ones in their cradleboards upon a tree limb where they could be easily watched. A mixture of pleasant smells drifted through the site. The air was fresh, the sky blue.

Yes, Skyraven thought to herself, *it is a good place for us. I think I will like it here very much.*

Everyone seemed to be enjoying their new surroundings. Even the dogs scampered about. Only one face looked sad and melancholy. Whispering Wind sat alone brooding over her lost love. Skyraven felt sympathy for her, but as she caught the Indian girl's eyes, the look of glaring anger reminded her that the she-cat had gotten her due.

But what of Lone Wolf? She couldn't help but wonder, hoping against hope that he wouldn't turn out to be a renegade. It would have been a sorry end for Left Hand's son, and a humiliation for a chief who prided himself on being peaceful. Skyraven decided that it was best to put the matter out of her mind, and yet a few days after they had arrived at their destination near the sandy creek area, some scouts returned with a report that they had seen a few lone riders far out across the Arkansas River and on the ridges along the southern skyline. Skyraven hoped that Lone Wolf had come to his senses.

Chapter Eighteen

Major John Hanlen was miserable, and he was bored. He had been in the guardhouse at the far end of the fort for almost a week now. His cell was large enough but it was completely constructed of adobe with only a solid wooden door and a small, barred window. There was not much to see and nothing to do except when the young lieutenant, Sam Dunham, came to see him. He looked forward to the stout, amiable lieutenant's visits, for it was the only time he could indulge in friendly conversation and also find out what was happening outside his tiny prison. To Sam, John was still a hero in spite of what had happened, perhaps more so. He confided to John that he had heard the whole conversation with Chivington and that he was on the major's side. The colonel was being unreasonable and shortsighted, he had said. John readily agreed. If Chivington was any example of the commanders in the area, then the cavalry was in a great deal of trouble — not to mention the Indians.

Last night, when Sam had come to see John, he had brought him a mug of beer from the sutler's store and told him that a small force, under the command of a Captain Wilson, was sent out to investigate his story of the ambush and had returned to report that they had seen hundreds of milling Indians but no bodies of white soldiers. According to Sam's story, Frank, his trumpeter friend, had gone with them.

"Frank said that the captain didn't want to go too far," Sam informed John. He told them that the remaining fighting men left in the garrison were diminishing and they would be of more use to their country if they stayed alive. A streak of yellow down his back if you ask me! Anyway, they galloped back to the fort with inconclusive evidence which will go bad for you."

"What in the hell did they expect to find?" It was the most idiotic thing John could think of, sending out a party to gather evidence. "As if there would be anything left, for God's sake." He shivered. "The vultures and crows would have made certain that there wasn't anything left of my men, and the Ute would have taken weapons, clothing, or anything of use."

"I guess Chivington expected to find skeletons clothed in uniforms or some such thing."

John Hanlen plopped down on a stool, the only furniture in the boxlike tiny room besides a narrow, rock-hard bed. "I told him about the Indians taking my boots and hat. They would have stripped my soldiers clean since army uniforms are quite a treasured item for them."

Sam Dunham shrugged. "Maybe Chivington didn't want to find evidence but was covering his bacon by sending out that search party! Or maybe he was hoping to find a body or two so that he could bring the gruesome things back to aid his vengeful cause."

"I hadn't thought of that." Covering his face with his hands, John let his breath out in a deep sigh. "Dear God, I'd thought to find a rational man. I wanted to tell the truth of what happened, but maybe by my honesty I've somehow endangered

167

Skyraven. Seems to me that there isn't much distinction made between tribes. But I suppose I thought so, too, once . . ."

Sam went on with his story. "Anyway, Wilson didn't even follow the route you described to them." John could not miss the expression of concern in the young lieutenant's eyes. "He can be a hotheaded son of a bitch. Now the talk around the fort is that you are a deserter, that you ran away from your men and then conjured up a cock-and-bull story to cover your actions."

John Hanlen bolted to his feet. "That's a damn lie!"

Sam made himself comfortable on the bed, the place he seemed to claim whenever he visited. "It just isn't fair for you to be here in the first place — not after what you witnessed and went through yourself." Lowering himself into a reclining position, he put his hands behind his head. "It must have been sheer hell to see your comrades slain before your very eyes and then captured and beaten nearly senseless yourself. Chivington is being as ruthless as an old snarling wolf, but then I guess only a fool would expect justice from that fanatical old Bible thumper."

"He isn't punishing me for what happened to my men but because I spoke kindly of Skyraven's tribe." In frustration, John struck his fist into his open palm. "Can't anybody else see that, or are they steeped with hatred, too?"

"There are many soldiers who don't agree with the colonel's Indian policies, but nobody dares to cross that big bear of a man. Why, hell, he's six feet five and weighs at least two hundred and sixty pounds — his size alone is enough to frighten anybody."

Sam filled his friend in on the details of the man in whose hands his fate rested. When the War Between the States started, Chivington had been offered a chaplain's commission. He had made it clear from the first that he preferred fighting to preaching. Apparently he had meant every word of that statement. Everybody knew, however, that the trouble with the Indians had increased since he became commander of the garrison just last year.

"Some people say Chivington has his eyes on a political career and is using the military as a stepping stone. The talk is that he wants to become a congressman if and when the territory becomes a state."

John's answering laugh was tinged with sarcasm. "Oh, and he would be just the man Colorado would need." He guessed many military men did want political careers, but that route never held appeal for him. His own father, who had risen through the military ranks to become a general, had held such ambition.

Sam wiggled his feet, making himself comfortable. "Let those that want it have it. As for me, I'm reasonably content. Food and a bed is about all I need." He looked up at John Hanlen and grinned. "I guess by now you've realized that I have an ulterior motive in these visits of mine. Give me time to relax."

"I wish *I* could!" Worry about what might happen to Skyraven played on his mind. Never would he want her to be at the mercy of a man like Chivington. Thank God she was where she was. It seemed a safe enough distance away, at least until he could make somebody see reason. He hadn't given up hope that he could help to bring about a peaceful solution—if they would only listen to him. A parley with Skyraven's grandfather and the chiefs could be the answer.

Hell, what did they expect the Indians to do when the government kept chiseling away at their hunting grounds, confining them to smaller and smaller portions of land? Sam Dunham had given him a great deal of insight into what was happening. The situation reminded him of dogs and cats baiting each other into trouble. The soldiers would do something to cause anger, then the Indians would retaliate. There would be a moment of peace, then the whole thing would start up again. If incidents provoked by both the whites and the Indians continued piling up, there soon would be an all-out war that nobody could stop.

"Colonel Chivington is constantly calling for increased troops when he knows full well that the government can't spare any more men," Sam observed.

"We're fighting a war, for God's sake. The government needs more men themselves." He thought a moment. "But he knows that. He's trying to call attention to himself and make it look bad for the Indians."

"Leave it to Chivington," Sam said sarcastically. "Somehow he'll get just what he wants. He always does."

John was to learn very quickly just how right Sam was. When Chivington's plans for more men did not materialize, he demanded authority to raise more troops from the Colorado Territory. He got his authority and his one-hundred-day volunteers — a sad assortment of riffraff, yet probably the best they could get on such short notice and to serve for such a brief time. The pay for enlisted men was poor. Nobody could survive on thirteen dollars a month, or so it was always grumbled. Most soldiers couldn't even afford to get married and support a wife on a salary like that, John thought. That was why the enlisted men's barracks was known as Suds Row. The few wives who were here at the fort had to work in the laundry room to supplement their husbands' meager earnings. John, on the other hand,

170

made a good salary. Were he to marry, his wife would never have to perform such a demeaning task.

Placing his hands on the bars, he put his nose close to them and looked out. He could see the parade grounds from where he was. The new recruits, known as the Colorado Third Cavalry Regiment, were practicing out on the field. What an odd assortment of men, he thought. Mainly settlers, miner, and farmers. There wasn't a real soldier in the entire bunch. There was an atmosphere of contention at the fort, the enlisted men against the officers, and both sticking their noses up at the new men. And all the while Chivington growled like a bear, trying to mold his hodgepodge into some kind of manageable unit. There was an atmosphere of tension and conflict at the fort. He suspected the truth was that Chivington was feared, but also hated.

The staccato rhythm of snare drums sounded like volleys of gunfire as the new group of men marched back and forth. Left, right, left, right, marching on and on. Marching. Drilling. Marching. Drilling. Monotonous and tiring. Even so, John thought he might as well watch them for a while. There wasn't anything else to do. God, but they were a disorderly bunch. Although Chivington didn't know it yet, the colonel needed him.

John watched now as a tall, lanky, red-haired recruit who wasn't watching where he was going ran smack-dab into the man in front of him. "No, no, look out, you fool," he shouted out on impulse, relieved that nobody could hear him since he was too far away. The discipline was so terrible as to be almost funny. And these were the men they were going to send to fight Indians? Remembering the Ute and their well-organized maneuvers, he knew at once that the cavalry was in a whole lot of trouble.

There really wasn't much hope for any kind of future unless the cavalry could do better than that. But at least these bumbling fools would ensure Skyraven's safety, and that was his foremost concern. Skyraven! Oh, how he wanted to see her again. It was a need festering within him. He had to get out of here. He had to warn Skyraven's people about Chivington and talk about peace. If the Arapaho made it absolutely obvious that their intentions were to remain friendly with the white man, then perhaps there was hope that they would not become victims of Chivington's obsession. With Skyraven's help, he was sure that they could succeed. The alternative was so odious he hated to think about what would happen if something wasn't done soon. Chivington had already proven to be as touchy as an old bear disturbed in hibernation.

Oh, Skyraven. I told you I'd come back for you and I will find some way to do it, John thought as he sat on the small stool, staring at the earthen floor. He couldn't dig his way out. The floor was as hard as baked clay. He put his head in his hands and began to think. No, he'd have to do this legitimately. Legally.

A name popped into his head. Maybe he could get his father's friend, Henry Sedgwick, to put in a good word for him. He might pack some weight. He was only a lieutenant colonel and so didn't outrank Chivington, but Henry had some high-ranking friends, including John's own father, and had always been a help to the Hanlen family whenever possible. He had spent a great deal of time at John's home in Missouri when John was just a boy, and his promotion to lieutenant colonel had been the senior Hanlen's doing.

He hadn't seen Sedgwick very often since then. The lieutenant colonel had been transferred from Missouri to a place near Fort Lyon a couple of months ago when the call for some good officers went out. John hadn't thought much about it then, but it could prove to be a godsend. Asking his help now seemed the logical thing to do. The next time Sam Dunham came to see him he would send a message via Sam to Lieutenant Colonel Henry Sedgwick asking for his help in getting him out of this hellhole.

Chapter Nineteen

Life at the new Arapaho village, nestled among the cottonwoods, settled back into a normal routine as the days passed. Skyraven continued to tan hides, do porcupine embroidery and other works of art when she had a few moments to spare. There were many chores that had to be performed each day, however. Only after taking care of the day's necessities could she spare time to do the things she truly enjoyed. But no matter where she was or what she was doing, she was never too busy to think about her white soldier, wondering where John Hanlen was at that moment and if he was all right. He was like the sun's light, warming her heart, her soul. Oh, how she wanted to be with him again. Would he come back to her as he had promised? She wondered. She had to believe that he would.

A long, peaceful quiet settled over the area. The braves who had agitated contention had left with Lone Wolf. If Skyraven could not be truly happy without John Hanlen by her side, she had at least settled down to a semblance of contentment. Now that Lone Wolf was gone, it did Whispering Wind no good to belittle Skyraven. She had tried to find new ways of finding fault and blaming Skyraven for Lone Wolf's disappearance at first, had tried to make life miserable for Skyraven, but it did not work. Skyraven was well liked by the village women. Whispering Wind was not. Her sharp tongue had stung too many, too frequently. Nor had her emotional display endeared her to the other women. It had shamed them that an Arapaho woman would act in such a shameful manner. It was no wonder then that Whispering Wind pulled herself into her own little shell and refused to mingle with the others.

Today, as Skyraven walked along the creek collecting driftwood, she felt vibrantly alive. Last night, for the first time, there had been a lessening of the tension between her grandfather and herself. She hoped that she had softened his heart and that he at last fully understood how she felt about her soldier. With a long, drawn-out sigh he had agreed to approve of the marriage when John Hanlen came back, had even said he would perform the ceremony. Was it any wonder that this morning she smiled.

In moments such as this, when her work was completed and she had time for pleasure, Skyraven had time to let her thoughts wander. At such times, she usually thought about John Hanlen. As she thought about him now she knew why she felt so vibrantly alive. She was in love, and it was such a wonderful feeling. As she passed by the men and boys who were watering their horses, she waved, giving vent to her heartfelt joy. Perhaps it was time for her to gather together what possessions she had so that when John Hanlen came for her she would be ready for the ceremony. That thought was on her mind as she bent down to take a drink of the clear water. Could anything in this life taste as refreshing? And just as the water soothed her thirst, so did John Hanlen enrich her soul.

It was a perfect day. Autumn had turned the leaves of the trees red, yellow, and a pleasant shade of brown. Just like her tribesmen, the animals were preparing for the change in the seasons. How she loved to watch the wildlife scamper about, she thought as she picked up dead twigs and branches, gathering an armful for the fire. The beaver were busily building a new home for themselves, the squirrels were storing food in a hole in a tree, a large mother raccoon was teaching her little ones how to fish.

"Ah, that is just what I should be doing," Skyraven said aloud. "Thank you for the splendid suggestion, Sister Raccoon. Grandfather would enjoy a fine young trout for his dinner tonight." She hurried back to the tepee, dropped the driftwood she had collected near the entrance and entered just long enough to get a net in which to catch a fish.

"Where are you off to in such a hurry, Skyraven?" one of the young mothers called to her as she dashed past her tepee.

"I'm going to offer Grandfather a slight change in diet tonight. I'm off to set a net to catch a large fish for his dinner."

"Oh, what a fine idea. Will you take my net along with you and catch a fish for my husband's dinner, too?" The young mother did not wait for an answer but went into her tepee and returned with a small net which she handed to Skyraven. "You are always so good about helping others, Skyraven. I knew you wouldn't mind."

"Of course I don't. I can just as well catch two fish as one." Skyraven took the other net, chucked the baby under the chin, and dashed off toward the creek again. It was the Indian way to help the others of the tribe. She had little doubt but that in some way the young mother would repay her for the fish in a similar act of kindness.

She walked toward the grazing horses on her way to the stream. Although she missed her brown-and-white mare and knew that no horse could ever replace her, she was sure that John Hanlen would take good care of Running Antelope. She found her new mare, one she was training herself, and patted her gently on the nose. The white horse was graceful and gentle, whereas Running Antelope had been powerful and strong. Skyraven loved them both. Her instincts told her that the new horse would be a good riding horse in time, and with enough training. When John Hanlen came back with Running Antelope, she would challenge him to a race, just to see which horse would win.

It was a cool day, the air was filled with earth smells. "Mother Earth has been very good to the Arapaho," she sighed to herself. As she sat on the edge of the bank, she thought how she loved to look up at the trees rising high above the tepees. They reminded her of tall, strong warriors. Dipping her nets in the water, securing them with rocks, she contented herself in watching the breeze stir the brightly colored leaves and branches. One slim tree swayed gently in the wind, ending its branches as if reaching out toward another tree. The symbolic embrace made her blood run hot as she thought about the lovemaking she had shared with her golden-haired lover. At night sometimes, in her tepee when she was lying naked beneath her buffalo robe, it was the same. An aching hunger she could not fulfill. A longing for her soldier.

"Hurry back to me, John Hanlen," she whispered to the wind. As if in answer, she seemed to hear him answer, "I will," then drew back in surprise. It was as if somehow she had actually heard his voice. Strange, but a sudden discontent pushed away her

177

sense of well-being. She had a chilling feeling that John Hanlen was in some kind of trouble. Peering into the water, she tried to see a vision in the water as she had once before, but all she could see were two fish, trapped in the nets she had set. Then just as quickly as the feeling had come over her, it vanished, leaving her trembling and confused.

Skyraven hurried back toward the tepees, stopping by to leave one of the fish she had caught at the tepee of her friend. When she reached her own tepee, she brought out the lightweight leather cooking pouch, placed it upon a tripod over the fire in front of the tepee, cut up the wild vegetables, and started supper. She scaled and gutted the large trout, placed a skewer through it, and hung it over the flame along with the pouch of vegetables.

"John Hanlen, John Hanlen," she whispered. "If you are in trouble, let me feel it. Think of me as strongly as I am thinking of you." She tried to renew the strange vibrations she had felt at the stream, but somehow the feelings eluded her. She hoped she had only been imagining. Wherever John Hanlen was, she wanted him to be safe and comfortable.

Suddenly she knew she must see him, just to assure herself that he was not in trouble. But how could she? Surely she could not go to the fort. She would be afraid. Besides, her grandfather would never allow it. He said that too many of the white men came without their women, that there was a shortage of women of their own kind, which caused them to cast lustful eyes at the Indian maidens they encountered. Should she wait for her yellow-haired soldier to come for her? But how could she arrange to let John Hanlen know her whereabouts now that the tribe had moved? Several of the chiefs and her grandfather would soon be going to meet with an

Indian agent about the slaughter of the buffalo. Perhaps she could figure out a way to go with them.

Perhaps because she was so anxious to pose the idea to him, it seemed to take Buffalo's Brother an inordinately long time to return to his tepee. When at last he did return from his meeting with the chiefs, he was in a jovial mood. He gave her a pat on the shoulder and a wry grin, then, as always, he walked slowly toward the cooking pouch and peered in. A man's stomach, he said, was all too often the real ruler of his being.

"What is this, Skyraven?" When he spotted the succulent morsel roasting over the fire, he cried out in delight, "It looks like a fine trout will be our supper tonight."

"I thought that you would like something different. We haven't had fish for a long time, and I know how much you like it." Skyraven thought for a minute, then smiled cajolingly as she had as a child when she had wanted her way. "Since I fixed such a nice supper, do you think I could talk you into taking me with you when you go to the Cheyenne camp?"

"What?" Throwing back his head, he laughed. "So, my granddaughter, you haven't changed a bit in all these years. You think you can bribe me."

"No, I don't . . ." But she did. Hanging her head, Skyraven took on another look from childhood, one she had always assumed when she had been caught doing something her grandfather might not understand. "My heart was not filled with wiles when I went to the stream, but I thought . . ."

The hand on her shoulder was warm with affection. "Don't look so downhearted, Skyraven. I had already decided to take you with me. Your girlhood friend Desert Flower is expecting a baby. She asked if I would bring you. She would like to have you with her when the baby is born. Not only because you are such a good medicine woman but because you are her trusted friend."

"Desert Flower is with child?" A smile as wide as the overhead sky beamed across Skyraven's face. The young Indian girl had longed for a baby. They had often talked about such things. Now Skyraven had something else to discuss with her. There were times when only another woman could possibly understand. Flinging her arms around her grandfather, she hugged him. "Oh, Grandfather, can I really go with you to Sand Creek?"

"I said that you could, and so you can." His eyes were gentle. "I think it will be good for you to see her and for her to have you by her side. That is why I told Desert Flower that you were coming. The news made her joyful. She wants you with her at this very important time in her life."

"I can stay with her while you and the chiefs discuss buffalo with the white men." Already she was making plans. Somehow she would find out about John Hanlen and get a message to him. The very thought of just seeing him again caused her lips to sweep upward.

"I am glad I have made you smile, little one." Cupping her face in his hands, he looked deep into her eyes. "And have you some news for Desert Flower?"

Skyraven nodded.

"Then the two of you will have much to talk about to occupy your time." As was her granddaughter's habit, he opened the flap of the tepee and went inside to rest and relax before eating his supper. He always told her that it was a sign of his old age that he needed to nap so often.

"You are not old, Grandfather. Not in your heart you are not," she whispered softly.

180

After he had gone, Skyraven sat by herself, allowing her thoughts to wander. It did seem as if the Great Spirit was helping her. Skyraven had given her word when Desert Flower, Lone Wolf's cousin, had married the Cheyenne chief's son, Blue Fox. She had promised Desert Flower that she would come when their first child was born. It was a matter of honor to keep such a promise. How was Skyraven to know that the child's birth would come at so opportune a time?

"A child!" Living proof of the love between two people. Now, as she thought about it, she wished for a child of her own. John's child. "John," she murmured, closing her eyes for a moment and letting the cool moist air caress her face. She just might see John Hanlen again very, very soon. Each day was bringing her closer to Fort Lyon and the man she loved.

Chapter Twenty

Early the next morning the small company of Arapaho crossed the dividing ridge between the valleys of the South Platte and the Arkansas rivers and proceeded to the Cheyenne camp on the edge of Sand Creek. As they traveled, the men did most of the talking. The buzz of their voices sounded like angered bees. Skyraven garnered much information just by listening. It seemed, she learned from their conversation, that the white men were at it again, going into the buffalo hunting grounds and shooting the buffalo. The chief and her grandfather had decided that joining with the Cheyenne in protesting the matter might make it a more emphatic gesture to the white men in charge that they were angry.

"It is a matter of considerable importance to prevent encroachment of the white man upon our hunting territory," Chief Left Hand said. With the thought in mind of impressing the white men with his importance as chief, he had worn his best buckskin and headdress.

"Yes. We have given the white man authority only to cross over our land, not to infringe on our hunting ground," another chief, Arapaho, added.

"The Cheyenne tell us they are finding more and

more white hunters leaving the territory carrying many buffalo hides with them. The white eyes have no right to hunt on our ground and to steal away buffalo hides to sell to the eastern markets." Buffalo's Brother looked very unhappy as he spoke. "That is, from what I have learned, their intent. The white men in the white man's villages pay much for such soft skin. But even so, it is not right that they break their word. It is one of the only places where the buffalo still roam in large numbers."

The favorite hunting ground of the southern herd was the very section of the plains they were on now, the land about the Republican River between the Arkansas and South Platte. This land had been granted to the Arapaho and Cheyenne as a hunting reserve established by the treaty of Fort Wise in 1861. So soon the white men wanted to break their word.

"I signed that treaty," Lame Bear, the Cheyenne chief who had ridden out to greet them, said. "The treaty promised the Indians could hunt buffalo on the land north of the North Platte and on the Republican Fork of the Smoky Hill River, so long as the buffalo were in such numbers as to justify the chase."

"This is just the reason we must stop the white man from hunting here," Left Hand shot back. "The treaty gives us the right only as long as the buffalo are in such numbers as to justify the chase. If they keep killing our buffalo at such an alarming rate, soon we will not have any rights or any buffalo."

Buffalo's Brother reined in his horse and raised his hands toward the sky, knowing instinctively that the tribe needed help on this matter. He let out a sharp yell that startled the others in the party. When they realized what he was doing, they, too,

183

paused and turned their eyes skyward. "Oh, Great Spirit hear me. Do not allow the white men to do this terrible thing," he chanted.

Skyraven said a similar prayer. If the white men continued to do such a deed, it would not only anger her people and possibly diminish the buffalo but might endanger her happiness with John Hanlen as well.

The chanting done, Buffalo's Brother gestured for the party to move on. The small band of Arapaho neared the village and could see the Cheyenne assembled to greet them. Desert Flower, although large with child, rushed up to Skyraven before she could even dismount and cried out how glad she was to see her. There was a special glow to her face that spoke of the contentment of the lifegiver.

"I am as round as a pumpkin but happy," she called out, putting her hand on her belly as she smiled. When Skyraven had slid from her horse, Desert Flower took her hand and led her toward the tepee she shared with her husband. "I'm so glad you have come. Already I can tell the little one wants to make his appearance very soon. You will know just what to do."

"You are not afraid?" Skyraven asked.

"Not now."

There was a large lodge in the middle of the camp built especially to entertain a dozen or more visiting chiefs or other dignitaries. The two young women watched as the men immediately went into the lodge. There would be a council, and they would decide what to do about the white man's infringement. She found Blue Fox staring at her with piercing eyes which nevertheless held some kindness.

"I saw Lone Wolf. He is miserable without you," he finally blurted out. "Everyone thought the two of you would marry."

So that was the reason he was staring at her. How could she make this Cheyenne warrior, husband of her best friend, realize that she couldn't help loving someone else. Even if he was a white man. She could no more stop loving John Hanlen than she could stop breathing. He had become as necessary to her as the air of life itself.

His dark brows furled. "Why? How could you — ?"

"Do not question her, Blue Fox, and do not judge her too severely," Desert Flower said quickly. "I am sure that Skyraven will tell me all about it, and we will understand her feelings in time." The hand holding Skyraven's squeezed tightly with affection.

Blue Fox only looked at his wife, then, with a shrug, left the tepee to join the other men in the meeting lodge.

Desert Flower touched Skyraven's arm gently. "My husband does not understand, but I do. To him, Lone Wolf is the most glorious specimen of manhood and he cannot but wonder how you could choose someone else." Lifting the flap of her tepee, she drew Skyraven down to sit upon her buffalo robe. "We can talk now, you and I. Tell me about your soldier."

"His name is John Hanlen. He is a major. I will tell you about him, but first I must know about your life with Blue Fox and about the baby you are carrying."

Desert Flower blushed. "My husband wanted the child very much, but he says that making the baby was equally pleasurable. And I agree. I want many, many children."

Skyraven remembered the soul-shattering moments with her white soldier in the cave. "So do I," she whispered.

The two friends talked long into the night, Sky-raven telling her Indian friend about her rescue of John Hanlen, how she had carried him back to the cave. To Desert Flower she could open her heart; thus it was only to her that she would tell the whole story. Now that her friend had also enjoyed the passion of love, they could talk about woman things.

"He loves you?"

"Yes. He told me so, and I believe him. There was such tenderness in his embrace that I cannot think he lied. He will come back and bring the horses with him just as he promised."

"And then there will be wedding." Desert Flower seemed excited by the prospect.

While the warriors and chiefs held their meeting in the friendship lodge, the two young women made their plans. Skyraven made herself comfortable in her friend's dwelling, thinking to herself that Desert Flower would be a pleasant companion in the days spent away from her own tepee.

Chapter Twenty-one

Lone Wolf and his good friend, Red Dog, clad only in leggings and moccasins, were crouched upon their haunches side by side watching the activity in the valley down below. The ridge upon which they were crouched had an almost perpendicular cliff at the back and a steep slope on either side, and thus made a perfect place of concealment.

The braves had come from across the Republican River several days ago following the buffalo carcasses that were strewn across both sides of the river. Their group of warriors had ridden hard and had picked up fresh horses from some of the ranches nearby as they needed them. Horse-stealing had been going on between the whites and the Indians for quite a while now so Lone Wolf had no qualms about what he had done. The white men stole from the Indians and the Indians from the whites. Neither side was less guilty than the other. But now there was a more urgent matter to be taken care of—the needless slaughter of the animal the Indians held sacred.

Since early morning, the two braves had watched while three white hunters took stretched buffalo skins from the frames beside a small, sod-roofed shanty. Now they were tying them in bundles upon the two horse-driven wagons. It was obvious these white men had been the ones to leave the decaying buffalo bodies for the vultures.

"See. The white eyes cannot be trusted under any circumstances." Lone Wolf shook his closed fist as he spoke. All the while he had been thinking that the white eyes steal everything, even the Indian women. He was still bitter about Skyraven's refusal to marry him. That she preferred a white man stung his pride.

"It is bad enough that these intruders are diverting the river water away from our hunting grounds for their own use and cutting the trees and other vegetation that offer us protection, but to indiscriminately slaughter the buffalo and leave the carcass to rot in the sunshine is unforgivable," Red Dog hissed.

Turning to his companion, Lone Wolf bared his teeth in anger as he spoke. "I am not surprised. Just as I told you, the white eyes are liars. I have never trusted them as our fathers do. Their treaties are useless. They are much too greedy to keep their word."

"Nor have I trusted them," Red Dog sneered. "Those men are killing our buffalo for the robes right on our own hunting reserve. We were right to leave our fathers' village. We cannot live in peace with the white man. We have to drive them out of our country while we are still strong enough to fight."

"My father, Left Hand, and yours, Lame Bear, both tried to tell us that the Indian agent is in control of the business of trading." Lone Wolf spit on the ground. "Indian agents are no better than any other white man. They have tried to keep us

188

ignorant of what is going on. But now we have seen for ourselves."

"You are right, my brother, we had better hang on to the few guns, knives and other things we have received in trade. It looks as if we will come out the losers in our dealings with men such as these."

"Both of our fathers were there to sign the treaty and we know what it said; that no white man without just cause and without consent of the Indian agents is to set foot upon this hunting reserve." And yet here the men were, Red Dog mused, doing as they pleased without any interference.

Lone Wolf shook his head in despair. "What is the matter with our fathers that they cannot see? It is not good to trust the white eyes. We come from two different worlds. They are like vultures. With them there can be no peace."

"Come. We have watched their treachery long enough," Red Dog called to Lone Wolf over his shoulder as he started toward their tethered horses. "Let us ride back and tell the others that we must drive these white hunters from our hunting reserve."

The two braves rode at breakneck speed back to the narrow valley on the other side of the ridge where the others were camped. It was a perfect spot for the tepees. The cliffs on each side offered concealment, there was an abundance of food and forage for the horses, and there was a stream along which delicious fruit grew. The stream gave them water and a place where they could bathe and catch fish if needed.

"Here at least we are free," Lone Wolf cried aloud as he slid from his war pony, "without fear of white men's lies. They will not cage me." The few times he had been in the square dwellings of the white eyes he had found them hot, dark, and stuffy.

A subchief of the Cheyenne by the name of Spotted Eagle had seen how excited the returning braves were when they returned and had heard Lone Wolf's voice. Now, he walked over to them. Spotted Eagle was a powerful figure. Over six feet tall, large of frame but with no fat to mar the beauty of his body, his shoulder-length hair was braided. His appearance differed from that of Lone Wolf in that he was older and not as handsome. His nose was broad, his mouth wide, and his skin a shade darker.

Spotted Eagle was leader of the Cheyenne dog soldiers, Lone Wolf the acting chief of the few Arapaho who had joined them. More young Arapaho had become dissatisfied from time to time and were coming to join Lone Wolf's band. Right now there were only ten, but the Arapaho were gaining in strength.

"We have seen them and what they do." Lone Wolf and Red Dog told the assemblage of braves all that they had been watching since early morning. "Three white men are murdering our buffalo. It is they who leave the skinned bodies of the dead buffalo behind them."

"Ugh. I thought as much," Spotted Eagle grunted.

"The white eyes do not share like we do," said another brave. The hunters of the Arapaho and Cheyenne always saw to it that every family received a fair share of the kill. The white men took the skin and left the meat, yet they did not even think to offer that which they did not want to those in need.

"And they will keep demanding more and more of our ground," Red Dog grumbled. "Has it not already been proven so? Peace, they say. Ha."

"But what can be done?" a young brave, barely into manhood, asked.

All three of the Indian chieftains exchanged glances. Lone Wolf and Spotted Eagle uttered simultaneously, "Let us sweep down and drive these white men away."

Lone Wolf was a respected leader among the Cheyenne as well as among his own Arapaho. Together, he and Spotted Eagle made all the decisions. They were responsible for defending their land and for the general welfare of the others. Quickly they prepared themselves for a confrontation. Telling the other braves to follow them, they gathered together their war regalia, including rifles, lances, bows and arrows, war paint, and war bonnets.

When they were well prepared, they rode to the ridge, where they watched and waited astride their war ponies until the white men had loaded both wagons and started to leave. Then, with wild, shrill war whoops, they galloped down the sides of the steep cliffs.

The three hunters saw them coming and whipped the horses into running as fast as was possible while pulling a wagon full of buffalo hides. The Indians slowed down purposely and did not follow. They did not want to get close enough to shoot or be shot at. Any disturbance in their own territory might give the soldiers reason to come in and shrink their hunting grounds even more. The area of the buffalo herds was not their choice of place for an all-out war since war in the hunting grounds would scare away what buffalo were left. They just wanted to frighten the white men enough so that they would be reluctant to return and would caution others to remain well outside of Indian territory.

Their plan worked well, or so Lone Wolf boasted. The three white men were frightened nearly to death when they looked behind them to see so many painted faces, war bonnets, and feathered lances. They made a comical sight as they ran, each one in a different direction.

"Like prairie chickens!" Lone Wolf observed, and that was exactly what the Indian warriors had intended. They enjoyed seeing the enemy shake in their shoes and scurry away. "Now let us go back to camp." The time would come when there would be an all-out war, but not here and not now. With a signal from their two leaders, the warriors retreated to the bluffs as soon as the wagon had crossed over the Sandy River. The braves rode triumphantly back to camp knowing that their mission had been accomplished.

When the white men returned to their own camp, they did not tell the story as it really happened, however. Since they did not want to appear cowardly, they greatly exaggerated, insisting that there had been more Indians than there actually were, nearly a hundred, they said, and that the entire episode happened *outside* the Indian territory. The outright falsehood was told that the Indians had fired for no reason and had stolen horses and buffalo hides that were rightfully theirs. The hunters hadn't really meant to start a furor. The lie just grew in their effort to save their own skins and to make themselves look honorable and brave. They knew that they could get into a lot of trouble for hunting on the Indian hunting reserve.

"They were on the war path all right," one of the men had said in ending the story. "You should have seen those horrible painted faces. Why, there were probably Sioux, Kiowa, Comanche, Cheyenne, and Arapaho. I'll just bet any man here that the tribes have all got together and decided to kill every one of us."

Within an hour, Colonel Tappan, the officer in charge of Fort Lyon while Colonel Chivington was in Denver City, had sent men out along the Arkansas River to investigate complaints. A seed of fear had been sown by three greedy men. The people living nearby were sure that an all-out war with the Indians was about to take place.

Chapter Twenty-two

It was a cloudy day with just a hint of a chill, but even so, John Hanlen had never been so appreciative of fresh air in his life. He had been released from that unnervingly confining cell, and, stepping through the doorway, he filled his lungs, savoring the air in great gulps. Freedom. Perhaps a man didn't truly appreciate such a gift until he'd been cooped up for a while.

True to his word, John's old family friend, Lieutenant Colonel Henry Sedgwick, had convinced Colonel Chivington that John would be of more value to the cavalry outside of the brig than in it. With the War Between the States still raging strong, the regiment was short on skilled manpower. Keeping him incarcerated would serve no purpose, he had said. There were only three hundred soldiers stationed at Fort Lyon and even fewer at Fort Wise, near Denver.

Every man was needed just to keep the fort running smoothly. There were gates to be mended, food to be prepared, clothing to be patched and sewn, stables to be cleaned, horses to be fed, groomed, and watered, water buckets to be filled, wood to be gathered and stacked and a million small jobs which had to be accomplished daily. And, even more important, officers were needed to supervise the routine work. John Hanlen had no doubt that his being a major had been an added help.

Sam had filled him in on the meeting with Colonel Chivington. There was really no reason to hold him in jail any longer, Sedgwick had argued. There was no charge against Major Hanlen, and no evidence could be found to warrant a charge of desertion. Drawing himself up to his full height of five feet four, Sam had given his best imitation of the lieutenant colonel.

"Now, Colonel Chivington, I can understand how you could have been bitterly upset at the time Hanlen was sentenced, what with those marauding tribes of Indians giving the United States Cavalry and the settlers out here such a bad time, but I have known John since he was a boy. His . . . uh . . . father is quite influential. Perhaps you didn't know. A *general* in the United States Army." Sam had looked at his friend with a new sense of veneration. "General's son, are you? Why didn't you tell Chivington that yourself? Would have meant fewer days in here, I would reckon."

John hadn't wanted to mention his father, didn't want the old man poking his nose into the situation. But now it didn't matter. Sedgwick had been all the help he had needed. All he cared about now was that he was free.

As for Chivington, he had handled the situation with political dexterity. He merely said that he had now discovered that many times when soldiers were presumed killed in a battle, the bodies could not be found. The steep terrain and gulleys prohibited much exploration, he had mumbled. He said he had been told that in one instance, in order to cross a deep ravine, the soldiers had to attach a rope to the wagon tongue and hand-pull it over the trouble spot. There had been no apology; in fact, Chivington seemed to want to act as if a "misunderstanding" had never happened at all.

"Ah, well!" John had a happy skip to his step as he walked near the edge of the parade ground. It was good to be out of jail where he could exercise his legs. Now he could plan to take some of the leave he had earned in order to go to Skyraven's camp. He was determined to do just that as soon as he could. He hoped that she didn't believe that he had forgotten his promise to her. Well, he'd soon prove to her that he had not. He had some money saved, and just as soon as he could, he'd go about buying those horses to give to her grandfather. He didn't want to wait too long. She was a beautiful woman, and he had no doubt but that Lone Wolf, the brave Skyraven had said wanted to marry her, would quickly gather up horses if he did not.

"Skyraven . . ." He whispered her name softly. All the time he was in the brig he had thought about her. In the long, lonely moments when it was quiet and he was in solitude, she had played on his mind and on his body. His skin flushed hotly as he remembered that just the memory of her soft curves had aroused him, made him ache for her. "Yep, it's about time to think about getting those horses," he said to himself.

It was a long day. Just because he'd found out he was a general's son didn't mean the colonel intended to make things easy for him. In fact, it seemed as if he had been given enough chores to make up for lost time. He had just finished work at the quartermaster's where he had been stacking ammunition in

196

a storage shed and was walking along whistling a happy tune when he encountered Sam Dunham.

"My, my, my, you sound happy, Major." Sam winked at him. "Glad to see you so cheerful. Don't suppose I can guess why?"

"Feels great to be out of that cage. And I was just thinking about a pair of big blue eyes and hair as black as coal." John winked, knowing Sam would realize immediately that he meant the Indian girl. Certainly he'd talked enough about her. "A woman like that will put a man in a downright agreeable mood every time."

Sam's smile changed abruptly to a cautioning frown. "Shh. Don't speak too freely, Major." He laid his hand on John's arm. "Evidently you haven't heard what Colonel Tippan's scouts are saying."

"Colonel Tippan? I haven't heard a word all day, Sam. All I have heard is the sound of wooden crates being piled on top of one another." A deep sense of foreboding took hold of him. "Why? What's going on? What are they saying?"

"It seems a large band of Indians robbed some white men of their provisions a few miles east of Sand Creek a few days ago. They stole some horses, a wagon, and buffalo hides, too. Blatantly attacked the three men. Whooping. Hollering. Colonel Chivington has already sent out several groups to scout the territory and find out where those braves could be. He wanted them followed and brought to punishment but the men came back empty-handed with no Indians or any sign of sighting any. The terrain is so steep and rocky that some of the units had to turn back. But they did spot some Indian villages."

"Indian villages?" The muscles in John's body all tensed. He had been listening to every word without blinking an eye or uttering a sound, but now he couldn't hide his emotions. "Do they know what tribes were responsible?" The thought of Skyraven's people being punished worried him. "It was probably Ute. Those savages are capable of almost anything."

"No it wasn't the Ute. Colonel Chivington had had several reports of skirmishes that took place between the Colorado troops and the Cheyenne dog soldiers. Some men are already out with the order to burn villages and kill any Cheyenne they may find, men, women, and children."

"Women and children? Oh, my God!" It was just the kind of event he had feared. Pacing back and forth like a caged bear, he wracked his brain for a way he might be able to help. "There has to be a better way. There just has to."

"Sergeant Andrews was in several such fights. He was the one who reported this incident. He says that everyone he has talked to thinks the Cheyenne are hatching up a plot with the other tribes to run the whites out of the country. Heard it said that some Arapaho are suspect. There is even talk of an all-out Indian war. The people up and down the Arkansas River are scared to death. Colonel Chivington is on his way back from Fort Weld, near Denver City now. He sort of bounces back between the two forts from time to time. Prefers the more 'civilized' fort near Denver City. Guess it really is an emergency if he is leaving his beloved Camp Weld to come back here."

John Hanlen's face turned an ashen white. "There has to be some mistake. Both the Cheyenne and Skyraven's Arapaho tribe are peaceful. I remember her telling me so. They do not want war." He didn't have to be a military genius to know there was

198

going to be trouble on a large scale. "I have to get out of here, Sam. I have to go warn her." He looked around as if trying to find some means of escape, but the guards and the walls gave proof that it would be dangerously difficult.

Sam grabbed John's arm and spun him around. "Don't do anything rash! If you do, that time you spent in the guardhouse will seem like paradise. Just hold your shirt on, John." He gulped and stammered as he looked down at his hand and realized what he had done. Quickly he pulled his hand back. "I'm . . . I'm sorry, Major. I had no right to hold on to a superior officer like that. It's just . . . well, it's just that we are sort of friends and well . . . somebody has to talk some sense into you." As if to make amends, he quickly saluted. "Sir!"

John shook his head from side to side. "After what we have been through together I wouldn't dream of pulling rank." How quickly things could turn topsy-turvy, he thought. When he'd stepped out of the guardhouse he had been so filled with hope; now all he could think about was that all his dreams could quickly crumble into dust. His fingers trembled slightly as he combed them through his hair. He had to stay calm. A foolish action on his part now could snowball into tragedy. "You are the best man for talking sense into me. You're right. I'll use my head."

"Can't you go to Chivington and ask him to send you on a peace mission?" Sam was quick to pose the idea. "Lame Bear's Cheyenne village isn't more than a day's ride from here. So far, at least, the fort has a reasonably peaceful relationship with them. They're said to be friendly."

"Lame Bear? Cheyenne. That might help some, but I need to talk to Skyraven's grandfather and the

Arapaho, not the Cheyenne." He supposed it was selfish of him, but all he could think about was Skyraven. First and foremost her face hovered before his eyes. "If there is any danger, I don't want her to be anywhere near it."

"Sure. Sure. I understand. But listen to me. One of our Indian scouts told me that the Arapaho and Cheyenne are like one tribe. They always travel and hunt together. Maybe you can at least send a message on ahead with a Cheyenne, to warn the Arapaho. It's worth a try. And maybe the Cheyenne chief would offer you a guide to Skyraven's camp, so if there is trouble, the Indians will know you are on a peace mission. It wouldn't hurt to have a friendly Indian with you."

"No, it wouldn't," John replied thoughtfully. He realized that while Sam was thinking about the matter objectively, he had let his emotions rule him. Going to Skyraven's camp might be just the wrong thing to do. Perhaps Chivington wasn't even aware of her people's camp. The Cheyenne camp he already knew about. Going there would be a cautious beginning. He turned to the lieutenant. "Thanks, Sam. It's worth a try."

But though the plan had seemed so simple, it turned out to be filled with complications. While Chivington was away, none of the other officers would ever dare think about approving such a mission, because they knew how the colonel felt about Indians, John supposed. Two days dragged by, seeming more like two months, but as soon as Chivington returned from Denver, John hurried to his headquarters and told him of his plan, cautiously choosing his words.

"You want to do what?" Colonel Chivington looked at John with annoyance.

"I would like your permission to visit Lame Bear's camp," John repeated.

"For the love of God, why?" Chivington's cold eyes surveyed him. *Like a weasel's,* John thought uneasily.

"To seek peace between our people and the Indians."

"Peace? Peace, you say?" The colonel's face was slowly turning a deep red, and for a moment John was certain if he had not been a general's son he would have ended up right back in the brig.

"I heard about what happened. About those three men being attacked. Perhaps a peaceable chief can help by talking sense into them. I've heard such things have happened before. Just give me two weeks to see if they will council with us. That's all I ask."

The sudden silence was unnerving, but at last Chivington asked, "Just what is the reason for such an unexpected request?" Though it appeared he was trying to keep his anger under control, nonetheless he spoke in a low-throated growl. "Is it possible that you are a seeker of glory and want all the honors for yourself? Are you trying to usurp *my* authority. Do you want to prove that you can handle these savages better than *I* can? Trying to get yourself promoted, Major?"

John Hanlen did not answer immediately. What did one say to a colonel who was himself a seeker of glory and an avowed Indian hater? The truth was he did think he could do a better job in managing the peace. He had absolutely no respect for Chivington and his kind, yet he couldn't say that. Chivington was an ass! Such a man could not be expected to understand rational reasoning. Above all, how could he tell the colonel about Skyraven and his love for he? Love was undoubtedly a word not in the colonel's vocabulary.

"No, sir. I am not after a promotion," John said carefully. "It is just that I have been over the area before and know it quite well. I believe that I can be of some help. And I would like to offer my services."

"Your services! As I recall, you lost a whole unit to an ambush and nearly got yourself killed as well. That really doesn't qualify you as an expert on the terrain here."

John's face flushed. He knew that what the colonel was saying was true, but somehow he had to find a way to go alone, first to the Cheyenne village, then to warn Skyraven and her people to seek peace as soon as possible. "What you say is true, sir. But perhaps a man who has learned by his mistakes will not repeat them. Perhaps having experienced what I did will give me insight. Knowing the penalty of violence makes me value peace all the more highly."

For a while the silence between the two officers was unnerving as the colonel looked John Hanlen over from head to toe. *Is he trying to read my mind?* John thought to himself, hoping all the while that the colonel could not see through his facade and remember about the Indian maiden. Well, it really didn't matter what the colonel thought as long as he was able to go on ahead. The cavalry units were being ordered to bring fire and death to the tribes. He had to warn Skyraven in time to save her life.

Chivington circled round and round John, his hands clasped tightly behind his back. The boards of the wooden floor creaked beneath his great girth. He couldn't hide his irritation, and for a moment John lost all hope. But strangely enough, instead of denying his request flat out, he said merely, "I'll have to think about your suggestion."

"Yes, sir. Thank you, sir."

"Don't thank me until after I decide. And *if* I decide to allow you to go on ahead, Major Hanlen, just be sure that *if* you reach the village," he emphasized the "if" again with a scowl, "you save some of those heathen savages for us to deal with later." John wondered what on earth he meant by that but didn't ask. "Leave me now, Major. I have to think about this." He dismissed John without another word.

John hurried from the room, fearful lest his presence do more harm than good. Perhaps he would use Sedgwick's influence again. There really was no time to waste. And then again, if the colonel didn't decide soon well, he would have to go anyway. John knew that he could be sentenced to death for any deviation from orders but already some troops were out scouring the countryside with the order to burn villages and kill troublesome tribes. He couldn't let such a terrible fate ensnarl Skyraven. She had saved his life, her tribesmen were peaceful. If he had to, he would act now and suffer the consequences later. "Oh, Skyraven, Skyraven," he murmured. "You gave me back my life and now I must save yours."

Closing his eyes, he remembered her lovely face, her smile as she talked about her people. She truly thought the spirits had brought them together. Well, perhaps they had. If that was so, then he prayed with all his heart that they would intervene again, that all would go well and that he would see her again soon.

Chapter Twenty-three

Close to the time he had made up his mind to find a way to sneak out of the fort, Major John Hanlen was summoned to Colonel Chivington's headquarters. Lieutenant Colonel Henry Sedgwick was also in the room, and as John stepped inside he smiled a friendly greeting. Sedgwick's presence served as a buffer to the tension Hanlen felt.

"Tell me, Major, do you still want to go on your peace mission?" Chivington asked with forced politeness.

"I do."

"Then I have decided to give you permission. Hopefully I will not regret my decision," he looked toward Sedgwick, "and have to tell your father you are coming home without your scalp, in a pine box!"

"Believe me, you won't, sir!" It was all that John could do to contain his excitement. He grinned at Henry Sedgwick, knowing well that the final decision had somehow been his doing. He didn't care how he had managed it or what he had said. All he knew was that he had been given a chance to save Skyraven and her people, and that was all that really mattered.

John Hanlen set out from Fort Lyon at five

A.M., driving himself onward at a steadfast pace, following Andrews's directions. He felt compelled to reach Lame Bear's Cheyenne camp as quickly as possible, perhaps because he feared that somehow Chivington might change his mind and send someone after him to bring him back to the fort. When no riders appeared on the horizon to follow him, however, he guided Running Antelope along at a more leisurely pace.

A stillness hung over the wide stretch of land he traveled, a quiet that seemed to contradict the threat of violence which threatened the area. The Republican River flowed peacefully like a shimmering ribbon, reflecting the light of the midday sun. Cottonwood and willow trees dotted the landscape. Indian territory, John mused, land they wouldn't want to give up. But could he blame them? How sad, he thought, that there were men among his kind like Chivington, who just couldn't seem to understand. But then hadn't he been just as biased in his opinions until Skyraven had opened up his heart and mind?

John traveled up a path that took him to a valley beside a busy stream, listening to the jingle of his horse's harness and the clomp of Running Antelope's hooves. As he went along, he played over and over again in his mind just what he was going to say to the chief when he met with him. Strange how he'd tried to convince Chivington that he was an expert on Indians. The truth was, except for Skyraven, he'd never even met any Indians before. He was merely going on what she had said, and yet her word was enough. Skyraven valued honesty, perhaps that was the answer. He'd confide in Lame Bear that he cared for an Indian maiden and then let their talk go on from there.

Skyraven. The closer he approached the Indian

encampment, the stronger his memories of her became. From the very first he had been drawn to her, had sensed that she was different from any women he'd met before. There was an innocence about her that brought out his protectiveness. He admired her integrity, her womanliness, her knowledge, her way of speaking frankly without playing at games. There was no coyness, no batting eyelashes, no feigned fainting spells to try to get her own way. She just spoke the truth from her heart. It was to her inner qualities as much as her startling beauty that he responded. He doubted she even knew just how beautiful she was, but he'd be sure to tell her emphatically when at last they met again.

It was now about three in the afternoon. He had made very good time, but then, he knew he would, for there was no faster horse around than Running Antelope. Not only did she know every inch of the terrain with an instinct that was uncanny, but she was in tiptop shape. She had been given the best of care even while John was in the brig. Lieutenant Dunham had taken it upon himself to see to her grooming, her feeding, watering, and exercise.

In some ways he wished that the young lieutenant was with him now. He had wanted to come, but John thought it would be better if he traveled alone for this mission. Indians were not as apt to fall upon a single man as they were two or more, or at least so he had been told. Besides, he hadn't wanted to press his luck in asking for anything else. Henry had just so much influence on the colonel after all.

John had traveled along on the east side of the big Sand Creek being careful not to trespass on the Indian hunting reserve. If those red men had taken off after the three hunters, it was probably because they had been within the hunting reserve and not outside of it as they had claimed. John knew Gustave Flinch, one of the hunters, was known for telling tall tales containing little truth if any. Just why the colonel had chosen to take his word in the dispute was something John could not understand. Everyone knew it was against government policy to interfere with Indian rights. God only knew, much of their land had already been stolen from beneath their feet. It would seem someone would listen to their side of things once in a while, but the authorities never seemed to. It was always assumed that the Indians were in the wrong.

Continuing on, John stopped by the side of the Sandy River only long enough to rest Running Antelope. Finding a shallow place in the stream, he cupped his hands and drank of the cool water. He brushed himself off a bit and splashed water over his head, arms, and upper chest. He had not seen a single soul as he traveled northward looking for the Cheyenne village. Things had been very peaceful and serene, though at times he had the feeling he was being watched. He couldn't be certain. Running Antelope was tired and thirsty; thus, he waited a bit longer than he had planned. Spirals of smoke gave proof that the Indian camp was right over the next hill. The thought that he had at last arrived scrambled his emotions. Anxiety and excitement ran rampant.

"Whoa! What is this?" he muttered in startlement. There were footprints in the wet sand. They had been made quite recently from the looks of things. Apparently they were the prints of only one person, but he couldn't be certain. John's curiosity was piqued and he thought he had better check it out. Suppose, just suppose there really was a band of renegade Indians about the area? He'd have to make certain that he didn't have any unwelcome

207

surprises.

John took Running Antelope's reins in his left hand and led her along the wet, sandy shore following the footprints. All the while his other hand gripped the pistol in his hip holster. In this country he did not want to appear warlike. It was best to have any weapons out of sight unless needed. His rifle and sabre were both in saddle holsters where he could get to them easily enough in case of trouble.

Chapter Twenty-four

Beams of sunlight danced erratically across the stream. Skyraven shaded her eyes with her hand as she looked down the river. She had been at the Cheyenne village for six days now and still Desert Flower's baby had not made its appearance. Everyone was anxiously awaiting the blessed event, but it was just as well that it had not occurred already, Skyraven thought, for the delay gave her more time to prepare and more time to engage in conversation with her young friend. Too soon it would be time to leave. She decided to enjoy her stay until it was time to return. The invitation had been extended by Lean Bear that she stay as long as she wanted. Skyraven had it in mind to come as close as she dared to Fort Lyon. Lean Bear knew an Indian who had been at the fort once or twice, and it was to this scout she thought she would give a message for John Hanlen.

Desert Flower had laughed when she told Skyraven that the braves would stumble over themselves for the honor of accompanying her home. "You have the reputation of being an independent woman. They all know that you are in no hurry to marry even though you are the oldest of the unmarried women at the age of nineteen summers. Still,

209

each of them would like to change your mind."

Desert Flower's husband, Blue Fox, reminded her that Lone Wolf had become annoyed with her refusal of marriage, but that he still admired her and wanted her. Blue Fox had spoken with the renegade brave and told Skyraven that he was nearby. It was her only cause of unease. Hopefully Lone Wolf would not press his proposal again. But if he did, she would again tell him no.

A rustle in the undergrowth behind her caused her to stiffen. She turned around but saw that it was only a small rabbit in search of its dinner. "I saw some wild lettuce over there, Rabbit," she said, pointing to a spot a few feet away. The animal's nose twitched as if in anticipation and she laughed softly, returning to her own foraging.

This afternoon she was by the river with the intent of gathering a bit of the yucca plant, or soapweed as it was sometimes called. The plant gave forth a slippery substance and could help in the birthing. Earlier she had explored the area near a prairie-dog colony and gathered some milkweed. After the baby came, the substance would help increase Desert Flower's milk to feed the little one.

Spotting the coveted spiked green leaves, she knelt and opened her leather pouch, carefully selecting the strongest-looking plant and tugging until the thick woody base was uprooted. "This will do," she said to herself. A whisper of wind answered, lifting several strands of her hair, tickling her neck as she sat back on her heels. For just a moment, a tingling feeling swept over her, a sense of anticipation, but since such feelings had stirred her before she merely shrugged them away.

Rising to her feet, she brushed dirt and leaves from her doeskin dress and tied the pouch around her waist. She had seen some puff balls a little distance away. While she was out gathering herbs, she might as well pluck one or two of them for her collection. Stepping through the thick foliage, peering out from between two cottonwood trees, she paused for just a moment. Her pulse quickened as she caught sight of a brown-and-white horse being led by a tall cavalry officer. Running Antelope! It looked so like her. If it was her horse, then the officer just had to be . . . Did she dare to hope? Her heart skipped a beat at the very thought.

No. It just couldn't be. Her eyes were playing tricks on her. It was but another one of her visions, this one come to cruelly taunt her. When she looked again, there was nothing in sight but the bend in the river and the thick groups of cottonwood trees. Even so, a jolt of fire coursed through her veins. Potent memories invaded her mind. Memory of John's tender kisses flooded over her. Although they had only been parted a short while, it all seemed so long ago. Still, she had lived those moments over and over and had kept them alive.

She looked down the river again, still hoping, but the foliage blocked her view. She came to the conclusion that she had just been imagining things because she wanted to see John Hanlen so very much. She had just turned to retrace her steps back to the village when a hand grabbed hers from behind. Fearing it to be Lone Wolf, she fought like a wounded bear, kicking, biting, and scratching. Her dark hair fell into her eyes, the fringe of her leather dress entangled her legs.

"Please, I come in peace," a voice exclaimed. He turned her around slowly to face him. Skyraven brushed her hair from her eyes and let out a gasp. Her blue-eyed gaze was wide in disbelief as she looked up at the man who held her by the wrist.

"John Hanlen!" Her voice was just a whisper. She

drew her face closer and looked more intently. What cruel trick was this? Surely the spirits were taunting her with visions from her heart. And yet . . . "John Hanlen, is that really you?"

"Skyraven!" Had she just dropped down from the sky, he couldn't have been more stunned. He most certainly had not been expecting to find her here, poised like some heavenly gift. His breath caught in his throat as he stared at her loveliness. "Skyraven?" Their eyes met and held, caressingly. "What are you doing here?" He trembled from the shock of seeing her. With the late-afternoon sun casting light upon her dark hair, she looked like some Indian goddess, even more beautiful than he remembered.

Skyraven's throat suddenly went dry as she stared back at him, mesmerized by his stare. In his face she read her own longing and her heart gave a crazy leap. Somehow she managed to answer him. "I am visiting my grandfather's friend, Lean Bear's Cheyenne camp. Desert Flower's baby is—"

Then there was not time for words as he swept her into his arms, gathering her close. He was content for just a moment to do nothing but hold her, then his mouth closed hungrily over hers in a deep, probing kiss that left her senses whirling. His lips were warm and firm. Skyraven welcomed the sweet bolt of fire that jolted her as her lips parted to receive him. His arms were tight about her waist, as if fearful that she might somehow slip away from him, elude him like a haunting dream. He kissed her hair, her eyes, her lips, and the softness of her neck, murmuring her name over and over. Skyraven clung to him, never wanting to let him go. She belonged in his arms.

When at last he pulled away, she told him about journeying to the Cheyenne camp to aid her friend in the birth of her baby. "That is why you find me here," she finished.

John reached for her hand and brought her down to sit beside him on a large rock by the river's edge. He listened patiently to all she had to say, brushing her long raven tresses back from her face from time to time while she talked. She had the most beautiful face and the most expressive eyes, he thought.

After a while it seemed that the entire world had ceased to exist and there was just the two of them here together, as if there were no warfare between their peoples, only this fire which burned in them whenever they were together. When she had finished her story about her friend Desert Flower and the coming baby, however, the world intruded again as he explained his own reason for being there. He talked about his first meeting with the bigoted colonel, his imprisonment.

"You were held captive?" Skyraven was horrified. She had once heard about the white man's jail. "Because you spoke kindly of my people?"

"Yes. But I don't care about that now, only that you are safe." He told her about the supposed attack on the three hunters.

"Lone Wolf!" she exclaimed. "But Blue Fox said that Lone Wolf told him that the three white men were on our hunting ground. Lone Wolf and his band were trying to frighten them away."

"Hmmm . . ." John murmured in puzzlement, but, in truth, he wasn't really surprised. Hadn't he suspected as much. "It has stirred up the countryside nonetheless." He told her about Chivington and his unreasonable dislike of her people. "And so you see, your people are in great danger. You must either leave or hide yourselves until this all blows over, or put down your weapons and make a great show of peace. If you don't, you may all be killed."

Skyraven looked at him quizzically. "Weapons?

213

We carry no weapons for warfare, only to hunt. Would you take our means of feeding ourselves away?" She fought against her anger, knowing that the words he was saying came from another's mouth. Even so, she frowned. "Hide? We are not cowards. My people are peaceful. It is the soldiers who bring danger, not the Arapaho. Never us." She turned her back, got up from the rock, and started to walk away from him, talking over her shoulder. "Just as I told you back in the cave, we are already peaceful. It is the white man who must make peace."

He forgot for the moment all gentleness as agitation at the situation gripped him. He got up, grabbed her by the shoulders trying to make her understand. "Can't you see that I am trying to protect you? I love you!"

For just a moment Skyraven looked up at him, her eyes touching on his blue coat, the gold buttons decorating it in a fine, straight line — as rigid as the white man's rules. "If you feel as you say, you will tell your white chief to order his hunters to go away. To leave our land."

"I wish I could promise you that I could tell him such a thing and that he would listen, but I cannot."

His eyes looked so sad that Skyraven was deeply touched and her anger melted away. "John Hanlen!" she whispered. With a sob she ran into the circle of his arms, felt herself engulfed within the strong arms of his passion. All her resistance ebbed. Her lips found his, her body arched against him.

"I know that what you say is true. That is why I am here," he breathed, brushing back her hair. "I have talked my chief into allowing me to try to arrange a peace council."

"A peace council?" She looked deep into his eyes.

"Lean Bear is peaceful, yes. So is Left Hand and my grandfather." *Peace,* it was a hopeful word. "I will take you to the village and there you can speak with Lean Bear." She smiled. "I should never doubt you, John Hanlen. You taught me the joys of love. Now we must bring our two peoples together. I could never stand for us to be enemies when being lovers is so much more enjoyable."

With a sigh of relief that they were once more in accord, she cuddled into the circle of his arms. Her lips found his, her body moved against him. He crushed her within his embrace, kissing her hungrily, fiercely. All of his past misery, his days spent away from her in a damp jail cell, the hours of worry, everything else dissolved. All that remained was his love and longing for her.

Groaning, he suddenly tore his lips from hers and whispered, "Let us find someplace where we can be alone without fear of discovery. Our love is too precious to share with any watching eyes."

Skyraven whispered in his ear of such a place. Picking her up in his arms, John carried her to a soft, grassy spot surrounded by trees and caressed by the gentle sound of the rushing water.

"I want you to make love to me. I have needed you so." Skyraven was not shy. She was in love with John and wanted him to know it. She did not want to lose him to any misunderstanding. It had been so long, too long without him.

"I have dreamed of this moment all the time we were apart. I love you, Skyraven. I love you so." John moved his mouth on hers, pressing her lips apart, seeking, exploring the softness.

The ground was soft and damp, but they were aware of nothing but each other. His kisses made her dizzy and sparked a fire deep within her, an ache that wanted to bring him closer and closer

215

until they became one. She could think of nothing but that she was here in John Hanlen's arms. He was finally here and they belonged together. His nearness was a healing thing, washing away all the loneliness she had felt while he was away.

He kissed her neck, her shoulders, then drew down the scooped neck of her doeskin dress to kiss the swell of each breast. Finding the material cumbersome, John undressed her slowly, reverently, feeling the need to woo her all over again. "I want to look at your lovely body."

The soft breeze gently caressed the lovers. A warm intimacy was slowly, sensuously surrounding them as they lay side by side. Desire sweet and warm as honey flowed through them as John kissed her once again. Skyraven felt his hands fumbling anxiously at her garments and lent her own fingers to aid him in his quest, freeing herself of her soft doeskin dress. Then she was lying next to him, naked. The very thought of his touch on her bare skin made her veins flow with liquid fire. It was as if her body had been asleep all these months, but now her breath caught in her throat as she saw the look in his eyes.

"You are even more lovely than I remembered," he breathed, feasting his eyes upon her bare body. He felt himself blessed to have her love, to be experiencing this enactment of his dreams. In the muted sunlight her long legs gleamed like pale bronze, the thrust of her breasts invited his touch.

John's lips closed over Skyraven's in a kiss of urgent sweetness and frantic hunger. His mouth kept hers a willing captive, probing, exploring, making her vibrantly aware of how much she wanted him. When he drew his mouth away, he gathered her breasts in his hands, burying his face in the softness, trailing kisses over the soft mounds until she

216

nearly went mad with a feverish longing to feel the strength of his love deep inside her. Needing desperately to touch him, she pushed the cloth of his jacket and shirt aside and let her fingers explore the expanse of his chest, caressing him as he was caressing her.

"I love you. I love the taste of you, the feel of your body next to mine. Oh, Skyraven, my beautiful Skyraven," John breathed, then he sat up, removed his own clothing, and returned to his place beside her. In turn, Skyraven admired his lean, muscular body as she reached out to caress him, touching his back, the muscles of his thighs, his buttocks, and his flat stomach.

Again and again he kissed her, enveloping her in his embrace. Her arms crept around his neck, her fingers tangling and stroking his thick golden hair as she whispered Indian love words. As his hands moved over her body, she explored his maleness as well. Her mouth opened to the probing of his tongue, then shivered as his mouth went on to other delights.

He trailed hot kisses across her breasts, her stomach, down her slim legs to the core of her being. Arching closer to him, Skyraven delighted in the tantalizingly pleasurable arousing sensations. She gasped with pleasure as John gently parted her legs and gently plunged deep within her.

With a groan of passion, John savored the tightness of her surrounding him. All coherent thought fled his mind. It was as if for a moment their hearts rose up to embrace. Their bodies moved together like a summer storm, gentle at first, then becoming more demanding. He murmured sweet words of love into her ears over and over, sending shivers of delight up and down her spine. She raked her fingers through his hair, rubbed her hands over the flesh of his back, down his muscular thighs and over his buttocks, drawing him deeper and deeper within her. Their senses whirled and soared to the highest height. They both felt that they were joined in spirit as well as flesh. They moaned with pleasure as wave after wave of ecstasy washed over them.

At last when they returned to this earth, they clung together savoring the rapture of their lovemaking. John cradled Skyraven's head on his shoulder and gently rubbed her back while she smiled and repeated over and over again how glad she was that they had found each other once again. They remained contentedly locked in each other's arms for a long time before they dressed. Just before she slipped her dress over her head, she drew his head down between her breasts one more time and he kissed each peak lovingly.

Then as the sun dropped farther down on the horizon, the spell was broken. They realized that they must move quickly. They had many things to do if John Hanlen had only two weeks to bring the plans for a peace council to his superior officers at Fort Lyon, Skyraven knew. She would take him to the village, speak a good word for him, and arrange an audience with Chief Lean Bear. So thinking, they started back to the village together.

Chapter Twenty-five

From a high mesa overlooking the Sand Creek area, Lieutenant Colonel Henry Sedgwick sat astride his horse looking through binoculars, his tall, lean form casting a long shadow on the sandy ground. On the flat land just north of the river he could see many cone-shaped lodges and several trails leading to the river. The Cheyenne Indian camp.

He hated waiting, but he had come all this way and he wasn't about to turn back until his curiosity had been satisfied. He had never liked these hostile savages or this damned flat prairie country they were so proud of. He agreed with Colonel Chivington that the only way to make a lasting peace was to exterminate every one of them, for these rebellious heathens could never be subdued for long.

Henry Sedgwick smoked cigarette after cigarette while he waited. It seemed like hours. Down the river he could see the figures of a soldier and an Indian girl walking along holding hands. Finally the two of them had emerged from the thicket, and Sedgwick recognized John Hanlen. He was even helping her up onto his horse. Now she was riding off and he was left without a horse to carry him back to the fort. He certainly wasn't going to let himself be seen until he knew what this was all about.

The Indian girl rode a little ways, then turned back. Bending down, she embraced Hanlen, then rode away again, glancing back from time to time. "So, what I heard is true," Sedgwick mumbled to himself. "He does have a squaw. Randolph Hanlen's son is an Indian lover. That old windbag would probably have apoplexy if he knew his Johnny boy was cavorting with a savage." He couldn't keep from smiling. Someday when it was to his advantage he just might tell the general.

Sedgwick had followed John Hanlen all this way along the trail he had chosen, carefully avoiding the chance of being discovered. He'd masquarade as a loyal friend for a while longer. He had a scheme up his sleeve and he didn't want anyone to know of it just yet. *Well, we shall see what else you are planning, my friend,* he thought, his mouth twisting in a smirk. *For I doubt that it is peace that you are seeking.* Neither had Chivington thought so, that was why he had so easily agreed to Sedgwick's plan. Give John Hanlen all the freedom that could be allowed, to do as he wished, Chivington had told him. But he would be followed. Give a man enough rope and he would hang himself, or so it was said.

But what are your motives, Hanlen? For the life of him, Sedgwick couldn't fathom the major's intent. Could it just be the girl and nothing more sinister? He had seen the two lovers go into the thicket together, but he couldn't tell what they were doing because of all the foliage. They had been in there a long time before coming out. *And I don't think you were just picking berries.* Some of the men said that the Indian squaws were a hot-blooded lot. No doubt he was savoring her body.

A little bedsport, eh, Hanlen? he concluded. Strange that he thought that John had to relieve his desires on an Indian. Being the son of a general, a handsome one to boot, had given the young man every advantage possible. But maybe the Indian girl was worth it. Sedgwick whistled beneath his breath with a chuckle and muttered, "Well, have your fun while you can. It just might be that before this whole matter is through, fornicating will be the last thing on your mind."

Sedgwick was uncomfortable in the saddle, but still he waited, watching Major Hanlen. The major was acting as if he had all the time in the world. Now he was sitting on a rock as if he were waiting, but for what or for whom? At last he thought he saw some movement on down the trail toward the Indian village. Picking up the binoculars again, he held them to his eyes. He could see a small band of braves approaching. Three of them and the woman proceeded in the young major's direction. The rest of them turned back.

What on earth had come over Major John Hanlen? The next thing, he would be leaving the cavalry to become a squaw man! Henry's cold blue eyes continued looking at the scene before him. My God! The three warriors were shaking hands with John. Now he was getting upon the horse with the woman. They were all riding toward the village like they were long-lost, good friends.

How big was the village? How many braves? Sedgwick tried to calculate. If Chivington decided to strike, it would have to be determined that the soldiers could win. A defeat could be disastrous. Victory was what was needed. He had to get away from here and report his findings. No doubt Chivington would find them very interesting. Turning his horse around, he went down the other side

221

of the butte and urged his horse into a fast gallop.

All the way back to the fort he was thinking what a wonderful hero's welcome he would get after he had led a cavalry to that village and killed those damn hostiles. He'd talk Chivington into letting him take command. It would be his reward. Yes, sir, he thought, he was going to use the relationship between the major and that Indian girl to further his own goals. Well, at least the young Major Hanlen had led him to the village he was looking for and given him a chance to ingratiate himself with Colonel Chivington and with the restless settlers near the fort.

Sedgwick's head was filled with dreams of glory as he galloped onward. He kicked the horse in the side to urge it to go even faster. He could see himself riding through Denver City in a parade in his honor. Every citizen for miles would come to see him, would laud him as the great Indian fighter. There would be marching music, flags flying, and much cheering. He might even receive the distinguished service medal for bravery.

Colonel Chivington and the governor of Colorado, John Evans, had not shared with the soldiers the fact that killing Indians was against government policy. The soldiers were there to protect the white population but they must abide by the treaties that had been made and seek peace not war. Both Evans and Chivington thought those policy-makers in Washington, D.C., had no idea of how hard life was out here in the West. What the territory needed was statehood, with Evans as senator and Chivington as state representative. They understood western problems. The government had their hands full with a war of their own right now. As soon as the War Between the States was over, both John Evans and Colonel Chivington wanted to see the

Union Pacific Railroad go right through the Arapaho and Cheyenne hunting reserve. There really wasn't anyplace else for it to go if they wanted it to come to Denver City.

As he neared the fort, he thought that he must write to Major Hanlen's father just as soon as he could find the time. It would break the old man's heart to finally realize that his son would never become a real soldier. Too bad that he was he one to have to tell him, but then, someone had to do the dirty work. Perhaps then old Randolph would take him under his wing again. His son wasn't a good soldier, but Henry certainly was, and he was determined to prove it beyond a doubt and reap the benefits.

The stone structures with their flat sod-covered roofs looked mighty inviting as he passed through the gates of the fort. He had run the horse so fast that the poor thing was ready to drop from exhaustion. Its coat was wet with sweat and its mouth lathered with foam for lack of water.

"Here, do what you can with him, Corporal." He dismounted and threw the reins toward a blue-clad soldier standing nearby.

Lieutenant Colonel Henry Sedgwick hurried toward the colonel's headquarters. This bit of information about Hanlen rolling around with a squaw was just too good to keep to himself. And he'd have a few other things to talk about as well. Those wild brutes would soon pay for causing so much trouble to their betters.

A commotion up on the lookout tower distracted him before he could walk through the door. "Lieutenant Colonel Sedgwick, sir, a band of soldiers is approaching," a young soldier said when he inquired. "They have an Indian with them."

"Oh they do, do they?" Climbing up the ladder of

the tower, he took a look for himself. The Indian warrior was dressed only in leggings, a breechcloth, and moccasins. His glistening braids were each tied with strips of otter fur and feathers. Although his hands were tied behind his back, he held his head high and proud. Arrogant bastard, Sedgwick thought disdainfully. He had heard that there were rules of conduct which the warriors followed. They were known for their bravery and courage even in the face of great danger. Well, he'd soon have this one down on his knees, begging for mercy.

"Our men captured him during a raid to steal horses at the Dennison place near Beaver Creek," the officer leading the small party of soldiers said. "Some of the Cheyenne dog soldiers were with him, but we don't think he is Cheyenne. We questioned him, but he didn't seem to understand and none of us can understand that dialect he is speaking."

"Good work, Lieutenant." *Maybe we can get John Hanlen to talk with him*, he thought sarcastically. He seemed to like Indians—or maybe only the females.

"We followed his companions but lost track of them. We did come upon their abandoned lodges, though, and burned down the whole damned mess."

By now, the white men had taken over the North Platte country. The Cheyenne claimed only the country from the headwaters of the Republican River and Smoky Hill River southward to the Arkansas. They had vowed never to give it up.

"So you don't think he's a Cheyenne, huh, soldier?"

"So far the Arapaho and the southern Cheyenne have remained peaceful in the midst of the hostilities," the commanding soldier said, "but if the stealing and disruption goes on much longer, they are bound to be drawn into it, too." The lieutenant shook his head as if trying to think what could be done about the whole situation.

Another Indian lover, Sedgwick thought. Too many bleeding hearts. "If the Arapaho and Cheyenne make war on us, then they'll have to pay the price, won't they, soldier?"

"I guess so, sir."

"That's why we're here, aren't we? To rid the area of these red devils?" And surely a devil is what this well-muscled brave seemed to be. "Look at him staring back at me. What I wouldn't give to know what he was thinking."

Though he was tempted to let the white man know that he understood every word, the Indian didn't speak their language. It would be to his benefit to play ignorant. But if these white men thought the Arapaho and Cheyenne would ever abandon the best buffalo hunting reserve in the entire plains area, they were loco. Somehow he'd stop them. It was a vow Lone Wolf made as he was marched roughly along.

Chapter Twenty-six

Clouds floated gently across the blue sky like huge puffs of smoke. Chirping birds sang cheerful melodies as they flew from tree to tree. The air smelled of pine and flowers. No day had ever seemed so perfect. Running Antelope moved with agile grace, carrying Skyraven and the man she loved back to the Indian village. Riding behind John Hanlen, Skyraven took comfort from his nearness, yet the brush of his legs against hers was very stirring, especially after the moment of love they had shared.

John was equally aware of her as they rode. Their bodies touched from shoulder to knee, her firm breasts crushed against his back, her thighs hugging him with a familiarity that threatened to make it impossible for him to control his desires. He glanced at the three Indian braves out of the corner of his eyes, wondering what their reaction would be if they knew he and Skyraven had just made love. What were their customs about matters like that? Until he knew for certain, he thought it best to maintain the strictest sense of propriety, but God that was going to be difficult when every one of his senses cried out to her, when he wanted to lean into her embrace, touch her, give vent to his affections. Keeping a firm hand on the reins, he tried to think of other things.

"So you are Skyraven's white soldier," one of the braves said, a bronze-colored giant with muscles that rippled as he guided his horse alongside Running Antelope. His eyes were piercing black, boring into John Hanlen.

John smiled in an attempt to be friendly. "My name is Major John Hanlen . . . and you are called?"

The brave's lips were drawn into a tight line. "Blue Fox! I am Chief Lean Bear's eldest son."

"I am pleased to meet you." Never having met any Indian braves before, John reacted spontaneously, holding out his hand, feeling like a fool the moment he initiated the gesture. What was he thinking of? This man wouldn't understand that custom of the white man. He was surprised therefore when Blue Fox grasped his hand in return, squeezing so tightly that it caused a flash of pain. John refused to flinch. Looking the brave directly in the eye, he clutched with equal pressure. Blue Fox's eyes shone with a measure of respect.

"Blue Fox is my friend Desert Flower's husband," Skyraven interceded, her arms tightening around John's waist with a feeling of pride, knowing that Blue Fox's first appraisal had judged him worthy. "And about to become a new father."

Puffing out his chest with pride, Blue Fox announced, "It will be a son."

"Or perhaps a daughter," Skyraven amended. "If my calculations are true, we will know now very soon." Playfully Skyraven nudged Running Antelope on ahead of the other three riders. Unprepared for the horse's sudden jolt, John grabbed tightly to the reins.

"Your friend Blue Fox is a grim man," he confided, looking over his shoulder as the Indian sought to catch up with them.

"He and Lone Wolf are friends and, by marriage, cousins. While you were gone, Lone Wolf made preparations to ask for me. He even gathered together the necessary horses."

"I see!" John tried hard to fight his jealousy, but it surged through him nevertheless. He thought how it might be timely that he think about gathering up the necessary mares and stallions to present to Skyraven's grandfather. "And . . . ?" he asked.

Skyraven leaned forward, tickling his ears with her breath as she answered. "I refused him, for I will have no one but you, as you must well know after our love at the river."

Her answer renewed John's feelings of just what a beautiful day it was. It was as if Running Antelope floated on air, for certainly his heart had wings. Was that why they managed to stay at least a horse's length in front of the others? As they rode along, he took in the view of the countryside wondering if the leaves of the trees always looked so green, if the sky was always tinted so deeply blue.

When they reached the Indian encampment, John saw before him what looked to be a city of tall, pointed tents nestled in among a grove of trees. As they rode closer, he could see the village come alive. Fires flamed as the nightly dinner was prepared, the women busying themselves at their work, cooking or sitting with large pieces of leather in their laps. It appeared they were doing some kind of embroidery, not too different from the women at the fort. He could see two strong braves carrying a large haunch of deer which had been spitted toward the largest fire. It was much like any other group of people gathered together. Why then was it always said that the Indians were so different? Children played, their

228

laughter bubbling in the air. Was there anything as uplifting as the sound of high-pitched giggles of happiness. No. John had always loved children. Now, as they circled about the small returning party, he turned his attention to them.

"They are fascinated by your sword, the way it glitters in the fading sunlight," Skyraven said. "And by the gold buttons on your jacket. The children have always liked buttons. And by your hat."

Sliding from his horse, John dismounted, then helped Skyraven down. Taking his hat from the saddle horn, he knelt and placed it on the head of one young boy child. A beaming smile was his reward, though when the youngster ran off, John felt a moment of anxiety "I'll be taken to task if I come back without it," he said to Skyraven.

"He'll return it," she promised. "He has gone to show his brother, that is all." Skyraven led him to the center of the camp and paused before the largest and most ornate of the tepees. "Lean Bear's lodge," she said. Hearing her voice, a tall, graying, big-boned Indian emerged from within. The pride with which he held himself, his stance, the deference the others showed him, proclaimed him chief even had John Hanlen not known who he was. He reminded John more of an eagle than a bear.

"So, who have you here, Skyraven?" he asked, his deep, commanding voice silencing the children's laughter and the women's chattering.

"My soldier. John Hanlen."

The chief's assessing eyes were not unfriendly, just stern. "I know many soldiers from the fort." He pointed to a medal that he wore hanging around his neck. "This was given to me last year by the Great White Father, Lincoln. Have you met him, John Hanlen?"

"No, sir, I have not."

229

The chief grinned. "Then I have scored a coup," he said.

"A coup?"

"A victory, Skyraven's white man," Blue Fox said with a smile, coming up behind him. "Skyraven scored a coup when she laid the Ute warrior low with a tree limb to save you." He laid his hand on Skyraven's shoulder with friendly familiarity. "Most women would have fled, but not Skyraven. You have found yourself a good woman."

"I know." John's look of gratitude was from the heart. "I guess you could say that *I* scored a coup when I was fortunate enough to be found by her. Your Great Spirit smiled on me."

A group was forming around John Hanlen, Skyraven, the Indian chief, and his son. A joyful greeting rent the air as a plump, obviously pregnant young Indian woman came forward to take her place at Skyraven's side.

"I hope that you do not mind that I sent Blue Fox and a party of braves in search of you, Skyraven. When you did not return promptly, I was afraid you had lost your way." Desert Flower looked at the soldier in their midst and back at Skyraven again, then smiled a wry smile, as if sensing full well why Skyraven had not returned promptly. The white soldier standing next to her had to be the reason.

"We sort of found one another, the braves and me," Skyraven laughed. "I had already been back here, but I simply didn't have the heart to wake you. You were sleeping so soundly. I was searching for the yucca plant and milkweed when John Hanlen made himself known." Her eyes sparkled as she looked at him, giving full vent to her feelings. "I rode back to bring Blue Fox, Spotted Pony, and Night Hawk with me—and now here we all are."

She flung her arms open wide to indicate that they had returned to the fold.

"Then this white man with you is the John Hanlen we have talked about?"

Skyraven flushed, remembering the intimate details she had discussed with her friend. "Yes, my dear, dear friend. This is Major John Hanlen of the United States Cavalry."

Desert Flower studied the man standing in front of her for just a moment before she spoke. "It is unusual to see a blue coat such as you are wearing here in our village. As you know, we are sometimes not too fond of the horse soldiers. However, since you are a friend and a guest of our dear Skyraven, you are most welcome."

"I thank you all for that welcome," John replied. He had a sudden idea. "Since the blue coat makes you uneasy, let me remove it and prove once and for all that there should be no barriers to friendship." Undoing his gold buttons, he stripped off his jacket, shirt, and yellow neckerchief. Seeing that the braves were bare-chested, he also removed the top half of his underwear and his suspenders and likewise bared himself to the waist. A twittering followed his actions as the women of the camp came closer to get a better look at him, their eyes focused on his chest hair. Indian men had no such growth. The braves, however, appraised his shoulders, neck, and arms, sizing him up as men do other men. One young brave was even so bold as to feel the muscles of his arm.

"Strong man," Blue Fox said, grunting with approval. "But how well can you fight, white man?" He crouched to a challenging position. "Shall we see?"

"All right!" Though this was far from the greeting he had envisioned, John sensed he could not back

231

down, not now. The Indians admired two things, Skyraven had told him—strength and wisdom. This was then to be his first test. Controlling his breathing, ignoring the pounding of his heart, John hunkered down.

The large brave shouted what sounded like a war cry. His long hair flew wildly about him as he moved forward, circling John like a wolf about to snare his quarry. Then he pounced. Locked together in combat, the two men rolled upon the ground. Freeing himself from the Indian brave's grip, John pushed himself to a partially standing position, changing his weight from foot to foot as he awaited the Indian's next move. He'd wrestled before—it was something the soldiers sometimes did to wile away the time—but never with an opponent like this one. Still, he had only such combat to aid him now.

Desert Fox lunged again, moving with the swiftness of a sprung arrow. He gripped John by the wrists trying to pull him down. "The winner is he who touches his opponent's arm to the ground and holds it there," he said. With that instruction, he tugged and pushed, trying to knock John off balance. John retaliated. Catching the brave by the foot, he sent him sprawling to the ground.

"I hope that is allowed," he said. That the move wasn't contested told him that it must be. Seemingly anything within reason was allowable.

"You are quick, like the fox I am named for, but my strength is greater," Blue Fox warned, bounding back to his feet with the agility of a cat. He lunged at John again, but the major, the thinner of the two, danced out of the way. Crouching down, he waited for the brave to come closer, for then he would show that he had other surprises.

The wrestling match moved like a dance. Blue Fox would pounce, John would sidestep him again

232

and again, remaining alert. It at least kept him from being pinned to the ground, yet John knew he couldn't win the combat this way. To win he had to keep the Indian down upon the ground and he wasn't going to be able to do that. What's more, he was tiring.

A howl of excitement rose from the onlookers. John felt Skyraven's eyes upon him and felt the depth of his love strengthen his resolve. He didn't want her to think him weak. He had to prove himself worthy of her.

"Come on, Blue Coat! Do not fear to let me touch you?" Blue Fox taunted.

The Indian's confidence made him careless. He moved closer to John, making himself an obvious target. In that moment, John bounded forward, pinning the brave to the ground with his weight, holding his arm. It was like wrestling with a lion. The brave bucked and thrashed, trying to get up. John Hanlen steeled himself to the brave's great strength. Just when he was certain the Indian was going to pull free, Lean Bear stepped forward, declaring John Hanlen the winner. Slowly both fighters struggled free of each other.

John extended his hand, helping Blue Fox to his feet. "You gave me quite a fight."

"I fought like a woman, else *I* would have won," the brave said sullenly. Nevertheless he was a good sport about the match. "We will fight again, you and I, yes? You must give me a chance to prove myself the best warrior."

That being decided, Lean Bear led John and Skyraven to the area where the aroma of cooking food tantalized the palate. John's stomach rumbled with hunger, and he realized that he was famished. "You will stay with us, John Hanlen?" Lean Bear offered an invitation which John readily accepted. It

233

would give him time to make the chief's acquaintance, for there was still the matter of the peace discussions.

"To eat supper?" he asked. "Yes, thank you."

"For as long as you would like," Lean Bear answered. "Skyraven is like one who shares my same blood. My son's wife and she were raised in the same camp. You are the man she has chosen. I would like time to get to know you."

The Indian women were carrying wooden bowls to the men who had taken positions around the fire, whom John concluded were either their husbands or relatives. Skyraven likewise brought a steaming portion to him. For just a moment their eyes touched, then she smiled. "You will stay?" she asked.

"Yes, I will stay. The colonel gave me two weeks." At that moment, looking into her eyes, he knew the time was going to move too fast. It was going to be the two shortest weeks of his life.

Chapter Twenty-seven

The night was ebony-black, dotted with stars. The mist-ringed moon shone through the branches with a silvery haze. A lover's night. John sat across the fire from Skyraven, watching as the flames danced up toward the sky, wishing he could pick her up in his arms and carry her into one of the cone-shaped tents and make love to her again. God, how he wanted to. Each time their eyes met, he knew that she felt the same. An impossible dream. The Indians kept the strictest propriety with their unmarried women and were fiercely possessive of their wives. The stories of Indians bartering their woman was pure tomfoolery, one more story circulated to slander them and somehow make them less than fully human.

Sleeping arrangements were not what John might have wanted, though he appreciated the chief's hospitality. John was to share a tepee with some of the unmarried braves. Skyraven was sharing Desert Flower's tepee. She had told him that she would be by her friend's side morning and night as the time for the baby's birth crept nearer. She enjoyed the responsibility and the honor granted to her in fulfilling such a mission. With such close scrutiny, lovemaking tonight was out of the question, but

John was determined to find a way. Tomorrow perhaps? The memory of their tryst by the stream would give him treasured dreams that would have to last until then.

After dinner the braves talked among themselves while their women stayed together. But like Skyraven, however, here and there a woman sat beside or behind her man. Desert Flower leaned against her husband, displaying her respect and affection. Skyraven had spoken with admiration about Blue Fox. He was a good husband and loved his wife very much, showing deference to her condition and more than a modern amount of devotion. Some of the things he did for her now would have been considered woman's work at any other time, but even so, he took over her tasks without complaint. Carrying water and collecting firewood was too hard for her now that her belly was big with child, he had said. Blue Fox had given up his bed to Skyraven so that she would be nearby at all times, but he came to his wife's tepee every day to help in any way that he could. A man couldn't be more attentive than he.

Lean Bear dominated the attention of the braves now. He had promised John that he would talk with him at the same time tomorrow night in his tepee about the subject of the white man's peace. John had also been introduced to Skyraven's grandfather, who had made the same promise of a powwow. "You want to speak to me of horses?" he had said. Meeting him had made John understandably nervous, yet the medicine man had been more than amiable, as if he had resigned himself to the situation. Still, every once in a while John could feel his eyes touching upon him and wondered what he was pondering.

John smiled, thinking to himself that this wasn't

really much different from sitting in the parlor hoping that your chaperone would leave you alone with the woman you adored. For just a moment he viewed Buffalo's Brother much like any other stern grandfather. He made it obvious how much he loved his granddaughter and how he wanted what was best for her future. John vowed that he would prove to him that their love could buffer any problems.

Like a warm blanket, the cordiality and friendliness of the Indians enveloped John as the night progressed. It was as Skyraven whispered in his ear, he was earning their good will. She said further that Blue Fox had talked with the other warriors and told them that if Skyraven trusted this white man named John Hanlen, then so should they. She had loaned him her horse, her robes, and other belongings.

"Would Skyraven trust anyone who would harm her people?" Blue Fox had asked.

The braves murmured that she had been led by the spirits to save the white soldier. In so doing, she had kept a war party of Ute away from her own village. Such bravery was not common among women. John found out quickly that one of the Indians' favorite pastimes was telling stories, and now recounts of Skyraven's bravery seemed to form one of the tales, embellished each time it was told so that her valor and daring steadily increased.

"She fought three braves single-handedly and took the white man away, out from beneath the very noses of those Utes," Blue Fox was saying now.

Other stories abounded. John listened as several of the braves told their tales, his eyes caressing Skyraven. She sat with a young child upon her knee, crooning in its ear, and he couldn't help thinking about how it would be when she was the mother of

237

his children.

"Tell us a story," the wide-eyed boy said. "About the search for the buffalo."

"You want to hear that one again?" she asked the boy, then explained to John, "It is an old Blackfoot tale. They, like the Cheyenne and Arapaho are plains people."

Enthusiastically he nodded. Skyraven moved closer to John as the other children, just as anxious to hear the story, gathered round, sitting at her feet as she began to speak.

"In the old days," she began, "vast herds of buffalo, often as thick as a swarm of bees, roamed the grasslands. The lives of our ancestors revolved around the movements of those herds just as ours do now, for those generous animals provide the Indians with life's necessities. Which are. . . ?"

"The meat," one boy said, his eyes bright, "to be dried and stored for the long winter months when hunting is difficult."

"The skins, for clothing, bedding, tepee covers, bags, and riding tackle," added a little girl.

"Tools are made from the bones, ropes from the hair, thread and bowstrings from the sinews, and cups and spoons from the horns. Not one hair is wasted," said the boy.

John listened attentively. If that was true, then it was no wonder the Indians were so angry at those three hunters. If only Chivington could hear this story, perhaps he would understand.

"But there came a time when there were no buffalo. Day after day hunters scoured the plains, but every evening they returned empty-handed. The people grew pale and thin, and the children cried with hunger. In despair, their chief decided to enlist the aid of Napi, the Old Man of the Dawn, who set the world in order and caused things to be the

238

way they are now."

As she told the story, Skyraven used a different pitch of voice for the characters, much to the children's delight. It was a charming story, yet sad, too, for John remembered her having told them that her tribe had moved because there had not been enough buffalo nearby to last them through the winter.

"And Napi listened sympathetically to the chief's pleas for help and told him to go beyond the Sweet Grass Hills to the lodge of the shaman, Crow Arrow, who he suspected had stolen the buffalo. Napi told the chief that he would take it upon himself to search out this Indian, and he took with him the chief's son, Little Dog, who told his father that when he became a man and went into the mountains, the spirits had granted him powers. What were they, Lame Beaver?"

"Strength and courage. And . . . and he could turn himself into a swallow or a spider or a dog."

"That's right." Skyraven smiled. Putting her hand behind the log they were sitting on, she touched John's hand, her fingers entwining with his. "Napi turned himself into a horsefly and Little Dog into a swallow, and together they flew over the hills in search of the evil Crow Arrow."

Taking a deep breath, John relaxed, relishing the touch of Skyraven's hand. John enjoyed the story, yet it troubled him, too. Strange, but as she told the story, Chivington's face flashed before his eyes, taking the place of the dastardly shaman who was responsible for the misery of the chief's people.

"Not wishing their approach to be seen, Napi became a pine tree and Little Dog a spider. They crept close enough to hear the murmur of voices and to smell the smoke from the campfire but saw no sign of the buffalo. Only three people were present: Crow Arrow, his wife, and their little daughter. Napi bent his head to catch the spider's tiny voice. "I am certain that the buffalo are hidden somewhere nearby," he said. "After much discussion, they came upon a plan. Napi would change himself into a stick of ashwood and Little Dog into a small brown puppy whose actions attracted the attention of Crow Arrow's little daughter. The puppy became her best friend, and she confided a secret. She knew where there were many, many animals, much bigger, she said, than the puppy."

It was a charming tale which made use of Skyraven's talent for mimicry. The child led the puppy, the stick in his mouth, to where the buffalo were hidden. The dog tumbled down into the cavern where thousands of brown beasts stood pawing the earth.

"Napi could hear them snorting and stamping their feet and ignored the child's pleas to climb back up the mountain. Together, he and Little Dog carefully rounded up the buffalo, Napi in human form and the chief's son in the form of a huge dog. Shouting and barking, they drove the buffalo up the slope and out through the hole in the rock."

Crow Arrow was vindictive, determined to wreak vengeance, just like Chivington, John thought as he listened to Skyraven's description. Thankfully, however, Napi and Little Dog changed themselves back into the stick and the puppy, leaped upon the largest buffalo's back, and made it past the furious shaman. Just like Chivington, again, Crow Arrow did not give up but changed himself into a gray bird, hovering over the buffalo in an attempt to herd them back to his hiding place. To counteract the shaman, Napi changed himself into a beaver and lay down in the grass as if dead.

"The bird, thinking this an easy meal, swooped down upon him. Quick as lightning, Napi changed

MORE PASSION AND ADVENTURE AWAIT... YOUR TRIP TO A BIG ADVENTUROUS WORLD BEGINS WHEN YOU ACCEPT YOUR FIRST 4 NOVELS ABSOLUTELY *FREE* (AN $18.00 VALUE)

Accept your Free gift and start to experience more of the passion and adventure you like in a historical romance novel. Each Zebra novel is filled with proud men, spirited women and tempestuous love that you'll remember long after you turn the last page.

Zebra Historical Romances are the finest novels of their kind. They are written by authors who really know how to weave tales of romance and adventure in the historical settings you love. You'll feel like you've actually gone back in time with the thrilling stories that each Zebra novel offers.

GET YOUR FREE GIFT WITH THE START OF YOUR HOME SUBSCRIPTION

Our readers tell us that these books sell out very fast in book stores and often they miss the newest titles. So Zebra has made arrangements for you to receive the four newest novels published each month.

You'll be guaranteed that you'll never miss a title, and home delivery is so convenient. And to show you just how easy it is to get Zebra Historical Romances, we'll send you your first 4 books absolutely FREE! Our gift to you just for trying our home subscription service.

BIG SAVINGS AND FREE HOME DELIVERY

Each month, you'll receive the four newest titles as soon as they are published. You'll probably receive them even before the bookstores do. What's more, you may preview these exciting novels free for 10 days. If you like them as much as we think you will, just pay the low preferred subscriber's price of just $3.75 each. *You'll save $3.00 each month off the publisher's price.* AND, your savings are even greater because there are never any shipping, handling or other hidden charges—FREE Home Delivery. Of course you can return any shipment within 10 days for full credit, no questions asked. There is no minimum number of books you must buy.

back into a man and seized Crow Arrow's legs in a powerful grasp. Ignoring his squawks and thrashing wings, he carried him back to the camp and tied him in the smoke-hole of the chief's tepee, where by evening he was a sorry sight. The smoke from the fire had turned his gray plumage jet-black. Napi looked up at the dejected bundle of sooty feathers and said, 'You see where your wickedness and greed have brought you?' Crow Arrow begged to be set free, promising never to steal the buffalo again."

If only the white men would make such a promise, John thought sadly. But then if it wasn't buffalo they wanted on Indian land, it was gold, and if it wasn't gold, it was access to the railroad.

"Napi cut the ropes that bound Crow Arrow," Skyraven continued. "But ever since that time, the crow's feathers have always been black." The story completed, Skyraven motioned for the children to follow her. "Now, it is time for bed." Once again the scene struck John in it similarity to his people — young ones listening to a bedtime story, then hustled off to bed. Standing up, he followed Skyraven and her group, hoping to have at least a moment alone with her. As if Napi was granting his wish, he waited until all of the children had gone into their tepees, then stood in the shadows of a cottonwood, looking down into her face.

"You are talented at storytelling."

"My grandfather used to tell me many such stories when I was a child. I am merely repeating them." She turned to him and closed her eyes, knowing that he wanted to kiss her. His chin just touched the top of her head as he gathered her into an embrace. He felt the soft contours of her body against him and melted into the warmth of her. He felt her breath ruffle his hair, felt the sensation continue down the whole length of his spine.

241

"Skyraven, that story . . . it made me all too aware of why I am here. I have to warn the chiefs and your grandfather about the hostilities brewing. Perhaps they can find out which Indian braves attacked those hunters and bring them forward to tell their side of the story."

"Shh . . ." She lifted her head, her face in shadow. "Let us not talk about such things now. We have so little time before I must return to the fire. I am just so glad that you are here at last, with me."

He bent his head and felt her mouth brush lightly against his cheek. The world narrowed down to the touch of her lips, the fragrant smell of her skin. He was lost. His lips found hers, and in that moment he knew she held his heart captive. His fingers toucher her arm and moved to wrap her tiny waist. For the moment at least Chivington was forgotten. But for how long John Hanlen could only wonder. Then the passion of their kiss chased even that thought from his mind.

gove nearly that story, I would like all and
more of it why I am here. I have to warn the chief
and to inquire about the time there is between
Perhaps there is little more—more—

Chapter Twenty-eight

The air was fresh, as it can only be early in the
morning. Following their routine, Skyraven and
Desert Flower had just returned from their daily
walk. Skyraven had explained the baby grew strong
at sunrise and would be better formed; thus they
walked along with the unborn child's welfare in
mind.

Dogs were gnawing at bones and growling, children were playfully chasing one another, they could
hear the whooping and hollering of some of the
braves as they raced their ponies just outside the
campgrounds. Some of the men and women they
met on their way back to the tepee stopped to talk
with them for a minute or two before continuing on
their way to do their early-morning chores. Skyraven spotted John Hanlen among a group of young
braves saddling their horses. The young men had
promised to take him on a small game hunt to
observe them use their bows and arrows.

"I like your John Hanlen. He is not like most
white men," Desert Flower confided. "There is a
gentleness in his eyes when he looks upon you. I
think in some ways he is like my Blue Fox."

"I think from the first moment our eyes met, our
souls cried out for each other. But it took us some

time to listen to our hearts. I was afraid because of my mother . . ."

"But each man must be judged for . . ." Desert Flower paused in midsentence, putting a hand to her stomach.

Today, during their walk, Desert Flower had suffered a severe pain or two, but they had not lasted long. Even so, the cramping feelings were warnings. Both she and Skyraven knew it was just about time to convert the tepee into a birthing lodge. During the weeks before the birth, the mother-to-be had observed the taboos, just as Skyraven had instructed her to do. She did not look at any fearsome animal or other object which might mark her baby. She tried to remain in a happy frame of mind so that her baby would be happy all through its lifetime.

Now the child was making it known that it wanted to make its appearance. "My little one is anxious to come into this world," Desert Flower sighed in anticipation. "I can feel more movement than usual." She placed both hands on her well-rounded belly and smiled. "I hope, Skyraven, that when you have a child, our young ones will be good companions and form a bond of lifelong friendship as we have done."

"I am sure that they will. They will race their ponies and play games just as we did, and dream of days to come."

"But if you marry your John Hanlen, he might take you back with him to his home in Missouri." Though she tried to hide her feelings, it was obvious that Desert Flower found this most distressing.

"I do not want to leave my people. I am hoping after John Hanlen has spent time among us that perhaps he might want to live with us at my camp." *Was that a foolish dream?* she wondered.

"But if he does not want to live as an Indian—if

244

he can not—what will you do then. I would miss you terribly were you to move so far away."

"Then I will send for you and the baby and you can visit me there. We will never be parted for long, Desert Flower. And if Blue Fox cannot leave the buffalo hunting long enough, then I can come to you." Suddenly Desert Flower almost doubled over as a series of pains came upon her. "The pains!" They were coming in intervals closer together, a sure sign that the baby was soon going to be born. "Come now, we must get you inside and prepare for the young one's birth."

Skyraven helped the young expectant mother into the tepee and laid her upon the bed of tree boughs and furs. "I'll be back in just a minute. I must tell Blue Fox that he is soon to see the face of the young one you both have waited for so long." It was a custom for the father to be the first man told; next would be the chief.

Skyraven left to fetch Desert Flower's husband, but returned quickly, bringing two older women to assist in the birth, relatives of Blue Fox who were mothers themselves of several children. "We must bring in some hay and the birthing pole," the oldest and stoutest of the women, called Running Brook, said. "Eyes of Night and Skyraven, you both stay here with Desert Flower. I can bring the hay and the pole." The woman hurried away determined that she would be the one to oversee the birthing. A battle of dominance appeared to be brewing, but Skyraven took it in her stride.

"So, my wife, you are soon to birth a little chief." Blue Fox came in and held his wife tenderly in his arms, whispering into her ear from time to time. The look of pride on his face was mingled with compassion, knowing that this greatest of treasures would be brought forth from great pain. It was the one time when a woman proved herself to be just as courageous as a warrior.

Running Brook returned with the hay in a small wagon and a long pole with two leather thongs attached. It was set into a sturdy log which had been cut in half to make it free standing. Clucking her tongue, she tried to shoo Desert Fox's husband out. "Go now, Blue Fox, this is a time for women."

"But . . ." Blue Fox was reluctant. He looked over in Skyraven's direction as if to question if he should leave. He was very aware of her friendship with his wife and trusted her judgment.

"We three will take good care of your wife." Running Brook was impatient. "Men only get in the way. This is a thing only women understand. Go."

Skyraven answered his questioning eyes with a nod. "Do as Running Brook says."

"We will let you know the minute the baby comes. You are just in the way. There is woman's work to be done here," the other Indian woman said as she gently pushed Blue Fox out of the tepee.

Lifting the tepee flap, Blue Fox started to go out, then looked back in. "I will be at the lodge of the other men waiting for the news of our son, Desert Flower." Then he was gone.

Both the Cheyenne and the Arapaho warriors considered Skyraven a leader of the tribe just as her grandfather was. It took bravery and courage to lead the life of a medicine man or woman. It took a strong spirit in order to acquire the ability to communicate with the otherworld spirits and to heal wounds. She was Buffalo's Brother's granddaughter and had gone on a vision quest to receive the power of prediction. Blue Fox felt confident in leaving his wife in Skyraven's capable hands.

"Kneel, Desert Flower." The young Indian woman did as the three women instructed her to do. She knelt on the hay-covered robe for the delivery, firmly holding the center pole placed in front of her for balance as she positioned herself. Skyraven placed her hands upon Desert Flower's head as the young woman knelt and put her wrists through the leather thongs hanging from the birthing pole. Soothing her with loving words, Skyraven administered herbs as they were needed—rosemary for the pain, and slippery soapweed to hasten the delivery. Then she crouched beside her friend softly shaking rattles and chanting.

"Pull and bring your baby into the world," the two other women repeated over and over.

Desert Flower was very brave and despite the pain, she endured. She pulled and she pushed to bring the baby into the world never uttering a cry. After a long time of straining, she gave out with a loud moan and the baby's head came into view. A final push delivered the child into the morning air. Skyraven held the baby in her two hands as the cord was cut, then laid Desert Flower upon her bed of furs.

"Rest now, you have done your part."

After the baby's delivery, one of the midwives tickled Desert Flower's throat with a feather to make her expel the placenta. Skyraven placed the afterbirth in a buckskin pouch, drew the drawstrings shut. To bury the afterbirth would cause the baby's death, so later she would hang it in a tree branch.

As soon as the baby's umbilical cord had been dusted with puffball fungus to hasten the healing, Skyraven placed the newborn upon his mother's chest. "It is a boy just as Blue Fox wanted. A Cheyenne brave for his father to train in the ways of a warrior," she said. "But for now your infant son is hungry and wants only his mother."

Desert Flower looked at her son with love and

admiration. "He's a big boy, isn't he, Skyraven? He weighs almost as much as a buffalo hump roast. According to white man's measure, that would be about nine pounds." She smiled as her good friend wiped the sweat from her brow and made a face to indicate that the delivery had been difficult.

"He is very big and strong and will make his father proud. Now you must rest and gather your strength," Eyes-of-Night instructed sympathetically, herself only recently having gone through the same ordeal.

"By the time he is four summers Blue Fox will have him upon a pony's back and he will become as expert a rider as his father is," Skyraven whispered. Bending down to her friend, Skyraven smiled. "And when I, too, have a child, they will ride together, as I have promised. And when it is time for more children, I will be there, as I have been today. Friendship is a potent thing."

"Yes, as I have found out." Desert Flower motioned her closer. "What would I have ever done without you, my dear friend?" Holding the baby in the cradle of one arm while the infant suckled at her breast, Desert Flower reached out to take Skyraven's hand in her own.

"You would do the same for me," Skyraven said, patting Desert Flower's hand. "You should rest now. It looks as if your young one has had all the milk he wants. Let me take the baby and show him to his father. Then I must hang the afterbirth in a tree." The dried-out afterbirth would later be placed in the pouch to be worn around the baby's neck as a charm to bring a long life.

The baby was wrapped in a fine deerskin which had been prepared with great care by his mother before his birth and exhibited to a grinning Blue Fox who, after holding his son and visiting a short while with his wife, fired his rifle into the air. Walking through the village, he invited everyone to come to a feast in celebration of his newborn son who had been named Big Bear. "The birth of a child is a joyous occasion," he said to everyone he met, pounding them on the back and giving free vent to his happiness. He bragged that soon the other braves would give him many horses. Having sons could be very profitable, he announced with a wry grin. Then when the news had been narrated all over the camp, Blue Fox returned to the tepee to look upon this new son of his, sleeping in the crook of his mother's arm.

During the day, the new baby would be strapped to his mother's back on a skin cradle, a gift which Skyraven had made. She had embroidered it with black cattail roots and porcupine quills dyed red and yellow. She had also made a pouch in the shape of a turtle, a special gift for Lean Bear's grandson.

It was now just midday. Since the new family needed some time alone, Skyraven decided to take another walk down by the river to look for milkweed, or at least that was the excuse she gave to the other women. In truth, she hoped to encounter John Hanlen. She was certain his heart would lead him here as hers had. It was the only spot secluded and far enough away from the Indian camp that they could meet safely. And the hunt should be over by now. She remembered yesterday, and felt a hot shiver flash through her. Bending down to cool herself off in the stream she looked into the river, combing her hair with her fingers, trying to make herself pretty just in case he came to her.

She was enjoying the water when she thought she heard the sound of horses' hooves in the distance. Putting her ear to the ground, she listened intently. One horse. She knew even before the horse and rider came into sight that it would be her soldier.

"Skyraven!" Slipping from his horse's back, securing the animal tightly to a tree, he moved toward her. In his hand was a large leather pouch from which he pulled a length of brightly colored blue cloth. "I was going to give you this cloth yesterday, but we . . . we had other things on our mind, and then last night we had such a short time alone."

"Cloth?"

"Calico. Blue, to match your eyes."

Skyraven ran her fingers over the material, then smiled. "It is very pretty. Some of the Indian women who live with the traders wear such colorful cloth. And I have seen your white women in long, fine dresses made of its lengths. Thank you."

"And I have other presents as well." Reaching in the bag, he carefully brought forth a piece of glass, painted with black paint on one side. "A mirror. So that you can see how very beautiful you are."

"A mirror. I have also seen such things at the trading posts." She laughed softly, holding it up, peeking at her image. "Much better than a pool of water, is it not?" Seeing a smudge of dirt on her nose, she wiped it away. "Once we were fearful of such a thing, for it was said that the glass stole away the soul and held it captive. But now I know that it is just my reflection, like I see within the stream."

"I would have brought you flowers were it the season," he said, "but there just weren't any blossoms left at this time of year. But come spring I will bring you a bouquet of the brightest colored flowers." He explained, "In my world, when a man is paying court to a lady, he brings flowers."

"Then we are 'courting,' John Hanlen?" She smiled her gratitude, pleasured by his gesture. "I truly like flowers, but I like this cloth and the mirror, too." She took his hand and led him to the secluded spot among the trees where they had made love before, drawing him down upon the ground. The leaves of the trees formed a leafy canopy high overhead. Dead leaves and velvety moss formed a bed. For a long while they did nothing but sit beside each other, holding hands. She thought what a fine Indian he made, bared to the chest, the only evidence of his being a soldier his boots, blue trousers, and leather belt. Her admiring appraisal completed, she asked, "How was the hunt?"

He laughed. "I'm afraid I'm not very good with bow and arrow. I had to cheat and use my gun, but I did get a small deer."

"Then you can bring it to the special feast tonight."

"Feast? What is the occasion?"

"Desert Flower had her baby. A son." She lowered her eyes. "It made me think of how much I would like to have your child, John Hanlen."

"Skyraven, are you. . . ?" he asked, remembering their night together at the cave. "I must waste no time in giving your grandfather those horses."

"I'm not with child, though when we are married—"

"It will be our first priority," he finished, his lips moving to hers, his mouth warm and soft. He did want to marry her, to fall asleep with her slim body cradled in his arms, to wake up beside her, to know she would always be with him. She was everything he had always wanted. "We were meant for each other, do you know that, my pretty Skyraven?" he breathed huskily. "I knew it the moment I saw you bending over me. My flesh, my heart, my soul, belong to you."

He reached up to caress her and found that she was stripping away her garments. She held the

251

length of calico up to her bosom, fashioning it around her body like a dress. "Do you like it, John Hanlen?"

"You look very pretty." There was a woman at the fort, one of the officer's wives, who had skill with a needle. He would see about having it made into a dress for her. "Although you look just lovely without it . . ." he added, slowly reaching up to pull the calico from her body, then letting his eyes caress her softly curved form. Her body glowed in the hazy afternoon light with a golden hue. Slowly, leisurely, he traced the lines of her body, then pulled away as he remembered. "The braves . . . ?"

"Are busy preparing their kill for the evening meal," she answered his unfinished question with a smile. The warmth in his eyes made her feel beautiful. She didn't want to go back. "And there will be much excitement with the birth of Blue Fox's son. I do not believe we will be disturbed."

"I hope not, and yet at this moment, I can't even think of being cautious." He leaned against her, caressing her every part, his lips devouring hers. Then, in a heat of anticipation he stripped off his own clothing, longing to become one with her and knowing there was little time before they had to return. If they were gone too long someone might come out to look for them.

Skyraven's eyes and heart, her very senses, were filled with him as he lay naked beside her. Flames of desire consumed her and she reached for him. "I love you, John Hanlen."

"And I, you," he said with deep emotion. "Someday I'll have you all to myself so that we can make love for days in a row and not have to think of the time." He stretched his tall form to his full height as he lay beside her. He branded her flesh with his lips, kissing her stomach and thighs. Skyraven reached out to caress him, moving from his hard-muscled shoulders to his taut, firm buttocks. They were swept up in the fire which ignited their desires. John remembered that Skyraven had told him that the Arapaho and the Cheyenne were a sensual people, making love day or night, whenever it seemed right.

Moving over her, seeking entry, he glided into her, welding her tightly against him. When he entered her, it was as if she felt her heart move. She sighed as she arched herself against his hardness, delighting in the feel of his flesh expanding inside her, filling her with flame. He penetrated to his full length, moving with her in a rhythm that brought forth exquisite sensations, supreme pleasure. She strained against him, anxious to take him even deeper inside her. A gust of passion surged up and rocked them like a mighty wind, enveloped them.

When at last their passion was spent, John placed a whisper of kisses on her brow and snuggled against her. Skyraven's hands moved down the apex of their thighs where they were joined and breathed a sigh. "I think now I will always feel empty when you are not there," she said. Languidly she stroked his smooth back, answering his lips as they sought hers. Lying face-to-face, they held each other, with closed eyes, feeling fulfilled and content.

Chapter Twenty-nine

When Skyraven and John Hanlen arrived back at the village, the preparation for the baby's feast was underway. A fire blazed in front of the tepee of Blue Fox and Desert Flower. The aroma of food drifted through the air, foretelling the celebration. The couple's female relatives were busy cooking or scurrying about helping Desert Flower and the new baby wherever they could, just like any aunts and cousins from Missouri might have done, John thought. People were already beginning to arrive from their own tepees bringing gifts and food for the festivities. Everything from horses to smaller personal items had been brought for the new infant, grandson of their chief, Lean Bear.

Desert Flower sat outside the tepee upon a finely embroidered buffalo robe with a woven willow-branch backrest behind her. She held the sleeping infant in her lap. From the radiant expression on her face, no one would have ever dreamed that just a few hours before, she had been in great pain and had delivered a nine-pound baby boy. The Indian women had wonderful recuperative powers, as well as much good medicine to help them through such trying times. They had been taught to be strong.

Still, a trusted medicine woman was most necessary, and her good friend Skyraven had given her much strength and encouragement, which had greatly helped her through her first birthing experience.

Desert Flower smiled knowingly as Skyraven and John walked down the path together and came toward her tepee. Nervously, Skyraven reached up to brush her hair back from her face wondering if the afterglow of love was visible for all to see. Sensing that someone was looking at her, she turned her head and met the eyes of her grandfather. *He knows,* she thought. *Somehow he knows.* But that was always the way with him, a certain sight. Flushing, she turned away. John Hanlen had spoken of meeting with Buffalo's Brother later in the day. It would all be settled very soon and then she need not feel such guilt.

Blue Fox kissed his wife's forehead and that of the sleeping infant and took his seat beside Desert Flower. He turned to Skyraven. "I did not know where you went off to," he said to his wife's closest friend. "I was afraid you would miss Big Bear's celebration."

Desert Flower lifted an eyebrow as he spoke, for she knew full well why Skyraven had not returned promptly. The white soldier standing next to her was the reason. *Foolish man not to see and remember how it was before we were married and had to share stolen moments,* she thought with fond memory.

"I was out gathering more milkweed," Skyraven said.

"More milkweed?" Desert Flower smiled slowly. "It will be a blessing, for the little one is very greedy."

John had been told at the fort how much the Indians enjoyed receiving presents. He had come prepared, and now made an unexpected offering to the newly born child. Though he had intended to give Skyraven a leather horse's bridle for Running Antelope, he placed it before the baby instead. He would get her another one later. He had asked her permission as they had walked the path back to the camp, and she had agreed, delighted at his kindness.

"For your child, Blue Fox."

Reaching down into the leather pouch he was carrying, John pulled forth and presented a beautiful string of beads to Desert Flower, and two engraved armbands to Blue Fox and the chief. He had come well prepared with gifts for everyone, to show his sincerity and goodwill. Placing the open leather bag upon the ground, he informed the Indians gathered about that they could help themselves to whatever they wanted. There was a flurry of excitement as the men and women searched through the pouch. Much like overeager children, John thought, touched by their naiveté in the matter of worldly goods.

Just as they had the night before, John and Skyraven sat beside each other by the fire, relishing every moment of the time they could spend together. As Skyraven explained the ministrations of the feast, Blue Fox came to John's side. "Come," he said. "You have said that you want to talk with my father. I will take you to him now. We will have time for eating, dancing, and festivities later, when we have learned more about each other, my friend."

Blue Fox led him to the large tepee he had seen upon his arrival at the camp. John wondered if he would be able to do some good in this situation between the soldiers and the Indians or would his meddling be seen as intrusion? Well, he couldn't back out now.

256

Blue Fox entered his father's tepee first, then beckoned John to enter also. Lean Bear sat cross-legged in front of his tepee fire. He did not rise when the two younger men entered but bid them sit down beside him.

"This is the man Skyraven told you has come in friendship, Father. He would like to seek peace between our people and his," Blue Fox explained.

"I, too, want peace," the chief said, lifting his head proudly. "This is Chief Black Kettle, John Hanlen," he said, indicating the stern, dignified Indian who sat beside him, a man of medium height and physique in the autumn of his years.

Major Hanlen had heard the names of Black Kettle and Lean Bear before. Both men were well known and widely respected among the plains tribes and at the fort as well. Like the Arapaho chiefs Left Hand and Little Raven, it was said they were deeply concerned about peaceful relations with the white community but were having some difficulty controlling the young braves.

Lean Bear *and* Black Kettle, John thought. Two powerful chiefs in the Indian nation! Taking a deep breath, he began, telling the two men why he had come. "The attack on the hunters has caused anger. The soldiers are seeking to make retaliation, and I fear they will take action endangering some of you who had nothing at all to do with the scrimmage."

Lean Bear spoke up at once. "I have talked with the braves who are accused. The men you speak of were hunting on Indian land."

"Then have them come forward," John suggested, "and travel to the fort to tell their side of the story. They must clear the matter up or there will be lives lost. Innocent lives."

Lean Bear replied quickly. "One of the braves has

already been taken to the fort. That is why Black Kettle is here."

"I see. Hopefully then this will all be cleared up." Suddenly it seemed a simple matter. But then again that was contingent on Chivington's acting rationally.

"He was taken as a *prisoner*, John Hanlen, not given any chance for explanation. My scouts tell me that he has been locked in one of your jails. Hardly a show of justice."

"I will give you my assurances that the matter will be straightened out. I'll see what I can do about having those three men brought in and questioned."

"They will lie, like all white men. Lone Wolf and his braves will be found at blame."

"Lone Wolf?" For just a moment, John had a flash of recognition at that name, but shrugged it off to coincidence. "Colonel Chivington has made a gesture of understanding and peace by sending me here. It is a beginning. Perhaps the President himself will intervene."

"This medal I wear around my neck with a likeness of your White Chief Buchanan . . ." Lean Bear took the medal off and handed it to John, then continued. "That was given to me, as I told you, by this President you speak of." The chief turned and pointed at the tepee wall, "and that American flag was also a gift from the Great White Father. But if such gifts are meant to entice us to sell our birthright, and that we cannot do. Our land is not for sale. And what land we have we will guard."

"I understand, but hear me, please. You must not take up arms. Tell your rampaging braves this as well. It only increases the chance for misunderstanding. Make a great show of peace and then

258

there will be no fighting."

"We already have, John Hanlen. My village, and that of Black Kettle's, is peaceful. For the young braves whose blood runs hot with anger I cannot answer. It is out of my hands. But know that more than anything in this life I do not want our mother the earth to tremble. I do not want trouble with the soldiers."

John liked Chief Lean Bear. He was an affable and courteous man who had made himself clear. He liked his white brothers, wanted peace but stood firm in his belief that the land belonged to the Indians. He could not control those braves who fought to keep their rights of possession of the buffalo hunting grounds.

"We cannot get used to the white man's way of dealing with the land. To us this is the land of our ancestors. Their bones lie beneath its surface. This land belongs to the whole tribe, not to individual owners. A man can own bows, arrows, horses, or his tepee, but the land is not meant to be bought or sold," Black Kettle said, speaking for the first time.

"Yes, I understand that your feeling for your Earth Mother runs deep. Skyraven has explained some of your beliefs to me. I will try to make my white brothers understand how you feel. We must do everything we can to stop the killing and the stealing and try to live peacefully together."

Blue Fox was not convinced. "Please hear me, my white brother. The white man is trying to change our very way of life, the proud life of a plains buffalo hunter. We enjoy the exhilarating gallop after the buffalo, the dawn raid on an enemy camp, telling our young men of the brave coups while they are all ears. The women and children also listen to

259

us and feel pride and admiration and respect for the way we live. The whites would turn us into rabbits."

"The soldiers have already invaded our land with their forts," Lean Bear said sternly. "The buffalo hunting grounds are the only places that remain sacred. We do not want to see them spoiled."

John could sympathize with the chief's point of view. "I know that the army posts dotting the landscape throughout your ancestral lands are unpleasant sights to your eyes, but as you know, Chief Lean Bear, all of the tribes are not peaceful. The soldiers watching from along the riverbanks are necessary to protect the lives and property of the white settlers." John tried hard to protect the Army's reasons for being there. After all, he was a soldier.

Lean Bear's eyes held sadness as he spoke. "You speak of white man's possessions? These settlers and the soldiers cut down our timber, burn our grama grass, kill our buffalo, steal our horses, fence us out of our own territory, and even rape our women. When I see such things, my heart bursts and bleeds for our people."

"I have heard talk that your people intend to settle us upon reservations," Blue Fox added. "We are hunters, Major John. If we settle down with no activity we will grow pale and die." The chief's son was almost imploring John Hanlen to understand that they could never become a stationary people, for the need to roam was a part of their very being.

"I do understand. I will carry what you say to my chief." John decided at that moment that he needed to go higher up the rank than Chivington. "We have come to an understanding, and I want you both to know that I will do my best to relay your message to my chief so that he, too, may understand." John was sincere in his feelings for the chief and his son. They deserved better than to be stripped of their ancient homelands by methods fair or foul without their consent.

"Then let us smoke the pipe of peace together." Lean Bear took his own personal pipe from its leather case. It was a long pipe beautifully decorated with feathers, strips of leather, and beads. He filled it with kinnikeneck and tobacco mixed with rye grass, then he raised it toward the sky, touched it to the ground, and pointed it in the four directions—east, north, west, and south—while chanting a low, melodious chant. The eerie tones were echoed by Blue Fox and Black Kettle.

Chief Lean Bear took the first puff, passed it to John, who took a puff. John then passed it to Black Kettle, who passed it on to Blue Fox to complete the small circle. When they had completed their smoking, Lean Bear stood up and shook hands with John in the white man's manner.

"I am glad you have come to talk peace with us. Tomorrow we will meet with other chiefs and, if all goes well, we will prepare for a council meeting with your people some time soon. You are right. This matter of the three men who have told lies must be concluded," Blue Fox said.

"But I must let you know that we make no decisions without the vote of the others in our tribe," Chief Lean Bear explained. "Within the next few days, we will send a runner to seek the meeting of the medicine lodge council with the Arapaho chiefs Left Hand and Little Raven."

"I will tell my chief that we must wait," John said, hoping Chivington would be not pigheaded on the matter.

From outside the tepee, drums could be heard,

their staccato sound echoing the beating of John's heart. Was he foolish to truly believe there could be peace and tranquility here on these lands without bloodshed? "I hear the drums beating. We must go now and join my new son's celebration," Lean Bear said, standing up. As if dismissing John, he opened the flap. John took the hint and stepped outside, followed by Blue Fox and the two Indian chiefs.

When they returned to Desert Flower's tepee, the dancing had already begun. The older people sat at the edge of the flickering flames or reclined on thick, soft buffalo robes while they shared stories or reminisced about days gone by. Many removed their moccasins and danced in bare feet in order to be closer to the Earth Mother. The younger people danced and played games. Skyraven quickly chose John for the blanket dance, in which the women chose partners to share their blanket with them while they shuffled around the circle. When the dance was over, Skyraven pulled her blanket over their heads so that they could steal a quick kiss.

"How did your council with Lean Bear go?"

"He listened and talked about peace, but I'm still uneasy." He clutched at her hand. "If anything happened to you, I don't know what I would do."

She smiled. "Nothing will happen. I will be safe. That is why the Great Spirit sent you to me. I can see that now."

"Tell your grandfather to be careful, nonetheless."

"You can tell him yourself, for even now he is motioning for you to join him."

John looked in awe toward the old Indian. Whether he and Skyraven would live happily ever after or face heartache rested in this man's hands. Squaring his shoulders, he walked briskly over to join him, hoping to make a favorable impression.

"Good evening, Buffalo's Brother."

"You have said you wanted to talk with me?" The crackling flames of the fire cast eerie shadows on the face of Buffalo's Brother as he stood scrutinizing the man who might become his grandson-in-law.

"I have spoken about peace with Lean Bear and Black Kettle, and I want to speak with you about peace as well." John reiterated much the same story as he had in Lean Bear's tepee earlier, feeling more and more nervous under the medicine man's piercing gaze.

"I have spoken with the chiefs. My people will also abide by their decision."

"In the meantime be careful that no violence will be instigated. Any show of weapons might be misunderstood."

"And that is all you want to see me about?" He looked for just a moment like a bird with ruffled feathers.

"I want to speak with you about your granddaughter. She must have told you how we feel about each other." Dear God, the man's frown wasn't making this any easier.

"Your attraction to each other has been as silent as the thunder." His granddaughter's blood burned for the white soldier, that was clear to him. "Yes, I know."

"Then I'm certain it isn't any secret that I want to marry her." John decided to come right to the point.

Buffalo's Brother nodded grimly. "She has told me." Crossing his arms across his chest, he looked very formidable.

"And do you approve?"

"I want my granddaughter's happiness above all else."

John breathed a sigh of relief. Skyraven's grandfather had not told him no. "She has told me about the matter of the horses."

"Four is what I ask for."

"She is worth more than that. I'll bring you six, just to show you how much I think of her. Six of the finest horses the territory has to offer, and leather saddles for each of them. Agreed?" He'd never thought it would be so easy.

"It will be as you say." The gray eyebrows furled. "And if Skyraven agrees to go with you to your world, what then, white man? Will you make her happy. Can you love her as deeply as I believe she loves you?"

"You would allow her to go?" John had been afraid that he would not agree to this and had wondered how he was going to solve the problem. He would hate to resort to abducting her, though he knew that had been done before in other similar situations of mixed love matches.

"I would sacrifice my very heart if it would make her happy. Indian ways are the only kind of life my granddaughter understands. The others will shun her—those of *your* kind." His face was so expressionless as to have been cut out of stone. "You whites can be cruel in your treatment of those who are different from yourselves."

John thought about the South where men kept other men enslaved because their skin was black and about Mexico and the way part of the Mexican's land had been stolen by those whose motive was greed. Now it was the Indians. "I know, and for that I am truly sorry, but . . ."

"Never would I want Skyraven to be wounded by such sharp barbs. And it is thus I make my plea, that you will join *us*."

264

John was taken aback, though he'd feared that such a proposition might be made. "Become an Indian?" It was out of the question. Although he truly liked these people, theirs was a primitive way of life. Interesting, soothing, uncomplicated, carefree, yet a manner of living that was going to become obsolete by mankind's progress. Times were changing. Once he might have been content to fish and hunt and live as the Indian braves did, but now, with so many eyes focused covetously on Indian lands, it was impossible to act as if the world could stand still. And most important, he was a soldier who had sworn to serve his country. He couldn't just up and leave the fort.

"It is a good life. A life of freedom." Buffalo's Brother's eyes flickered in the firelight, yet the medicine man did not betray any emotion. John started to speak, but, waving his hand, Skyraven's grandfather silenced him. "Do not answer hastily, John Hanlen. I will give you time to think it over. That is how it must be."

John Hanlen knew it would be foolish to argue now, that it would make it look as if he somehow scorned the Indian's way of life. Instead, with shoulders straight, he gave the medicine man a level look and nodded. "I understand. It will be as you ask." What would happen when he gave his answer, an answer that inevitably had to be no?

The festivities lasted well into the night and it seemed as if it were going to be an eternity before John had the chance to be with Skyraven again. Like the other women, she took her turn preparing the food that was to be partaken of at the feast. John was greatly impressed that the Indians were not at all wasteful. Whereas he had seen much food thrown away at the fort, the Indians made use of every inch of an animal, including the deer he himself had killed that afternoon. It gave him a feeling of pride to know that every bone and sinew would find a use. Perhaps his deer would end up as a pouch, its bones as eating utensils. He had, in fact, never seen a more ingenious and industrious people, taking from the land only what they needed for survival.

"Join us . . ." he remembered Buffalo's Brother saying. Strange that tonight those words sounded so appealing. He had to force himself to remember who and what he was before he promised something foolish.

"John Hanlen . . ." John turned around to see Blue Fox standing in the shadows, holding a bow and a quiver of arrows in his hands. "You have been most generous in giving gifts to my family. I would like to give you a token of friendship in return. This bow is the proper size and weight for you." With a smile, he presented the bow and arrows. "I heard the braves talk about the hunt. They said you made an attempt to try and use our method to kill your quarry."

"It takes great skill. I'm afraid I made a poor showing." His arm muscles were still slightly sore from his attempt.

"After our fight, I know that you have the strength. I will show you." He drew John into a well-lighted area of the camp and pointed toward a large knot in one of the trees. "The curve and tension of bow and string is very important. These arrows are straight, the feathering just so, for accuracy." He showed the white soldier how to hold the bow and draw the bowstring properly, the correct way to nock the arrow. "The position of your arms and shoulders must be just right. And you must

266

practice. Next time you are at our camp, I will take you hunting."

John was deeply touched by Blue Fox's show of friendship. "Thank you." Having watched the special hand grip the braves used as a gesture of friendship, one that looked a bit like arm wrestling, he initiated the handhold. "From this moment on, we are friends, Blue Fox. I have asked for Skyraven in marriage. I want you to know. Perhaps that will make of us even closer friends."

"I have heard." Blue Fox smiled. "Six horses are enough to have married an Indian princess. I fear that wily old wolf made a good bargain for himself."

"I am the one who made the good bargain, as you say. I love Skyraven very much. He asked for four but I offered six as token of the high esteem with which I hold my future wife." John wanted everyone in the tribe to know how honorable his intentions were.

"Mmm. You are generous, John Hanlen, but, as you say, Skyraven is a special woman. Perhaps it *is* you who made the good bargain. Now, go to her. At last she has pulled free of the women and she is looking your way."

John didn't have to be told twice. Hurriedly he hastened to Skyraven's side, his smile as radiant as the stars that shone in the sky. "I was afraid I wouldn't get a chance to talk with you."

"I would have found a way." Her fingers caressed the bow. At the back of her mind was the thought that little by little John Hanlen seemed to be taking to Indian ways. Her heart held hope. "It is an honor to be so gifted by Blue Fox. He does not offer friendship easily, particularly to whites."

"Then I will value his friendship all the more." Reaching down, he took her hand in a show of affection. "I have made arrangements with your grandfather to give him horses. He has approved of our marrying."

"I know. He told me." The love in her heart was mirrored in her eyes.

Sitting on a log, they made tentative plans. Skyraven wanted an Indian wedding, with her grandfather performing the ceremony. John was as eager as a young boy to please his intended in any way possible. He was not overly religious, although he had been raised as Methodist. It really didn't matter to him who married them as long as they were legally wed and could spend the rest of their lives together. He looked deep into the beloved blue eyes. "I can only truly find happiness when you are my wife," he said to her. He might have said more, but the couple's solitude was disturbed as several of the Cheyenne sought them out. It was the one time John wished the tribe wasn't quite so friendly!

The night seemed to fly by. John and Skyraven were too closely watched to be able to steal away and had to content themselves with the kiss they had stolen while dancing under her blanket. When the celebration was all over, the two young lovers went their separate ways reluctantly. John would again sleep in the tepee with some of the young unmarried braves. Tonight Skyraven would no longer be in Desert Flower's tepee, but instead would be with Morning Dove, one of Blue Fox's aunts, and her family. John and Skyraven had only tomorrow to be together before John would be on his way back to Fort Lyon to report to Colonel Chivington about the possibility of a peace council. Skyraven would be accompanied back to her own village on Smoky Mountain.

They were completely happy when they parted,

each of them determined that there would be peaceful relations between their peoples. They both knew that now was not the time to speak further of a marriage ceremony. For now the peace council was very important to their future plans, for if there was no peace, there could be no thought of a life together. Peace. Could he really make such a promise? He knew he had to try everything within his power.

Lying on the floor of the tepee, John slept poorly, a fact not aided by one of the brave's snoring. So, he thought, in that, too, they were just like his own kind. He was tormented by the needs Skyraven's loveliness had awakened. At last, after tossing and turning for a long while, he slipped out to calm his ardor in the icy stream. While some men might have counted sheep, he counted off the days, the hours, the minutes until he could make her his forever.

Part Two:
Darkness Before the Dawn

"The sun's rim dips; the stars rush out:
    At one stride comes the dark."
— Samuel Taylor Coleridge, *The Rime of The Ancient Mariner*

Chapter Thirty

Lieutenant Colonel Henry Sedgwick rode his horse into a lather as he approached Fort Lyon. He'd just been out on another scouting mission, this time with three of his men, and had left them in a hurry so he could deliver his news. There were several ranches in the area whose cattle had been stolen, and the ranchers questioned gave testimony that they had seen Indians doing the evil deed. On the pretext of punishing the culprits, the colonel would be able to get rid of at least a few of the heathen brutes. It didn't really matter to him that nobody was exactly certain just which Indians had been responsible. *Hell, Indians were Indians, weren't they?* he smirked to himself, then hummed a cheerful tune as he stabled his horse.

It had worried him when Major Hanlen had come back a day or so ago, spouting off about peace and telling everybody who would listen just how noble the Indians were. Still, he had smiled politely and listened, as if he agreed with every word, just biding his time until just such a chance as this thing about stolen cattle presented itself.

Sedgwick's optimism quickly evaporated, however,

273

when he arrived at Colonel Chivington's headquarters. He was informed that the colonel, his wife Martha, and their three children were in Denver City. No doubt on another little political excursion with the hope of feathering his own nest, Sedgwick thought. He fumed and shouted that someone must ride into Denver to bring the colonel back. He was needed here and not in Denver. But no one wanted to disturb Chivington, who was a guest at the home of Territorial Governor John Evans. Colonel Chivington had been leaving another officer, Colonel Tippan, in charge of Fort Lyon quite frequently of late and had left specific orders that he was not to be disturbed unless there was an extreme emergency.

"But that is exactly what I have to report. This *is* an extreme emergency." Henry was red in the face with anger because nobody would listen to him. He seemed to forget, for the moment at least, that he was talking to a senior officer.

"Colonel Chivington has made two points very clear, Lieutenant Colonel Sedgwick." Colonel Tippan emphasized the word "lieutenant." "John Chivington and Governor Evans have very important business to discuss, and both he and his family are badly in need of a vacation."

Realizing that he had forgotten himself for a careless moment, Sedgwick was contrite. "Yes, Colonel Tippan, sir. I understand that, but if no one else will go to Denver City, then I request permission to ride there myself. I have to talk to Colonel Chivington. The news I have is so important that it can't wait." Henry was not going to take no for an answer. He had an opportunity to make a name for himself and, come hell or high water, he was going to do it.

Colonel Tippan tried to get him to reveal the urgent matter, but Henry insisted that it was for the ears of Colonel Chivington and no one else. Thus Colonel Tippan had no choice: he must either grant the lieutenant colonel permission to go to Denver City or have him thrown in the brig for insubordination, for Sedgwick insisted he was going no matter what.

"Permission granted." The truth of the matter was that Colonel Tippan was anxious to get the unreasonable Sedgwick out of his hair for a while. He could never quite understand why Chivington had befriended this obnoxious, overbearing man, but then again, he really didn't know either the colonel or the lieutenant colonel very well. It seemed that both of them had been away a good deal of the time since he was assigned to Fort Lyon just a month ago.

"Thank you, sir." Henry knew he had been unreasonable, but he wasn't planning on taking a chance that anyone else would get the credit for the information he had gathered. By God, he rightfully deserved the honor of leading the soldiers out to engage in battle with those brazen cattle thieves. And he knew just which brazen Indians he would choose — Hanlen's Indians!

He would destroy that Indian village he had seen. It was the closest one at hand and would make an easy target. Why subject himself and his men to a long, tiring ride when there were Indians practically under their very noses? He knew that Colonel Chivington would agree with him, for they had talked at length about the Indian problem. Why, the colonel practically hated those beastly savages as much as he did. Tippan, however, was of a different ilk. He was not so sure that Colonel Tippan would agree with what he wanted to do. Some people had even said that Tippan was soft on Indian rights. He would have to work it out very carefully. If he just happened to be on his way to Denver and if he just happened to encounter a hostile band of braves, well . . . Some people had seen Indian warriors in that area. Many settlers were certain that they were planning an all-out war with other plains tribes against the whites. To Henry's way of thinking, such a report would not be too far from the truth.

He finally decided to send a message to Chivington telling him about the cattle raids and asking for permission to proceed, just to cover his ass. It would give what he was planning an air of respectability — all official and proper. Perhaps he'd even ask for reinforcements and insist that the urgency of the situation demanded immediate action.

Chapter Thirty-one

Daybreak swelled over the land, hinting that it was to be an unusually hot day for this time of year. Skyraven clothed herself in her lightest buckskin dress and leggings and did what she could to make herself comfortable for the journey. One last time she checked the knots to make certain that her precious bundles were properly tied for the traveling ahead. Then, patting Running Antelope's neck affectionately to let the mare know she was glad that they would be riding as one again, she mounted.

As the caravan moved northwestward across the tree-covered sand hills, Skyraven turned her head. She was moving away from Fort Lyon and John Hanlen. That thought made her sad until she forced herself to realize that when next she saw him she would be closer to becoming his bride. *And perhaps then he will bring with him my grandfather's six new horses and saddles,* she reflected with a smile.

Chief Lean Bear, Blue Fox, and many other braves were accompanying Skyraven back to their own village in the Smoky Hills, since it was not deemed proper for a woman to travel alone. Her grandfather had gone back a few days before, feeling his presence was necessary at the Arapaho camp. Skyraven, however, had wanted to spend a few extra days with Desert Flower. Lean Bear and a few of his braves planned to continue on with Skyraven so that he might meet with Chief Little Raven and Chief Left Hand concerning John Hanlen's proposal for a peaceful settlement.

Skyraven sat astride Running Antelope, her buffalo robe and the length of calico John Hanlen had given her safe within her parfleches. Her horse pulled a travois loaded with gifts from Desert Flower's family, as well as her personal belongings. Blue Fox had laughingly teased her about returning with so many possessions, saying she would not be able to fit them all in her lodge.

A warm, comforting thought stayed with her as she traveled along. Her spirits were high. Lean Bear had assured her that the Cheyenne chiefs would somehow be able to talk sense into their rebellious young braves. Somehow they would make them see that as chiefs they were responsible for the entire tribe, which included the women, children, the old, and the sick. Surely the young braves would fall into line when they knew that peace with the whites was the only answer.

"I have thought about what your John Hanlen has said." Lean Bear looked back as he slowed his mount and waited for Skyraven to catch up with him. "If we lay down all our weapons except for those necessary for hunting, then how can there be any misunderstanding? Without weapons there can be no war. The white men will know we want peace."

"At least it will be a beginning," she answered back.

278

"There is nothing in this life worth having that does not command a great price. And yet, it will not be easy. Living with the white man can be a test of our patience and our wisdom. There will be times when their greedy ways might cause anger. Some of the braves have tempers that are hot as a summer fire. It will take skill to keep them in line."

Skyraven smiled as she saw that Team Bear had carefully shined and polished the medal the Great White Father had given him. Of all his possessions, this was the one of which he was most proud. As it caught the gleam of the early-morning sun, it glittered with radiant lights. Seeing it prompted her to ask, "What is he like, this Great White Chief of all the white men?"

"Tall, very, very tall. At least two heads taller than our biggest braves. Thin of body. He holds himself with the grace of the Cheyenne and Arapaho."

"Does he have hair like the sun, like John Hanlen?"

"No, it is dark like an Indian's." He laughed as he confided, "He has hair all over his face. Like some of the traders. It is his eyes, however, that drew me to him. They look deep into your soul without looking away. I knew in my heart that he was a man to trust. And I felt the same about your John Hanlen. Such men are all too rare."

They galloped across the land for what seemed to be hours, bouncing over the uneven ground. Skyraven's teeth seemed to rattle in her head, her muscles ached, yet she kept a smile on her face, determined to bear her discomfort as well as any brave. A slight breeze brought a measure of comfort as it touched Skyraven's face and rippled through her unbound hair like a lover's caress. Her eyes touched on the rugged beauty of the land, a vast terrain of browns, greens, and yellows. Ahead of them the hills stretched out like a multicolored ocean, rising up and falling, an area usually peaceful, but which now swirled with clouds of dust.

"Horses!" she heard Lean Bear exclaim.

Skyraven squinted, adjusting her eyes to the glare of the sun. A dark-blue blur merged with the light brown of the earth. Soldiers. The thundering hooves of their horses echoed violently through the stillness. Thinking the group perhaps was led by her yellow-haired soldier, Skyraven felt her heart skip a beat. For the moment she knew no fear, at least until the swirling depths gave proof they were attacking. They were coming in four groups with their cannon rolling along behind their horses like huge logs. Like a swarm of raging bees they came closer, closing the distance little by little, forming into straight lines.

"They are attacking!" she heard Blue Fox exclaim and in that moment remembered a vision her grandfather had had once — of the white men sweeping over their land like a great cloud.

Still, she did not want to believe. "It is a mistake!" she cried out. *It had to be.*

"We must do as John Hanlen said. We must show them that we are peaceful." Lean Bear fumbled in his saddlebag for the piece of paper he always carried, the treaty he had signed while meeting with the whites in Washington. He held it in his hand. "Stay behind me. Do not draw any weapons. I will go forward to show these papers from Washington which will tell the soldiers that we are friendly." Taking one warrior named Star, he started toward the troops, waving the paper as proof of his goodwill and proudly pointing to the medal hanging around his neck. A few of the other Indians rode several yards behind him.

The grisly scene unfolded slowly with a horror that made Skyraven cry aloud. When Lean Bear was twenty or thirty paces from the line of soldiers, the commanding officer shouted out an order. The soldiers lowered their rifles, took careful aim, then all fired together. An explosion more fierce than thunder boomed out. Lean Bear and Star doubled over in pain and fell from their horses, their blood spilling out over the ground.

Skyraven choked back a sob. A cry of anguish rose up from her throat. "Nooo!" She gulped in a mouthful of air, holding it in her lungs until she had calmed her fear. She must ride quickly to their sides and see to their wounds. Nudging her heels into Running Antelope's sides, she started forward, then stopped abruptly. With muted alarm, she saw that it was too late. As Lean Bear and Star lay on the ground writhing in agony, several soldiers rode forward and shot them again.

"Skyraven, move back." Only Blue Fox's barked command could have pierced through her trance. Riding to her, he took hold of Running Antelope's horsehair bridle and led her away from the danger.

"It cannot be!" She prayed that her eyes had deceived her, prayed for a miracle to stop the carnage. Suddenly the soldiers scattered, retreating hastily in the face of their own danger. Looking toward the hills, Skyraven saw the reason for their hasty retreat: A large party of Cheyenne, led by the Cheyenne dog soldier, Bull Bear, had heard the shots and now came to aid their brothers, whooping and firing their guns. In that moment Skyraven knew her prayer had been heard.

As if the wind had drawn the current, the tide changed. The blue-coated soldiers sought to pull back and return from where they had come. Though Bull Bear ordered his warriors to cease their attack, a group of renegades defied him and kept up a volley of fire. When the smoke of the guns had settled, the bodies of seven Cheyenne and four troopers were strewn upon the ground.

Lean Bear had suffered a volley of shots. Surely, Skyraven thought in horror, he could not have survived. Even so, she held on to that hope, until it shattered when at last the soldiers had vanished and she went to Lean Bear's side. His eyes were still open, staring in disbelief. Clutched in his hand was the treaty he valued so highly. He who had spoken of peace had been killed violently, senselessly.

The Indians rode in silence. Lean Bear's body was dragged back to the village on Skyraven's travois behind Lean Bear's own horse. With sad faces and downcast eyes, Skyraven and Blue Fox followed close behind. Next came the small number of braves who had been chosen to accompany the chief on his mission.

I cannot believe that this has happened, Skyraven thought. Surely she would awaken to find it had only been a very bad dream. But no, it was true. How would she ever forget watching Lean Bear shot before her very eyes? An anger festered inside her that could not be soothed.

As soon as the body arrived, it was carried to the burial lodge on a blanket. Four braves, each holding one corner of the chief's own red blanket, carried it inside while the keening of the women rent the air.

In the burial lodge, the Cheyenne medicine man chanted and rattled gourds while presenting a sweet grass offering. Skyraven, Desert Flower, and the women relatives washed the body. They dressed the chief in his finest ceremonial clothes, then wrapped him in a buffalo robe. His war bonnet, his buffalo-hide shield, his many decorated buffalo robes, his bows, his own personal peace pipe, his arrows—all of his personal possessions were wrapped in rawhide bags to be placed beside his body, which was then placed on a platform high upon four poles on a hill overlooking the village. His war pony was shot and left near the platform, provided with everything he would need in the next life.

A lone Indian went to stand on the hillside. Skyraven could see from the markings on his headbands that it was Blue Fox. He had a single white feather in his hair, his blanket was held close about him. In sadness, she listened as he sang songs, chanted, and began to speak half to his father, half to himself. Leaning back into the shadows, he promised that soon he would see to it that none of the white soldiers who had killed his father would remain to tell about it. Wanting to offer words of comfort, Skyraven kept her distance instead, sensing that he needed to be alone with his anger.

When he returned to the village down below, he went to comfort his mother, his wife, and to hold his baby son. Then he talked with the other warriors long into the gray light of morning about what they would do to retaliate for Lean Bear's senseless murder.

"Lean Bear told me to always remember the treaty that had been made at the Big Council in Washington. It concerned the lands that belonged to all of us and to our children, he said. In return for letting the white man pass over our land, we were promised annuities and protection by the soldiers from every enemy, red or white." Blue Fox growled in anger at the thought of how trusting his father had been. "Lean Bear said that fighting would only bring more and more grief and heartache to everyone. Perhaps so, but his peace efforts have brought nothing but grief this night and for many more moons."

Many of the gray heads—the older members of the tribe—plus Desert Flower, Blue Fox's young son, and Skyraven were all with Blue Fox's mother now, but Skyraven knew there was little they could do to comfort her. In her heart she was all alone. She would not sleep this night.

"Ey-ee." The air was shattered by the soulful wail of Lean Bear's wife mourning her husband. It was a sorrowful sound repeated over and over as she rocked back and forth on her heels. A sound as if she, too, were dying.

Drums beat, voices chanted, expressions on all faces showed disbelief and anger. The Cheyenne were enraged by the death of their beloved chief. They were only kept from immediate revenge on the whites by Black Kettle, who had come to pay his last respects. Had it not been for him, Skyraven was certain that the braves would have ridden out and made retribution for the killing.

"And now it seems right that Blue Fox become chief," one of the young braves whispered.

"No," Blue Fox said, rejecting the suggestion. "If it is a peace council you want, I will let Black Kettle go from his camp on Smoky Hill near Hackberry Creek," he said. "But hear this, and let me make it clear: I will not attend another peace council. The white man's hands are dripping with my father's blood. Perhaps Lone Wolf is right after all."

"We can understand your anger and desire for revenge, but let us give peace a chance, as Skyraven's young man has suggested. I like him and I trust him. You seemed to take him to your heart also, Blue Fox." Desert Flower said, thinking past the passion of the moment.

"Our white brother John Hanlen is not like other white men. I do think we can trust him. It is too bad that he is not of Indian blood. I tell you this now, we have lost our lands along the North Platte, but we will not give up one inch along the Republican or Smoky Hill rivers. If we must fight the white men for that hunting ground, then we will also have to fight John Hanlen."

No, Skyraven thought. Not her soldier. He couldn't be blamed for what had happened. He had not even been among the soldiers. Was it not possible that just as there were renegade Indians, so were there renegade soldiers?

"You are right in what you say. The buffalo herds here can last a hundred moons or more," one of the young braves said. "Be not troubled that we would not be with you on that. Each of us here would fight to keep this sacred ground."

Runners were sent out to each village with news of Lean Bear's death. Bull Bear reminded the people that his brother Lean Bear had been a friend of whites but nonetheless had been killed by them. "No peace can be had with the white men!" he shouted. Bull Bear was leader of the dog soldiers, the skilled Cheyenne fighting group with which Lone Wolf had often mingled. Lean Bear's brother would not speak of peace. He began holding war councils and his followers voted to retaliate against the whites.

To most of the Cheyenne tribes the incident was like waving a red flag in front of a bull. It was unforgivable that their great, friendly chief had been murdered by the white man, he who had gone all the way to Washington, D.C., to smoke the pipe of peace with the Great White Father! Many of them felt that they must band together. The Cheyenne nation should go to war with the white eyes. Treaties apparently were only for the white man. Thus it was that almost immediately, bands of Bull Bear's Cheyenne attacked ranches that lay along the stage road, killing one white and running off several others.

Blue Fox, however, once his anger had cooled, was willing to give peace another try for the sake of his son if for no other reason, but in his heart he was certain that while the whites were talking peace, they were preparing to bring big guns into the Indian country. Not now, for winter was fast approaching but as soon as spring came again, they would be there.

Skyraven sat close to him as Blue Fox sat alone, pondering. He seemed to be confused. He wanted peace for his wife and son but he also wanted revenge for his father's death. The terms of the treaty had promised that each side would punish their own for wrongdoing. Since the treaty was signed, the Cheyenne and Arapaho always released their captives to the forts. They no longer took prisoners of war, but the whites had Lone Wolf in prison and had made no effort to release him to his tribe for punishment.

"Lone Wolf is caged like an animal, punished by the white men." Blue Fox said that he did not feel that Lone Wolf needed to be punished for just stealing a few horses, not after what the white men had done. "The whites do their share of horse stealing from the Indians," he explained. "Besides, many of our horses were wild before being taken into the white's possession and those horses had been taken from land that was supposed to belong to the Cheyenne." He said further that Lone Wolf had not killed anybody. It was his belief that the treaty seemed to be a one-sided affair. Blue Fox was not so sure that another treaty would be any better, but he would let Black Kettle decide. "For now, I will do what the elders of the tribe want me to do," Blue Fox concluded.

An uprising had not taken place because of the efforts of Left Hand, Buffalo's Brother, and Black Kettle. They had gathered enough support among the other chiefs and their people to force the young hostiles to remain quiet while peace was negotiated. Still, Lean Bear's death had undoubtedly marked a turning point in the dealings of the Arapaho and Cheyenne with the soldiers. If the whites struck again, what would happen? It was a thought that chilled Skyraven as she looked upon the Cheyenne camp from her special spot by the river. In her mind she heard her grandfather's voice, telling her that there would be death and destruction. Was this what he had meant?

Chapter Thirty-two

Fort Lyon was abuzz with the rumors. It was said that Chivington, just returned to the fort, had received a communication from two of his commanders who had joined forces in the Smoky Hills area. It seemed, went the rumor, that Lieutenant Colonel Sedgwick and another officer had been attacked by Indians.

"Attacked?" John was completely taken by surprise when he overheard snatches of the conversation. "Which tribe? When? What exactly happened?" he asked frantically, understandably confused and fearful.

"Your *peaceful* Cheyennes, Major," Ben Staltwort said with a condescending grin. "So much for your claims of their being peaceful."

"They *are* peaceful, at least Lean Bear's tribe," he countered, annoyed by the young officer's cockiness.

"*Lean Bear?*" The name struck a chord of recognition in the lieutenant. "It was Lean Bear's braves who attacked the joint regiment of troops commanded by Lieutenant Colonel Sedgwick and a Lieutenant Eayre who headed the Independent Battery of Colorado Volunteer Artillery."

Staltwort repeated the story he had heard. Sedgwick had been on his way to Denver to meet with

288

Chivington when he was joined by Eayre, who was in pursuit of the Indians who had reportedly stolen one hundred seventy-five head of cattle. "There were four hundred of your *peaceful* Cheyennes. They swept down on Sedgwick and Eayre without provocation."

"I don't believe it! There has to be some kind of mistake!" John's face turned red as he blustered his indignity.

Turning his back on Lieutenant Staltwort, he hurried to Chivington's headquarters. There he read a transcription of Eayre's and Sedgwick's reports. The account stated that when the soldiers were within three miles of Smoky Hill they were attacked by the Cheyenne Indians, about four hundred strong, and after a persistent fight of seven and a half hours, they succeeded in driving them from the field. The Indians, the report stated, had lost three chiefs and twenty-five warriors in the battle; the wounded couldn't even be estimated. The white soldiers' losses included four men killed, three wounded, and multiple losses of weapons and animals.

Chivington's staff officer had written back that the colonel commanding the district was highly gratified at the conduct of Eayre and his command and would commend the lieutenant in his report to department headquarters.

So, Eayre claims that the Indians attacked first, John thought. He didn't even know the lieutenant yet he doubted his word. He could not believe that Lean Bear would do such a thing. John remembered how proud the old chief was of his medal; it had been given to him by the Great White Chief, he had said. And what of Blue Fox, Black Kettle, and the others? And yet he *did* trust Sedgwick's word. The man had been a family friend for a long, long time.

Over and over he pondered the matter, trying to sort out the details of the report. He thought of Skyraven, and above all, the love he held for her in his heart caused him to reject the authenticity of that damned piece of paper Chivington held in his hand. That Chivington openly crowed about how right he had been all along goaded John into investigating for himself the truth surrounding the atrocity. Although there was much doubt as to who had actually stated the trouble, one thing was clear to him: Eayre had been out to kill Indians. Several of the soldiers told John the lieutenant had made his intentions clear.

Having heard that the major was asking questions, one young soldier who had been in the battle sought him out and confidentially told his side of the story. His was an entirely different report from the one documented. He said that the original party of Indians was much smaller than reported and that *they* had been the ones attacked. He also made mention of the fact that a few women were with the Indians.

"Sergeant Fribbley was approached by Lean Bear and accompanied by him into our column, leaving his warriors at some distance," the soldier recounted. "A short time after Lean Bear reached our command, he was killed and rifle fire opened upon his band."

"And Lean Bear did not give an order for his braves to fire?"

The young man was obviously shaken. "No, sir, he did not. He was waving a piece of white paper, shouting out that he was peaceful, that he didn't want any trouble . . ." The young soldier looked bewildered. "Why did we shoot him? He didn't mean any harm, he wasn't even carrying a gun."

"I hope this was nothing more than a big misunderstanding, soldier," John replied, seething inside as he thought about the murder of that noble old man. "Then what happened?" he asked the soldier.

"There was another band of Indians up on the ridge who Lieutenant Eayre hadn't seen when he gave the command to fire. They pursued us until we . . . we ran." Taking a deep breath to compose himself, he said, "I think we did wrong, sir. Shooting a man when he isn't aiming to harm you, well . . . it . . . it just isn't fair." After a pause, he continued. The next morning about nine o'clock we were attacked by about seven hundred Indians, and fought them until dark. We lost four men. We . . . we had no interpreter along with us, but when two Indians came to meet us, they appeared friendly and ran off. Anyway, Lieutenant Eayre didn't even try to hold a talk with them, either time."

"Some of the Indians speak English, Soldier, nearly as well as we do. Lean Bear did, that I know for certain." John couldn't help but feel bitter and angry. He felt a little guilty, too. He had been so emphatic about there being peace, about not making show of weaponry. Was it possible that he had in some way contributed to the death of Lean Bear? Would Lieutenant Eayre have been as bold about confrontation if the Indians had been brandishing arms? He would never know, but the question haunted him and he was determined not to let the matter rest. He owed it to Lean Bear, to Desert Fox, to the entire tribe to exonerate the good name of their chief.

In an effort to get to the truth of the matter, John questioned Colonel Henry Sedgwick, and was troubled when he seemed to vary in his account. One time there were two hundred Indians, the next moment three hundred. The time and details of the orders that had been handed down changed in the telling a number of times. Another thing that bothered John was the way Henry always avoided his eye. John was determined to keep careful watch on the lieutenant colonel.

It seemed that the whole fort was divided over the matter of the Indian situation. Some still blustered that the only good Indian was a dead one, others took a more lenient view. Nevertheless, Chivington was the one in command and his contempt for the "savages" obviously influenced the decisions made in the next few days. The Indian captive was moved from the brig to a windowless cell thought to be more secure, his food rations cut in half. *As if he were responsible for the trouble in the area!* John thought with compassion in his heart.

Though John tried to get leave to visit Skyraven's village, his requests were denied, not once but several times. Chivington made it only too clear that he had the upper hand. Nevertheless, John did what he could from the fort, including sending messages to Washington. In the end, though Chivington resented his interference, he did get a special investigator to take interest in the matter, Major T. I. McKenny, who talked to members of Eayre's and Sedgwick's command.

McKenny reported back that Lieutenant Eayre, with two mountain howitzers and eighty men, went in search of Indians with instructions to burn villages and kill Cheyennes whenever and wherever they were found. With his men and fifteen wagons, he had wandered out of his district and come upon the band led by Chief Lean Bear. After the "unfortunate" incident regarding that chief, Eayre's soldiers had scattered and the Indians, taking advantage of the situation, made an attack. It was in this skirmish and not in the one involving Lean Bear that the soldiers under his command had been wounded and killed. Eayre was cited for irresponsibility but not punished. Sedgwick's part in the fighting was deemed merely coincidental, being at a certain place at a certain time, and the lieutenant colonel was declared guiltless of any wrong-doing.

It was hardly the report that John had hoped for and indeed only seemed to fire Chivington's determination. Instead of discontinuing his tirade against the Indians, he now openly engaged in fighting them whenever he got the chance. In only a few weeks' time, officers under the colonel's command engaged in major fights with the Cheyenne three times, burned four of their villages, and killed a number of their people, among them Lean Bear, who had prided himself on his peaceful relations with the whites. In John's opinion it was hardly a record of which the soldiers should feel proud. His only consolation was that at least there was no stain of blood on his hands. His "softness" toward the Indians was no secret and he had been ordered to stay at the fort at all times.

Chivington's efforts had much the same effect as poking at a hornet's nest with a stick. The warriors of the Cheyenne finally reacted in anger. John heard that the Cheyenne dog soldiers and young warriors were striking out in retaliation at last, though it was Kansas which suffered the main part of their vengeance. Some men at the fort whispered behind their hands that "old Chivington" was stirring up an Indian war so that he could bask in the glory of being a hero. Other soldiers were certain that the Cheyenne were working out a plot to run the whites out of the country. There were those who lauded John's recent peace efforts and those who condemned him as an "Indian lover." John, for his part, continued his efforts to find a solution to the brewing storm. He wrote letter after letter, only to be dealt a crushing blow. The Commissioner of Indian Affairs, himself a personal friend of Chivington, basing his conclusions on findings from the territorial governor's report, wrote that from a careful examination of the papers, reports, and letters from Evans was unable to find any immediate cause for the uprising of the Indian tribes of the plains except for the active efforts upon their savage natures by emissaries from hostile tribes to the north.

"Has the whole country gone mad?" John asked Sam Dunham angrily as they walked together after a shooting drill one afternoon.

"Sometimes it seems that way. A person just doesn't know what to do." Just like some of the others, Sam was torn between the loyalty he had sworn to his country and his sense of right and wrong. "I used to think it was all so simple. Guess I was just as pigheaded as Chivington. But ever since you told all about those Indians, well . . ."

"They are people like you and me, Sam, and as such they deserve respect. They were here first and no matter what Chivington would like to have you think, they have been pushed and provoked into dangerous behavior." John wondered what Skyraven's reaction to him would be now. *Would she shun him? Would she see him as her enemy?* Dear God he hoped not.

"I think Chivington wants to exterminate them so that all this land can be divided up. He wants them to be angry. Why else would he be threatening to hang that Indian brave we have imprisoned?"

"Hang him?"

"That's what he said. I have no doubt but that the arrogance of that Indian fella is really what's bothering old Chivington. Either that Indian doesn't know English or he's just being stubborn. He won't talk to anyone, hasn't said a word in all the time he's been here. It's driving the colonel wild. He thought he could get some information from him and now he's been threatening to hang him publicly outside the fort as a warning to the Indians." Sam mimicked Chivington's voice. "It will strike the fear of God and the Army in their heathen hearts."

"That will mean there can be no turning back, no hope at all for peace. He can't do it, Sam."

"If that's what he wants to do, then he'll do it. Right now he is drunk with power."

"Yes, he's drunk all right, only it's the rest of us who will feel the effects of his stupidity." John thought a moment. "What do you know about the captive

Sam. Do you think it would be worth it for me to talk to him?"

"Talk to him? Why?" Sam shook his head. "I don't think that would be a very good idea. He does seem rather wild. Probably a Ute or a Sioux."

"I have to try something, Sam. Chivington hasn't issued the order for the hanging yet. Perhaps if I could convince the brave that if he at least acts as if he's cooperating then his life might be saved. It's worth a try."

Chapter Thirty-three

Lone Wolf paced back and forth in his makeshift jail cell like a trapped animal. Being caged like this made him rage inside. The soldiers had transferred him from their prison to this small boarded-up part of the stable. It was cramped, dirty, and had no windows so he was unable to see the sun or moon, could not tell if it was day or night. White men — how he hated them! They hadn't given him any decent food — no buffalo meat, just beans and something they called hardtack. Now they threatened to give him nothing at all if he didn't loosen his tongue. Well, he would die before he would ever give them any information.

From the first, their manner of treating him had done little to mask their contempt for Indians. They had attempted in every way to humiliate him into compliance, but he wouldn't break. Foolish white men, didn't they know that the Arapaho braves were strong? One of his guards had kicked him, but he had not even cringed. They had asked him question after question, but he had stared into their faces, his own face as hard as stone, pretending that he didn't understand. They had grumbled and they had shouted, but this had only made him laugh.

In the first days of his captivity, the soldiers had made threats, ranted and raged. Now they didn't even come to look in on him. His punishment, he supposed. Was his isolated incarceration supposed to frighten him? If that was what they intended, then they had made a very bad mistake, for all it sparked was his fury. They only proved that they were cowards, afraid to deal with him as a warrior. Now they only pushed his meager food offerings through a slat at the bottom of the door. No one even looked in on him. He could be dead by now for all they knew. How he wished that someone would come and open the heavy door of this stockadelike cage. He could easily overpower any of the white men he had seen so far, any but that big giant everybody referred to as Colonel Chivington. He had never seen such a big man, except perhaps Roman Nose, the northern Arapaho chief.

Lone Wolf walked up and down, wearing a path across the hard-packed dirt floor. What were they planning to do with him? Keep him locked up until he withered away and died? Starve him? Kill him? Their attitude infuriated him, as if he and not they were the intruders. They had no right being here in the first place. This fort was built on Indian territory. The tribes should have run the whites out a long time ago. How foolish of his tribesmen to think they could make peace with coyotes.

He knew he had to get out of this square log box, but how? Maybe he could dig out from beneath it or through the sod roof. Most of the other buildings were of stone, but this one, down by the stables, was part of the stable itself. He had heard one of the bluecoats making a joke, saying that it was only fitting that he be placed with the other animals, away from their own quarters up at the other end. It had taken all of Lone Wolf's self-control not to pounce on the bluecoat. If they said he was an animal, he could act like one, could kill. He had instead ignored their insult, for he was only interested in one thing: escape. If he could figure a way to get out of this stinking cell, at least the horses would be close by.

He was looking up studying the roof and trying to judge its strength when he heard a creaking sound. At last someone was opening the door. Folding his arms across his chest, he sat down on the hay floor and awaited his visitor.

The soldier standing at the door of Lone Wolf's cell held a gun pointed right at the Indian's heart, ruining any plan he had of fighting his way to freedom, at least for the moment. "I don't know about this, Major, even for an extra ration of tobacco." he said to the other white soldier beside him. "He's a dangerous one all right. I've been given strict orders not to open this door."

"I'll take full responsibility, sergeant. If it makes you feel any better, you can stay here while I interrogate him." Lone Wolf glanced up at the tall, yellow-haired bluecoat, the man who was talking.

"Interrogate him? Hell, he don't know no English! Been silent as a mute all the time he's been here except for a grunt and a growl or two. A savage if I ever saw one. One thing for sure I can say. He's stubborn as a mule and downright unpleasant."

"Maybe you would be, too, soldier, if the boot was on the other leg." John looked at the tiny room

298

in disgust. There was no furniture, not even a chair, just dirty hay. The room hadn't been cleaned and stank of horses. "If you were a prisoner of *his* people, shut up and half starved, you might not be cordial, either."

John knew the soldier fully intended to stay, and he shut the door with his foot. He would have preferred a private meeting with the Indian, but he was lucky to be able to talk to him at all. What he had to say would just have to be said in front of the sergeant.

"Well, I hadn't quite thought of it that way. Guess I would be angrier than a polecat." Despite his apparent empathy, the sergeant kept his gun sighted on Lone Wolf's chest. "Whatever it is you have to ask him, it better be in a hurry. I'll be off duty in fifteen minutes and George Herbert just might not be as obliging as I am."

"I won't take long." John appraised the Indian and noted that he himself was being scrutinized also. The Indian was strong and his face exhibited a great deal of pride. John wondered what tribe he was from, but didn't know enough about the various tribes to tell. Sioux? Not Ute, he wasn't dark-skinned enough. Cheyenne? Arapaho?

I must be careful with this soldier, Lone Wolf thought. *The yellow-haired man did not look like the other foolish bluecoats.* Intending to prove beyond a doubt that he was not intimidated by the white soldier, Lone Wolf stood up and faced John man-to-man.

"Careful . . . !" warned the bluecoat guard.

Even now, though he was within the sergeant's site, the Indian showed no fear. He was a brave one, all right, John thought. How tragic that he

299

must be treated this way. Though his buckskin leggings showed the dirt and tears of his fight with the soldiers, and he appeared unwashed, there was still a certain nobility about him, as if he were one at the top of his tribe's hierarchy. Remembering his stay at Lean Bear's camp, John made the hand gesture for peace he had seen the Indians use, trying to communicate with the prisoner, and saw a gleam of recognition in his eye.

Lone Wolf was surprised by John's sign language. None of the other bluecoats had known the gesticulation for peace. Still, he would not let his heart be softened. This man was a soldier, just like all the others and therefore just as guilty of putting him in this cage.

"He ain't gonna answer, I tell you. He hasn't up till now."

"I want to try." John felt like a fool as he went through hand motions as best he could in an attempt to get his meaning across. He made a sign like a tepee, trying to communicate that he had visited an Indian village. He would never get anyplace unless he managed to win the Indian's confidence.

"Aw, you're wasting your time, Major. He's either ignorant or just plain mean. Like them two Cheyenne ole Sedgwick and that other officer killed. Lame Dog, or whatever he was called."

Lone Wolf attuned his hearing. What was this?

"His name was *Lean Bear*, Sergeant."

Lone Wolf's blood pounded in his temples like war drums. Lean Bear had been killed! Now more than ever, he knew he had to get out of here. The dog soldiers would never allow the death of their beloved chief to go unpunished. Bull Bear, the dog soldier leader, was the brother of Lean Bear. Now was the time of retribution for the whites. They would drive them all from the land. No more talk. The Indians needed him now more than ever.

"And Lean Bear was far from being ignorant or mean. He was a very noble, peace-loving man," John told the sergeant. Strange, John thought, but for someone who supposedly was unable to understand English, the Indian seemed to be reacting — and strongly — to the news of Lean Bear's death. Maybe his not knowing English was all a ruse so that he wouldn't be badgered by his captors. If that was so, then he was a damned sight smarter than anybody else at the fort, for most assuredly he had fooled them. John was determined to watch him carefully to see if his theory was right.

"Aw, I know what you and all the do-gooders say, that there are good Indians and bad ones. Only problem is, how the hell are we gonna tell the difference. There sure as hell are those that rampage and scalp. How we gonna know if they are peaceful or not?"

Skyraven's beautiful face flashed before John's eyes. They had been so close to finding happiness. "From what Skyraven told me, the southern Arapaho and southern Cheyenne are peaceful, the northern denominations of those same tribes tend to be a bit more troublesome. And of course the Utes are warlike."

Skyraven? Lone Wolf glowered at the yellow-haired soldier as he suddenly realized that this was Skyraven's soldier, the man she had chosen over him. He couldn't control the low-throated growl that came from his throat, a noise John Hanlen didn't fail to notice.

301

"Don't know what it is you said, but something sure riled him. Hell, maybe he does understand."

Realizing that he had nearly given himself away, Lone Wolf sat down again, turning his back to the two soldiers.

John was certain that the Indian did understand, yet he played along with his game. "Oh, I don't know. I doubt it, soldier. He probably just didn't like the way I was looking at him."

"Yeah, maybe . . ."

"If he did understand," John continued, "I'd sure tell him that he'd better cooperate with the chief of this fort. It means his life. And I'd sure urge him to tell us about what happened that day of the Indian raid so that if he *is* innocent of any wrongdoing, it can be known."

"Innocent? Innocent! Makes me want to puke when you and all them Indian lovers try to take the Indian's side. Truth is they are thieves. They steal cattle. They steal horses."

And we have stolen their land, John thought. "Ah yes, the cattle. Tell me something, Sergeant. You were at the battle. Did you see any of the Indians leading any cattle? According to some of the other soldiers, there isn't really any proof of that. The Indians we questioned say they found the cattle wandering about loose on the plains. Isn't it possible that somehow they got out of their pen? It wouldn't be the first time."

"Begging your pardon, *sir,*" the sergeant spoke up, "but I think you are gullible if you think that, but don't let it be said that I argued. Anyway, it don't matter. It's time for you to go. Even if he did know what you were saying, it doesn't matter. From what I hear tell, you're wastin' your time.

Chivington has given orders that this one is to be hung."

Lone Wolf picked up his ears. So, they were going to hang him. He must get out of here *fast*.

John knew he had done everything possible for the Indian without completely compromising his already tarnished reputation. If the Indian could understand what had been said—and John had no doubt that he indeed could—then perhaps he would think about the danger he was in and at least be cooperative enough to save his life. Taking just one last look behind him, John followed the soldier out the door.

Later that evening, in the quiet hours, Lone Wolf gathered every ounce of his strength. The soldier's chief had tried to shame his pride, but instead he had inflamed his heart like red coals thrown into dry grass. They would not get the chance to hang him like a dog. He would be a prisoner no more. He wanted to hear the noise of the victory dance when he and his band triumphed over these bluecoats. It was time for his brothers to set their feet on the warpath.

Using a log he found lying on the ground nearby as a battering ram, he jammed it over and over against the ceiling. At last he broke through the sod roof. The hole was just large enough for him to climb out of, then he jumped to the ground outside. He silently slid along on his stomach the short distance to the horses, cautiously listening for even the faintest of sounds that might be made by a human. Only the horses' nickering came to his ears. Moving with the quietness of a mountain lion, he selected a sturdy-looking animal, and when he was sure that his actions had gone undetected,

303

he guided the horse to wait in the shadows near the fort's big double doors. Using his skill at hunting to move soundlessly, stealthily, coming up behind first one guard then another, he rendered them both senseless. Opening one gate, he mounted his horse and rode away from the fort as fast as the wind.

Chapter Thirty-four

The blast of a trumpet tooting over and over again summoned the men to the parade grounds in the twilight hours of the morning. There, a scarlet-faced Chivington raged and roared to the still sleepy-eyed gathering. "That Indian has escaped! God damn it all to hell and back." His eyes scanned the crowd, touching on each face. "I want some answers. Whoever was responsible is going to lose his head. Well . . . ?" His attention for the moment was focused on the unfortunate private, George Herbert.

"I . . . I don't know, sir."

"You don't know. You don't know. Hell, Soldier, as I remember, you were on guard duty last night. Are you trying to tell me that red devil just jumped right through the roof, stole a horse, knocked the guards unconscious without anyone being the wiser?" Chivington's ruddy face turned nearly as bright-hued as his beard.

"Well no, sir. That is, sir, I . . . I just wasn't expecting that he would escape."

"So you let down your guard."

"No, sir." Herbert thought a moment, trying to

come up with an explanation. "Sir, I heard a noise, but, hell, he's been doing that for a long time. He's always causing commotion tryin' to get out. I just never thought—"

"That's the problem, Soldier. You *didn't* think! I ought to put you in that stinking stable to take his place."

"But, sir . . ." Frantically the soldier looked around him, trying to find another scapegoat, certain that Chivington would carry out his threat. His eyes touched on Major John Hanlen and his face lit up. "It ain't my fault. If you ask me, the Indian-loving major had something to do with it. Sergeant Riker told me when I came on duty that Hanlen had been talking to that Indian. We had quite a laugh about it."

"What?" Colonel Chivington screwed up his face into a hateful expression. "You had better have some explanation, Hanlen. I knew that savage was dangerous and I gave orders that no one was to go anywhere near him. Why were my orders disobeyed?"

John forced himself to remain calm. He would not let the old goat frighten him. "Your exact orders, sir, were that he was not to be alone with anyone. If you will question Sergeant Riker, you will learn that he was with me the entire time, his gun pointed squarely at the Indian's chest."

"A moot point. What I meant was that I wanted him thrown in there and treated like the wild beast that he is, that they all are!" The colonel paced back and forth trying to cool his temper. "I ought to have you put in the brig. I won't this time, but if you ever disobey me again, or bend my rules to suit yourself, I'll see that you rue the day you were born. Is that clear?"

"Yes, sir," John answered, saluting.

"Meet me in my quarters just as soon as this little gathering has cleared. I want to talk with you further about what happened. *In private!*"

"Yes, sir." John knew that if anyone knew his true feelings, he would *really* be in hot water. In truth, he was glad the Indian had made his way out of the fort. He would have hated to see him hang—a sorely unjust punishment for the situation. Besides, except for the theft of a horse and several sore heads, his escape hadn't caused much damage, just a prick to Chivington's pride. But he knew he had better choose his words carefully when he talked about his meeting with the brave or he would find himself in bad trouble.

"That one of the enemy has escaped is a serious problem." Chivington was addressing the group again, holding up a long piece of paper. "And he *is* the enemy. I have here an official letter from the territorial governor John Evans. He has declared that the war with the Indians has opened in earnest."

His words were met by just the reaction he had hoped for. All discipline was forgotten as the assembled men made their feelings known, responses running the gamut from surprise to fear, from sorrow to outrage, bravado, anger. At that moment Chivington knew he held every one of the soldiers in the palm of his hand, and so he played on their emotions.

"As you well know, those savages have gone on a rampage from here to Kansas. Stealing cattle, looting, scalping, burning down buildings. If we don't do something soon, this whole territory will explode

307

with fear. The folks hereabouts are scared half out of their wits thinking there might be a repeat of the atrocities committed by the Indians in Minnesota. Hundreds of people were killed there. The whole situation is causing havoc and panic, even as far as Denver City, where the people practically stampeded the town."

John had heard all about that from Sam, who had accompanied Chivington on one of his jaunts to the city. A rancher had seen "dark shapes" on the horizon and had run with the news, causing panic to break loose. The streets had become crowded with carts, women, children, horses, wagons, and horseback riders trying to move to safety. The iron shutters on windows and doors had been bolted shut. People went down on their knees in prayer. A mob had tried to break into the military ordnance storeroom, demanding the issue of arms and ammunition. No Indians had appeared, and the men who scouted outside the city could find no evidence of any in sight. It was just such stupidity that was adding fuel to an already raging flame.

True, there *had* been scattered Indian attacks, but Evans and Chivington had blown them all out of proportion, certain in their own minds that the Indian tribes were going to unite and force the whites from the territory. The truth was, John thought, that atrocities had been committed on both sides.

"In order to combat the reported alliance of the tribes," Chivington continued, "Evans is putting into operation a plan designated to separate the friendly Indians . . . if indeed there really are any." Chivington said the last beneath his breath, looking in John's direction. He cleared his throat and began reading from the piece of paper he clutched. "Our intent is to separate the friendly tribes from the others so that a vigorous war can be waged against the hostiles. Agent Colbey at Lyon has been directed to arrange for feeding and support of all friendly Indians of the Cheyenne and Arapaho tribes."

A chill ran down John's back as he stood at attention listening to Chivington's words. Something terrible was brewing, but he didn't know what to do to stop it, or how to ensure that Skyraven would not be caught in Chivington's spiderweb.

"Evans is depending on our efforts to keep the nucleus of the friendly Indians away from those whose minds are set on war. Therefore he has ordered that this proclamation be made known to the Indians."

He read the missive which said that agents, interpreters, and traders were to inform the friendly Indians of the plains that some of their tribes had gone to war with the white people, that they stole stock and ran it off hoping to escape detection and punishment, that in some instances they had even attacked and killed soldiers and murdered peaceable citizens.

"For this the Great Father is angry, and will hunt them out and punish them. But he does not want to injure those who remain friendly to the whites. He desires to protect and take care of them."

Chivington revealed that for the purpose of keeping the friendly Indians away from those who were at war, Evans wanted to direct them to places of safety. They were to go to Major Colley, U.S. Indian agent at Fort Lyon, who would give them provisions and lead them to a place of safety. The same would be done for the Kiowa and Comanche who came in friendship. They would be placed at other designated places, he said.

"The object is to prevent the so-called peaceful Indians from being killed through a mistake. None but the friendly must come to these places. The families of those who have gone to war with the whites must be kept among the friendly Indians. The war on hostile Indians will be continued until they are all subdued. Any questions?" he concluded.

"Does that mean we can use hostile savages for target practice?" The first question came from one of Chivington's Colorado volunteers, a man of little intelligence.

"If the situation warrants gunfire."

"Are we gonna have reinforcements?"

"Evans has written to General Curtis expressing our needs. Troops are on their way." Colonel Chivington answered several other questions posed by the soldiers, then dismissed them. Chattering with excitement, they formed into groups to prepare for the upcoming Indian war, some taking their places for drill practice, others at the six straw-filled targets to make sure their aim was true. John saw Sam Dunham walking hurriedly across the rutted gravel and went to meet him.

"What do you think of that?" Sam asked John.

"At least he's making a distinction between those Indians who want to be peaceful and those who are causing the trouble. I have to give him that." John knew he had to make certain that Skyraven and her tribe knew about the proclamation, and Lean Bear's people as well.

310

"Yeah, I guess." Sam was quiet as he looked up his friend, then he asked, "Did you?"

"Did I what?"

"Have anything to do with the Indian's escape?"

"No. I just tried to make him understand that he should cooperate. Actually, I think it was Sergeant Riker who was indirectly responsible. He mentioned that Chivington had plans for hanging our silent brave. It must have prodded him into making an escape. Which reminds me, I'd best be getting to Chivington's headquarters before he has me skinned alive." John started to leave, then took a few steps back, touching Sam on the arm. "If I can convince the old bastard to let me take part in getting the word out to the peaceful tribes about the protection Governor Evans is offering, would you come with me?"

Sam thought a minute. "Sure. I'd rather be talkin' than shootin' any day. But if you can get Chivington to let you go, it will be a miracle. I think he'll probably say no just to prove his power. He'll know at once that you want to see that little Indian girl again."

But Chivington didn't say no. Egged on by Sedgwick's influence and a reminder that John had visited the Cheyenne before and that he knew an Arapaho medicine man, Colonel Chivington was in fact very obliging. After listening to John's explanation about his talk with the Indian brave and issuing him a severe reprimand, he agreed.

"The sooner we separate the docile ones from the troublemakers, the sooner we can begin this war, with Washington's approval, of course," Chivington crowed. "They'll soon see the Confederates aren't the only threat. And once the Indian menace is over, we can think of making Colorado a state."

And you can use these Indian wars to catapult you into a senator's seat, John thought, but he held silent, making a request instead. "I'd like to take Lieutenant Sam Dunham with me."

"And a few others. Ten men. In case you run into any trouble."

Though he hated to arrive at Skyraven's camp with an army, there didn't seem to be anything he could do but agree. If he couldn't convince Skyraven and her people to take advantage of Evans's offer, it could very well mean their deaths.

Chapter Thirty-five

The morning was clear, without any sign of clouds. Still, the air held a chill which warned that the time of cold would soon be approaching. There would be so many things to do before winter came. Drying meat, fruits, and vegetables, tanning hides, making certain there were enough buffalo robes to guard the people from the icy breath of the wind. Skyraven paused in her chore of boiling meat for the morning meal to look up at the sky, wondering if John Hanlen was even now at his fort looking up at the deep azure blue, too. Had he heard about what had happened to Lean Bear? Was he saddened, or had the white soldiers fabricated a lie so that even he now believed that the killing of such a great chief was warranted, as Blue Fox said would happen?

Life had settled back in a familiar routine for Skyraven and her people, and though the death of Lean Bear had not been forgotten or forgiven, it did not weigh as heavily on their minds. Time healed the soul's wounds, her grandfather always said. Buffalo's Brother and Chief Left Hand were still determined to remain at peace with the white men and thus had resisted all invitations from the northern Arapaho, Kiowa, Comanche and hostile Cheyenne to join forces with them in fighting the soldiers. Left Hand had told his people to keep to their village, to avoid avenging soldiers and hostile raiders. He abhorred the violence and said that to retaliate would only bring death to the Arapaho.

Skyraven wiped out the wooden bowls, preparing one for Buffalo's Brother and one for herself, then used a sharpened stick to pull the meat from the pot. She was just about to call her grandfather when a cloud of dust announced a rider. "Lone Wolf!" she breathed.

He rode into the camp like a whirlwind. Seeing the two bowls Skyraven held in her hands, he slid from his horse and tore them from her hands. He wolfed down both portions, then wiped his lips with his hand. "Good. Very good."

Skyraven noticed that he was dirty, that the buckskins of which he was so proud were torn. He was bruised and he was bloodied. "Lone Wolf, what has happened?" Skyraven was astounded to see him, and more than a little apprehensive, for Lone Wolf was a disruptive force among the younger braves. "You look thinner and act as if you are starving."

Lone Wolf stared at her with a look that held neither malice nor gratitude. "I am half starved, like a stinking animal. And like an animal I was put in a cage." He spat at her feet. "By the white soldiers."

"Caged?" In spite of what had happened between them and his anger at her refusal of marriage, she was horrified. Lone Wolf was bold and brave and was not one to be so treated. "Why?"

He told her the story of the three men who had defiled the buffalo hunting grounds and his retaliation, then about his capture by the white soldiers. "They kicked me, hit at me, and treated me with scorn. I was put in a stone box with a tiny little square hole, and bars just like a cage. Like little children they chattered, asking me question after question, but I fooled them. I played a game and pretended I could not understand their words."

Lone Wolf looked around him for just a moment, pleased that his presence was creating a stir in the camp. The people had ceased their activities and now thronged around him like a returning hero. All eyes were upon him as he continued his story.

"I angered them by not acting like a trained dog at their heels. They moved me to a dirty, stinking, place of horses, a box even smaller than before with no opening for the light. And then they practically starved me."

"They were going to let you go hungry?" a little Indian boy asked, horrified at such a thought. No Arapaho would treat even a prisoner like that, for starvation was an agonizing death.

"They had condemned me to death. When a yellow-haired soldier came," Lone Wolf looked upon Skyraven with a frown, remembering that the man was *her* soldier, "he tried to get me to loosen my tongue. I fooled him, too. I heard him talking to another soldier. Their chief was going to hang me to vent his hatred on our kind." His voice grew louder as he tried to stir the others into anger. "But the Great Spirit would not let that be. He gave me strength to break free of their cage so that I could return to you with a warning. We must

315

stop them. Drive them from our land. Kill them if we must."

"No!" The word was a sob which tore from Sky-raven's throat.

Lone Wolf ignored her outburst. "The whites have a chief who is touched with an evil spirit, a huge, tall giant with eyes that glow with hatred. I heard the soldiers talk. He wants to rid the land of Indians so that the white men can roam freely here. But we will not let them. We must be like those who follow Bull Bear and strike a blow that will be felt all the way to the Great White Father in Washington." He raised his fist. "Ayeeee, it must be so."

The war cry was met with blood-chilling enthusiasm as the memory of Lean Bear surfaced. "Ayeeee!" Several of the braves mimicked Lone Wolf's gesture. Hurrying into their tepees, they gathered together bows, arrows, rifles, and what white men's weapons they had. Had it not been for Chief Left Hand's entrance at that moment, they might have been incited to ride out and do mischief, but, like a steadying force, the chief swept forward.

"My son talks with brave words, but words from his heart and not from his head. I say it is too late to fight with the white men and win. There are too many of them and they are much too strong. It would be much like using a woman's wooden spoon to spar with a bear." His voice was sharp and decisive. "As long as I am chief of this band of the people I will call for peace."

"Then perhaps you should no longer be chief!" Lone Wolf's voice was steeped with his bitterness. "A man who would not make war on those who planned to hang his own son is an old woman!"

All those watching stood in stunned silence as Chief Left Hand took a step forward. "I will allow no man, not even you, to say such a thing. You are the seed of my loins. When you were born, you were the joy of my heart. I looked upon you with pride. Now I know only shame that you can be so foolish."

"Foolish, am I?" Lone Wolf fought a duel of eyes with his father, yet in the end he backed down. "Well, we will see, for I believe all the white men to be like the jackal. Soon you will see that what I have told you is right. The red men and white men can not co-exist in peace." With that, Lone Wolf stalked off into a clump of trees at the edge of the camp. Skyraven found herself following him though she could not say why she did so.

She came upon the brave as he was cleaning his wounds in the river. "You are wrong about the white men. They are not all like wolves," she felt compelled to say. "You have suffered, and for that I feel much pain in my heart, but do not let what happened blind you."

"It is you and my father who are blind," he grunted, splashing water over his face and shoulders. As if to impress her with his manliness, he slowly stripped to just a loincloth. "Look. These cuts and black-and-blue marks are reminders to me of how peaceful are the white men." He traced the outline of each and every wound.

"John Hanlen is not a man who would do such a thing," she whispered beneath her breath.

"I say he is! Like the others, he came to gloat when I was held captive."

Skyraven's heart skipped a beat. "You saw him?"

317

"He was the one who brought word that I was to be strung up like a piece of sun-dried buffalo. Aye, I saw him." He fought with his emotions, his jealousy. Skyraven was his, had been since they were children. He would not give her up to the man with hair like the sun. "That wasichu!" He spit the Indian word for white man like an insult.

"How were you certain that it was him?" Her eyes met his and did not falter. She had to know.

He stood up from the stream and pushed his wet hair back from his face. "Because he spoke your name." He seemed to see into her heart. "I suppose that you believe this white man will return for you."

"I do so believe."

Lone Wolf laughed contemptuously. "You will never see his face again. White men bed our women and make of them whores and concubines but never wives. You will see that I am right. Your world and his can never be the same. You will see."

"I hear your words, but my heart will not listen. My love is strong for this man. I would be with him, among his people or mine. I care not what I am called, only that I cannot live without him!"

Lone Wolf trembled with his anger. "So, you would rather live with him as his whore than live with me as my honored wife?"

Skyraven's face took on a pleading expression as she tried to make him understand. "Someday you will feel as I do about someone, and then perhaps you will understand," she said softly. "I love you as a brother, Lone Wolf. I care for you, and it was never my intent to cause you this pain. Please let there be friendship between us, for I need your love and your trust."

Lone Wolf looked for a long time at the face of the woman he had known since his boyhood. She was a woman to honor and respect as well as to love, and yet he could not soften his resolve, or his rage. "I cannot feel love or friendship for anyone who has a softness for the whites. Listen, and listen to this well. The yellow-haired white man is no different from any of the others. This you will see. Someday when he has proved that he speaks as the others with a forked tongue, then remember this day and remember that I told you it would be so." Thus said, he dove into the water.

Skyraven watched him as he swam with long, easy strokes across the deep part of the stream and knew a sense of sadness disquietude.

Skyraven's white man did come, however, putting to lie Lone Wolf's prediction. But John Hanlen did not come alone as she might have hoped, but rather with several of the bluecoats. Even so, she ran to greet him and was met with the white flash of his smile.

"Skyraven!" Trying to maintain an air of dignity he dismounted slowly. He did not gather her into his arms as she ran to him but merely squeezed her hand affectionately. "It's good to see you again. How good you will never know." He turned to a dark-haired, short, stocky man who had ridden a half a horse's length behind him. "Sam, this is the Indian girl I told you about, the one who saved my life. What do you think?"

"That she's even prettier than you said, Major." The man bounded from his horse with cheerful enthusiasm and came over to where they stood. "Long dark hair, and look at those blue eyes! A real treasure. Wish she'd saved me instead of you. Beggin' your pardon, Major." Grabbing her hand, he pumped it up and down. "Pleased to meet you, Skyraven, ma'am. Indeed I am. All I've heard about since the day the major and I met is you."

Skyraven flushed her pleasure at his words, then, remembering hospitality, gestured toward the fire. Although her grandfather, the chief, the braves, children, and women had already eaten, there was enough food left over with which to make an offer. "You must be hungry after your long ride."

Sam Dunham quickly took her up on her offer, competing with the camp dogs which hovered about hoping for their share of what was left. "Thank you, ma'am. I'm as hungry as a bear."

Sam and several of the other men partook of boiled antelope meat and wild vegetables, but John hung back. How he wished he could be alone with Skyraven, he mourned, but it seemed there were too many eyes watching to even steal a kiss. For the moment at least he had to be content just to look at her. "I've thought about you every day," he said, brushing her dark hair from her eyes.

"And I, you." His being here was as warm as basking in sunshine.

"I'm sorry about Lean Bear." For a moment he hung his head as he remembered what he had heard.

"I was with him when he was killed. We . . . we were not armed."

"I didn't think you were."

His fingers traced the line of her jaw, then gently touched her lips as if in a kiss. "I can't find the

320

words to explain so that you can understand this travesty of justice. All I can do is repeat that I am deeply sorry. Lean Bear was an example of what all men should be. God knows I wish my chief was even half as wise. But sadly he is not."

"Lone Wolf says that your chief is touched with an evil spirit."

"Lone Wolf?"

"He was locked up by your chief but broke free. He came back early this morning."

John raised his eyebrows in surprise. So the Indian brave he had seen at the fort prison was an Arapaho. Now that he thought about it, the name seemed familiar. Then he remembered. The brave Skyraven had once talked about, the one who had wanted to claim her for his wife. So, he had ridden back here. He hoped Chivington did not get wind of this or there might be trouble.

Skyraven noticed the furl to his forehead. "Something is wrong. What is it, John Hanlen?"

"Skyraven . . ." He didn't know how to begin. How was he going to tell her of the danger? How could he tell her that he had come with a proclamation that would herd her people onto an area of land like so many sheep, to wait docilely by while the United States Army went in search of her own kind. While her people hunted wild game, his had taken it into their heads to hunt human beings. "Our people are soon to be at war." He felt her stiffen. "That is the word of my chief. I have been sent to talk with your chief, to give him a message from the man he calls the Great Father. I'm here to save your people, Skyraven."

"To save us? How?" She listened patiently while he spoke about the proclamation. "We cannot stay here?"

"No. A rancher and his family were killed by Indians, the bodies taken back to Denver City and exhibited. It has angered my people against yours, and now there is going to be big trouble. There are Indians who are going to be punished for the deed. My chief promises that you will be safe if you do as he says." It was the only way, though he knew it was a great deal to ask of these people. The citizens of Denver and the outlying area stood behind Chivington and Evans's decision to not only punish the Indians but to drive them from the territory, to exterminate them if necessary. He had to protect Skyraven and her people at any cost. "All Indians refusing to come in will be considered hostile."

She looked at him in anger. "That land you speak of is dry, without much water. There are no buffalo, only a few small game. How are we going to survive? How, John Hanlen?"

"There has been money set aside. My chief will see that you are fed, at least until the fighting is over." He knew his own sense of anger. Why had Evans chosen such a barren area? He should have placed the Indians near the buffalo range so that they could have provided for themselves. Instead, they would be dependent on the fort's charity.

For just a moment Skyraven looked at John as her adversary. *Lone Wolf had given warning.* "You and my people are enemies," she exclaimed bitterly. Once before he had come talking about peace. He had spoken to Lean Bear about putting aside their weapons. Now Lean Bear was dead, and yet that was not enough for the whites. Now they wanted to put the Indians on land even the prairie dogs

322

did not want, to be as little children dependent on them for their food. It was degrading. Humiliating. "You are my enemy, John Hanlen. You and all the soldiers you bring into our camp."

For just a moment he forgot all gentleness as he shook her roughly by the shoulders, trying to make her see what must be done. "Skyraven, listen to me. If you do not go, if you make any show of carrying weapons, you will come to harm. Can you understand that? My chief is touched by the evil spirit, just as Lone Wolf says. He is just waiting for you and your people to make a wrong move so that he can sweep you out of his way. But if you prove to the Great Father that you are peaceful, you will . . ." Helplessly he stood there searching for words and then remembered. "You will score a coup. You will make that red-haired devil who wants to play at war look foolish. Please see that what I say is true. Trust me, Skyraven. The soldiers will go out on their rampage, and when they have sufficiently meted out what they think is rightful punishment, they will cease. The war to the south has drained us of men. Soon they will have to leave."

Looking into the depths of his eyes, she saw the glitter of sincerity, yet her voice was cold. "It is not for me to say but for Chief Left Hand."

"I know, but I was hoping that you would talk with him, with your grandfather. Help me make them see . . ."

Skyraven didn't answer or say a word. Instead she took his hand and led him toward the center of the camp.

Chapter Thirty-six

The veil of night fell over the village. Skyraven listened to the voice of the camp crier. The old man shouted out the recent news, the mandates of the chief, and the orders of the day. Skyraven awaited the meeting of Chief Left Hand's council with great anxiety. Feelings ran strong among the tribe members, since Lone Wolf's return. John Hanlen's proposal had been met by scoffs and then laughter among the younger warriors. Give up their weapons and go to the fort? The white men must think them to be as foolish children, they said, echoing Skyraven's own thoughts. The Indians had eyed the soldiers in their midst with undisguised hostility and anger, even going so far as to form a circle around them. Only respect for Left Hand's leadership had deterred them from making any show of violence.

Skyraven took great care in choosing her ceremonial garments, knowing John Hanlen would be able to see her. Because there were so many people involved in this meeting, it would be held outside where all members of the tribe could listen. Though she would not have any say in the matter, she still would be able to hear every word. Looking into the polished silver mirror John Hanlen had given her, she studied herself. She had chosen to wear a new buckskin dress, a gift from Desert Flower, one of lightest beige, fringed and studded with embroidery and beads in a myriad of colors. The glow of her large, ornate necklace fashioned of white bone and her elk's-teeth earrings shone in the light of the fire. Her hair was left hanging long, a headband with a swirling design worked in turquoise and coral beads adorning her head.

The full moon shone brightly down on the earth. Skyraven could see as they approached the fire that the warriors were all wearing feathers in their headbands, the number of feathers and the color signifying the society to which they belonged. The men of the tribe were divided into eight age-graded societies, and all of these were represented now — the Fox Men who were the lowest in rank; the Star Men society of young warriors who venerated Lone Wolf; the Club Society of warriors in their prime; the Lance Men Society who enforced the orders of the camp chief; the Crazy Men who had served their time in battle; the Dog Men Society who were the four principal leaders and four lesser leaders; the Sweat Lodge Society who were a secret order of mature men; and the Water-Pouring Society to which her grandfather belonged, whose members were the seven venerable priests, each keeper of an important medicine bundle. The faces of all the braves assembled were stern, causing Skyraven to feel cold within. She didn't want any harm to come to her yellow-haired soldier.

Chief Left Hand stood tall and proud, magnificently attired in full ceremonial clothing. His feathered bonnet reached all the way to the ground. Buffalo's Brother, too, was in full ceremonial clothing, his buffalo-horned headdress atop his head, the peace pipe secured within an elaborately embroidered carrying case.

Drums, always there were drums when there was anything important going on in the camp, a mournful thump. Now they grew louder as the rhythm of Buffalo's Brother's rattles echoed their beat. A chant, a wailing, filled the air. Skyraven searched for the golden hair of John Hanlen among the soldiers seated around the fire and found him with her eyes. He looked so troubled, so sad, that any anger she might have felt melted as quickly as the spring snows.

Left Hand came forward, standing in a position to block her view of John Hanlen as he began to speak. At that moment Skyraven felt proud, for he was said to be one of the finest-looking Indians who roamed the plains. He was of muscular build and over six feet tall, both adding to his aura of authority. Dressed in his full regalia of feathers, buckskin, and beading he looked every inch the chief. His English was fluent with no trace of accent, for he had learned it from traders in his boyhood. Firelight danced on his face as he abruptly raised his hand.

"Let the soldier's chieftain speak," he said in a deep, resonant tone.

John Hanlen stood up from his cross-legged position. "The governor of the territory of Colorado wishes you to go to a place of safety," he began. "There has been trouble here. Raids, burning, scalping, and the like. Soldiers are out scouring the area to bring the offenders to punishment, but in the doing they have punished those who have done no wrong—Lean Bear, for example. I am here to make certain that such a thing does not happen again, that your people can live in peace, within the security of the governor's protection."

Lone Wolf's eyes looked with hostility at his adversary. "You want us to give up our weapons, to be toothless and clawless like old men and old women. Isn't that what you want, Soldier?" He stared down at the fire. "The truth is that you want the yellow metal and title to the land you now call your own. Well, I say no. Man Above has given this land to all Arapaho and Cheyenne. We do not sell what Man Above has given."

Left Hand was stern. "Yours is not the only vote. Let us hear what the white man has to say." He nodded to John to continue.

"You will be given food and be looked upon as friends. Already there are supply wagons coming with provisions . . ."

One weathered old warrior stood defiantly in front of him. "And what else does your chief want of us? Far more than a promise to lay down our arms I would wager."

"They want to shear us as the shepherd shears a sheep. Never!" Lone Wolf shouted. His fists were clenched in anger as he glared again at the white man. "Lean Bear listened, and he is dead."

"A regrettable and tragic thing to have happened." John tried to maintain his calm as he read from the proclamation. His recitation created a stir.

"If we do this thing, we are growing soft!" came a voice out of the darkness. "Someday this peace will reach up to strangle us and will be the death of us all." With a show of disdain a young warrior walked to the outer circle of the council, leaving behind him an uproar of discussion. Turmoil broke out, shouts of anger that no true Arapaho warrior would ever agree to such terms, that they should join with the Kiowa and Comanche in making war. Other voices joined with the chief's to make a cry for peace. Each warrior took his turn to say what was on his mind. For a long time the arguments raged. Then suddenly all was silent as Left Hand spoke again.

"I understand your feelings," he said sternly, holding his head up with the dignity befitting a leader of the people, "but we must think carefully before we decide what is to be done." Buffalo's Brother took the peace pipe and lit it with a burning stick from the fire. He offered it to the earth and the four directions, took a puff, then handed it to Chief Left Hand. Skyraven knew that those who were for peace would take a puff of the pipe, while those who were for turning down the white men's proposal would leave it untouched.

Each member of the eight societies took his turn with the pipe as it went around in a circle. Then it was Buffalo's Brother's turn to speak. Skyraven could see that he was carefully weighing every word. "I have listened to all of your words," he said. "I, too, have pride, I, too, love my people, I, too, want what is best for us all. I have had a vision of the whites coming to our land. Though we push away the fog, it always returns. So it is with the whites. We cannot stop them."

"Then if we cannot stop them there is no hope." One of the older warriors added his voice to the council. "We must come to an understanding with the white men. The traders have been our friends.

328

If we show that we have peaceful intentions, so will the soldiers come to terms of peace. No soldiers would make war upon unarmed people."

The next three warriors smoked the pipe, but it was passed over by a fourth and a fifth. Peace. War. Again peace. By the time the pipe was returned to Chief Left Hand, the verdict was to try the white man's way. The chief's deep voice stirred like a ripple of thunder. "Go. Tell your Colonel Chivington that we want peace. We will come to this land he marks for those of us who want to create a bond with the whites. The warriors and the medicine men have spoken."

Skyraven watched and waited as the gathering slowly dispersed. *So be it,* she thought. *My people's answer to the soldiers is that we agree to peace.* It was the answer she had hoped for, and yet suddenly she was nearly overwhelmed by a vision of mayhem and slaughter. Trembling, she put her fingers to her temple to try to block out the sight. No, it could not be. Logic told her that Chief Left Hand and the elders were right. There could be no harm in seeking peace.

Blending with the night, Skyraven waited until the camp quieted. When at last everyone was asleep, she approached the area where the soldiers lay sleeping. She looked at every soldier's face and saw at once that John Hanlen was missing. Then she was out into the night again, running down to the river where the high grass grew, and though she could not see him in the darkness beneath the huge cottonwood, she knew he was there. Her heart told her so.

"Skyraven . . ." He pressed his lips against her neck as his arms went around her. The village slept in the distance, the river murmured, night birds serenaded as the lovers kissed and embraced. "It must be this way . . ."

"I know . . ." Her arms went around him as her hands caressed his wide, strong back.

"I wish I could take you away with me, this very minute," he murmured with conviction. He was tempted to forget the oath he had taken as a soldier and abandon everything to marry her and take her far from here and the danger that surrounded them. "Would you go with me?"

"Yes, oh, yes!" At that moment, she would have gone anywhere just to be near him.

"I'll come to you, after you are settled near the fort. I'll send for a preacher, or I'll get married by your laws, anything. Then we can be together. I'll take you into the fort where you will be protected." At that moment he felt it was the only way. Inside Fort Lyon, with the protection of his name, no one could harm her, not even Chivington.

"Yes . . ." She was lost in the sweetness of his kiss. Her fingers found the ridge of his spine and followed it down.

He drew her down onto the soft mat of grass beneath the cottonwood. Knowingly, his fingers worked magic upon her body, sliding down her breasts, her hips, and thighs. He wanted her, more so than he ever had before, and yet for some reason he held himself back, contenting himself just to touch her, hold her, talk to her. For a long time they just lay there, looking up at the mist-shrouded moon.

Loving was just being with someone, Skyraven thought, then whispered to John, "This war. It cannot touch us if we do not let it. If we always remember our love, then somehow it must survive all."

"I hope and pray that you are right." For just a moment, John held a doubt. Had he done right in convincing these people to trust Chivington? What if they were in some way betrayed? He pushed the thought out of his mind. Just as one of the Indians had said, soldiers would not make war upon unarmed people. It was a thing that just wasn't done, not even by an Indian hater like Chivington.

She started to talk with him about her grandfather's vision of the white men but thought better of it. What good would it do but worry him now? As her grandfather said, no one could control the future. Instead, she snuggled against him. They lost track of time, forgot all else but that they were in love. Delicately, slowly, they gave of themselves to each other. They were woman and man coming together with passion, love, and joy—ultimate joy at the beauty of their love. The night shattered into a thousand stars. No more words were needed. The rhythm of their passion, the meeting of their gaze as they looked at each other said it all. There was an old Arapaho saying that Skyraven thought of now: "Let tomorrow take care of itself."

Chapter Thirty-seven

The sun glinted through a mist of rain the next morning as the tepees were pulled down and loaded on packhorses and the travois. At last all that was left was a hodgepodge of bent branches, rocks, and stakes. All the women worked together with the cadence acquired by people who were constantly on the move. John Hanlen was surprised at just how quickly and easily the process was accomplished.

"I wish that the men in my command could be as disciplined," he said to Skyraven as he helped her load her parfleches onto Running Antelope.

"We have had a great deal of practice," she answered, taking great pride in showing him off to the other women. Her white man was very attentive to her. She noted how Whispering Wind in particular stared with admiration and perhaps even some jealousy.

"Your people never cease to amaze me." There was none of the laziness he'd often seen among his own, those who tried to shirk their duty. Everyone, even the children, pitched in to ready the tribe for the journey.

"We are used to packing quickly. It has been our

way of life for many moons." Skyraven made a check of her bundles and those of her grandfather, making sure the knots were secure.

"If only my people could really take the time to know yours, I think they would see how very foolish they are being. There are so many things we could learn from each other." John had been impressed at the dignified and democratic manner in which last night's council meeting had been conducted. And to think that Chivington insisted these people were savages!

Lacing his fingers together, John made a step for her foot so that she could more easily mount her horse, then he climbed up on his own mount. He had taken it upon himself to give Chief Left Hand's people an escort to the lands they were now to occupy, just in case there was any chance of trouble. Not only did it seem the logical thing to do since he and his men were going the same direction but it gave him more time to be in Skyraven's company as well.

"Fall in, men," he said, giving a signal to the others to likewise mount up and ride. He led the procession, followed by Lieutenant Sam Dunham. The soldiers rode in a line, two by two, with the Indians following. It was a parade of men, women, and children off to seek refuge.

They traveled south, stopping only a few times to rest the horses, in which times John made it a point to check upon Skyraven with a protective eye. It was a difficult journey, made more so by the haste, but it was important to get to their destination before there was any sign of trouble.

Near the end of the day, they left behind the gently rolling hills, wending their way slowly over rocky and rutted ground. The scenery changed dramatically from the verdant spot where the Arapaho and Cheyenne villages had been nestled. This land was dry, with its mesquite-spotted sandhills instead of lush willow and cottonwood trees. A range of bluffs halted the southerly meandering creek, forcing it to an easterly course for nearly a mile before it once again turned southward. The spot where the Arapaho were to make camp was an area with few cottonwood and willow, a place bare of foliage.

John eyed the area with alarm. Chivington had been far from generous in the land he had bequeathed the Indians. John felt much like Moses condemning his people to the wilderness. It looked dead here, with little sign of life except the few conical tents that dotted the land and glared white in the fading sunlight.

"Look, it is Chief Black Kettle," Skyraven said, interrupting John's bleak thoughts. Noting the large-brimmed black hat the chief always wore, decorated with its feathers, she waved cheerily at him from the distance and he responded. "Perhaps it will not be too bad here."

"I hope not," he replied, not voicing his reservations.

Chief Left Hand chose to pitch his camp southwest of Black Kettle. John watched as the new camp was erected with the same efficiency with which the old had been torn down. Once again, the women held everything in control. He wanted to lend a hand to Skyraven as she put up her grandfather's lodge and then her own, but she told him sternly that it was woman's work.

"In my world, a gentleman helps a lady," John said, holding the poles together as she tied the top of the tripod.

She shook her head, gently pushing him away. "In our world, a warrior considers it beneath his dignity."

John soon saw that it was up to the woman to unload the horses, unpack the baggage, and set up the entire camp. Though he wanted to help Skyraven, he conceded to her wishes, however, realizing that to go against Indian custom was unwise. He had to admire the women's tenacity and strength. No swooning females here. Soon the tepees dotted the sandy ground, fires blazed, food bubbled in the pots placed over the fire. Children scampered, dogs barking at their heels. The camp of the Arapaho had come alive.

"I will miss the trees. There is no shade here, no birds singing." Skyraven's voice held a hint of sadness, though she held her head up proudly. "Your white chief is not good at picking campsites."

"You should not be here for too long. Soon you will be back among the cottonwood trees you so love." John wasn't as certain as he sounded. For just a moment he wanted to lead them back to where they came from, where they could live off the land, but reasoned that the die had been cast and the only safe place for Skyraven's tribe was here in this designated place. Still, as he took his leave of Skyraven and her people, he had a foreboding that he tried to set aside. Telling himself that Evans had already sent three thousand dollars to Colley at the fort instructing him to use it to feed the Indians, he convinced himself that everything would be all right.

Chapter Thirty-eight

For a few weeks after the proclamation and the Indians' relocation to the Sand Creek area there was peace in the territory, interrupted only by two minor Cheyenne attacks. John breathed easier, hoping perhaps the war that Chivington envisioned would not happen after all. The threat that a contingent of rebels were again marching on Colorado pressed upon Chivington's mind and made him temporarily forget about the Indians.

Feeling that Major John Hanlen had experience dealing with rebels, Chivington sent him to Cimarron Crossing, east of Fort Lyon, where it was reported that a band of rebels had plundered a wagon train. John was assigned to take a unit of men and follow the trail from the location the train was attacked. He made his investigation and duly reported that the tracks led southward toward Texas, across the Cimarron, and beyond both Canadian rivers to the Red River where they turned back. He made a further report. He had learned through questioning the people in the surrounding area that the attack on the train at Cimarron Crossing had been made by a party of twenty-two rebels led by a former

Coloradan who had escaped from Denver's prison two years before. Though their original intent had been to recruit for the Confederate Army, the band of men had taken to outlawry and robbing trains, dividing up the spoils among the gang.

John was kept informed of the gang's activities, which included the holdup of a stage and several other robberies, acts that infuriated Chivington. The colonel was further incensed when one of the gang was shot in a gunfight and it was found that he was wearing a blue United States soldier's coat. He raved and he ranted when John returned to the fort, and the only respite from his anger was when five of the gang were captured by a Lieutenant Shoup near Beaver Creek. John thought it to be the end of the matter when Chivington took it upon himself to try the men. Issuing an order that he was taking the prisoners into his custody, he proceeded to appoint a military commission in the absence of the United States attorney general. John intercepted a message Chivington sent to headquarters at Leavenworth. "If convicted, can I approve and shoot them?" it asked. The answer that came back was that the authority to confirm sentence of death was vested in the department commander and could not be delegated. Only the attorney general could pass a death sentence.

The official answer slowed Chivington down, but it did not stop him. He instructed that the prisoners be turned over to a Captain Cree of the newly formed third regiment of the Colorado Volunteers who left Denver with a large escort of troops to take the prisoners to Fort Lyon for trial. They never arrived at the fort, for near Russellville, still in chains, the prisoners were shot "while attempting to

337

escape." John was suspicious of the matter. He took it upon himself to look into the situation and found that there had been no rations drawn for the prisoners. Chivington never planned on them making the journey much less completing it.

"He had them executed, Sam," he said to his friend when they were alone in the stables after a short ride. "I have a feeling there was no attempted escape."

"That riffraff he calls his Colorado Volunteers are nothing but a bunch of thugs. They make the rest of us wearing blue look bad." Sam brushed at his uniform with a snort. "Anyways, I think you're right. Rumor is that those men were taken several miles off the road and lined up for a firing squad, that they were left unburied on the plains. Hell, they're probably still there unless they've been devoured by the beasts of prey—the kind that don't have bars on their shoulders."

"A hell of a stiff penalty for nothing more than robbery. I guess Chivington appointed himself judge, jury, and executioner." The thought only served as a reminder of how ruthless the colonel could be. How then was he expected to show any mercy to the Indians, a group of people he did not consider fully human?

Sam had still more news. "I heard," he said to John, "that when the news of the deaths and the manner of how it was done was brought to him, Chivington sneered and remarked to bystanders that he told the guard when they left that if they did not kill those fellows he would play thunder with them."

A chill shot up John's spine. This, this was the man to whom he had delivered Skyraven's people. "I think it's about time I wrote to my father. Something has to be done and quickly."

"Chivington is dangerous when crossed. And I would warrant that he would do much the same to you if ever you got in his way. Be careful, John . . . er, Major."

John did send a letter. He had never asked his father for anything and hated to do so now, but something had to be done quickly to save Skyraven's people. He asked him to investigate Colonel John M. Chivington. "The man is dangerous," he wrote. "His bouts of temper border on insanity. He seems to think that he can do anything with impunity, including execute men without trial, as he did recently in the Reynolds gang case. As for the Indians, he is aggravating an already dangerous situation. The Indians requested that the Smoky Hill Trail through their buffalo country be closed, the hunters driven out, and the soldiers taken away. Nothing was done and thus there was retaliation by the young Cheyenne braves who started raiding. Even so, peace could have been maintained by a leader with a cool head and a knack for diplomacy. Chivington reacted like a bull in a china closet, blustering and talking about punishing all Indians for what a few had done and fanning the flames of fear. I think to the contrary that caution must be exercised on the United States' part or there will surely be a bloody war. This man is at the head of his so-called army 'volunteers,' who are nothing more than troublemakers in some instances. All too frequently they can not tell one tribe from another and have regrettably shot at anything in the shape of an Indian, then asked questions later. I know myself of one Indian chief who meant to make peace and was shot down. It will only take a few murders of such peaceful Indians to unite all the Indians into a warlike state. Many of them want peace, but any group of people can only take so much. It seems that every time the peaceful chiefs manage to quiet their young men, the Army shoots some more women and children. Please do what you can to expedite this matter, Dad. My suggestion is that Colonel Chivington be removed as commander of Fort Lyon and the area at once."

John sealed up his letter and gave it to the soldier in charge of the fort's mail, feeling a little better. He might have had his disagreements with his stern father, but the senior Hanlen was a wise man. At the very least he would put Chivington under scrutiny. Then John felt it would only be a matter of time before he would be released from his command.

But the murder of the five Confederate prisoners and the scattered raids on Indians was not the only critical matter. John learned that Evans was increasing the pressure upon Washington for full authority to organize an army of more volunteers, with the express intent of killing Indians because he was certain that the tribes of the plains were intent on combining into a warring force. Some said it was an obsession with him, no doubt egged on by Chivington's reports. Evans's plan to separate the friendly Indians from the hostile ones was not even given sufficient time to work. Evans impatiently abandoned the plan and issued a second proclamation, this time to the people of Colorado Territory, without even notifying the Indians that his previous declaration promising friendly Indians safety had been voided.

John and Sam stood together, listening in stunned

horror as the second proclamation was read by a grinning Chivington, who had at last been given his way. "As you know, special messengers have been sent to the Indians of the plains, directing the friendly to rendezvous at Fort Lyon, Fort Larned, Fort Laramie, and Camp Collins for safety and protection. We have warned them that all hostile Indians would be pursued and destroyed. The last of said messengers having now returned, the evidence is conclusive that most of the Indian tribes of the plains are unprincipled savages who are at war and hostile to the whites."

John piped up before Sam could stop him. "By God, they're not, and you know it! I myself took a large group of the southern Arapaho under Chief Left Hand to the area you instructed. They are living there peacefully!"

Chivington thundered in response, "Say one more word, Major, and you will find yourself in the brig!"

"But . . ." John was silenced by Sam Dunham's rough nudge to his ribs. Wisely, he held his tongue, though his blood boiled as he listened to the contents of the proclamation. Evans said that he had induced the Indians to come to the designated area, but that they had, with a few exceptions, refused to do so. It was a lie. John had seen Black Kettle's camp, had led Chief Left Hand to the area. He had also been informed that Chief War Bonnet, Chief One-Eye, Chief White Antelope, and a few of the others had camped there as well.

"John Evans, governor of Colorado Territory, issues this proclamation, authorizing all citizens of Colorado, either individually or in such parties as they may organize, to go in pursuit of all hostile

341

Indians on the plains." Chivington read from the proclamation that as the reward, he authorized such citizens to take captive and hold for their own private use and benefit all property of said hostile Indians that they might capture and to receive for all stolen property recovered from said Indians such reward as it was deemed proper.

"Dear merciful God." John's face turned white. Evans was giving as a reward for killing Indians permission to their killers to keep the property of their victims! "He's authorizing anarchy. Doesn't he realize that, Sam? He's handing the citizens, every one of them, a license to hunt and kill Indians with no questions asked."

"What are you mumbling, Major?" Chivington paused to look at John.

"I said that whether he realizes it or not, Evans is making it possible for men to kill even peaceful Indians and profit by it," John answered back. The colonel couldn't put him in the brig for answering a question. "He stipulates that pursuing friendly Indians is to be avoided. It says it right here." He held up the document, pointing to that place. "If you ask me, that stipulation is ineffective at best, at worst almost cynical. In fact, *sir*, whites can kill any Indian, enrich themselves with robes, horses, jewelry, and food, and claim the victim was hostile." Though John's comments angered Chivington, it did some good in that it made some of the soldiers think. John had found that there were many who disliked Chivington and sided secretly with the Indians. "Who could dispute such a claim?"

"That is not my concern!" In a fit of temper, Chivington crinkled up the missive. "A few months of extermination against these red devils will bring quiet. Nothing else will."

His answer chilled John to the very bone. He trembled with suppressed rage. "I've got to do something, Sam. And quickly," John exclaimed softly. He put his face in his hands. "Dear God, I've brought Skyraven and her people here to be sitting ducks. But I didn't know. I couldn't have guessed. I thought Evans meant what he said about protecting them, and I thought it was the only way . . ."

"What are you going to do?" Sam whispered behind his hand, keeping his eye on Chivington's face.

"I don't know, but I've got to think of something. I've got to get out of here and ride to warn them. They don't know of Evans's latest proclamation. They don't understand that they are fair game for any white man with a gun."

That night John made good on his word, deciding that if Chivington confronted him about his absence he would tell him that he had gone to see William Bent at his trading post. It wasn't unusual for some of the officers to frequent the place, purchasing items they could not get at the fort. It was the only way, for he knew that Chivington would never give him leave to warn his Indian friends. In actuality, he would ride like hell to Skyraven's camp and warn Chief Left Hand to be careful, to be ready in case there was trouble. In the meantime, he would try by every legal channel he knew to stop this all-out rampage against the Indians. Even if he had to write to President Lincoln himself!

Saddling his horse, an animal that was black and therefore nearly invisible in the dark, he rode up to the gates, thankful that Sam was able to finagle it

343

so that he was on guard duty. "Open the gate, Sam."

"I always obey my superiors, sir," Sam answered with a wink, knowing full well what John was up to. "I'll try to cover for you while you are gone. If I'm clever enough, the old toad won't even realize you're not here. I'll tell him you're in the infirmary or something if he starts asking questions."

"Thanks, Sam." John waited as the heavy doors creaked and groaned.

"If I tell him you've got food poisoning, he'll undoubtedly believe it," Sam was saying. "Food around here is—"

Suddenly, as if from out of nowhere, Colonel Chivington stepped forward. "Are you going somewhere, Major?"

John turned around on his horse very slowly. "Thought I'd visit Bent's Fort, Colonel," he said, trying to maintain his smile. "Seems there isn't any tobacco here."

"You don't smoke, or even chew, as I recall," Colonel Chivington said caustically, moving out of the shadows.

"No, he doesn't, sir, but *I* do," Sam said quickly. "Got a hankering right now, as a matter of fact. Makes me fidgety and nigh on as cross as a bear. The major was doing me a favor."

"The major was going to see those Indians of his. I'm not a fool. I thought he would do just such a thing. That's why I've had him watched. The minute he saddled his horse, I knew I had him." He stepped out of the shadows, hovering ominously over the two men.

If only I weren't commissioned in the army, John thought. *Just an uppercut to the chin and I'd soon have*

344

him out of my way. But to dare to touch a man in Chivington's position was pure insanity, and all he could do was to get down off his horse. "Perhaps you would like to come with me," he said, thinking quickly. "That way you'll see that it was to the fort that I was headed."

"Even if you *were* going there, it would be just as damaging to your reputation. William Bent is married to a squaw and has children of mixed blood. To my mind, that brands him a traitor. He is clearly on the Indians' side." Chivington called the men standing nearby together and issued an order to all in range of hearing. "Now hear this. Major John Hanlen is hereafter confined to this fort under my direct order. He is not to leave under any circumstance. Any man opening the gate to him will himself be considered insubordinate. Is that clear?"

"Yes, sir." Sam said, hanging his head.

"Yessss, sir!" the rest of those assembled answered one by one in echo.

"Tomorrow I'll advise every soldier of my order, Major."

"And just what are the charges, Colonel?" John asked coolly. He imagined he would soon find himself in the brig again as threatened. If so, he'd get word to his father. Surely he would have received John's letter by now.

"No charges, Major." Chivington smiled like a cat cornering a canary. "I am merely assigning you duty here." With a wave of his hand, the colonel dismissed the soldiers lurking nearby.

"Yes, sir." Well, John thought, at least he wasn't going to be put in the brig. He wouldn't have been much help to Skyraven and her people from there. He'd wait until Chivington's anger cooled and find a way to sneak out by climbing over the wall if necessary. "Yes, sir," he said again, saluting.

"Oh, and Major . . ." Chivington withdrew a piece of white paper from the inside lining of his jacket. I just wanted you to know that your father won't be getting this."

"What?" John gasped in surprise, recognizing his letter. Somehow the old bastard had intercepted it. He flinched as he remembered all he had said, yet he kept his jaw from ticking somehow. "That letter is personal, sir. I would appreciate it if you would send it on."

"Send it on? I think not, Major. You see I consider it to have matters within that are of a sensitive nature. Were it to fall into enemy hands it might prove to be detrimental. Am I understood?"

"Yes, sir." John reached for the paper, longing to have it again in his possession, but Chivington playfully held it just out of reach.

"I think it better to keep this letter on file, if you know what I mean," Chivington said warningly. At that moment, he fully realized just how cunning and devious the colonel really was. He realized something else as well: He had just targeted himself for severe trouble and had made himself Chivington's foremost enemy.

Chapter Thirty-nine

It was growing cold. Skyraven hugged a blanket around her as she sat huddled in her tepee. She was growing thinner day by day, for although John Hanlen had promised that they would be given food, the white men had not kept their word and no supply wagons had brought in food to the camp. Still, she would not listen to any criticism against her white soldier. Such things took time, she argued, and was supported in what she said by her grandfather and Chief Left Hand.

"The war to the south is still going on. Perhaps the white men have not been able to get their wagons through to us," Buffalo's Brother had said. "And those of our tribe who make war on the soldiers are not helping the matter."

Were the soldiers having a hard time with the other Indian tribes? Skyraven supposed that they were, and she worried about her yellow-haired lover, hoping that he had not been injured in the fighting far to the east. Chief Left Hand had kept the tribe informed of what was happening and had even made a journey into Kansas to see for himself. The Kiowa, Comanche, a large band of warring Cheyenne, and a small band of Left Hand's braves led by Lone Wolf, had been causing much havoc, joining with Chief Bull Bear's dog soldiers again. Horses and cattle had been stolen, ranches raided, many whites had been scalped, men, women, and children killed, white hostages taken. He said it caused him shame that any of his own had taken part in these atrocities after it had been decided to live in peace. Indians did not break their word, he had said. He had denounced Lone Wolf as his son.

Skyraven had been very proud of Chief Left Hand, for he and Black Kettle had acted as mediators and been instrumental in securing the release of a white woman hostage and three little children. He had ridden forward to parley with the dark-haired major and had assured him of his intent to remain at peace. Because of this effort, he had been taken to the white man's city of Denver and spoken with the chief called Evans. Left Hand had promised the white leader that he would keep the peace.

Skyraven had asked Chief Left Hand if he had seen John Hanlen, but the major said no and that worried her anew. That she had not seen her white soldier in several weeks was a source of worry to her. He had told her that he would come to her, and yet not once had she seen his face.

In the meantime she did what she could to help the others, rationing out the meager foodstuffs they had and sharing them with Black Kettle's Cheyenne. Sugar, coffee, flour, rice, and bacon were often swapped back and forth when one of the Indians was able to find something the white man wanted and traded it for food. One thing that gladdened Skyraven's heart was that Desert Flower and Blue Fox were not very far away, close enough, in fact, that she could walk to their portion of the village and talk with them. Black Kettle had absorbed Lean Bear's people into his band, since Blue Fox had not wanted to be chief and no other had yet been chosen.

As if her thoughts had caused her to materialize, she looked up now to see Desert Flower standing at the entrance to her tepee. "Blue Fox caught two squirrels this morning. We thought that you and your grandfather would like to have one." She held the small animal up like a treasured prize.

Rising to her feet, Skyraven took the offering. "And I have something for you." She rummaged in a leather pouch and came up with the oblong brown vegetables. "Potatoes. Chief Left Hand has recently made friends with the men at the post. They allow him to trade buffalo skins for provisions." She didn't want to demean her chief by telling her friend that as a condition of receiving such foodstuffs they had had to give up their weapons, horses, and mules, as if they were prisoners. Left Hand had complied, giving up three rifles, one pistol, sixty bows and quivers, four horses, and ten mules, saying they would not need them where they were.

Desert Flower bit into the potato and cocked her head. "Strange-tasting, but not unpleasant."

"The white men like them so much that some of them grow them outside their homes. If you take off the brown skins and boil them with meat, they taste very good."

"Hmm." Desert Flower laughed. "I cannot help but think how very strange the white ways are.

They live in boxes that cannot be moved, keep their animals confined, think they can own the land that Man Above gave to every man. Now you tell me they plant these brown vegetables. Why, when the earth is filled with plenty in spring if you just know where to look?"

"I suppose they want to keep control of their world. They seem to value freedom not at all. In truth, it seems they even want to control us. Why else would they have put us here upon this land?" There were times when Skyraven wished the council had voted to stay just where they were. The Indians near the Smoky Hill area were protecting their camp. How, in fact, did the white men expect the Indians to prepare for the winter when they had no means to shoot fresh meat to be dried?

"I do not know," Desert Flower sighed. "I only know that I am anxious to leave. I do not like the way the white soldiers look upon the women whenever they come to our camp."

"Nor do I. I hope that soon we will be able to go to our winter grounds in the Far West, where the red rocks form those beautiful mountains. The traders called it 'Boulder.'" She thought about taking John Hanlen there and climbing with him all the way to the top of one of the mountains where they could be alone and make love in a place where they could nearly touch the sky.

"You have that look in your eyes," Desert Flower said with a smile. "You are thinking of your white soldier, aren't you?"

"Yes," she answered truthfully. "I am worried, for I have not seen him in so long. I wonder just where he is."

* * *

At that moment John Hanlen was marching back and forth with the other soldiers at the parade grounds, wishing he could find a way to slip free and vault over the wall. He paused for just a moment in his stride, an action that sent several pair of eyes in his direction. It was useless to even think of leaving the fort. He was being watched like a hawk by those anxious to find favor with Chivington. His only consolation was that, so far, the Indian camps on the sand creek had come to no harm.

Even so, he was beginning to fit together all the pieces of Evans's "proclamations." The governor was anxious to enlist his hundred-day volunteers, as the Colorado Third Regiment of Volunteers was being called. Posters had been put up all over Denver, or so he had heard. There were war meetings being held, speeches made. In order to promote enlistments, the businessmen of Denver had petitioned the colonel to establish martial law. Indeed, he had heard from Sam, who had made a trip to Denver, that the whole affair was being treated as a business proposition. Entrepreneurs had begun scrambling for contracts to equip the new outfit. It was beginning to look as if quite a few people were going to be making money on Evans's "little Indian war." Indeed, the process of equipping the outfit enriched many a greedy Denver merchant who had busily scrounged government contracts.

As for Chivington, it had been proven that he had no scruples when he had so brutally ordered the execution of the Reynolds gang. The man who had carried out his gruesome orders was the very same man he had chosen to head the hundred-day

351

volunteers. Lieutenant George L. Shoup had even been made a colonel. Quite a promotion, though John didn't envy him his command. It was the sorriest collection of flophouse scoundrels, claim jumpers, street thugs, and assorted riffraff ever to put on the blue uniform of the United States Army. But then, steady, reliable men did not rush off on one-hundred-day forays to kill and maim.

"The bloodless third," some had taken to calling Evans's and Chivington's pet army, since so far no blood had been shed by any in their ranks. Along the Platte, things had been relatively quiet except for a small party of ten Cheyenne who had raided a ranch. It seemed that Chivington and Evans had made a major miscalculation. With the winter coming up, the Indians would not choose to fight but would be more prone to peace. The terrible Indian war that Evans and Chivington had predicted just wouldn't materialize after all. The "bloodless third" would find themselves without any adversaries. John could only hope that it would stay that way. Even so, he still wanted to go to Skyraven, just to advise her of all that was going on.

"Walk lively, Major. You're getting out of step." John was startled by Sam's fervent whisper and hurried to keep up. Bless Sam Dunham! He was John's only haven of security in a raging storm, the only one he knew he could trust. It was Sam to whom he had given another letter to his father, as close to a duplicate of the first letter as he could recall. Sam had sent it by mail from Denver. It well might be John's only hope, if only it didn't arrive too late.

John had heard the talk around the fort. The men of the hundred-day volunteer army were beginning to complain strongly that they might never be given the chance to kill Indians. They were as Sam called it, "chomping at the bit." John was beginning to realize that all the hostile Indians were moving out of Colorado, or at least taking refuge for the winter in the mountainous areas of the territory. The others were readying themselves for the pre-winter buffalo hunt and thus behaving more peacefully than they had in some months. He thought about it all as he carried out his rifle maneuvers. A hell of a time to put together an Indian-fighting regiment, especially a disorderly crew, into the field, he thought.

As soon as the practice drilling was over, John sought out Sam in their favorite meeting place, the stables. "Have you heard anything more about what's happening outside? What has William Bent told you?"

"It seems that Evans is involved in a heated controversy over statehood, but it was defeated. And . . ." Sam grinned, "Old Chivington was badly beaten in the election for the postion of delegate to Congress representing the territory of Colorado."

"I almost wish he had won. That would have gotten him out of here," John quipped dryly.

"But our friend Chivington hasn't given up. He got enough votes to give him hope. He's still counting on that Indian war."

"I think Evans is, too. He made a big show of getting men to fight Indians, insisted they were needed here. He's going to be a laughingstock if he never engages the 'third' in any fighting. The hundred days is almost . . ." Sam hushed his voice to a whisper as they heard someone coming. Knowing it wouldn't be wise to let it be known they were meeting clandestinely, they both shrank back in the shadows.

"Yeah, that's what I heard," a deep male voice was saying. "The Third Colorado Volunteers, the hundred-dayers, are headed this way. Gonna at last kill themselves some Indians."

"Is that why all this hay and corn has been issued for Chivington's stock?" The man who asked the question had just a hint of a lisp. "And why I had to load all those rations of bacon and hardtack into wagons today? God Almighty!"

"The only problem I have with that, is to my way of thinking they're peaceful Indians."

"There ain't such a thing."

"Oh, yes there is. They seem kinda peaceful to me, these Indians old Chivington is gonna attack. They ain't hurtin' nobody." There was a pause. "Ya know I don't rightly know just how he is gonna justify it, them having taken refuge under the governor's proclamation and all. But then I guess it is a technicality. They really aren't directly at the fort, but forty miles outside. That's how Chivington will get around it, I suppose. Old Chivington is gonna find himself some Indians, mark my words. He plans to attack the Indians at Sand Creek. The ones outside our fort."

Chapter Forty

John and Sam stood in frozen silence, listening to the two men. When they were out of earshot, John gave vent to his rage. "I'll kill him!" he whispered, his entire body trembling. "If what they say is true, I'll shoot that bastard before he gets the chance to even go near that camp. I'll ride out there and—"

"And do what? What can one man do against six hundred? If he intends to make war on that camp, then where can they run?" Sam gripped John's shoulders hard. "Think, John. If you go racing out of here, you'll be court-martialed before you can blink an eye. What good will that do Skyraven?"

"I can warn her people."

"And then what? If they fight back, even more will be killed. Chivington is probably just talking and those soldiers just misunderstood. We are civilized men, after all. You can't leave the fort without condemning yourself to a hell of a bad time. These things take care of themselves."

"No, Sam, they don't." In frustration, John flung out his arms. "Look at what's happened.

355

Chivington's Colorado troops have been sent out to punish the warrior tribes, but with a combination of cruelty and stupidity, they have attacked peaceful Indians who counterattacked in retaliation. Why not again?"

"Why not find out for yourself what is going to happen instead of depending on hearsay?"

Find out for himself? That seemed to be good advice. With that thought in mind, John made his way at once to Chivington's headquarters. There he found a few of the other officers waiting and listened in on their conversations.

"Chivington has thrown a cordon of pickets around the trading post with orders that no one is allowed to leave under penalty of death," one officer was saying. "Lest the Indians be warned."

"Sedgwick is certainly making his feelings known. He met the members of the 'third' and welcomed them heartily, saying openly that he felt the Indians should be punished and that he would have attacked them long ago had he had the force."

"If you ask me, Sedgwick will prove his true colors. He's been an Indian hater all along."

"He said he was eager for the troops at Fort Lyon to join in, every man of which he claimed would go. But I don't cotton much to killing peaceful Indians."

As Chivington walked up the steps, each officer to a man quieted. Ah, but Chivington looked smug, John thought angrily. Well, it would be seen just what was going to be done. Surely the sane men here would refuse any controversial orders. He waited for Chivington to tell him to leave, particularly since he'd made an enemy of the man by writing that letter to his father, but, strangely

Chivington greeted him cordially. Indeed, John was actually invited to attend the meeting where the plan to attack the Indians was going to be discussed. He could only suppose that Chivington thought to get some sort of perverse satisfaction from his presence. Or perhaps it was to keep an eye on him. Whatever, John followed the other officers into Chivington's conference room.

Events moved all too quickly. Soon, the cigar-filled room was reminiscent of an Indian Camp, the tobacco smoke floating up like Indian smoke signals. John found himself wishing he knew that Indian way of sending messages, for he would have gone to the top of the tallest tower and done just that. Instead, he leaned back in his hard wooden chair and listened, praying all the while that his worse fears would never come to pass. Regrettably they did, for Chivington did indeed plan to attack the Indians at Sand Creek.

"An eye for an eye," he exclaimed, hovering over the assemblage like some evil angel of death. "The Indians have spent the summer and autumn making trouble. Now they should be punished."

John stood up. "I agree," he said slowly, "that there have been brutal attacks on whites by Indians, but not by *these* tribes."

"It doesn't matter. The example will be made so that all these rampaging savages will be taught a lesson," Chivington said coldly. "Besides, it's been proven that the Arapaho and Cheyenne are responsible for some of the atrocities."

"Not *these* Cheyenne and Arapaho! You don't punish peaceful Indians for what the hostile ones have done."

John sat back down and watched as some of the

others took their turn at arguing with the colonel. Captain Soule, who likewise abhorred the plan to engage in the campaign, backed John up. As the discussions raged, John found that he was not the only rational man there. A Lieutenant Cramer also tried to reason with Chivington, stating that Chiefs Left Hand and Black Kettle had acted in good faith.

"I believe it to be murder. We are under obligation to those Indians. I brought them here to comply with Evans's proclamation. I made a promise to Black Kettle," Cramer said.

John watched as Lieutenant Colonel Henry Sedgwick stood up, expecting him to speak rationally too. He was disappointed. Sedgwick held to Chivington's view, supporting him enthusiastically, but tempered with the promise to Cramer that Black Kettle, Left Hand, and their friends would be spared and that the object of the expedition was to surround the camp and take stolen stock. Only those Indians who had been stealing or otherwise doing wrong would be killed.

Chivington used harsher words. Threats were made against any soldier voicing opposition to the plan. "I believe it is right and honorable to use any means under God's heaven and kill Indians who would kill women and children if given the chance. And damn any man who is in sympathy with the Indians," Chivington thundered. Slowly his eyes touched on John, on Cramer, Soule, and any of the others who had voiced even mild objection in the Indian's defense. "Such men as you, Hanlen and you, Cramer and you, Soule. And Johnson and Vickery. All of you should get out of the United States Service if you can't do your duty.

That duty includes killing Indians."

"Not unarmed ones, sir," Captain Vickery said, looking toward John.

A final attempt to divert Chivington was made by a contingent of officers who stated that it would be a crime to attack Indians who had come to the fort in peace.

"They are prisoners of war!" Chivington growled, "and as such I will do with them as I see fit!"

Chivington, livid with anger at the opposition mounting in the room, walked excitedly around the room and ended the meeting abruptly, once more declaring "Damn any man who is in sympathy with an Indian."

John hurried from the room and stood on a ladder beside the stables. He could see the Colorado Third camped outside the fort, their campfires dotting the area. As he watched, the fires were snuffed out, an ominous sign. He knew in that moment that Chivington, afraid his orders might be contramanded, had commanded the volunteers to break camp and move out. As if to prove him right he could see the parade wending into the distant horizon like fireflies, their torchlights reflecting on the flakes of snow that had started to fall from the sky.

"So much for reason," he whispered, hurrying into the stable.

Sam watched John saddle up, all the while clucking his tongue in warning. "You know the orders. Anyone trying to leave here to give warning is to be shot, no questions asked. You'll come back with bullet holes plastered all over your body." His voice grew sadly quiet. "If you come back at all, that is."

"I have to go, Sam. There is no other way." John thrust his foot into the stirrup and climbed onto his horse. "I couldn't live with myself if I allowed this thing to happen. I can't just sit by while Skyraven and her people face slaughter."

Thus spoken, he fiercely nudged his horse's flanks, watching for an opportunity to ride out of the fort when the gates were opened for a supply wagon. John ducked as a barrage of shots were fired at his retreating figure. He could hear shouted commands that he stop but paid them no heed. Though he risked his life, he didn't care, for doing the right thing was more important and he was certain he was doing just that right now. Urging his horse on at a frantic pace, he braced himself against the icy wind and followed after the ragtag soldiers of the Colorado Third.

Chapter Forty-one

The night sky was clear, the stars bright, the air biting. John Hanlen rode on, shivering against the chill but refusing to go back. He paused only long enough to pull a saddle blanket up around him, then galloped on. Snow was falling, making it difficult to see where he was going, yet somehow he managed to follow the parade of Chivington's men, wishing he had a head start on them. His only hope was that the howitzers they were pulling behind them were slowing them down. If he were persistent, he might well be able to come upon the village before them. He held on to that hope.

The command traveled in columns of fours. It was a rowdy group of men who headed for Sand Creek, men who carried whiskey in their saddlebags and didn't bother to wear their uniforms, who often refused to obey their officers. Now they sought their whiskey bottles for warmth, shouted out bold comments about all the Indians they would kill. John could only hope that their drunkenness would make them careless and alter their aim.

The dark forms of the soldiers were black against

the snow. John tried to calculate just how many there were and judged them to be about five hundred. Five hundred men to swoop down upon a slumbering Indian village! Another column, coming from the direction of the fort, looked to be about a hundred. Reinforcements from the fort. Chivington didn't want to take a chance on defeat.

It was a long ride to the camp, much longer than John remembered. Perhaps it only seemed that way because of the circumstances. As he traveled he construed a plan. He couldn't save the whole camp, he knew that to be an impossibility, but if he could find Skyraven, he would put her up behind him and ride like the wind as far away as was possible. That was the overriding thought urging him on. Save Skyraven and somehow manage to escape being caught. If he were apprehended, it would surely mean his life.

A faint glow of light at last arose from the flat horizon to the east and spread over the sand hills. To his right, John could see the tree-marked course of the river. The river had no prominent north bank, the sand hills to the south having caught the main force of past flood waters. The riverbed was low and flat with only a faint trickle of ice-crusted water snaking along the creekbed. In the bend grew the scattering of cottonwood and willow that he remembered. Through the bare tops, a horse herd could be seen grazing. To the west, less than a mile away, the village of Black Kettle's Cheyenne speckled the river's bend on the north bank. And to the west beyond . . . Skyraven's people! From the ridgetop, John surveyed the quiet camp. The Indians would be sleeping. They wouldn't know Chivington was coming unless he raised an alarm.

But how? Guiding his horse down the bank, he decided to take a shortcut. Meanwhile, from a hilltop above the Indian village, two units of the Colorado Third Cavalry Regiment waited patiently for the sunrise. None of them were really soldiers or had ever fought Indians, but most of them disliked the red-skinned savages. On the other side of the river there was one regiment of the First Colorado Cavalry. Now, in the chilly dawn of the late fall, the creeping sunlight made the tepees visible.

"They're all beddybye, just like the colonel said. And look at them horses down there on the other side of the river, grazin' as if nothing was gonna happen," one of the volunteers of third unit said as he pointed in that direction.

"Ride over and tell Major Anthony to cut that herd of ponies off from the village and then proceed up the other side of the creek." Colonel Chivington gave the order to the sergeant directly in back of him. "And tell him everything else will go according to our original plan. We will ride up through the middle of the camp and Lieutenant Folley can circle around the other side."

"Yes, sir."

"Sun up, Sergeant. Then I want you to kill and scalp all, big and little. Kill all you come across."

"Yes, sir."

The young sergeant headed toward the hill where the howitzer cannon was being set up without stopping to look back. He had a message to deliver to Major Anthony. The shooting would start at sunrise.

Unaware that her village was under surveillance, Skyraven slept soundly. Long into the night she tossed and turned, assailed by a feeling of apprehension, not knowing why she felt as if something terrible was about to happen? Long after the others had gone to bed and the camp was hushed, she received her answer. A noise. She was certain she had heard something. The barking of the camp dogs announced the presence of intruders.

"The dogs . . ." she said sleepily, wishing they would cease their yapping.

She turned over but stirred when she thought she heard the sound of a bugle. Thinking that she was just dreaming about John Hanlen, she pulled her buffalo robe up closer around her shoulders and snuggled down to continue her sleep. He had told her that in the cavalry everyone lived by the sounds of the bugle. "You wake up to that sound and you go to sleep to it," he had said quite emphatically. "Sometimes you just wish the bugler would take a leave of absence for a while."

"Imagining . . ." she breathed into her robe.

In a matter of just a few minutes her dreams were shattered again. This time there could be no mistake. Suddenly shots rang out and there were more bugle sounds. There were voices and neighing horses. The approaching hoofbeats sounded like a distant roll of thunder, yet she knew instantly that this was not the rumble of the sky's fury. Skyraven was startled awake. Guns. Cannons. She heard them clearly. The shattering sound of hoofbeats and angry shouts assaulted her ears again and again. Danger. It was not in friendship that these riders had come.

Slipping from her bed of buffalo robes, Skyraven crept forward to explore. Most of the men were away hunting. It wouldn't be them. Those shots could not have come from their rifles and she cer-

364

tainly was not dreaming. Those were really bugles sounding. Carefully pulling aside the flap, she peered out and saw one of the soldiers scattering the horses so that no one could escape. There was hatred written on his face, on all the faces of the soldiers as they thundered into the camp. Why? What had her people done?

Scrambling to her feet, Skyraven lifted the flap of the tepee and stuck her head from the opening. Everywhere her people were running for cover. The soldiers were charging from three directions, cutting off the horses so that the few men left in the camp could not ride to get help. At first there was only confusion. There had been no warning. Since the Indians believed themselves to be at peace, they had posted no guards other than boys tending the pony herd. What kind of hateful men would sneak up on others while they were at sleep?

Skyraven grabbed her clothing. Hobbling about on one foot, she hurriedly dressed and pulled her leather pouch from its place on the pole. Then she rushed outside to join the other women.

In the event of attack, every member of the tribe had been assigned a duty. Women were to bring their children to shelter, what braves there were at the camp took up weapons to fight, but most of them were away, trying to forage meat. It was a frightening thought, that the healthy, skilled men were away from the camp in this the hour that they were most needed.

The thunder of hooves filled the camp. Pools of blood spread through the camp in their wake. She saw an old woman rush accidentally into the horses' path only to be mercilessly trampled. Skyraven fell backward, narrowly escaping the trampling hooves of another attacker. She could feel the warmth of the horse, could smell the sweat of it, felt the swish of air touch her body as the animal thundered by, and knew the sharp pang of fear. Bullets were hitting the lodges like a hailstorm and only by a miracle was she spared.

Chief Black Kettle, thinking there was some mistake, ran outside his tepee shouting, "No! No! Go back. Go back. We are friendly." As Skyraven ran by in frenzy, he tried to reassure her. "This village is under the protection of the United States Government. They gave me a medal and a flag. There is no real danger. The soldiers will soon realize that they have made a mistake."

He had no sooner gotten the words out of his mouth when his own wife fell to the ground, a bullet barely missing her. Running forward, Black Kettle yelled, "There are one hundred and fifteen Cheyenne lodges and eight Arapaho lodges here. We are friendly. We came to seek the protection of your proclamation." But the firing continued. The Indians, now fully roused, watched in alarm. When a volley of grapeshot was hurled upon the village from the creekbank and gunfire shots began missing him only by inches, Black Kettle rushed inside and came out with his American flag, which he hoisted hurriedly on a tall lodgepole. Beneath the flag was a piece of nearly white, tanned buffalo hide. A flag of truce. Some of his people huddled under the flags as Black Kettle told them the soldiers would not hurt them while they were under the two flags. Gunfire quickly proved them wrong.

Black Kettle put down his flag and commenced his death song: "Nothing lives long, except the earth and the mountains."

Skyraven could see the familiar figure of her grandfather. Standing tall and proud in the melee, he was looking up at the sky and chanting, but he broke his concentration when he heard her cries. "Run, Skyraven."

"No. I cannot leave you." She was too numbed by what was happening to realize fully what all the commotion really meant.

"You must. That is what I tell you. Obey! I will join you later."

Her instinct warned her to do as her grandfather asked, yet her sense of loyalty kept her hovering near. This time his voice was a loud boom of thunder as he repeated his command. Heeding his wishes, she ran into the cover of sheltering trees and there watched the destruction of the Indian camp. Carnage. Death. Before her was a tangle of dead bodies. Women and children.

Like a madman, John rode into the fray, searching frantically for any sign of Skyraven. He couldn't quite believe it when he had heard the signal for attack. How could Chivington have done this? The man was as vile as a serpent. Even from a distance he could hear the screams and the pleas for mercy, see the bright scarlet staining the snow. His eyes were nearly blinded by tears at this senseless bloodletting. With a scream of anger and anguish, his heart was grieved that his own people were the agents of such brutality. And *they* called the Indians "savages!" Was it worth it for these people to be sacrificial lambs just so that Evans could save face, so Chivington could justify keeping his precious hundred-dayers? Apparently there were those who thought no price too costly for their own glory.

Fearfully he searched among the dead, feeling blessed relief that he could not find Skyraven among them. She must be alive, but where was she? His instincts told him that she would have tried to protect her grandfather, and so he sought out the form of the noble old man as well.

Fighting against the blue-coated volunteers cursing them aloud for their stupidity, trying to do whatever he could to minimize the carnage, he fought like a courageous gnat against a swarm of flying ants, saving what women and children he could. It sickened him to hear the soldiers making excuses for murdering Indian children.

"Nits make lice!" he heard them say. They were not reluctant to implement their leader's most savage intentions. One soldier fired at a child toddling in the sand and missed.

"You call yourself a soldier," another bluecoat said drunkenly to his comrade. "Let me try the son of a bitch." He also missed.

"You're both poor excuses . . ." Grunting in disgust, a third soldier took careful aim and killed the child. The wounded were killed and scalped, many of them ripped open with knives. Everywhere there was carnage.

The soldiers fired rifles, pistols, and cannon loaded with small shot. Terrified, the people ran, scattering, shrieking, and crying. The few warriors seized their weapons and gathered around the women and children, herding them up the creekbed.

John pushed himself through the soldiers, obsessed with finding the woman he loved. He was so intent, in fact, that he grew careless, not seeing the hate-filled eyes that watched him. But Lone Wolf, who had ridden into the camp to have council with his father and bring buffalo meat to the hungry camp, saw him. He vented his rage on the man who had brought his people to this camp. Skyraven's bluecoat! It was he who was responsible for this day of death and treachery.

Lone Wolf's long dark hair flew wildly about him as he ran forward, shouting his harsh war cry, pulling John off his horse. Locked together in combat, the two men rolled upon the ground.

From her hiding place, Skyraven gave a gasp, recognizing John Hanlen the moment he hit the earth. In the scuffle his hat had fallen off and his light golden hair gave proof of his identity. "No!" Seeing her soldier here among those bringing such tragedy, she felt pain grip her heart, mistakenly thinking that he was among the shooting, hollering, murdering soldiers. Covering her face with her hands, she sank down into the soft earth, sobbing out her grief. And yet even now she couldn't bear it in her heart if Lone Wolf killed him.

John fought hard against the other well-muscled man. He had to find Skyraven, he couldn't dally here. Skyraven. The very thought of her somehow gave him added tenacity and strength. Freeing himself from the Indian's grip, John pulled away. "I don't want to harm you," he said emphatically.

"You don't want to harm me!?" With a bellow of rage, Lone Wolf lunged again, a hunting knife poised high in his hand, his eyes wild with hatred. John ducked away just in time, and the blade found the earth instead of his shoulder, but the Indian was undaunted. Issuing another cry, he threw himself once more at John. Again and again he lunged with his knife, and again and again he missed, but only by a hairsbreadth. Lone Wolf was no longer thinking clearly. All he knew was that the bluecoats had ravaged his people's camp and that at this very moment he had one of their soldiers in his sights.

"I will kill you, white man!"

John could have drawn his pistol and yet he did not. "There has been enough killing. I don't want to shed your blood. Listen to me. I did not do this!"

His words were useless, for clearly the Indian was intent upon his death as vengeance for the women and children who had so mercilessly been slaughtered. John called upon some inner reserve of strength to ward off Lone Wolf. Kicking out with his foot, he pushed the Indian to the ground, but like a wounded lion, the Indian gathered his strength and jumped at John again, dealing him a blow to the stomach that made John curl up with pain.

He fought against the blazing pain, panting as he carefully aimed a kick which caught the Indian in the head. He struggled to get up, knowing that he was fighting for his life. He didn't want to die, didn't want his body to be used as justification for what had happened. That would be Chivington's way. To point out the body of one soldier and try to make it seem that this slaughter had been done in retaliation.

"Before this day is through, I will kill you . . ." Lone Wolf hunkered down, ready to spring again, but a gunshot stopped him in midair. Clutching at his chest, he fell.

"Got him, that goddamned Indian!" a voice shouted out in triumph. "Just like turkeys at a turkey shoot. Haven't had this much fun in a long while."

John's eyes met those of a young man who was so young he didn't even have whiskers. "Fun? You call this fun?" He looked at him with loathing.

"Sure is. And now I'm gonna get me some of his hair as proof of what I done." The young man thrust his chest out proudly.

John shouted out a string of curse words, damning the man for a barbarian and as fool. He was determined that there would be no such mutilation done to the body and moved forward purposefully to block the soldier, but when he looked again toward the spot where Lone Wolf had fallen, he saw that the Indian had somehow managed to drag himself away. Only the blood on the snow gave proof that Lone Wolf had ever lain there.

John pushed his way through the camp, trying to do what he could to counteract Chivington's attack, realizing that in the confusion no one would really know who barked out orders. He would attempt to give the Indians added time to get to cover. So possessed was John on finding Skyraven that he didn't see Chivington until it was too late. "You!" His hand shook as he gave his command. "Arrest this man!"

"You are the one who should be arrested. You fiendish bastard! May you rot in hell for what you have done!"

"He is a traitor. Shoot him! Shoot him!" Chivington warbled his command to a soldier, a young man who John had fortunately befriended at the fort. John's eyes met those of the soldier. He saw devastation written there, an unbearable self-loathing. The young man couldn't pull the trigger.

"I ain't doin' any more killing."

"Arrest him then." John was seized by four soldiers and dragged off to meet his judgment.

Chapter Forty-two

Skyraven knew if she lived to be an old woman, indeed lived through this day, she would never forget what the soldiers had done. The village was in panic, several lodges were aflame. The Indians were putting up a noble fight but they had few weapons and were outnumbered. They battled fiercely, but the strength and pride of her people were draining out with their blood.

Skyraven held her knife poised to strike as she ran, horrified as she saw that the enemy were as thick as the trees that rose from the forest. Birds screeched and shrieked, fluttering their wings in a frenzy as they darted from tree to tree, protesting the intrusion. Their angry voices blended with the other cries as the people sought places to hide. Women cried and the children wailed, a pitiful sound that tore her heart to shreds. Skyraven could hear the cries for mercy and knew that they would be given none. Just like prowling wolves, the white men were killing and maiming her people.

As she dashed through Black Kettle's camp, she saw that it was nearly as savagely ravaged as her own. Left Hand's camp had been hit especially hard by the ruthless soldiers' malice, located as it was in the center of the lodges. She fought total panic, reasoning with herself that it would do her no good. She must be strong. Somehow she managed to keep her calm until a hand clutched at her arm. Instinctively she reacted, slashing with her knife.

"Goddamn Indian bitch!" swore the man, who was stung by Skyraven's blade. Kicking out with his foot, he sent the knife flying from her hand. She winced in pain, holding her injured wrist, looking up into eyes that looked like those of a weasel, eyes looking through the site of a rifle.

The man paused, his finger resting on the trigger. "This one's got blue eyes." He put down his gun as if that fact troubled him.

"Doesn't matter. Shoot her or slit her throat. You know what the colonel said."

With that intent, he raised his gun again, but Skyraven was determined to live. She fought against her attackers, biting and clawing those who held her, wrenching away the gun. With a strength born of fear and desperation, she lunged free of her captors and took to her heels, running as if her feet had wings. Miraculously she escaped the man's bullet, but could hear it whistle over her head. She ran a long way, only to at last stumble over a body and fall to the ground. Quickly she got up, dodging the bullets that sent the dust flying around her. She heard a bloodcurdling scream. One of the Cheyenne women was struck down and killed before Skyraven's eyes, and there was nothing she could do except to mourn her.

What men there were in camp had managed a line of defense across the frozen river, but their bows and arrows were no match for the cavalry fire. Her people were fleeing in all directions now that they realized they had no chance. Skyraven saw that the main body of those still alive were moving up the creekbed, which alone offered some protection against the soldiers' bullets.

Everywhere women were running and screaming, children were crying, reminding her of Desert Flower and her little one. Before she thought of her own safety, she had to find a way to help her. Blue Fox was away on the hunting trip with the others. Desert Flower was not as independent as Skyraven, would not know what to do. And there was the baby. Desert Flower would need help with Big Bear. That was the thought which drove her on to run until she pushed through the flap of Desert Flower's tepee.

When Skyraven entered the lodge, Desert Flower did not even acknowledge her entrance. She was sitting with the baby in her lap, hardly moving, just staring straight ahead. Skyraven grabbed the horrified woman by the shoulders and gently shook her, then led her to the tepee flap. "I'm here to help you. You must listen. We cannot stay here." She took the baby from her arms. "Help me put Big Bear in his cradleboard," she said, placing him inside the woven wood pouch. "Lace it. Quickly." She aided Desert Flower's fumbling fingers.

Carefully lifting the tepee flap while strapping the cradleboard to her back, Skyraven peeked out to determine the best escape route. The balance of the soldiers had scattered in different directions, running after small parties of Indians who were trying to escape.

The riverbank. Even now she could see that some of her people had made it safely there and that they were digging into the soft sand for places to hide. "This way. Follow me." She led Desert Flower and her little son away from the line of fire only to run into more fire.

The soldiers were issuing no quarter, seemed to come from every direction. As the Indians moved, they followed and formed a line to block their path. "We'll cut them off, Captain Nichols," she heard a soldier yell. They began firing again at the Indians, even at the bank, picking her people off one by one. Even so, some braves were still fighting, shooting arrows. Skyraven felt glad when she saw two soldiers fall. At that moment she hated all who had white skin.

"We must go there," she said, pointing off to the right. Even though it was dangerous, Skyraven knew she had no other choice. The holes did seem to be saving some of her people. Those who did not reach them were killed, their bodies cut apart. A gruesome fate.

"Quickly, Desert Flower, we must go to the high riverbank. There are places to hide there." She changed directions once again, reaching behind her to take Desert Flower's hand to make certain she went in the right direction.

Desert Flower stumbled and fell once or twice but was soon upon her feet again. "Hurry! Hurry!" was all Skyraven could think to shout. Each time she heard the retort of a gun, she winced, fearing for Desert Flower and the baby, but the Great Spirit was with them. They ran until they thought their lungs would burst but did not stop until they reached the high riverbank.

Desert Flower was panting and looked as pale as the white of the tepees. "I . . . don't think I can . . . can run another step." She was indeed breathless. "I can't. I can't. You go on . . ."

They had reached the banks of the Sand River where vegetation grew in abundance. Dropping down in a crevice in the clean moist sand they both lay flat on their backs, exhausted. Their chests heaved in an attempt to consume more air. Skyraven's head whirled, her heart thumped wildly. She wanted to stay there in the shelter of the riverbank forever, but she knew there wasn't enough room for both her, Desert Flower and little Big Bear. One of them had to find another hiding place. Skyraven decided to make the sacrifice.

"You stay here with the little one. I'll find another place to hide." She squeezed her arm tightly. "Don't make a sound. Don't come out of hiding for any reason. Do you promise me?" Desert Flower shook her head yes.

After a short rest, Skyraven sat up and looked around her, then crept to the edge of the creekbank to look on the other side. There she saw the bluecoats still milling around the village. Some were committing terrible acts, looting, pillaging, setting fire to her village. Worst of all, they were yelling and hollering as they took scalps from those whose bodies were scattered about on the ground. She also heard the sound of hoofbeats, the clink of metal, and the sound of the bluecoats' angry voices, but she did not know where they were coming from.

"You stay here with Big Bear in the tall grass. Nobody can see you. You are well hidden. I am going to take a look farther upstream to see what our chances are for escape. If we can get away, we can at least try to make it to another camp," she whispered.

Crawling on her hands and knees, she left the clump of thick vegetation, behind which Desert Flower and the baby were well hidden. Thinking to lead any soldier who might be lurking about away from Desert Flower, she moved to a crouched position, then sprang up to run again.

"Oh, Good Spirit, please be with us now in our hour of need," she mumbled, raising her eyes skyward, praying that she would be spared. Now she would know the truth of the vision he had spoken of.

Hiding as best she could in the available foliage, she

followed along the riverbank for at least a half mile. Looking back, she could see soldiers following small bands of Indians who were trying to escape, but she was well in advance of them. "Please, Dear Spirit, be with me now," she repeated again, over and over. She had to live. She could do nothing for Desert Flower or for the others if she met her death now.

The sound of the hoofbeats were growing more distant now. She felt sure that she had gotten as far away from the soldiers as she could. Only then did she allow herself to stop and catch her breath again. She had seen no soldiers go anywhere near Desert Flower and the baby's hiding place. At least she could take comfort in that. Of her grandfather she did not know. The flames from her burning village made her shudder as she imagined it to be the medicine man's funeral pyre.

"Oh, Grandfather! Grandfather!" She felt tears sting her eyes but hastily brushed them away. There was no time for weeping. Not now. She was still not fully out of danger.

Skyraven hunkered down, making her way slowly. Was she imagining things or had she seen a horse? Reaching out to climb up the embankment for a look, she grabbed hold of a black rock, then gasped in horror as she realized that it was not a rock at all but the toe of a soldier's black boot. Her eyes traveled upward to meet the sneering gaze of a tall, lanky cavalry man and his evil-grinning companion.

"Here's one, Charlie. Can't let her get away that easy," he said, kicking his boot from beneath the grip of her fingers and sending wet sand flying into her face.

Skyraven reached up and brushed the damp sand from her closed eyelids, sputtering choked curses beneath her breath. So, she was to die after all. She had no doubt after what she had seen, that these soldiers would not show any clemency.

"What's that you say, girlie?"

Although every nerve in her body was taut as a bowstring by now and her mouth as dry as the canyon walls, Skyraven knew she had to say something. She had to know why the white men had done this terrible thing to a peaceful people, had to at least have her say before they killed her.

"We have done nothing to you. Why do you hunt us down like animals? The Great Spirit will punish you for what you have done," she murmured, trying to force a courage that she did not feel. She was frightened, more frightened than she had ever been in her life and surely not ready to die, but she would never let the white eyes know it.

"She speaks English, Boyd." The man took a step closer. Taking her chin roughly in his callused hand, he lifted her face upward. "And look at those blue eyes. This one is part white."

What a fascination the white men had for blue eyes she thought. One might have thought they had never seen eyes the color of the sky before. Even so, Skyraven scorned her white blood. The whites were murderers!

"Sure as hell she is, Charlie. We'd better take her captive. Colonel Chivington may want to question her, her speakin' English and all."

"Naw!" The man shook his head. "You know what he said. *No* prisoners."

"But . . . but, Charlie—she's so pretty, I haven't the heart to kill her. Can't we take her back? Maybe we can keep her. Hell, I'll take her back to Boulder with me. Sure would be nice to have her to keep me warm when the nights are cold."

"Aw . . . all right!" He nudged Skyraven roughly with the toe of his boot. "Come on, squaw. Get up off your knees and come with us." The big-boned, blue-coated soldier reached down and wrapped his hairy arms around Skyraven's waist and lifted her to her feet.

Skyraven was in a state of shock as the two blue-coated, white soldiers dragged and pushed her along to where their horses were tethered. The full impact of what had happened swept over her. The deaths, the killing! For the first time, Skyraven allowed herself to think, and it was a shattering thing to remember. Would she ever forget the sound of the screams, the shrieks? No, they would forever be branded on her soul along with her hatred. And to think that just a few days ago she had given her heart and complete trust to one of the white soldiers, had so trustingly allowed him to bring her to this place. Peace, he had said, making a false promise.

"Oh, how could he have betrayed me so?" she breathed, falling to her hands and knees once more. The thought of what John Hanlen had done defeated her as no white man's bullets could do. Beating her breasts in a show of grief, she at last gave in to tears.

"Come on. Come on. Get up and follow me or I will have to shoot you," Boyd commanded.

At that moment, she nearly told the white man to do just that and might have if not for the memory of Desert Flower. She did have something to live for. Defiantly, she stood up, thrust back her shoulders, and walked along.

John Hanlen! John Hanlen, I curse you, she thought. Somehow she still wanted to believe that he had not had anything to do with the killing and yet how could she not believe when she had seen him with her very eyes. Lean Bear had trusted the whites and he was dead. Black Kettle had held out his hand in peace to the whites, had even received a medal, a flag, and papers from the Great White Father, saying that his

380

tribe was friendly. That hadn't stopped all of this. The white man had fired on Black Kettle even though he waved the American flag, even though he waved a white flag of truce. Both he and Left Hand had gone to Denver City and had eaten in the white man's homes. Left Hand had welcomed the miners, had left them in peace. Now they had all paid the price for showing any friendship to the whites.

"Come on. Walk a little faster. You ain't exactly a lady out for a little stroll and we ain't got all day." The tall, thin man pushed her forward causing her to lose her balance and fall to her knees. Ignoring the pain, brushing herself off, she rose again. They said nothing more to her, but pushed and shoved Skyraven along. Finally, they got to the clearing, where two horses stood patiently chewing on tree bark.

"Guess she'll have to ride with you, Boyd. My saddlebags are too full of souvenirs. That buffalo robe I took from the chief's place before we burned it down is rolled up across part of my saddle already."

Skyraven recognized Black Kettle's favorite painted buffalo robe. There was not another like it anywhere around. She wanted to ask if Black Kettle was still alive, but decided against it. These cutthroats would never tell her the truth.

"Did you take any scalps?" Boyd asked Charlie.

Skyraven paled at the question and drew back.

"Naw. Somehow taking hair just isn't my way of doin' things. I've knowed a few Indians in my day, some of them peaceful up around Boulder way. Well, I guess I just kept remembering."

"Ya know, just between you and me, I don't remember seeing very many braves in that camp. Mostly women and children. Kinda takes all the whoop-de-doo of the victory out of it. Kinda makes my mouth go dry . . ." Without another word, Boyd jerked Skyraven onto his horse.

Skyraven closed her eyes as she sat in front of the stocky man in the blue coat. She had been through so much on this day. All thought of running away had fled her. She knew she wouldn't have the strength to go very far. Her body was sore, she had several cuts and bruises. She was uncomfortable as they proceeded down the narrow trail along the river's edge. She really didn't have enough room sitting in front of the heavyset man. Even so, she realized how lucky she was. She was alive! Alive! At the same time, she grieved for those she loved who had been cut down. She felt her body pump with blood and gave her thanks to Man Above. Now she owed it to the Great Spirit to do something to help her people, to make her having survived worthwhile.

"Steady there, girlie. Don't fall off." As they went down the hillside, the man placed his big arm around her, but still his body slid into hers causing her to be caught between his girth and the saddle horn. The saddle horn pressed into her tender stomach, rubbing a new sore spot on her body. Even so, Skyraven welcomed the pain. It was a tangible sign of life and how very precious it was. Life! Once again she mourned those who had not been given the gift of life, shuddering as she thought about those who had been scalped. By doing terrible deeds, the soldiers had condemned them in the afterlife.

"Sure is flat country hereabouts. Not at all like those Flatirons we have up Boulder way," her heavyset captor was saying. "I sure am in a hurry to get back. Seems more like a thousand days than a hundred."

Skyraven managed to smile as they passed the place where Desert Flower and the baby were hidden. The two soldiers had not noticed that there was anyone in hiding. They obviously did not look very closely and did not see the dark eyes peering out and the hand raised in a waving position. But Skyraven did, and rejoiced in her heart to know that Desert Flower and Big Bear were still there and were all right. She was not alone after all. From wherever the soldiers took her, her heart would reach Desert Flower's and be glad.

Chapter Forty-three

John was tied securely and pushed into Chivington's tent. He posed no danger to the colonel, though he would have liked to have wrung his neck, for they had bound his hands and feet so tightly that he had gone beyond pain to numb fingers and toes. Even so, it was his heart that pained him, as well as his soul. Skyraven! Her face came back to haunt him again and again. He had so wanted to save her, to carry her away with him, but fate had not been that kind. Though it pained him to even think of it, he felt certain that she must be dead. He had watched the slaughter from a hill with his captors and knew there were very few survivors. He was afraid to hope.

And Skyraven's grandfather, Chief Left Hand, Blue Fox, and Desert Flower . . . What of them? he wondered. Had they been victims of this senseless act of violence? A great evil had been perpetrated today that he knew could never be fully rectified. Murder was the name he had for it, though Chivington called it "glory," and John was the one facing punishment.

"Inventory has been taken, sir." A young sergeant

entered the tent and addressed the balding lieutenant in charge of the records. "Four hundred fifty head of captured animals."

"And the lodges?" Chivington had ordered that a complete inventory of "recovered" articles be detailed.

"Sixteen buffalo robes, twenty finely tanned and embroidered deerskin dresses and skirts, sixteen buckskin breechcloths, ten pair of moccasins. Add to that some food, utensils, tools. And quite a lot of jewelry. Them Indians sure do like beads."

Were any of the purloined articles Skyraven's? John wondered. The very thought made him rage. Not one of these so-called "heroes" had been worthy to kiss her feet. Now the most wonderful woman who had ever touched his life was probably dead— dead while all these skunks were living.

"Dead . . ." he whispered. *Would death be his fate, too?*

John knew that his only redemption lay in the fact that Chivington had pushed southward. The colonel was heading toward the Arkansas River, or so he had said, in search of Little Raven and his band of Arapaho. *Another triumphant victory?* John wondered dryly. Perhaps the colonel would not be so determined to fight the Indians if they were armed. Shooting at women and children seemed to be his specialty. Had Chivington not left Sedgwick in command John had no doubt but that he would have met death at the hands of a firing squad much the same as the Reynolds gang had.

However, Sedgwick at last proved his true colors. He was no friend to John, and now he showed it as he entered the tent. His first order was to make certain the prisoner's bonds were secure.

385

"I want you to contact my father," John said, certain that when he revealed to his father exactly what had happened, it would be Chivington and not he who would be facing censure.

"I'm afraid not, John." Sedgwick's expression was uncompromising. "It would be against Colonel Chivington's orders."

"For God's sake, man, my life is in the balance." John tempered his shout, lowering his voice so that the others could not hear him. Another prisoner, an Indian, had been shot to death by a rowdy bunch of soldiers. He had to be careful not to get any of Chivington's remaining rowdies stirred up. "I think my father has a right to know."

"That his son is a traitor? Would you really want to do that to that proud old man?"

John's jaw ticked in anger. "I'm no traitor, and well you know it! It will be proved when I reveal what really happened here."

"We punished a band of rampaging Indians" was Sedgwick's response. "Chivington has written a letter attesting to the fact that scalps were found in the camp."

"That's a lie!" John retorted with furor. "If there are any, he planted them there to whitewash the fact that he just massacred a village of peaceful Indians."

Sedgwick smiled slowly. "Peaceful? Why, there are rifle pits dug in the bank."

"Rifle pits be damned. They were digging holes for themselves in which to hide from that devil's brutality." John shook his head. "Why am I talking to you? You know as well as I what happened here. As for me, my conscience is clear. I wonder if you will be able to sleep nights."

386

"I'll sleep very well, but, as for you, with so many marks against you, I would think you would be having nightmares." Sedgwick's eyes were as cold. "Consorting with the enemy for starters. To be exact, consorting with the enemy in time of war, which in itself carries a death penalty. Disobeying a direct order. You knew very well that no one, I repeat no one, was to cross that cordon and go to the Indian camp." His brows furled together. He thrust his face close to John's. "To warn them, I have no doubt." Before John could defend his actions, Sedgwick hurried on. "Cowardice. It is obvious you had no stomach for killing Indians and I can only think that to be because you feared for your own scalp." He paused, his face relaxing its stern lines as he thought of yet another charge. "Ah, yes. I forgot. Fleeing to the enemy with a national secret."

"Your charges or Chivington's?"

"I fully intend to back him up." Sedgwick strutted about, reading from a letter Chivington had dictated. In it, the colonel bragged about the defeat he had handed the Cheyenne and southern Arapaho at Sand Creek, calling it a "brilliant thing" which would make him a brigadier general, or put a star on his shoulder.

"We'll see," John mumbled, longing for freedom. If he could only get away, perhaps he could get together some of the soldiers who had been abused by the senseless violence and convince them to testify. He heard that Captain Silas S. Soule, one of the soldiers who had tried to talk Chivington out of his campaign, proved that a resolute commander could keep his men under control, even during hysteria. Through the hours of battle and butchery,

Soule had steadfastly refused to order his men to fire, making it known that he opposed killing peaceful Indians. Nor was Soule totally alone, for several of the men from Fort Lyon had been severely troubled over the matter. But would they tell anyone?

Sedgwick seemed to read John's mind. "Oh, now don't go thinking about stirring up a hornet's nest. You see, we have a trial all planned out for you, me and the colonel. Only we're going to keep it very secret. Just a few officers. Wouldn't want to ruin morale."

"If I reach the fort alive, is that what you mean? Well, don't think you can shoot me in the back on the way back to Fort Lyon and bury me out in the sand. If anything peculiar happens, there will be a full investigation."

For the first time since entering the tent, Sedgwick's self-confidence faltered. "What do you mean?"

"I mean that the letter from me to my father that Chivington has in his possession wasn't the only copy. I sent another, listing all of Chivington's little idiosyncrasies, such as what happened to those five Confederate outlaws."

"I see." For the moment at least, John knew his hide was saved. As he was hoisted on one of the fort's horses to head back to Fort Lyon and the brig, he had hope that the letter he had sent to his father would ensure his safety, at least for a while.

Chapter Forty-four

Skyraven's eyes opened wide as the small band of soldiers rode through the double gates of Fort Lyon. The sight of the cannon they pulled behind them made her flesh crawl. She gripped the saddle horn, feeling an all-consuming urge to flee, but the soldier behind her held onto her like a great big bear, making escape impossible. Hiding her trepidation, she held her head high, determined that the whites assembled to witness the return of the soldiers would see that the Indians were not cowards.

"Here they come!" Excitement swept through the fort at their approach. News of the soldiers' arrival had been sent on before them by a messenger who had come with a small band led by Lieutenant Colonel Henry Sedgwick. The whole situation just got more interesting all the time, it was whispered. Skyraven felt the heat of many eyes pointed her way.

"Look, there's one of those savages now. Must be a prisoner," one white woman shrilled.

A prisoner. Yes, Skyraven thought, that was just what she was. Remembering Lone Wolf's words to

389

her about his stay at the fort, she wondered if she, too, would be put in a cage.

"Where's Colonel Chivington?" came a voice from the gathered crowd. The question seemed to intrigue everyone. It was asked over and over as if the man was a hero.

"He's out chasing some more Indians with a goodly portion of the third," another voice answered. "Then he's gonna return to Denver City by another route along with two regiments of his one-hundred-day volunteers."

The procession of soldiers passed by a long row of stone buildings. Skyraven's eyes caught sight of a tall, slim, fashionably dressed woman standing on a wood-planked walkway in front of the open door of one of the structures. Perhaps Skyraven noticed her because the woman took a step in her direction, staring at the Indian girl all the while, though in a much friendlier manner than the others. The woman was dressed in a shiny dress the color of a squirrel's fur, with a high collar, a bodice that buttoned down the front, and undersleeves all of white lace. The flounces on the skirt and sleeves were edged in black lace. Her small white caplike bonnet sat high upon her head and was trimmed with yellow roses and tied with a wide yellow ribbon in a bow beneath her chin. Her dark-brown hair was parted in the middle and coiled around each ear in the manner Skyraven had seen the white women do their tresses.

"Goodness above, who is that girl with the soldiers?" the woman asked in a voice that held a tone of gentleness. "What are they going to do with her?"

"One of the women of the Indian camp. A survivor. One of the soldiers says she's got white blood," someone in the crowd answered. "A half-breed."

"The poor little thing . . ." The woman wore a deep-brown shawl which she pulled up around her shoulders as she tried to get a closer look at Skyraven. "She must be frightened to death."

Skyraven was entranced by the sound of the low melodious voice, the tone of compassion, and she suddenly took a strong interest in the white woman. Her dress billowed out, for beneath was a hoop skirt, but Skyraven did not know about such things and thought the woman had a very oddly formed body, much like a tepee. Skyraven could see white shoes with inch-high heels peeking out from below her skirt. How on earth would the lady manage to walk in shoes with high heels like that? She had never seen clothes like these before, not even on the few white women she had seen. She thought the Arapaho mode of dress was much prettier and much more comfortable. So thinking, she rubbed both hands down the full length of her doeskin dress to remove some of the dust so that the woman could see the embroidery emblazoned there. How proud she was that she had done the quillwork herself.

The lieutenant who had been leading the group gave the order to halt and dismount. While the other soldiers scrambled off in every direction, he handed the reins of his horse over to a stableboy and hastened toward the fashionably dressed lady. "Is your husband here?" he asked, seeming to be bothered by something.

"He'll be here in just a moment. He wanted to greet you boys when you came back." Once again the woman looked in Skyraven's direction. "Why is

391

she here?"

"We were told not to take prisoners, but a couple of the boys just took it into their heads to claim her." He toyed nervously with his hat as he spoke, as if not wanting to speak with her about the matter. "That's what I want to talk to your husband about. What to do with her."

"Can't she go back to her people?"

"No, ma'am, she can't. They're . . . they're all dead."

The woman put a gloved hand to her mouth. "Oh, dear!"

As if to reassure her that she hadn't ought to worry, the bluecoat who had taken a fancy to Skyraven slid off his horse and walked toward the lady. "She'll be just fine. I'm gonna take her back to Boulder with me to be my woman. The colonel said we could lay claim to any property we wanted, and so I have." He grinned. "Yes indeedy, I have."

The woman drew herself up to her full height, showing her indignity. "You most certainly will not take her with you. Your property, indeed! I'll see what my husband has to say about that!"

Skyraven was uneasy about all the attention she was getting. But the fact that she hadn't been tied up or led to any of the buildings to be put in a white man's prison made her breathe easier. To her way of thinking, the fact that they were not confining her made it obvious that she was not a prisoner. She did not know where she was supposed to go, but at least it appeared that she'd at least be able to walk about freely. Finding a water barrel, she just sat there looking around at her new surroundings. Everywhere there were blue-coated soldiers but few women and children. One little girl clung to her mother's skirts as they walked past the wagon, another shrieked and looked at Skyraven as if she thought she would eat her alive.

What had this white mother told her child about Indian women to frighten her so? Skyraven wondered.

Several young soldiers walked past the wagon and eyed her up and down, then slapped each other on the back and guffawed. Once or twice they glanced back at her over their shoulders. One of the men turned around as if he was going to come back and grab her but continued on his way. It was just a gesture to amuse his companions.

Skyraven trembled her indignity. White men were all wolves! Resentment bubbled in her like a pot over a fire. She hadn't forgotten what white soldiers such as these had done to her village. And now to act as if she were something for their merriment further incensed her. She didn't need their amorous glances, nor did she welcome them. She wouldn't spit on any one of them. No, never again would she be taken in by a white man's sweet talk!

Oh, John Hanlen, her heart cried. *How could you have betrayed me so.* How often she had thought about this very fort, hoped to one day see it because he lived within. Now such thoughts were painful reminders.

Skyraven tried to push away the thoughts that troubled her, the visions of what she had seen in her village, and yet they tormented her. She wanted to put her hands to her ears to block out the sounds of the screams, and yet perhaps she would hear them in her mind even then. She was so immersed in her own thoughts that she had forgotten completely about the well-dressed woman until she saw a bluecoat all decked out in fancy trim walk over to the wagon where Skyraven sat all alone.

"Oh, look at the poor little thing, Henry. How forlorn she looks. Living with those savages must have been quite a trial."

Skyraven bristled at the woman's words. Her people were not savages, it was the whites who were. Yesterday and today they had proved it. Living with her people had been joyful. Whereas being among the whites was a trial.

The blue-coated man standing next to Skyraven eyed the Indian girl with disdain. "Poor little thing, my eye, Gwen Ella. She is an *Indian.*"

The woman clucked her tongue in frustration. "If what I heard is correct, she is only half Indian. The other half is white. Blood just like our flows in her veins, Henry, and she is one of God's creatures."

"And a fearsome one at that," Henry Sedgwick retorted. "If what those two volunteers from Boulder told me is correct, she put up quite a fight when they first came across her." He put his arm protectively around his wife's shoulders. "Remember, she is a *hostile.*" Henry Sedgwick was a known Indian hater, but appeased his wife because of her Quaker upbringing. "She is a squaw. An Indian. Probably a lie about her being white and all."

"I don't think so, Henry." The woman put her index finger beneath Skyraven's chin and tipped up her face for a better look. "Look at that pale olive skin and those enormous blue eyes. She is part white, all right. I can train her to be a good Christian woman. I just know I can. I feel it here." Gwen Ella placed her hand over her heart.

He grunted. "You'd feel it there, all right, if she ever got a knife in her hand. Bloodthirsty, every last one of them."

A low keening issued from Skyraven's throat at his words, a mourning for her people. Henry Sedgwick knew very well that the Indian maiden was not hostile and that the attack upon her village was without reason, yet he said not a word to his wife about what had been done.

"Bloodthirsty?" Gwen Ella Sedgwick shook her head. "I don't think so, dear. I don't think she would harm me at all. There is something gentle about her. Something noble."

"Noble?" He threw back his head and laughed.

"Oh please, Henry. Can't I at least take the chance. Can't I have her? I could use her as a maid and . . ."

"No! I don't want some Indian hanging around and getting in the way." In truth, he didn't want a reminder of his part in the killings. "We had to punish her villagers. She might take revenge."

"I don't think she would. Please give her to me."

Sedgwick looked at his wife, then at the Indian girl, and then at his wife again. Would he dare? Chivington would have a fit if he heard, and yet it appeared the colonel would be out of the way for a while. Perhaps he could give it a try, and then when Gwen Ella saw how unmanageable and unsuitable the girl would be, she would stop nagging him.

"All right!" His wife had just recently come from Missouri to live at the fort. Perhaps if she did have some help, it would make the fort seem more like home. She had told him she felt harried with problems because she had no place to put her belongings and that she had not been able to find a decent maid to come with her. If the Indian girl worked out, fine; if not, he'd send her to live with the half-breed Bent at the trading post.

Skyraven just sat there as the two of them discussed her future. She was tired, both physically and mentally. At the moment she didn't really care what happened to her. The world as she knew it had died when the soldiers had killed her people.

"Would you like to live with me? Would you like to be my maid?" Gwen Ella asked gently.

Skyraven did not understand what the word "maid" meant, but she shook her head wearily. Yes. Anything was better than that big burly soldier. She didn't want to be anyone's woman. Besides, it didn't matter. She had no intention of staying here among people who had killed her own. As soon as she could get herself a horse, as soon as no one was looking, she was going to ride out of here, back to the place she had left Desert Flower and her baby.

"All right then, come along with me." Gwen Ella held out her hand in a gesture of friendship. "Don't be afraid. We can become friends, you and I."

Friends? Skyraven would never show the whites friendship again. Still, she said nothing and stood up, placed her moccasined foot on one of the wagon wheels, and holding on to the rim of the wagon bed, let herself down to the ground slowly.

"By what name are you called?" Gwen Ella asked her. "That soldier you were with said you can speak English fluently. Will you tell me your name?"

"I am called Skyraven," she said proudly, without hesitation, as the two of them walked along the

396

graveled road toward the long line of stone buildings.

"Skyraven." Gwen Ella smiled. "That is a very nice name, but now that you are here, perhaps we should give you another name, one such as Mary, Estelle, or Jenny. A white woman's name."

"No!" Skyraven looked shocked at such a thought. "I do not want a white woman's name. I am Skyraven, granddaughter of the Arapaho's *wicasa waken*." She drew herself up to her full height and proudly raised her head.

Gwen Ella could see that she had offended the young Indian girl. "Oh yes, of course." She cleared her throat trying to recall Skyraven's words. "You are the granddaughter of the . . . the . . ."

"The *wicasa waken*, the medicine man," Skyraven explained.

"Yes, yes. Skyraven. To be sure. If that is the name you want to be called by, that is the way it will be. I do not want us to argue or have misunderstandings so early in our relationship. I so need another woman to talk to. There are other women here, but most of them are not officer's wives as I am. Most of the officer's wives prefer to live close to Fort Weld, you see. Many of the women here at Fort Lyon are married to enlisted men and live over there on Suds Row." Gwen Ella pointed to a group of run-down wood barracks at the opposite end of the fort.

Skyraven looked in that direction. Little boxes just like she had been told about, but what did the woman mean exactly? "I do not understand. What is this Suds Row?"

"Where the laundry is done."

"Like at the river with soapweed."

Gwen Ella chuckled. She was expecting too much from the girl. After all, they were from two different cultures. "We do our laundry in tubs. It is quite tedious work."

"Are we going there now to join the other women?"

Gwen Ella looked horrified. "Join them? Oh, no. The women are . . . are . . ." She didn't know quite how to explain. "Oh, dear, there is so much to teach you. Where do I begin?" She let her breath out in a long sigh. "Of course you don't understand, but you will after you have been here a while longer. Let me explain as best I can for now." She opened the door and gently guided Skyraven in the opposite direction, then led her inside one of the stone buildings. "This is where I live."

"Here?" Skyraven scanned the room but Gwen Ella didn't seem to hear the surprise in the girl's voice.

"My husband is an officer and receives much money, but the majority of men receive but thirteen dollars a month. Most of them have never married because they cannot afford to, but those who *are* married must put their wives to work in the laundry here at the fort in order to make ends meet. That is the reason their barracks are known as Suds Row."

Skyraven had lost all interest in Gwen Ella's explanation. When the white woman looked at her to see if she now understood the meaning of "Suds Row," she observed the girl looking all around her new surroundings. She had never been inside one of the white men's confining boxes before and found she did not like it at all.

"Perhaps it is too early to talk to you about such

398

things. Come, Skyraven, I will show you around." She led her to the largest room. "This room we are in is called the living room." Noticing Skyraven's expression as she looked toward the muslin-covered couch, Gwen Ella walked over and patted its cushion. "Would you like to sit down upon it?"

Skyraven sat down and bounced up and down several times but quickly got up. "It is like a wild horse that must be tamed." She sat down upon the floor in front of the couch. "In my lodge I sit like this upon soft buffalo robes."

Because Skyraven could speak excellent English, Gwen Ella had assumed that she had been around many white people. It was obvious to her now that she was wrong in her assumption. She would have to be patient.

"I'll show you the kitchen and the bedrooms if you will follow me."

Together they walked through the house from room to room. It was sparsely furnished because Gwen Ella had just recently arrrived herself. She had brought her trunks of clothing and her personal belongings with her as well as several well-packed boxes of china dishes and crystal glassware that were never allowed out of her sight for very long. They were her prized possessions. Many of their furnishings would arrive later, on the Over-land Stage.

"Now, this will be your room. You will be my personal maid and my companion when my husband must be away for long periods of time. You will sleep in that bed, in this room, and eat your meals with us in the kitchen."

While Gwen Ella talked, Skyraven's thoughts wandered. She had to get out of here, but how? As they had walked along she had noticed that the fort was heavily guarded. Men with guns were everywhere. She must be careful. It would not do Desert Flower any good if she got herself shot.

"Do you think you will be comfortable here with me?" Gwen Ella was hopeful. She just didn't want to find out the girl was unsuitable and have to give her up.

"I am not sure I would like being indoors so much of the time." What would her grandfather think when she told him? She put her hand to her throat. How could she have forgotten? In all probability, Buffalo's Brother was dead. The thought brought a mist of tears to her eyes. She would miss him so, and Desert Flower and her little one, as well as others of her tribe. She knew that Desert Flower and Big Bear were all the family she had now. Oh, Grandfather! Desert Flower and her baby had been spared, but she still knew nothing of her grandfather's fate. Perhaps . . . She could only hope that he had not been killed in the fighting. She had not seen him at all during the commotion, and all she could remember was that he had been standing in front of Black Kettle's lodge when she looked back over the river.

"And now if you will come along with me, Skyraven, I will show you where the privy is, and then you can carry some water for your bath. You are badly in need of one."

Skyraven knew it was so. No tribe of Indians were as clean in their personal habits as the Cheyenne and the Arapaho, but now she felt dirty, grimy, and had a keen desire to jump into some clear creek water. It would be so good to wash her body and her hair.

Skyraven just stood and watched as Gwen Ella stepped upon a stool, opened a small square door, and took down two large buckets and a wooden tub from the long narrow storeroom just off the kitchen. She placed them on the floor in front of Skyraven.

"Now that you know where these are kept, Skyraven, you can get them down yourself when we need bathwater." Gwen Ella was a little fanatical in her zeal. She felt it was her place to lead the savages into a different way of life, to eventually guide them in the ways of the Lord.

Skyraven was confused. "Why do we not just go to the creek?" That would give her a chance to escape, she thought.

Although Gwen Ella was trying hard to be a good Christian, she was having some difficulty accepting Skyraven's strange ways and her silly questions. She couldn't help looking at herself as the superior being. If only maids were not so hard to find out here in this godforsaken land. There were no white women to fill the job. Here there was but one woman to every hundred or so men, she judged. She had been told by several of her traveling companions that even the ugly girls were quickly snatched up as wives for the miners and other men in the district. The men didn't care what they looked like as long as they could cook and keep their beds warm. This one would just have to do.

"Because it would be indecent, my dear." That was her only explanation. Henry had said this girl was a savage. Was she, in spite of the way she could speak English? Like many other people in the States, Gwen Ella had never even seen an Indian woman before, much less talked to one. The fact that the girl could speak English, however, had to be in her favor.

"Indecent?"

"And we might catch a chill . . ." The feelings she was now experiencing were the consequence of long exposure to talk about the inferiority of the Indians, Gwen Ella reminded herself. Opinions were divided. Even she and Henry did not see them in the same way. Many of the people who talked about the Indians as if they were animals had never been in the West. And, after all, this girl was part white. Certainly she would be less of a savage because of her white blood. She deserved a chance. How proud Gwen Ella would be of herself if she could help Skyraven to see the evilness of the Indian culture and adopt white man's ways.

When Skyraven leaned over, picked up the water buckets as if trying to please, Gwen Ella's fears were laid to rest. She looked so very sweet and innocent, not at all like a hostile. She would clean her up and dress her like a white woman and see what would happen then.

Chapter Forty-five

Skyraven was used to heavy work, but making so many trips to and from the laundry on one side of the fort to the officers' quarters on the other side had taken a toll on her strength. White people were certainly strange, she thought. With all the water in the creek nearby, she had had to go back and forth, back and forth for water. Instead of going to where the water was to bathe, they made the water come to them. It seemed pointless and silly. Now she was tired. The buckets seemed twice as heavy as they had on her first trip. Nevertheless, she had completed her task and now stood proudly before the lady who insisted she call her Gwen Ella.

"Skyraven, you are back. That didn't take you any time at all," the woman said, eyeing her with relief, as if she had been afraid she might not return at all.

"Yes, I am back." Wanting to rest, Skyraven sat down on the floor, but the woman motioned for her to stand back up.

"No, no there is more to do."

Some of the water buckets Skyraven had carried

from the water-storage barrels in the laundry room were now poured into a large, oval-shaped copper boiler which was now placed on top of the kitchen stove. Gwen Ella lifted one end, Skyraven the other. Beneath it, a fire was lit, sending tiny orange-and-blue flames to lick at the boiler in fury.

"What . . . what are you doing? Cooking?" Skyraven asked. It was the only thing that made sense, for why else was water put on to boil?

"I'm readying your bath. When the water is hot, we'll put it in the large wooden tub over there," she pointed to it resting on the floor, "and then you can get inside."

The idea was terrifying to Skyraven. So, she had not escaped the white man's cruelty after all. They had just found another form of torture for her. They were going to boil her alive. They were going to cook her! As soon as the woman's back was turned, she fearfully slipped away, making a hasty retreat to her bedroom. Searching for a hiding place, she slid under the bed and lay on her stomach as quiet as a mouse, hardly daring to breathe.

"Ah, that should do . . ." When the water was boiling hot, using a large metal dipper, Gwen Ella poured dipper after dipper full of hot water into the cold water in the wooden tub to bring it to just the right temperature. Testing it with her elbow, she decided it to be perfect.

"Now, Skyraven, you may take your clothes off and . . ." She looked around, but Skyraven was nowhere in sight. "Skyraven. Skyraven," she called as she searched the house room by room. Where on earth could that girl have gone?

The door was still locked so she must be somewhere in the house. Gwen Ella called again but

Skyraven did not answer her. Then something led her to the bedroom, and the same intuition caused her to pick up the dust ruffle and lean over to look under the bed. Her look of astonishment was met by Skyraven's terrified look of utter fear.

"No! No!" Skyraven tried to wriggle out from beneath the bed away from Gwen Ella, but the bed was too close to the wall. The only direction she could go was directly toward where Gwen Ella stood. She was trapped.

"Whatever is the matter, child?" Gwen Ella was completely dumbfounded. "I'm not going to harm you."

"White men are cruel. I . . . I thought . . ." Skyraven was still not sure that she could trust this woman, though she had seemed kind. If the soldiers were so brutal what then of their women? The Ute women were often as violent as their men.

"Come on out of there this instant!" Gwen Ella decided to be firm with her. Even so, her voice held a tone of gentleness. "No one is going to hurt you."

Skyraven slowly crept out from beneath the bed. There in the corner of the room like a cornered animal, she knelt on all fours looking up at the white woman and not knowing what to do, which way to run. Her eyes searched for a weapon, yet she knew fighting was of little use.

Gwen Ella herself was filled with fear. She saw the direction of the Indian girl's eyes. A decorative knife that her husband had taken as a trophy from the Indian wars adorned the bedroom wall, and it was there that the girl was looking. Gwen Ella did not know why Skyraven was acting in such a strange manner, but she did remember her husband's warning. The girl might have white blood, but she was still an Indian.

The two women remained transfixed, simply looking at each other, neither speaking nor daring to move. Finally Gwen Ella dared to ask a question. "Skyraven, what on earth is the matter? Tell me. Please . . ."

"I will not let you cook me!"

"Cook you?" She didn't know whether to laugh or be angry. "I have no intention of doing that. How could you think such a thing?"

"Your people came into my camp bringing death. Why would I not think so?"

"Well, I assure you I have no intention of having you for dinner." Gwen Ella put her hands upon her hips. "Now, please get up from that uncomfortable position and come into the kitchen to take your bath."

Skyraven shook her head from side to side to indicate that her answer was no, then thought for a moment. "You are not going to cook me? Do you give me your word?"

Gwen Ella had to stifle a chuckle. The girl was not dangerous after all. She was just frightened. "Oh, my dear, of course not. You will enjoy your bath. The water is just nice and warm." She felt the need to explain. "You see, we do not like the water cold. I have made it as if you were in your . . . uh . . . creek on a hot summer's day."

"Like taking a bath in summer?"

"Come with me and you will see." As they walked together to the kitchen, Gwen Ella said aloud, "Well, my dear, I have crossed one hurdle but still have a long way to go. This is going to be quite a challenge after all, but I will teach you to accept the white world and our customs if it's the last thing I ever do." Skyraven's actions had made Gwen Ella even more determined. The girl was just too pretty to act like a silly savage.

Slowly Skyraven took off her garments, keeping her eyes on the white woman all the while. When Gwen Ella did nothing that appeared hostile, she relaxed a bit. Taking her finger, she thrust it in the water and was surprised to find it was comfortably warm. Skyraven put first one foot, then the other, into the tub, splashing around as she did when the women went wading in a pool, then slowly she lowered her body into the water.

"Mmm!" She leaned back in the tub and lathered herself with the sweet-smelling soap Gwen Ella had provided. "This smells better than soapweed."

"I'm glad you like it. I brought it with me from Missouri. It is lilac."

"Lilac!" Skyraven smiled as she popped several bubbles on her shoulder. She was enjoying herself so much that she didn't want to get out of the tub when Gwen Ella handed her the big white flannel bath towel. In rebellion, she sank down in the water to her shoulders, lifting first one leg, then the other to spread on the sweet-smelling bubbles. She didn't like the whites, but she did like this custom of theirs.

Gwen Ella felt triumphant. She had vaulted the first hurdle, but then what woman wasn't won over by lilac perfume? "If you will get out of the tub we will pour this water out and put in some fresh water to wash your hair with. I have some lilac shampoo."

Skyraven decided she would like to have some of

the bubbles put on her hair as well, so she complied and found it to be a pleasing experience, despite a slight sting of pain when she got some of the soap in her eyes. When all the washing was completed, Gwen Ella promised her yet another pleasant surprise.

"We'll make your hair curly," she said, "like mine."

"But . . . but I like my hair the way it is . . ."

"Nonsense!" The girl had beautiful, thick dark hair. She would tie strips of rags into Skyraven's damp hair to curl it, then she would look more like the other women in the fort.

After the rags were securely tied, Gwen Ella helped Skyraven into the clothing she had earlier assembled for her, cast off items that she had grown tired of. They wouldn't be a perfect fit, but that could be altered with a few pins here and there, or a little sewing.

For the moment, Skyraven was able to put the horror of the massacre out of her mind. There were so many new things being shown to her that it became an adventure. She recalled now that when she was a little girl she had gone to the trader's stores with her mother. She had admired the few white women she had seen dressed in calico and gingham. And then John Hanlen had given her the length of blue calico. But she would never be able to use it to make any garments now. Like all her other possessions it would either have been taken by the soldiers or else burned when the village was set afire.

Suddenly the painful memories came flooding back and she put her hands to her face. She could never forget that she had looked up and seen him fighting with Lone Wolf right in the middle of the violence. *What kind of man knowingly led people to their slaughter?* "Why . . .?" she cried.

"What, my dear?"

"Nothing!" Skyraven lifted her head. She would push the image from her mind lest she be consumed by her tears. With resolve, she tried, but she could not erase John Hanlen's name from her memory. What would he think, what would he do when he saw her here at the fort. Did he think that she would have been killed, that he would not have to face her, answer to her for what he had done? Well, he was wrong if he thought that. He would know the full fury of her wrath, this she promised.

"You will look so pretty when I am finished with you that all the men at the fort will stare," Gwen Ella said.

"I do not want them to look. I hate white men!" Her answer was so vehement that Gwen Ella was taken aback.

"Nonsense. There are some very nice enlisted men here." Her voice lowered conspiratorially. "And there are so few women you will have your choice."

"I do not want my choice." How could she even think of another man after what had happened? She should have married Lone Wolf. At least he fought for the village. He was one of her own kind. How could she have been so foolish as to ever give her heart to a white man? She should have listened to Lone Wolf, shared his hatred of the whites. Instead, she had succumbed to pretty words. And yet the saddest thing of all was that she still loved him even after what he had done.

Shaking her head to clear it of the image of

John Hanlen which danced before her mind's eye, Skyraven pulled on the knee-length, lace-trimmed muslin drawers that Gwen Ella handed her, thinking how foolish the white women were to wear something so pretty that would not be seen. Even so, they felt smooth to her skin. She tied the long strings that circled her waist to keep them in place. Next came a muslin shift, then wool stockings held up by round stretchable bands Gwen Ella called garters.

"White women's clothing is funny," she laughed as Gwen Ella held out a stiff, circular-shaped piece of material toward her explaining that it was a padded and horsehair crinoline with whale bone at its bottom to make the skirt of the dress stand out. Skyraven did not want to wear the hoop skirt nor the shoes with the high heels, and Gwen Ella did not insist, and fitted her instead with a soft flannel petticoat.

"Oh, Skyraven, you would look so much better if you would not be so stubborn. But then . . ."

Skyraven lifted one eyebrow as a smile tugged at her lips. "When I first saw you standing in front of your house, I did not know that you had on that big heavy tent like that piece of clothing. I thought you were built like a tepee, little at the top and big at the bottom." She circled round and round Gwen Ella, puzzled. "How can you sit down or even move around in that . . . that thing?"

"Somehow I manage." Gwen Ella laughed so hard that tears filled her eyes. Skyraven was absolutely right. There had been much discussion in the fashion world over the bulky crinoline hoop skirts the women were wearing. Not everyone liked wearing them. "Right now they are in fashion."

"In fashion?" It was a strange reason, but Skyraven didn't ask any more questions. She didn't like it when the white woman laughed. In truth, Skyraven thought how little she felt like laughing right now. Did this woman know what the men of her kind had done? She decided that she did not or she would not have given into her laughter. No, the white woman just didn't really understand. Perhaps her husband did not want her to know what he had been up to.

Gwen Ella hovered over Skyraven as if she were a lifesize doll, babbling on about her life. When she had decided to come west to be with her husband, she had determined that fashionable dress would be a way of keeping up her morale out in the dismal place she was going to live in, she told Skyraven. Gwen Ella had worn the simple Quaker dress when she was younger, but after her marriage, Henry had insisted that it would help his career if she were more fashionably dressed. It was expensive to dress in the manner befitting an officer's wife but Henry wanted it that way and that was the way it would be. "Even a yard of printed calico costs twenty five dollars," Gwen Ella was explaining to Skyraven.

Calico. Once again Skyraven remembered John Hanlen and his present. This time she could not help the mist of tears that stung her eyes at the betrayal by someone she had trusted and loved.

By the time the two women had completed Skyraven's attire they had become better acquainted, and if not friends at least closer to being so. The process had allowed them to know more about each other and to dispel some of the darkness surrounding Skyraven. A bond of sorts was formed when the women discovered they were just about the same size. Skyraven was fuller in the bust and Gwen Ella thicker around the waist and hips, but with slight alteration, Gwen Ella's clothes would fit Skyraven, as she put it, "quite nicely."

When at last the process of clothing the Indian girl was finished, Gwen Ella led her to a long mirror. "Well. . . ?"

Skyraven stared at her reflection, not really certain just what she thought. She was finally dressed in one of Gwen Ella's house frocks, a simple long-sleeved, red-printed calico dress with a white collar and cuffs, and a white apron tied around her waist. The only thing remaining was her hair. Certainly now, with the rags in it, she looked silly. As if she were going on the warpath, she thought.

"And now I'll work the finishing touch." She positioned Skyraven in front of the mirror, untied the rags, and began to style the long luxurious tresses.

Skyraven's hair was too abundant to pile in an upsweep so it was gently curled under in the popular waterfall style, with curls and ringlets over the ears. Most women wearing this style used a horsehair support, which they tied under their own hair to give it the added bulk, but Skyraven needed no artificial aids. Her hair was long, thick, and shiny blue-black. Gwen Ella felt a moment of envy, then pushed it aside. The girl was stunning, and she thought to herself she was partly responsible for the vision that stared back from the mirror. It gave her a sense of accomplishment. Henry would be very surprised.

And indeed he was. When he came into the house for dinner a few hours after the transformation was completed, he had hardly recognized Skyraven. His eyes raked over her. Why hadn't he noticed her slim waist and big bosom before? he silently asked himself. She was a beauty. Yes indeed, a real beauty. Perhaps having brought her here to be nearby was not such a bad idea after all. Looking at her now, she didn't look anything at all like a dirty Injun.

When they sat down to dinner, he could hardly keep his eyes off her. She was a pretty little piece. Gwen Ella was so cold, but he had heard that the Indian women were very passionate. He had to try extremely hard to cover up the lust he was feeling for the girl at the moment. It would never do for Gwen Ella to suspect such a thing. But he'd find a time when the Indian girl was alone and then . . .

"Well, my dear," he took Gwen Ella's hand and gently kissed it, "you have accomplished quite a miracle with this girl. She will fit in quite nicely after all. So you see, you were right." Gwen Ella smiled at his admission that she and not he had seen the girl's potential. "And I am glad you will have someone to help you now," he said pleasantly, hiding his true thoughts, that he would make of this Indian girl his mistress. His eyes met Skyraven's as he said, "I believe you can prepare yourself for a long stay with us. Indeed, I think you will be with us for a very long time . . ."

Chapter Forty-six

Escape! The word that pounded over and over in John Hanlen's brain as he rode back to the fort. He had to find out what had happened to Skyraven or be doomed to sleepless nights and an agony of uncertainty. But he had to be careful. Sedgwick had ordered his foremost prisoner to be surrounded by five armed men for the journey, one riding in front of him, one at each side, and two behind, all brandishing rifles. If he tried to ride away, John had no doubt but that he would be shot. Perhaps that was what Sedgwick really wanted and if so, he did not want to play into his hands.

Sedgwick. The very name stuck in his craw. How could he have ever trusted the bastard? Family friend, indeed! It was obvious to John now that Sedgwick had merely used his father's influential position to further his own ends. Now he was riding on the crest of Chivington's bravado and popularity, hoping it would reap rewards upon his own head. He had been put in command of the fort while Chivington had gone looking for Indians and was playing his authority to the hilt, insisting he

414

arrive back at the fort before anyone else on the pretext that he wanted to greet the brave men. Bullshit! Undoubtedly he wanted to ascertain that none of the soldiers, haunted by conscience, would shoot off their mouths. The truth would be the one thing both Sedgwick and Chivington would want to conceal.

John was glad that Sedgwick had gone on ahead. He knew the colonel all too well and knew he was a man who seldom let down his guard. Had he been along, John would have been under a scrutinizing, constant surveillance. As it was, the longer they rode, the more frequent were the times the men guarding John were distracted. He knew if he kept patient and focused a keen eye on his guards, he just might find a way out of this dilemma.

And John's patience paid off much sooner than he had anticipated. When they had traveled a third of the way to the fort, an image of some concern to the soldier leading the unit appeared on the horizon. Alarm coursed through the soldiers as the cry went out that a band of Indians was approaching.

Like a storm cloud, they swept down upon the mounted soldiers. The bluecoats were outnumbered. Far different from the incident at Sand Creek, these Indians were armed and therefore threatening. Fear that they might retaliate in kind for what their tribesmen had suffered prompted the soldiers into a near panic.

"Ride like hell!" The sergeant in the lead guided the men off to the right, hoping to outdistance the rampaging band. In the melee for self-preservation, John was forgotten for just a moment, but it was long enough for him to take advantage of the situation. With his heart beating wildly, he crested the top of a hill, and though he heard a shout and the retort of a gun being fired, he escaped being hit.

Nothing but wild grass and hills constrained him. Urging his horse onward, John plunged ahead to freedom. The wind tore at his face as he rode onward but he scarcely noticed, as he had no thought but to escape. Heedless of the rutted landscape, he rode faster and faster, looking back from time to time to see if he was being followed. He was, but not by soldiers. John thought he recognized the brave who had fought him at Skyraven's camp riding close upon his heels. So, he had been wounded but not enough to keep him down, he thought. Despite his predicament, he was glad, for it would have been tragic if a man of such fighting spirit and courage had been condemned to death and mutilation. For now, however, John would have to outride him, for he doubted any words could convince the brave that he was not involved in the atrocities against his people. He would have to get away or face death. With that thought in mind, he sought a firm grip on the reins, bending close to the churning muscles of his horse as if to become one with the animal.

The sound of approaching horses' hooves gave ominous warning that urged John to find a hiding place quickly. There was no way he could give a good accounting of himself were he forced to fight. Thus thinking, he guided his horse toward a clump of trees, where he would be able to seek the shelter of the trunks and branches, double back, make a large circle, and emerge from the thicket to take a different path. Though he knew how skilled Indians were at tracking, he could only hope that were he to disappear, his pursuer would lose interest in continuing the chase and seek others who were visible. With that thought in mind, he raced toward the foliage, reining in his mount to hide behind a tall, stout tree. From his position, he could see the shadow of his pursuer as he rode past him. Holding his breath for a long time, John at last gave in to his sense of relief, dispelling the air in his lungs with a sigh. With as much intensity as if he were an Indian, he trained his ears to the sounds. It was quiet, and he could only suppose that the soldiers had escaped any real danger. Still, he stayed where he was for many minutes, only emerging when he thought the coast was clear.

His own safety but of secondary importance, Skyraven's plight drove him on to retrace the path he had just ridden. From a vantage point on the hilltop, John could see a few of the soldiers still scavenging around. Once again he had to be patient, keeping out of their sight. When the last of the soldiers were gone, he stealthily led his horse down the hill. He found the Indian village in a smoldering ruins of death and destruction. Undoubtedly, the order to torch the village was to hide any evidence of what had happened.

In a daze he rode through the camp, revulsion overtaking him as he stared down at the bodies. Chivington had called the Indians savages, and yet the scalped and ravaged bodies revealed the savageness of the white man. Only now did the full realization of the horror strike him. His heart ached for the plight of these proud people. They had trusted, had wanted peace, and this is where it had led them.

"May God have mercy on their souls . . ." Crossing himself, he said a hasty prayer for the Indians who had died, and for the few white men as well.

Somehow managing to dismount, holding his horse's bridle tightly in his bound hands, John gave in to his desolation. Why? It was a question that had no logical answer. What added to his pain was the thought that he had been too late to save Skyraven. And yet his heart and soul cried out that she was not among those killed and in that then, there was still hope.

There were scattered weapons lying about. John used a discarded knife to work at his bonds, feeling a deep sense of calm once he was freed. The night seemed to be the coldest he had experienced so far, and he shivered, clutching the ends of a saddle blanket around his shoulders. Though he didn't know quite where to start looking for Skyraven, he found that somehow he just couldn't bring himself to leave. Perhaps he was hoping to find some clue to her whereabouts, he thought. Hunkering down, he picked up a discarded string of beads, and in that moment was fully lost to his pain. Though he had been told a man should never cry, he couldn't fight against the moisture that stung his eyes and blocked his vision.

A sudden noise warned him of danger. Looking behind him, he found himself staring into a begrimed face. The eyes were open wide in the shock of finding him here. Armed with a knife, the woman brandished it threateningly as if to protect the baby in her arms, yet something in her manner told him that in actuality she would not strike unless she had to. "I am not here with intent to hurt you," he said. His eyes met hers in stunned recognition. "Desert Flower!"

"You!" She stared at him in uncertainty. The uniform he wore marked him in her eyes as the very devil. "Why are you here?"

"I came to find Skyraven." He stretched out his arms in supplication. "Please, Desert Flower, tell me what happened to her."

Not knowing his motives, Desert Flower cried out at once, "She is dead!"

"Dead? No!" It was as if she inflicted a blow more fatal than any knife could render. Falling to his knees, John put his hands in his face and moaned. "Then I am too late to save her. Dear God!" In an outpouring of grief, he gave full vent to his sorrow, a sorrow that could only be soothed by his rage. "I'll kill him! I'll go after that bastard Chivington and I'll make him pay for what he did! The unfeeling bastard. How could he have been so ruthless? The filthy murderer!"

Desert Flower watched him warily. His grief was sincere, and yet how could she even think to trust a soldier? Coldly she said, "You have killed many, Bluecoat. Skyraven was but one among us."

John's eyes glittered with an angry fever as he turned to her. "I didn't, Desert Flower. It was not I. *I* took no part in any of this. You must believe me. Not all the soldiers are murderers. I did not fire any bullets in this slaughter. I did not kill any of your people. I was taken prisoner by my so-called chief because I would not have part in this atrocity. But I escaped when a band of Indians swooped down upon my captors. I came here hoping to find Skyraven. I had so hoped, but now I know that all is lost. All I can do now is avenge her, though it will mean my own death."

"Avenge her? You would do that?" Little by

little, Desert Flower's distrust was wavering. Skyraven's soldier was reacting as one would who spoke the truth. His eyes spoke clearly that what he was saying came from the heart. "Even though you would forfeit your own life, Bluecoat?"

"Even so." He closed his eyes. "I only wish that I could undo what has been done. I am sorry, Desert Flower. More so than you can ever understand."

"Then you have passed my test and I will tell you the truth," she said slowly. "Skyraven lives, though she has been taken prisoner by two men who wear the dress of soldiers."

"What?" His eyes flew open. For a moment John was afraid to believe, thinking that she was only trying to toy with him as punishment for the white soldiers' evil deeds.

"It is true. I saw her ride by with one of the soldiers and I heard the soldiers talking about taking her with them. I think one of the bluecoats wants to claim her, take her back to live with him in his lodge."

Dear God, what kind of man was she at the mercy of? What would they do to her? "Tell me, Desert Flower. You have to think and be certain."

"They talked about rocks. About boulders. They were headed in that direction." She pointed in the direction of the fort.

John motioned for the Indian girl to sit down beside him. "Tell me everything you saw. It is the only way I can even think to set Skyraven free. The chief of the fort is an evil man. I can't let her stay in his clutches."

Desert Flower took a seat beside him, her voice shaking with emotion as she relived the fear and revulsion she had experienced watching the slaugh-

420

ter of her people. She told him of Skyraven's bravery in coming to help her and her baby Big Bear flee to safety, how the soldiers were shooting at the running Indians, offering no mercy.

"We took refuge in the bank. Skyraven hid me and my baby in the weeds. I think she ran away to lead the soldiers away from my hiding place. It was then she got captured by the two soldiers. As I told you, they rode right by where I was hiding and it was then I heard them mention taking her with them."

"They did not say anything about going after Indians?"

"No."

"Then in all likelihood they did not go with Chivington. The fort is the only answer." John sighed wearily. Did he dare sneak into the fort to try to free her? What other choice did he have? After what he'd seen today, there wasn't anything he would put past Chivington or Sedgwick. He'd heard that several of the soldiers had even blatantly shot a man of half-white, half-Indian blood merely because they had some bone to pick with him. All Chivington had replied was "I have given the order that no prisoners be taken." What if, after having survived the massacre, Skyraven had been similarly murdered? He couldn't take the chance that she might be in danger. With that thought in mind, he bounded to his feet.

"You are going to free her?" Desert Flower tried to smile but managed only a grimace.

"What of you?" Knowing how much Skyraven loved her friend and the baby, he knew he couldn't just desert them.

"Some of us survived. Not many, but a few. My

421

husband and Skyraven's grandfather among them . . ."

"Her grandfather?" He rejoiced in that bit of news. Perhaps Buffalo's Brother did have some magic after all.

"I saw them from the hill, but I was too afraid to come out of hiding to join them. I returned to camp hoping they might still be here but found only you. They must think that I am dead."

"Where were they headed?" It was his intent to at least lead Desert Flower to her people before he started back toward the fort. He couldn't just leave her here all alone.

"I think they must be headed for the Smoky Hills, where some of our people are still encamped. The ones who did not want peace. We will join them there."

"Then I will take you in that direction. Once you are safe, I will go get Skyraven and we will join you. Would you take me in, Desert Flower. Can I become an Indian? In truth, I don't want to be a soldier. Not anymore . . ."

"Yes, we will take you in, John Hanlen." She reached out and took his hand as a sign of good faith, then followed him as he made his way to where his horse was waiting.

Chapter Forty-seven

Sounds travel far in the stillness of the plains. John soon learned that the Indians had honed their sense of hearing. To him, the night appeared silent, but Desert Flower listened keenly, and utilized the sounds she alone heard to guide John in the proper direction. Thus it took less time than he had thought possible to catch up with the party of surviving Indians headed northeast. Taking off his neckerchief, he waved it frantically in a sign of peace as he came upon them, though, as he came closer, he could see that he had little to fear from the pathetically ragged band.

"What do you want, white man?" Blue Fox's initial reaction had been hostility, but then he saw the precious gifts John was bearing as a sign of his goodwill. "My wife! My child! Why? How . . . ?"

John aided Desert Flower, who cradled Big Bear in her arms, to get down off his horse and responded to the question. "It's a long story, Blue Fox, one which your wife will tell you as she warms herself by your night fires. All I want you to know is that I was never against you, that just as you were betrayed by the soldiers' talk of peace, so was I. Words can never express what I feel at this moment, nor can my sorrow bring back those who died. All I can tell you is that not all white men are evil. I was not alone in còunciling against what happened, but men do not always listen to wisdom."

"Skyraven's soldier did not fight us, Husband. And because of that, he was taken prisoner by his own. It is as your father often said, that a man must be judged for what is in his own heart."

"Then to you I will offer my hand in friendship." Though Blue Fox never thought he could look upon a white man's face again without feeling hatred, with John Hanlen he made the gesture of peace.

They talked briefly, for John was anxious to see to Skyraven's safety, but in the short conversation he learned that news travels quickly among Indians and what had happened at Sand Creek was already being retold at the lodge fires of the various tribes. The reaction of the other plains chiefs was quick and violent: they were advocating an all-out Indian war.

"But that will mean more death, more destruction," John argued.

"That is what Black Kettle is insisting. He was deeply angry at the slaughter, yet still he does not advocate all-out war. He continues to believe that the destiny of the Cheyenne is to make peace, for both white and red men to live in peace."

"And what do you believe, Blue Fox?" John asked.

"I think Black Kettle is a fool. I will not make war on you, but I can not promise the same for other white men."

"I hope that time will cool your heart. That is my prayer."

John learned that Skyraven's grandfather was in charge of his people's move. He, as medicine man, was a man of great power whom the Arapaho would obey. Now he was leading his group of people in singing prayers to the Great Spirit to ensure a safe journey to their new camp. John made him the promise that if it was within his power the old man would see his granddaughter again.

After the massacre, many survivors of Skyraven's people had been given food, blankets, and clothing by other tribes who had seen what had happened from a distance. With winter fast approaching, it gave John at least a measure of hope that they would be safe, at least for the moment. He did, however, warn them to keep an eye out for Chivington's men.

"Lone Wolf is patrolling the area with his band of dog soldiers. We will be safe," Blue Fox answered. "But what of you? What will you do now, John Hanlen?"

"Now I will attempt to find Skyraven. If I am successful, I will free her and we will travel back here. Will you grant me asylum?" Desert Fox could not answer for the others, but after a hasty vote was taken it was agreed that John would be welcome. Then, with a nodded farewell, he set off in a southerly direction toward the fort.

The moon shone through the mist of the night, looking like liquid silver, shedding just enough light by which to travel along. John saw no sign of either Indians or soldiers until he came close to the fort. Then he had to be very cautious for most definitely he didn't want to encounter Chivington.

"So far, so good," he whispered as he came closer to the fort. He could see flags flapping in the crisp cool air, could hear the neighing of horses from the cavalry stables, but no alarm had yet been sounded and he knew the hope that he had not been spotted.

John thought quickly. Chivington knew he had been taken prisoner, Sedgwick knew, and a few of the other soldiers who had been on the Indian raid knew, but was it general knowledge at the fort? Had the soldiers who had been guarding him returned yet? If so, his return to the fort would be the last thought on their minds and they would be searching the territory *outside* the fort.

The doors were barricaded shut. There was no way of getting in without using subterfuge. Were he to try and climb the wall, he might be shot, but what if he entered at the gate . . . ? Pulling his hat low on his face, he pretended to be very drunk.

"Open up the gate to a returning hero," he called out. "An Indian fighter, that's me, yesiree . . ."

"Who goes there?" called out a voice.

Remembering that a few of the Colorado Third's men had returned and that they were not well known about the fort, he shouted out a fictitious name. "Herbert Booth at your service. From the bloody Colorado Third. Nope, after what we done, we're not the 'bloodless' anymore. No, sir. And I got me some souvenirs to prove it."

"Let him in," called out another voice. "He's obviously not an Indian. Let him settle with his commander later on for traipsing in at such an hour. For now, just write down his name."

As the gates creaked open, John put his saddle

blanket up to his face as if assessing his treasures. It had all been so easy he was nearly afraid to hope his luck would continue. Getting off his horse, he pretended to stagger as he headed for the stables and felt immense relief when he was not followed. Even so, he clung to the shadows as he put his horse in a stall. He had to find Sam Dunham. Sam was the only man he fully trusted inside the fort and he would know what was going on. If Skyraven was anywhere within the fort, he undoubtedly knew that, as well.

The fort was a rectangle of rock quarters, stuck together by clay mortar, with flat, dirt-covered roofs and dirt floors. Facing each other from the east and west were two rows of soldier's barracks. To the south were the corrals where John supposed the "stray" Indian ponies were being held, in the north were the officers' quarters, eight of them for the important officers who until tonight had included him. Sam's quarters were right in between the soldier's barracks and the officers' units, the place he headed for now. How he hoped Sam was inside and not out drinking.

Using the shadows to hide, John ducked from building to building. Upon reaching Sam's room, he paused to look over his shoulder, put his ear to the door, and hearing Sam's loud snoring, knocked loudly. He knocked again, calling out Sam's name. At last the door was opened.

"Maj—!" John blocked off his exclamation by putting his hand over Sam's mouth and pushing him inside the room. He kicked the door shut behind him, and only then removed his hand. "What are you doing here? Are you crazy? Have you taken total leave of your senses? Sedgwick is as mad as a hornet. When those men came back and told him you'd escaped, I thought he was going to have apoplexy right then and there."

"I came back for Skyraven. One of the Indians I talked with seemed to think she was brought back here as a prisoner. Is that so?"

Sam shook his head yes.

"Where is she?"

"Sedgwick has her."

"Sedgwick!" It was exactly what John had feared. "I'll wring his neck. Where have they taken her?"

Sam touched his arm. "It's not as bad as you think. Mrs. Sedgwick took a liking to her, wanted a maid."

"A maid?" John could never imagine Skyraven working in such a capacity with her fiercesome pride.

"Skyraven is living with the Sedgwicks. She has her own room. Actually she's being treated rather well." He sensed John's intent. "Don't—"

"I have to. I can't trust Sedgwick. If she were to anger him, he might harm her. I want to free her and take her away with me."

"As far away as you can go, Major. They're calling for your head on a silver platter."

"I'll take my chances. But I have to do this, Sam. I love her more than I ever thought it possible to love a woman. She's my life." He tried to smile. "Wish me luck. And don't get yourself involved in any of this. If anyone asks, you never laid eyes on me. All right?"

"Laid eyes on who? What?" Sam grinned. "Good luck. Get the hell out of here. You two try to be happy . . . if you can, after what has happened." He pushed John toward the door. "Now hurry!"

428

John didn't have to be told, though he knew that now he entered the most dangerous phase of his journey. How was he going to sneak Skyraven out from beneath Sedgwick's very nose? Undoubtedly they'd have her locked up somewhere, for Sedgwick wouldn't want her to escape. Then the thought entered John's mind, that it was possible Henry had an inkling that Skyraven was the Indian girl he loved. If so, her being under Sedgwick's care could very well be a trap. Could he take the chance? His heart answered for him. He had to.

John made his way to the officers' quarters cautioning himself to be especially wary. Undoubtedly anyone he met now would recognize him at once. He would not be able to fool those men into thinking he was Herbert Booth. Pausing for just a moment to slip back into the shadows, he took off his boots, not wanting the squeak of his soles or the clatter of his heels to give him away. Discarding them in a corner where he could retrieve them, he crept in stocking feet down the boardwalk. Was he crazy in thinking he could maneuver Skyraven's rescue. He was beginning to think that he was, yet knew he couldn't leave the fort without her.

Seeing the tall, lithe figure of an army officer in uniform, he hastily ducked behind a pole. Sedgwick. It had to be. Peering from behind the pole, he ascertained that indeed it was the lieutenant colonel. John didn't know where he was going, but certainly his absence would make everything much easier. He knew that Sedgwick's wife Gwen Ella was a sensible woman and doubted she'd give him much trouble. Of course he'd have to tie her up, which he deeply regretted, but it couldn't be helped.

429

Resolved, John hurried to the door of the Sedgwick quarters. Trying the doorknob, he was pleasantly surprised to find it unlocked, though it emphasized his need for speed. Apparently Sedgwick didn't intend to be gone long. He had to fetch Skyraven before he returned. With that thought in mind, he opened the door, walked boldly in the room, and headed immediately for the Sedgwicks' bedroom. Time was of the essence, good manners out of the question.

"Gwen Ella!" He called out her name as he pushed through the door and found her sitting up in bed, reading a book by lamplight.

"What . . . ? Major Hanlen! What on earth . . . ?" Clutching the bedcovers to her bosom, she looked on the verge of a scream.

"Don't make a sound." He put his finger to his lips, warning her to keep silent. "I don't want to hurt you. That is not my intent."

"Then what . . . ?" She didn't look as if she believed him.

"There is an Indian girl living here under your care. I want you to release her."

"What?"

"You heard what I said."

"Why?"

"I'm going to take her back to her people. That is where she belongs."

"No!" The word died on her lips as he took two steps into the room. "Major, do you understand what the consequences of such actions will be? They'll put you in prison for this. They'll . . ."

"I'm a wanted man already." He didn't have time to explain or to reason with her. "Now, do as I say. Quickly! There isn't much time." He took only one

430

more step, but that was enough to persuade Gwen Ella to follow his orders. Rising from the bed, she crossed the room and took a ring of keys from a peg on the wall.

"She's locked in the other bedroom. Henry insisted, you see, though I didn't want to treat her quite so harshly," she explained.

"Then unlock the door!" John was losing his patience. The woman was moving as slow as a snail. "Or give me the key! Hurry!"

"All right. All right." Her eyes were focused steadily on a point just beyond where John stood. He whirled around to see Henry Sedgwick standing behind him, pointing a gun at his back.

"Well, well, well, if it isn't Major John Hanlen paying call. A man can't even leave his own rooms to get cigarette papers without intrusion." He sneered. "If I were a jealous man, Major, I'd be livid right now, thinking perhaps you'd come to pay court to my wife. As it is, I know her loyalty to me is without question, and therefore I must ask just what you are doing here?"

"He came to get Skyraven, Henry. I . . . I don't really think he meant any harm. He was just acting impetuously. Please don't . . . don't shoot him! Why . . . why his mother would never forgive us. You know how she dotes on John."

John's eyes darted back and forth like a trapped animal searching for a way of escape. There was none. Sedgwick's tall frame blocked the door as he said, "Call the guards, Gwen Ella. Call them at once or I will shoot him, by thunder. He's a traitor and worse!"

As if fearing he might carry out his threat, Gwen Ella hastened to the door and soon had three stout

431

guards in attendance. And though John had had visions of a daring rescue of the woman he loved, he instead found himself being marched off toward the brig, a prisoner once again.

Part Three:
On Wings of Love

"And seem to walk on wings and tread in air."
— *The Iliad* of Homer

Chapter Forty-eight

It was cold in his jail cell. Winter had come upon the territory quickly and with a vengeance. Perhaps, John Hanlen thought as he huddled in the corner of his cell to keep warm, the Great Spirit was venting His anger at what had been done to His people. And the Great Spirit was not alone in his vengeance. On one of Sam's visits he had told John that two thousand Cheyenne, northern Arapaho, and Sioux warriors were gathering together in villages on the Republican River. "And I don't believe it's to make conversation," Sam had said. "After what has happened I really can't blame them. Bad thing about all of it is that the innocent on both sides are going to be killed. And all the time Chivington is eatin' it all up. Why, he's been hailed as a hero for God's sake."

Sam had related the gossip spreading around the fort. "The old buzzard was given a tumultuous welcome. He became the man of the hour, a hero. Why, it's said by one of the soldiers who was there and saw it that the colonel and his men paraded through Denver's streets, Chivington in the lead, holding a live eagle aloft and tied to a pole. And all the while the townspeople cheered wildly. Hell, Chivington and his gang of murderers even paraded their assortment of trophies on the Indian ponies they had stolen. Same thing happened nearby in Boulder. They received a rousing welcome there as well, before the men returned to their ranches, farms, and mining claims. A Captain Nichols and his men boasted that they had brought down the great southern Arapaho chief Left Hand."

So, John thought, Skyraven's chief was dead. He had held hope that perhaps, just like Chief Black Kettle, he might have miraculously escaped. Not so. Chivington and his mercenaries had killed and profited by their deed with impunity. There was no justice. Certainly he himself hadn't gotten any, though he expected better. A "kangaroo court" is what he called his trial, a travesty of lawfulness. The room had been packed with those soldiers who had been against the Indians all along. John's "peers" had been handpicked by Sedgwick. And just as he had supposed, he had been found guilty. Now he awaited the death sentence that was to come in just two days' time. Death by firing squad. Sedgwick, that perpetrator of mercy, had openly boasted of his leniency in giving the major extra time to, as he called it, "make his peace with God" before sentence was carried out.

"Your father will take some action. I have to believe that he will," Sam had said over and over, and yet as the hours passed by, John wondered. Sedgwick knew exactly what he was doing. He wouldn't allow him to have any contact with his father. He knew how long it took for the mail to travel east, if indeed it ever arrived there at all.

The War Between the States had things in a raging turmoil. If his father intervened, it would undoubtedly be too late, though Sedgwick would most likely make it appear as if he had done everything within his power to save the general's son.

"Indeed he did everything in his power to make certain I'd be put safely out of the way," John whispered beneath his breath. For the moment, it certainly appeared as if the world was ruled by the devil. As a child he'd been taught that right always overpowered wrong, but he'd learned firsthand that it was just a silly saying.

In the corner, crinkled into tight balls to reflect his outrage, were copies of newspaper articles — *The Rocky Mountain News* of December eighth and twelfth, to be exact. He knew the dates by heart as well as the unsettling headlines: "Great Battle With Indians! The Savages Dispersed!" "Five Hundred Indians Killed. Our Loss, Nine Killed, Thirty-Eight Wounded." The Denver City paper gave accounts of the battle, reporting the incident with great pride, though it was hardly the same account that John recognized. A thousand incidents of individual daring and the passing of events might be told, it said, had space permitted. All had acquitted themselves well, the paper reported, and the Colorado soldiers had covered themselves in glory. But then, as stated in the article, the primary source of the news had been a brief report by Colonel J.M. Chivington, a former Methodist minister, now commander of the military district of Colorado.

With the perverse intent of renewing his indignant anger, John read one of the pages again, noting that Colonel Chivington, whom it now called the "old war horse," would be in Denver City that very evening. The Third Regiment, which had made up the larger portion of his forces, would soon follow. A letter from one of Chivington's followers had exulted, "We have met the enemy and have gained the greatest victory west of the Missouri over the savages." The writer added his opinion that the brave soldiers had completely broken up the tribe so that the settlers would not be further molested by them. Worst of all, it detailed a parade through Denver in which the men had been cheered as saviors of the frontier. Some of them had appeared between acts of a performance at the theater, where they had shown off the Indian scalps and described their brave deeds to applause.

With the incident at Sand Creek had passed the last chance for reasonable men to come to an agreement that would allow for peace. John crinkled the paper up again in disgust. The article had also said that the campaign of the Colorado volunteers would stand out in history with few rivals, and none to exceed it in final results. If only he had a match, John thought in disgust, he would have started a fire with the article to keep himself warm, for it was worth nothing more than kindling.

John had become numb to his fear. At first he had wondered what it would be like standing before a line of soldiers, knowing they were going to bring his death. Now he wondered if he even really cared. His only regret was leaving Skyraven with no one to protect her, and yet Sam had given his word to watch over her from afar. The young soldier had even promised to take her back to her people if the opportunity ever presented itself. John trusted that Sam would keep his word.

John passed the time by pacing. Certainly there wasn't much else to do. The guards would not allow any visitors. It was as if Sedgwick worried that someone might take pity on the major and help him escape. What was even worse, without Sam's daily visits, he was isolated from the outside world. All he could do was wait, knowing the final outcome of the passing days would be his death.

Chapter Forty-nine

In her room, Skyraven felt miserably lost. She had never been so completely alone before. In her own lodge there were others of her own kind within a stone's throw from her tepee. The lieutenant colonel and his wife were right in the next room but their presence did not give her the same sense of security. She was as different from them as a deer from a horse. Their customs, even the way they thought, were so at variance with hers. They just didn't understand, wouldn't listen to her plea to be let go. Though they decried her protestations that she was a prisoner, they locked her in her room at night to keep her from escape.

She eyed the tall bed with distaste. Even in their manner of sleeping these white people were odd. Skyraven had made up her mind right from the first that she would not sleep on the foolish contraption. What if she should fall off? She did not trust it. She would be better off nearer the ground. Pulling the blankets from the bed, she had carefully spread them on the floor and, despite Gwen Ella's pleading that she would be more comfortable on the mattress, had made the floor her sleeping place.

Skyraven missed the comfort of her own lodge and the companionship of her grandfather and her friend, Desert Flower. How she would love to talk to her grandfather right now. She would like nothing better than to throw her arms around his neck and never let him go. "Oh, Grandfather, Grandfather," she sighed. "Please be alive and well." It was all she cared about now. If he was alive, somehow, they would be reunited.

The silvery moon shone down upon the officers' barracks, peering through the tiny window of her room. She snuggled down beneath the gray blankets marked "Property of the U.S. Cavalry" and tried to sleep, but just as last night and each previous night before, she was haunted by the visions in her dreams. She heard the cannons roar, saw people falling all around her. Desert Flower's baby cried and she could not keep him quiet. What if the enemy should hear him and find their hiding place? She called to her grandfather, but he did not answer.

"No . . . no!" She saw a soldier pull Desert Flower from her hiding place, saw him violate her, then slit her throat with a knife. "No!" Thrashing her head from side to side, she cried out, "Leave the baby alone! Please, have mercy." But the soldiers would not listen. Wrenching Big Bear from her arms, they dashed his head against a tree . . .

Skyraven awoke with a scream trembling on her lips. Covering her mouth with her hands, she forced herself to keep silent. It was just a dream. Desert Flower was safe. She had seen her hiding in her place of shelter as she had passed by on horseback. And yet what had happened to her friend after that? What if Desert Flower had been captured after all? How would she ever know her fate?

Although she was extremely tired, her sleep was constantly disturbed; thus she had taken to walking about at night until she was so exhausted she could sleep through the night. Several times throughout the night she would awaken in a cold sweat and walk to the window to look out, just as she did at this moment, wishing she could get free of the fort. If she knew her people, and she thought she did, she suspected they would return to the Smoky Hill camp and from there move on toward their winter camp. Oh, how she longed to be with them instead of being trapped here.

"If only I were a bird I would fly far away . . ." she whispered, peering out the tiny window. Indeed, the window was too small to have any hope of escaping through it.

Skyraven looked out at the white man's camp. All the lights were out, everything was in darkness. Only the shadow of the sentry walking along the tower parapet gave evidence of any life at all. Even the horses were quiet. Just as she had every night, she now had thoughts of escape, but also knew that they would do no good, that she would never be able to get free of the white man's watchful eyes. Besides, she did not even know how many of her tribesmen remained alive. Perhaps in truth there was no one, she thought in distress.

How she hated being here among people who had done such a treacherous thing to a group of Indians as friendly as Left Hand's and Black Kettle's bands. No one had worked harder for peace than those two chiefs, and yet she supposed they were both dead. She knew both of them well

442

enough to be certain they would still work for a peaceful settlement despite what had happened, were they alive. They would tell her to bury her hateful feelings and continue to strive toward peaceful relations with the white man. If living in peace meant not avenging what had been done to her people, then Skyraven considered her duty done. Though she saw the eyes of the other women staring at her, she had comported herself in a way that would have made her grandfather proud.

As the evening wore on, Skyraven made up her mind up once again to try to make the best of the situation. She was lucky to be alive. Gwen Ella had been very good to her. If everyone here was as understanding as Gwen Ella, perhaps she would learn to tolerate this new way of life. At least she had to try, for she had no other choice. With that thought in mind, she returned to her bed and huddled beneath the covers.

Morning came all too quickly. It seemed she had just settled down and dozed off when the bugle sounded. Half awake, she threw off the covers, stumbled over to the wooden bucket, and splashed her face with cold water. She scoffed as she struggled into her new white man's clothing, a dress of a checked yellow material Gwen Ella called "gingham," doubting that she would ever really grow accustomed to wearing such oddities. She longed for her own doeskin dress, leggings, and moccasins, but such attire had been strictly forbidden. At least Gwen Ella had not insisted that she wear the funny-looking hoop skirt. Skyraven wished she could tell Desert Flower about the garment. They would have been sure to have a good laugh.

While she dressed, the fort was coming alive.

443

She began to hear all sorts of sounds drifting through the window: horses' hooves pounding, trumpets blaring, voices shouting out orders, and feet scuffling.

The Sedgwicks were already up and about. She heard *his* muffled voice, first, then Gwen Ella's sounded from the kitchen area. "No, Henry, let her sleep. She was totally exhausted last night. It won't hurt me to get breakfast this morning. Skyraven will have plenty to do later on."

Skyraven made herself presentable, then listened to the sound of a key turning in the lock of her door. Strange, but she had the feeling that someone was peering through the keyhole but brushed the thought aside as fanciful imaginings. Tying the laces of the silly leather objects the white men called shoes, she opened the door. She was almost reluctant to enter the kitchen, and thus stood in the doorway.

Henry Sedgwick did not look nearly as imposing this morning as he had before when she had looked upon his slim form. He did not have on his complete uniform today. He was dressed in his blue trousers with the yellow stripe down the side, but he had only suspenders over his bare shoulders. He did not have on his hat with the plume, his blue coat with the large gold buttons and epaulets, his high-topped boots, his gloves, or even his neckerchief. Skyraven noticed that he was much too thin, not very muscular at all. His dark hair was thinning almost to balding on top. He had a full, dark mustache over his narrow lips, rather large ears, and deep-set brown eyes. Why had she been so afraid of him? His gruffness? The way he always stared at her? Because he was the leader to the soldiers? She determined that she would never again allow him to frighten her so.

He is an odd match for Gwen Ella, Skyraven thought, turning her attention to the white woman, who was dressed in what she referred to as a "wrapper." Her hair had not yet been styled and hung loosely down to her shoulders. The dark strands in front were streaked with some gray. Both of the Sedgwicks were seated at a makeshift plank table that would serve them until their own furniture arrived. The table, too, was a contraption Skyraven thought to be foolish. Why have such a thing when a person could just put their food on the ground. How strange that these white people always wanted to be so far away from Mother Earth, perched on their lofty pedestals even while eating and sleeping.

"My dear . . ." The lieutenant colonel cleared his throat when he saw Skyraven standing in the doorway. She looked very beautiful even this early in the morning, he thought, trying to win her over with a smile. "Come on in, Skyraven. I have just finished my breakfast so you can keep Gwen Ella company."

"Oh, no I just . . ."

He tried to hide his irritation. The little chit always acted as if he might bite her at any moment. How was he ever going to get close to her if she reacted to him that way? Though he had made repeated attempts, he just couldn't seem to win her trust. "I must get dressed and hurry over to headquarters," he said as much to himself as to the Indian girl. "There is much to be done to prepare for Colonel Chivington's return. He . . . he is coming to a little ceremony we are having." Major

Hanlen's execution he thought, remembering the night that foolish soldier had so blatantly broken in to the officers' quarters with the thought in mind of saving this Indian girl.

Knowing that she had been John Hanlen's lover somehow made her all the more interesting to Sedgwick. Only recently had he remembered her face; he had seen her with Hanlen the day he'd secretly observed the young officer's dealings with the Indians near Sand Creek. He'd seen their embrace and knew they were lovers. Certainly she must be a pretty hot little piece of tail for a man to risk his own life that way. Well, in time he would see for himself.

Gwen Ella was all smiles as she bade a good morning to Skyraven and indicated that she should sit on the bench next to her. Skyraven declined the invitation, taking her accustomed seat on the floor. "Skyraven, when are you even going to learn . . ." She clucked her tongue in frustration. "Oh, Henry . . ." She shrugged her shoulders helplessly.

"Let me take a hand." Coming to where Skyraven was seated, Sedgwick reached for her arm, allowing his hands to brush against her breasts as he helped her to her feet. And very nice breasts at that, he thought. Soft, yet firm. Much rounder and fuller than his wife's. Oh, to touch the bare skin of those tantalizing globes! "Come, sit here next to Gwen Ella, Skyraven." He attempted to guide her toward his wife. "It is time you learned our ways. You've been with us two and a half weeks now." Once again, he made use of his action of helping her to touch her breasts. "Gwen Ella has your day well planned no doubt."

"A very full day, dear," she replied. Seeing that

446

she was looking at him with suspicion, he quickly pulled his hand away, patting Skyraven's shoulder with an air of fatherly concern.

"Well, I'll leave you two girls alone so that you can get started." With that said, he was up and out of the room in an instant.

As soon as Henry had left the house, the two women tried to talk while trumpets blasted, carts rolled past the doorway, men called each other to assemble. It seemed their voices got louder and louder. Gwen Ella held her hands, palm up, in a gesture of defeat at the deafening noise. Finally they gave up the attempts at conversation and silently ate their breakfasts. When the noise had ceased, Gwen Ella went to the bedroom and brought two large canvas bags filled with soiled clothing into the living room.

"Today is the day for our laundry, Skyraven. Remember I showed you the building where it is to be done?" Skyraven shook her head. "The other women will show you everything you need to know."

Just as she handed the bags to Skyraven, Gwen Ella noticed that the drawstrings on one of the bags was tied into a tight knot. "Oh! How many times must I tell Henry!" She sighed in vexation. "Well, you will never get this undone without some help." She tried but was unable to get the knot undone and thus determined it must be cut. "There is a knife right over there near the stove on the wall, Skyraven. Just take it along with you to cut this string when you get to the laundry room, then bring it back when you are done." Henry would have her head for giving the girl a knife, she thought. He was convinced that she had a streak of savagery in her, but Gwen Ella thought otherwise. This would be a test. If she was right in judging the girl's character, the Indian girl would go and do the laundry and return with the knife. Skyraven had proven to be very obedient.

Skyraven picked up the knife and innocently stuck it down inside the strange band that held her stockings up, the band Gwen Ella called a "garter." As she walked along the dusty road, men weaved in and out of the barracks on their way to perform their chores. Everyone seemed to be in a rush and didn't give her much notice. They had grown used to seeing her and at least if they stared now, it wasn't with hostility. One company of the First Cavalry and one of the Infantry, with a buckskin-clad frontiersman for a guide, were getting ready to ride off somewhere. She tried to put it out of her mind that they might be hunting Indians.

As she came near the parade grounds, she noticed that the enlisted men's barracks were here near the dusty parade ground. The detached officers' quarters, which she had left far behind, was in the opposite direction, away from the stables, the dust, and the commotion. Just like at her camp, the men of importance had the most favorably placed lodges.

Suddenly Skyraven saw a man wave in a friendly manner and she stiffened, imagining for just a moment that the man was John Hanlen. Her heart seemed to come up into her throat as all the old feelings she had nurtured for him surfaced once again. But the man had dark hair, not golden, and he was stout, not as muscularly lean as her soldier had been. Still, she recognized him as one of the bluecoats who always seemed to notice whenever she was anywhere by. Fearing he might try to further a friendship for unwanted reasons, she quickly turned her back and continued walking.

Just left of the parade grounds there was a long row of quartermaster's storage buildings. Men were carrying supplies in and out of those buildings. A small military prison she had heard called the guardhouse was close by—surely the cage Lone Wolf had spoken about. She looked in horrified fascination but could not see inside. Did the white men have any Indian prisoners? Perhaps she would investigate someday when no one was around.

Outside the walled fort, but still part of it, were the frame stables built to house six hundred horses. Skyraven thought some of those must be the ponies that had belonged to her people. Strange how the white men never considered taking another's property as stealing. But the thought tugged her mouth into a frown, it was not considered stealing if something was taken from the savages.

Still farther back were the laundresses' homes and also a wide level plain which served as an extra place for drills, and the sutler's store with an attached billiards room. She did not know the names of all the buildings she passed, but she was carefully observing it all along her way to the laundry room. She must familiarize herself with her surroundings, the better then to make a plan of escape.

As she neared the barracks, the stable call sounded and the soldiers swarmed out like ants from an anthill. Skyraven had to step out of their way to keep from being knocked down. She watched as they formed lines and marched away to the sound of a drum beat. The stables, she thought. It was of utmost importance that she remember where the horses were kept, for without a horse she had no hope of ever getting far enough away from here.

John Hanlen. John Hanlen. His face and name haunted her as she looked around. She couldn't help but think of him every time she heard the bugle sound or saw a man in a blue uniform. Was he somewhere nearby or had Lone Wolf taken vengeance and killed him. That thought caused her so much pain that she quickly put it far from her conscious mind, but still she looked at each face, hoping she would see him, but though she did see a few other soldiers with sun-touched hair, John Hanlen wasn't to be seen.

Where was he? And had he truly been involved with the raid on her village? She didn't know what to believe anymore. She didn't want to believe the worst of him, and yet how could she think otherwise?

She pushed the heavy door of the laundry room open and looked inside. It was damp and musty and smelled of mildew. The floors were wet and slippery. Already four women were busy working. One heated water over the fire, another scrubbed on washboards over steaming hot tubs of water, still another stirred clothing in a big wooden trough and one more hung clothes over lines stretched upon pegs driven in the wall. There were many women working in the laundry room on Suds Row, but some of them were too busy with their own tasks to notice her. Others just looked but did not speak, then when their work was finished, they seemed to vanish very quickly as if to put the depressing room far behind them.

Skyraven went about her work ignoring the women, but one by one their disdain for her seemed to thaw. Soon she was joining in their chattering with a camaraderie that surprised her. She found herself thinking that, after all, the white women might not be as bad as she had first supposed. She soon learned that four laundresses were allotted to each troop. These women worked for troop eight, and all of them were married to men in that troop. Some of the laundresses had little babies or toddlers clinging to their skirts, not so very different from her own women cleaning their garments at the river, she thought. The women were very friendly and she listened as they explained the laundry process to her and helped her to get started.

They gossiped, chatted, and laughed as they worked, as if seeming to derive great pleasure from telling their stories about the white maids and how very much in demand they were in the officers' quarters.

"Nobody can keep a maid for very long because some poor enlisted soldier or miner or settler grabs the white girls up as soon as they arrive," said a dark-skinned girl.

"Ach, as you can see, there ain't very miny vite vomen around here," added a rotund woman with a thick foreign accent.

Two of the women were Spanish, Skyraven learned, one a Negress and the other Swedish. Their work was nearly done when they saw the covered wagons from the supply rooms pass by from the quartermaster's area filled with sacks and barrels. Kitchen utensils, shovels, axes, and other items were attached to the sides of the wagons.

Other wagons were headed toward the stables.

"Guess it's just about quittin' time. Ve be on our vay," the Swedish woman said as all the women pushed through the door, their youngsters in tow, clinging to their hands or carried in their arms.

"Are you comin', Skyraven?" the Negress asked as she held the door open for the Indian girl.

"No, not just yet." Skyraven was determined to do this job well. She had blundered at some of the tasks given her, and her pride demanded she do well at this one. "I still have some socks and white underthings to do. You go on. It won't take me much longer."

Indeed, it had taken the entire day, though only now did she realize it. Skyraven had had to take her turn at the tubs, then there had been the rinsing. Ah well, if Gwen Ella needed her, she would know where to find her.

Dusk was beginning to fall when the heavy wooden door of the laundry room squeaked open. Skyraven turned away from the wooden tub to find Lieutenant Colonel Henry Sedgwick standing there. He pushed the heavy wood door tightly closed and leaned against it. "Well, well, well. So at last I find you all alone. It's about time." He leaned against the door as if to keep Skyraven from leaving. As he started over toward Skyraven, something about his manner of approach cautioned her to be wary.

"I . . . I am through with . . . with the laundry," she said hastily, wringing the garments out as she had been instructed to do by the other laundresses. "It must be getting close to dinnertime. Gwen Ella will be looking for me."

"Don't worry about that, my dear. Mrs. Sedgwick is down with one of her headaches. Right

452

now she is napping. We will not be missed." His eyes were like a weasel's, hungry and ferocious, as he reached out to grab her. Skyraven tried to pull away, frightened at his intent, but he was stronger of arm than she might have suspected. "Oh, no, we won't be missed at all . . ." Feverishly, his hands moved over her body, tugging at her gingham dress. "But we will have to hurry."

"What are you doing?" As if she didn't know. "No!"

Oh you are a pretty little savage. No wonder John was so crazy about you. No wonder he dared . . ." He pressed his body close to hers, rubbing their lower portions together in a gesture that resembled some strange mating dance. The thought of what he meant to do was too terrible to imagine.

"No!" she said again, trying to control the hysteria that threatened to choke her. How could she have ever thought she could be at ease here? How could she have forgotten even for a moment?

His moist mouth fastened on hers so hard that she couldn't breathe. She struggled and fought like a bear to escape his grasp, but he had placed her hand behind her in such a way that it was nearly impossible for her to escape. He forced her to her knees and then into a lying position upon the damp wet floor. Pinioning her one hand to the ground, he placed her other hand upon the crotch of his trousers.

"Can you feel that I have a desire for you, my beauty? There is no need to struggle. Just lie down quietly and allow me to have my way with you. I have heard about you hot-blooded Indian girls."

Hot-blooded Indian girls! He was so smug, so sure

of himself. The loathsome snake! How she hated this arrogant man. She wanted to scratch his eyes out, to spit in his face. What would make him think that she would ever have anything to do with him?

He tried to kiss her again, but she moved her head from side to side, closing her mouth tightly to escape his probing tongue. Finally he managed to plant a slobbery kiss upon the side of her mouth. "Come on. Come on. Fight me. I like that. Show some fire."

Skyraven panicked. What could she do? If she screamed, nobody would hear her. This place was too far away from the mainstream of activity. She was helpless, and the feeling was demoralizing.

"Well, come now, let's get started. We must be quick about this." He relaxed his hold on her momentarily to unbutton his trousers. In that moment she remembered the knife. After cutting the knot on the laundry bag, she had placed it inside the canvas bag, which lay now by her left elbow. She could retrieve it if she were quick. With that thought, Skyraven positioned herself to reach the knife, then with her right hand, she carefully drew the weapon forth while he was looking down. By the time he looked up again, she was prepared to lash out at him with all her fury.

"What the . . . ?"

She plunged the knife into his arm several times, then ran from the laundry room like the hounds of hell were right at her heels. She was blurry-eyed from both the fright and the tears that stung her eyes. Not watching where she was going, she ran right into the arms of a short, stout, dark-haired soldier, the man she had seen watching her from

454

afar.

"Whoa, there Skyraven . . ." Lieutenant Sam Dunham had stayed at the sutler's store a little longer than he had planned, drowning his remorse at the major's certain fate. Just didn't seem fair that a man like that would meet such a ghastly end. Now he was on his way back to his quarters when the young woman he recognized all too well came flying into his arms as if from out of nowhere. Looking down, he saw she was holding a knife and that she was aiming it at him. "Whoa, Skyraven . . ." He gasped as her arm came forward.

Chapter Fifty

"Skyraven, don't!" The imploring tone in his voice caused Skyraven's reason to return. This man who knew her name was no enemy. Slowly she lowered the knife to her side. "That's better!" Lieutenant Sam Dunham held the trembling girl in his arms, listening to her frantic babbling until she had calmed down, then he drew her with him to hide behind a building, sensing that she was in some kind of trouble. "There, you see, Skyraven, I won't harm you."

Skyraven took a deep breath, fighting to compose herself. "How . . . how do you know my name?" she asked at last.

"Because I am a friend of Major John Hanlen."

She stiffened. "He told you about me?" She averted her eyes so that he would not see her pain. "He betrayed me. He led my people to the campgrounds near the fort and then . . ."

"No, he didn't betray you. He tried to persuade Colonel Chivington not to do what was done, but the old bastard didn't listen to reason. John loves you very much and loves your people."

Skyraven pulled herself out of his embrace. "He

loves my people so much that he came with the soldiers to kill them."

"No, that's not true."

"I saw him with my own eyes, there in the middle of the camp, fighting with one of the Indian braves." Even now, it made her heart ache to talk about it.

"He might have been there, but he did not come with the soldiers. He came afterward to try to save *you*. I know. He told me what he was going to do." Quickly Sam revealed the whole story of John's confinement to the fort. "He rode out with the intention of saving you and doing what he could to save your people. And as punishment he was taken prisoner by his chief."

"Prisoner?" Skyraven wasn't certain what to believe, her eyes and what she had seen, or this man's story.

"He got away when a band of Indians attacked his captors. Even then, he didn't think of his own well-being, but returned to your camp in search of you. There he found your Indian friend and her baby and took them with him up to the Smoky Hills to join the survivors of that . . . that killing spree."

"He took Desert Flower back? Then she and Big Bear are safe?" It must be true or how would this man know about her Indian friend. She had been so certain John Hanlen had deceived her. Now to find that he had placed himself in such danger for her was a balm to her soul.

"Yes."

"And John Hanlen?" She held her breath.

"He came back to the fort when he learned from Desert Flower that you had been taken by the soldiers. Now he is a prisoner again, and the same chief who killed your people has condemned him to death."

457

"No!" Skyraven put her hand to her throat. It could not be. To have learned that her soldier had escaped death only to be killed now was too great a shock.

"Yes. He was given a trial but the deck was stacked against him. A verdict of guilty was given out." The anger that Sam felt glowed in his eyes. "His execution is planned in two sunrises."

"Execution?"

"He'll go before a firing squad. They're going to shoot him."

"No, it cannot be." But now Skyraven realized why she hadn't seen him around the fort. John Hanlen was in the soldier's cage. "Since he is there because he sought to save me, I must in turn save his life."

Sam shook his head. "No, there is no way. God knows I've tried. I've even written to his father but . . ."

He peered around the corner. "Sedgwick! Another one of the vultures. He did what he could to put a bullet in the major's heart." Skyraven paled as he spoke the name. "Say, is that who you are running away from?" She didn't even have to answer. From the look of horror on her face, he knew at once. "Shh, he's coming this way."

Sam blocked her slim form from view with his girth just in case Sedgwick looked over, but he didn't, only muttered beneath his breath as he held a bloodsoaked towel tightly around his left arm. In that moment Sam knew what must have happened.

"You did that?"

"Yes. He . . . he tried to . . . and all I could think of was the . . . the knife."

"Whew! Skyraven, pretty little girl, you are in a heap of trouble, nearly as much so as John. With Sedgwick feeling as he does about Indians, he'll have

458

your ears."

"Oh, no!" Skyraven covered her ears in a protective gesture. She took him literally, having witnessed some of the soldiers taking bodily parts with the scalps as a prize of war.

"Well, at least he'll be screaming for your punishment," Sam said gently, seeing the stark terror written in her eyes. "How are we going to get you out of this trouble?"

"I do not care about me. Only about John Hanlen."

Sam sighed. "Strange, what love can do. He always says the same damned thing about you." He cautiously looked around the side of the building, then pulled his head quickly back. "He's going on up the road, but he keeps looking back. We will have to remain here until it is safe for us to go on. I don't know where I can take you then. He's on, but going to have every nook and cranny guarded. My quarters are in the officers' section, but . . ." It would have to do, at least until they could make other plans.

A timber wolf somewhere across the river gave a deep-throated mournful howl. Skyraven looked at Sam with despair in her eyes, fearful that the wolf was crying her doom.

"I must get free from here. And . . . and I must take John Hanlen with me."

He shook his head. "You are talking about miracles. There is just no way." And yet looking into her face he found himself believing anything was possible. Somehow, the way Skyraven held her head, the way she walked, even the tone of her voice inspired him with confidence. "I'll help you in any way I possibly—" Sam assured her.

"I have an idea," Skyraven broke in. "An old Indian trick . . ." She whispered her plan to Sam's ear.

It seemed farfetched, and yet . . . "Okay, but we must work fast before all hell breaks loose around here and Sedgwick calls out the guard." He was eager to get started on the plan. "You stay here. I'll go down to the stables and get two horses ready so that you can ride the hell away from here. And I'll find out exactly what is happening."

Skyraven watched as the dark-haired man walked away, sensing that he could be relied on. Perhaps it was time she learned to trust again . . . but would the plan work? If it didn't, then there would be two people awaiting their deaths. When Sam returned, she knew she must move quickly, but cautiously. If she were captured after her stabbing of Sedgwick, all would be lost.

"The horses are ready," Sam informed Skyraven when he returned. "I have them tied in a separate part of the stables so they can't run away with the other horses." He shrugged. "I don't want to put my own head in a noose, but I brought back this bottle. If you were to hit the prison guard over the head, I happen to know that the keys to John's cell are attached to his belt." He grinned. "It's the smallest key. And . . . and tell John I'll make certain the gates are opened. Who could blame me if I made a mistake and thought there was a loaded wagon just bustin' to get in?"

Skyraven peeked out from behind the wall, viewing the terrain like an Indian warrior. Many times she had witnessed the warriors' methods of stampeding the horses to cause confusion. She must do the same now, cause enough commotion to divert the soldiers' attention away from her. The cage in which John Hanlen was held was just a stone's throw from the open corral and reasonably close to the stables.

She must have courage, the attribute that counted the most among warriors. She must be brave, just as she had been when bringing down the Ute warrior when she had freed the man who turned out to be John Hanlen, her love, from his Indian captors. And the Utes had been more fiercesome adversaries than the white-faced soldiers.

"I'll stand guard and let you know when anyone is in sight." Sam took off his yellow neckerchief and waved it in the air to show what he would do at any sign of danger.

Crouching down on the ground, Skyraven cursed her white woman's dress as she crept slowly and silently toward the corral. Seeing that it was indeed the Indian ponies inside, she took it as a sign from the Great Spirit and that gave her added courage. With shrieks and whoops, she undid the gate, speaking to the animals in the language they had come to understand. The horses raised on their hind legs, pawed the ground, whinnied and at last broke through the fence and proceeded across the parade ground.

"The goddamn horses are loose. Who the hell. . . ?" she heard several soldiers yell as she moved quickly across the street, taking refuge behind a stone wall. Hefting the bottle in her hand, she moved quietly, as she had been taught to do since childhood. Coming upon the unwary guard, she cracked him hard across the head, then bent to fumble for the key. The small one, John's friend had told her. Her fingers were so clumsy as they trembled in anxiety that it took her much longer than she might have liked to find the right key. "This one." She remembered having watched Gwen Ella lock her in at night, and thus knew what to do with the strangely shaped piece of metal. Inserting it in

461

the lock, she gave a whoop of joy as the door gave way. She pushed it open. "Hurry, John Hanlen," she commanded.

John looked up at her in disbelief. "Skyraven. . . ? It *is* you. What are you doing here?"

"I have come to set you free." That was all she needed to say. Taking her hand, he followed her toward the stables but found one phase of her plan to be thwarted: Soldiers stood guarding the stable. "We cannot go that way," she said, leading John off in another direction, only to see that the way was also blocked by guards.

"Oh, Skyraven, I never meant for you to put yourself in danger." John thought quickly. "I'll lead the soldiers away. You run. Find Sam Dunham. He'll take care of you, he'll . . ."

"No." Skyraven wouldn't leave him. There had to be some way. What would Lone Wolf do in such a situation? she wondered. If only she could ride as skillfully as the warriors . . . "Do you remember when you were at my camp the trick Blue Fox showed you with the horses," she asked John. It was a maneuver the warriors often pulled in the heat of battle when the soldiers were firing at them.

John remembered all too well. Hanging from the side of the horse as it gallops. Yes, I remember. But . . ."

"We must do the same." Pursing her lips, she made a sound that was so high-pitched to be nearly undetectable to the human ear. The sound brought six horses galloping in their direction. "You must do this, John Hanlen. It is the only way we can be free." That the gate had suddenly been opened made her command all the more important. Sam Dunham had done his part just as he promised, yet she could not count on the gate being open for long. "Come.

462

Hurry."

John's heart was in his throat as he heaved himself upon one of the horses. Skyraven did the same. Clutching on to the horse's necks for dear life, trying to ignore the sound of rifle fire and the fact that the horses' hooves might well trample them if they fell, they both thanked the Great Spirit and God that some of the Indian ponies followed out the gate, giving them added shelter. They were free! At least for the moment.

As soon as they were out of sight of the fort, John pulled himself into a sitting position atop the Indian pony. Skyraven did the same. Riding as fast as the wind, they headed down the trail to the Arkansas River. Finding a shallow place to cross, Skyraven showed him another Indian trick, keeping the horses in the water so that there would be no tracks to follow. Then at last they crossed to the other side, feeling the exhilaration of knowing they had accomplished the impossible.

Skyraven and John rode at breakneck speed across the countryside. She could hear the thundering sound of their horses' hooves as they plunged down the hill, and she strained her ears to hear the echoing sound that would mean they were being followed. There was no such sound, yet even so she would not let down her guard. They pushed on, stopping only once or twice for a brief rest and to warm their frozen limbs by a fire. It was cold, brutally so.

"If the soldiers don't get us, then the cold will," John said warily, his concern for her evident. "We have to find some shelter before we are frozen to the bone." They were ill prepared for the cold. John was wearing only his shirt, having given up his blue jacket to Skyraven's shivering form. As he looked at her, her head slumped forward, her shoulders even now quaking from the cold, he knew they had to stop. Traveling at night in the cold was just plain suicide. But where could they go? The area they traveled was deserted, with no sign of life. The Indians had moved on, chased away by Chivington's march, and there were no white settlers about.

"I know of a cave." Putting her heels to her horse's flanks, she led him there, and though it turned out to be more an indentation in the hill, just big enough to crouch in, they decided it would do.

Dismounting, they carefully hid their horses, though John doubted anyone had followed them this far. Even Sedgwick wouldn't want his men to freeze to death. He would undoubtedly depend on Mother Nature and the time of year to thwart his two fugitives.

Skyraven gathered firewood, and once again used the Indian method of rubbing two sticks together to start the flames. John searched for and found dry grass and leaves to form a bed. What he wouldn't have given for one of Skyraven's buffalo robes at that moment, but realized they would have to do with the meager coverings they had—his jacket and her underslip, which they used as a sheet for their makeshift mattress. Clinging together, they soon felt the warmth of each other's bodies bring a measure of heat back to their bodies.

"John Hanlen . . ." Skyraven reached out to him, her eyes closing against her will. "I love you. Forgive me for doubting you, even for a moment. I should have known . . ."

"Hush, I love you, too, and I understand. I can't blame you for thinking I was part of it all. I am a soldier, or at least I was. But no more . . . I want to live at your camp. Your grandfather . . ."

"My grandfather?" Skyraven's heart sang with joy. "He is alive?"

"Yes. I saw him when I took Desert Flower to the Smoky Hills Camp. That's where we are headed now." John smiled. "I hope I can become a good Indian." He pulled her to his chest and cradled her head against it. Her body curved into his, and he smiled as he saw how they fit together so perfectly.

"I did not learn much of your white ways. They were so confusing," she sighed, nestling against his warmth. "But I will try."

"Sleep now. You'll be safe. I'll watch the fire and make certain it doesn't go out. We have the rest of our lives, Skyraven, the rest of our lives to love each other."

She fought to stay awake, but weariness overcame her. There was so much she wanted to talk about, but she was just too tired even to speak. Still, she knew that John Hanlen was right. They had the rest of their lives to be together. Days to make love, and to dream, and to touch each other.

The soft press of her body against him sent John's senses into turmoil, yet he breathed a sigh and closed his eyes. For the moment he would be content just to hold her and would worry about tomorrow when the sun came up. And yet the more he thought about it, the more he realized that running away, living in hiding with the Smoky Hill Indian tribes, was wrong. Something had to be done about Chivington. He had to be stopped. He had to pay for what he had done. The people of the United States had a right to know what really happened at Sand Creek.

I can run away and selfishly isolate myself from the real world, or I can take the chance of exposing Chivington for the lying, murdering bastard that he is, John thought.

465

What is it to be? Looking down at Skyraven's sweet face, it was difficult to make the choice, and yet he had to do the right thing even if it meant their daring dash for freedom had been all for naught. He had to go to Denver and tell his side of the story no matter what the penalty.

Chapter Fifty-one

A storm raged in Denver City. Snowflakes fell to earth with a wrathful fury. The wind howled, blowing the white, frothy ice into the eyes, mouths, and nostrils of those walking outside. But the fury of the weather was as nothing compared to the furor created by Major John Hanlen's visit.

"He's a liar!" was what the initial reaction had been at first. "Indian lover, that's what he is." Denver citizens, especially the men of the Colorado Third, expressed their indignation loudly, calling for his head. There was even talk of lynching him. Then suddenly, like a snowball, the truth began to be found out. Investigation after investigation took place with stunning conclusions, for it seemed that John's testimony was not the only one that claimed Chivington had been in the wrong. Repercussions of the Sand Creek tragedy were quick to be heard.

John's courage opened the matter to inquiry. A few of the officers and enlisted men were in anguish over the part they had played in the matter of Sand Creek. Some of them, it seemed, had written to officials in Washington. Now Washington and Denver both were alive with rumors that Sand

Creek had not been the glowing field of battle its commander had claimed. When all was said and done, the affidavits obtained from officers, including Lieutenant Sam Dunham, enlisted men, and civilians at the fort vehemently denounced Chivington's action, saying that the Indians were killed after surrendering and that a large portion of them had been women and children. These, too, were forwarded to Washington. Fort Lyon was reassigned to a new commander with orders to investigate Sand Creek.

Before the month of December was out, the people of the Colorado Territory were stunned to hear the unsettling details. It was now said that Chivington's men had murdered Indians who had thought they were under army protection. The testimony further showed that most of the Indian casualties were not warriors. Gradually the Indian side of the story was emerging.

As an eyewitness for the Indian's point of view, Skyraven gave an impassioned plea for her people, telling all that she had seen and heard. "The ground is still white with the bleaching bones of the slain," she said to the general hearing the case. "We came in peace, trusted your promises, and for that we were given death."

As for Skyraven's tribe, they as a people had not sought war and did not take part in it now, though other tribes joined in hostilities. Most of the tribe decided to remain with Chief Little Raven, who wandered the southern plains, remaining apart from the areas of conflict. Lone Wolf was the exception. He and a knot of warriors occasionally rode northward to join those who fought the whites in vengeance for the massacre.

John had taken a hotel room. Now as he sat on the settee with his arm around Skyraven, he read the headlines of *The Rocky Mountain News*, which told a far different story than previously. "Listen to this, my love. A dispatch from the capital heralds a different version of the affair of the Indians at Sand Creek." He squeezed her hand tightly. "The affair at Fort Lyon, Colorado, in which Colonel Chivington destroyed a large Indian village and all its inhabitants is to be made the subject of a congressional investigation. Congress has issued a report calling it a 'massacre of the Cheyenne and Arapaho Indians,' and scathingly denouncing Evans and Chivington. Even the President has heard about the inquiry."

"The Great White Father Lean Bear always spoke about?" Skyraven's blue eyes widened in awe.

"Yes. And so you see our coming here was right after all."

"Yes, it is what my grandfather would have counseled."

The future had looked dismal as the two had traveled across the snow- and ice-covered land, their feet and hands frozen, the wind whipping at their faces. More than once, John had been determined to turn back, to seek the protective shelter of Black Kettle's Arapaho camp, but Skyraven's courage and love had urged him on. It had seemed to be a journey that would never come to an end and then, as if in answer to a prayer, an old gold miner, heading back to his mine in Central City, had come upon them and offered them help. He'd given them food, blankets, and, most important of all, the shelter of his wagon when the nights were, as John put it, "as cold as hell."

Though it seemed they deserved to be together now without ever having to say good-bye again, John had been called back to active duty, but as an Indian agent and not as a soldier. He had proven himself a most respectable advocate of the Indian cause and thus was given a post that put to use his sincere liking for the Indians.

"It is a pity that what was done cannot be undone," he whispered. "The Sand Creek killings have driven a wedge between our two peoples, Skyraven. It's going to put our love to the test, but somehow I know the strength of what I feel for you and what you feel for me will cause it to survive. I love you so very much."

"And I love you." Touching his face tenderly, leaning over him, Skyraven gave promise of the future with her kiss.

Epilogue

A serene, unclouded, brilliant blue sky unfolded over the Indian village below. The wildflowers of summer emblazoned the hillside with a rainbow of colors. For the moment there was peace in the Smoky Hills beyond the Colorado boundary. Peace, what a precious blessing it was, Skyraven thought as she shaded her face against the sun's glare, watching the figure on horseback galloping over the crest of the hill. Her small two-year-old daughter was at her side, mimicking her mother's action, also watching the horizon.

"It's your father, Winter Fire. He's come home." She looked at her daughter, feeling a sense of pride and overwhelming love. She was a beautiful little girl with light-brown braids with just a hint of red, and eyes the color of the sky in spring. The child was proof of her ever-abiding love for her yellow-haired soldier, her husband now. Doubly so, John had said, for they had been married in two ceremonies, one by her grandfather and one by the medicine man of his people, a "preacher," John had

471

called the black-coated man.

Not that the years together had been easy. The last two years had been turbulent but happy. There were times when John's duties as an agent of the Arapaho and Cheyenne took him to see the Great White Father in Washington, away from his wife and child and the encampment. The division between their two peoples had caused hatred and prejudice to plague them. But, as John had predicted those few years ago, their love was strong enough to conquer all.

"John! John!" As he came closer, Skyraven waved her hands, trying to capture his attention. Leading his horse down the hill, he reined in Running Antelope, gathered his wife and daughter in his arms, and kissed them both, in turn.

"You don't know how good it is to know that the two girls I love most in the world will be here to greet me when I return," he said, smiling. His eyes touched on Skyraven's face. "I'm always amazed that you get even more beautiful with each passing day, my love."

His hands held her close in an embrace that spoke of his yearning, and that warmth spread to her, burning her where he touched. When he kissed her, it was with all the hunger of his soul.

Together they walked hand in hand, Winter Fire in the middle, toward the second largest tepee in the village. It was here they lived when they spent the time with her people. At other times they shared a small wooden frame house in Leavenworth. A compromise had been struck, for John had decided he could not ask her to leave the people she had grown up with. He would not take her permanently away from her own kind. Thus the spring and summer months were spent with the Arapaho, and the autumn and winter months among the whites. Winter Fire would have the best of two worlds, or so they hoped.

As an Indian agent, John had been fully accepted into the Arapaho tribe. He was known as "Tall Yellow Hair," the best and most honest agent they had ever had. Skyraven had taught him the Indian language so that he could speak in English, Arapaho, and Cheyenne. Together with the chiefs Black Kettle, Little Raven, Spotted Wolf, Storm, and the others, he worked to bring peace and prosperity to the Indians, no easy task considering the volatile emotions that flared between Indian and white man, particularly since Sand Creek. Now the southern plains of Kansas and the Oklahoma Panhandle had become home to the two tribes, not Colorado. After Sand Creek, they had never returned to the lands of their betrayal. It was a shame, Skyraven thought, for the winter camp of Boulder had been a most beautiful spot, one she could only reflect on in the dreams of her childhood.

"How did your peace mission go?" she asked John now.

"The usual grumblings and stupidity. Greedy men wanting more than their share of the pie. But I have hopes. There are plans for another treaty council at Medicine Lodge Creek, sixty miles south of Fort Larned." He sighed. "We will see . . ." Reaching down, he pulled at one of Winter Fire's braids. "I want to create a peaceful world for her, one where there is no hatred."

"Perhaps you will. We can only hope."

"At least there has been progress," John said.

"Remember that the committee investigating Sand Creek has given the opinion that in most cases, Indian wars can be traced to the aggressions of lawless white men. No longer are they blaming the Indians for every bit of trouble. Since Sand Creek, I believe my people have acquired a conscience and feel less cavalier about warring with those whose ways are different."

John was happy with the freedom he had found in the Arapaho village. He liked to walk with Skyraven and Winter Fire along the Smoky River and think of the earth and the dome of the sky as his home.

"John Hanlen!" Raising his hand in a gesture of peace, Skyraven's grandfather peered out of his tepee and came to greet his grandson-in-law.

Buffalo's Brother was getting visibly older and was not as active as he had been in years past. The sadness of Sand Creek and the atrocities he had seen had taken a toll on the man. Still, he loved his great-granddaughter with the same devotion he had loved her mother. At night around the fire he told the child Winter Fire stories about the brave deed of the Arapaho so that she would hold a pride in her heart for her heritage.

"President Johnson sends his greeting, Grandfather," John said, receiving a grin from the medicine man.

Buffalo's Brother had hoped he could go with John to see the Great White Father in Washington like Black Kettle and Lean Bear had done, but his health was too frail now and Skyraven had feared the trip would be too much for him. Thus he had waited patiently for the flag and medal that John had promised to bring back for him.

Now John held the medal out to the old man and Buffalo Brother's smile mirrored his pride as it was pinned to the buckskin of his tunic.

"Let us hope that this time these tokens will bring good luck," John exclaimed, trying to push from his mind that they had not brought much luck to Lean Bear or Black Kettle.

"We will hope it will be so." Buffalo's Brother looked from John to Skyraven to John again, and as if realizing they wanted to be alone, took Winter Fire by the hand. "Come, little one. There is a new little pony I want you to see."

"And I have some news for you." Skyraven knew John would be pleased, even as he looked down at her, Skyraven blushed.

"News?" In answer, she placed his hand on her stomach. His eyes swept over her, up and down, widening as they rested on her belly. "Another child?" Picking her up in his arms, John whirled her around as a piercing shout of happiness escaped his lips, then just as quickly he set her down and held her at arm's length, looking at her as if suddenly she had become as fragile as an egg.

Seeing his concerned expression, she smiled. I won't break, John." She held out her arms to him, tasting of his kisses as a gust of sudden wind ruffled her hair. The wind reminded her of the turbulent days still to come. Yet Skyraven knew they would always love each other. And where there was love, there was also peace, hope, and tranquility. In her heart she knew that as long as they had each other, all would be well.

Author's Note

The inspiration for my fourth historical romance novel was sparked by a recent controversy concerning a residence hall at the University of Colorado, named for David H. Nichols, a former Colorado lieutenant governor (1893-1895) who helped found Boulder's first school and the University of Colorado. When it was called to the attention of the citizens of Boulder that Mr. Nichols had served as a captain in the Third Colorado Cavalry and that he had taken part in the controversial Sand Creek Massacre (1864), a decision was made to rename the hall. It is now called the Cheyenne Arapaho Hall. This newspaper headline piqued my curiosity. I wanted to find out what had really happened in that tragic confrontation. After studying about the Sand Creek massacre, which happened one hundred and twenty-five years ago, I knew I had to tell this story.

The Sand Creek massacre is one of the most controversial of Indian conflicts. For nearly a full century the complete story has remained unchronicled, largely because of the prejudices which surround it. It was the subject of both Army and congressional investigators and inquiries, a matter of vigorous newspaper debates, political oratory, and gossip, biased both from the Army's point of view and from that of the Indians'.

The effects of Sand Creek extended far beyond the politics and borders of Colorado Territory. It meant the end of the Indian trader in Colorado, as well as the dominance of the Cheyenne and Arapaho tribes in the lands east of the mountains. It was influential in setting the stage for the years of bloody battle with the Plains Indians after the Civil War. In the aftermath and for years to follow, it remained in the Indians' mind as the foremost symbol of the white man's treachery. The fact that most of the dead were women and children and that Indian bodies had been mutilated made it a particularly horrifying occurrence.

Colonel Chivington is an actual person. With the expansion west, the Indians were seen as more and more of a problem, heathens who stood in the way of progress, who occupied territory coveted by gold miners, settlers, and the railroad. There was controversy as to what was to be done with them, some advocating a peaceful settlement and others favoring the more brutal solution of extermination. Chivington was of the faction whose point of view leaned toward a more violent end. To those who emphasize his responsibility for the massacre at Sand Creek it is sometimes referred to as the "Chivington Massacre."

Today the site of the massacre is dedicated by a compromising historical marker which reads: "Sand Creek Battle (or 'Massacre.' ") Willow trees and cottonwood still mark the bend in the creek. A faint trickle of water still moistens the sandy bend upon whose banks the Indians camped with the thought in mind that they were under Army protection and would be safe. Now a somber silence seems to hang in the air to remind us that once a Cheyenne band camped in peace and was struck down.